Coriolanus
at the National

Coriolanus at the National

"Th'Interpretation of the Time"

Kristina Bedford

With photographs by John Haynes

SUP

Selinsgrove: Susquehanna University Press
London and Toronto: Associated University Presses

Associated University Presses
440 Forsgate Drive
Cranbury, NJ 08512

Associated University Presses
25 Sicilian Avenue
London WC1A 2QH, England

Associated University Presses
P.O. Box 39, Clarkson Pstl. Stn.
Mississauga, Ontario,
L5J 3X9 Canada

The paper used in this publication meets the requirements
of the American National Standard for Permanence of Paper
for Printed Library Materials Z39.48-1984.

Library of Congress Cataloging-in-Publication Data

Bedford, Kristina.
    Coriolanus at the National : "Th' interpretation of the time" /
Kristina Bedford ; with photographs by John Haynes.
        p.   cm.
    Includes bibliographical references.
    ISBN 0-945636-18-0 (alk. paper)
    1. Shakespeare, William, 1564–1616. Coriolanus.   2. Shakespeare,
William, 1564–1616—Dramatic production.   3. Shakespeare, William,
1564–1616—Stage history—England—London.   4. Coriolanus, Cnaeus
Marcius, in fiction, drama, poetry, etc.   5. Theater—England—
London—History—20th century.   6. National Theatre (Great Britain)
7. Rome in literature.   I. Title.
    PR2805.B44   1992
    822.3'3—dc20   90-55697
                                                                         CIP

For my parents,
Harold and Hannele Bedford,
who supported me during the writing of this book.

Contents

Preface

It is a theatrical commonplace to say that the written text provides but half the ingredients necessary to fully experience any given play. Physical gesture, costume, localization of the action through the set and, if the director so chooses, the additional contributions of lighting, music, and sound all shape the audience's vision of the play and guide it toward a better understanding of the spoken word. Whether used to reinforce or to seemingly belie that word, physicalization of the play text ultimately has the same effect—it takes the action away from the comfortably abstract realm of the human mind and gives it concrete reality in the lives played out by the actors on the staging area before us. This physical reality becomes especially crucial in a complex work such as Shakespeare's *Coriolanus,* in which the major transitions (most notably the hero's decision *not* to forge himself a new name in the fire of burning Rome) are played out in silence. Here human emotion has reached such a degree of intensity that it refuses to be contained within the limiting structure of language. The moment can be transmitted to the audience only through gesture, facial expression, and body movement.

Accepted by the theater as an observer on Peter Hall's production of *Coriolanus,* I had the opportunity to witness first hand its development from the third week of rehearsals when the show was first put on its feet on a mock up of the set, through textual interpretation, technical rehearsal, the changes that necessarily arose when the set and costumes further specified the characters' identities. I also observed final alterations made during the week of previews when feedback from the first audiences revealed which moments needed fine-tuning and clarification. This book focuses on the finished work as it was performed in the Olivier Theatre, discussing the initial aims and ultimate achievement of the production, in an attempt to establish in what respects the National's staging illuminates and works with Shakespeare's text, and how well its vision is conveyed to the audience. Interviews with Ian McKellen and Greg Hicks offer an inside glimpse into their creation of the seminal roles of Coriolanus and Tullus Aufidius. And for those

9

interested in the practical mechanics of transferring a play from the page to the stage, the prose account of the rehearsal process is supplemented by a point by point diary report in Part Two. (Please note all dates are given in this order: day, month, year.) The resulting document is, I hope, a complete record of the production's journey from early rehearsals to the final performances in Athens— a written memory for those who saw Peter Hall's *Coriolanus*, a written recreation for the curious who didn't.

Acknowledgments

I am indebted to Methuen and Company Ltd. for permission to refer to the Arden Shakespeare editions of *Coriolanus* and *Richard III* in this book, and to the Grafton Books division of the Collins Publishing Group for allowing me to include a quotation from *The Empty Space* by Peter Brook. I would also like to thank the publicity department of the Royal National Theatre for permission to reprint both the program for *Coriolanus* and the handout distributed in the first scene of the production.

I am especially grateful to Sir Peter Hall for allowing me to sit in on his rehearsals for the play, and to the cast and crew for making me feel welcome. Their patience and kindness continued throughout the run and was deeply appreciated. The chapter describing the tour to Athens was made possible by senior stage manager Rosemary Beattie, who provided me with a ticket to the show on the shortest possible notice.

Finally, I would like to acknowledge the great debt I owe my friends and my colleagues at the RNT for their constant encouragement; thanks to Melanie Bedford, Philippa Carter, Joe Padovani, Diane Duquet, Nick Beale, and the Cottesloe Wardrobe past and present: Kathy, John, Annemarie, Jackie, Mags, and Hettie.

CITIZENS OF ROME:

Caius Martius is chief enemy to the people.

We want corn at our price.

We are hungry for bread.

The patrician storehouses are crammed with grain.

LET US REVENGE THIS WITH OUR PIKES!

Handout distributed to the stage audiences during the opening riot.

The *Coriolanus* Company in London:
(As on Opening Night,
15 December 1985)

Characters in Order of Speaking

First Citizen	Geoffrey Burridge
Second Citizen	Bill Moody
Menenius Agrippa	Frederick Treves
Caius Martius Coriolanus	Ian McKellen
Messenger	Mark Dowse
First Senator	Michael Barrington
Cominius	John Savident
Titus Lartius	Basil Henson
Sicinius Velutus	David Ryall
Junius Brutus	James Hayes
First Volscian Senator	Daniel Thorndike
Tullus Aufidius	Greg Hicks
Second Volscian Senator	Glenn Williams
Volumnia	Irene Worth
Virgilia	Wendy Morgan
Gentlewoman to Virgilia	Sarah Mortimer
Valeria	Judith Paris
Messenger	Paul Stewart
First Soldier	Lewis George
Second Soldier	Peter Dineen
First Roman	Brian Kent
Second Roman	Peter Gordon
Third Roman	Paul Stewart
Volscian Lieutenant	Timothy Hick
Herald	Geoffrey Burridge
First Officer of the Senate	Brian Kent
Second Officer of the Senate	Peter Gordon
Aedile	Peter Dineen
Volscian Citizen	Daniel Thorndike

First Servingman	Peter Gordon
Second Servingman	Bill Moody
Third Servingman	Paul Stewart
Lieutenant to Aufidius	Nigel le Vaillant
First Watch	Lewis George
Second Watch	Timothy Hick
Young Martius	Andrew Rigby/Tod Welling
First Conspirator	Desmond Adams
Second Conspirator	Guy Williams
Third Conspirator	Peter Gordon
First Volscian Lord	Daniel Thorndike
Second Volscian Lord	Brian Kent
Third Volscian Lord	Robert Arnold

Senators, Soldiers, Citizens, Etc.

Desmond Adams, Robert Arnold, Peter Dineen, Mark Dowse, Jenny Galloway, Lewis George, Peter Gordon, Timothy Hick, Brian Kent, Nigel le Vaillant, Bill Moody, Sarah Mortimer, Paul Stewart, Daniel Thorndike, Janet Whiteside, Glenn Williams, Guy Williams.

Musicians

Kenneth Bache (trumpet), Kenneth Browne (trumpet), Howard Hawkes (trumpet), Arthur Soothill (percussion), Terry Veasey (trumpet), Anthony Wagstaff (percussion).

The *Coriolanus* Company in Athens

Characters in Order of Speaking

First Citizen	Nigel le Vaillant
Second Citizen	Bill Moody
Menenius Agrippa	Frederick Treves
Caius Martius Coriolanus	Ian McKellen
Messenger	Mark Dowse
First Senator	Michael Barrington
Cominius	John Savident
Titus Lartius	Basil Henson
Sicinius Velutus	David Ryall
Junius Brutus	James Hayes
First Volscian Senator	Daniel Thorndike
Tullus Aufidius	Greg Hicks
Second Volscian Senator	Glenn Williams
Volumnia	Yvonne Bryceland
Virgilia	Wendy Morgan
Gentlewoman to Virgilia	Kate Dyson
Valeria	Judith Paris
Messenger	Paul Stewart
First Soldier	Lewis George
Second Soldier	Peter Dineen
First Roman	Paul Stewart
Second Roman	Peter Gordon
Volscian Lieutenant	Timothy Hick
Herald	Nigel le Vaillant
First Officer of the Senate	Glenn Williams
Second Officer of the Senate	Peter Gordon
Aedile	Peter Dineen
Volscian Citizen	Daniel Thorndike
First Servingman	Peter Gordon
Second Servingman	Bill Moody
Third Servingman	Paul Stewart
Lieutenant to Aufidius	Timothy Hick
First Watch	Lewis George

Second Watch	Alan Haywood
Young Martius	Andrew Rigby/Tod Welling
First Conspirator	Desmond Adams
Second Conspirator	Guy Williams
Third Conspirator	Peter Gordon
First Volscian Lord	Daniel Thorndike
Second Volscian Lord	Robert Arnold

Senators, Soldiers, Citizens, Etc.

Desmond Adams, Robert Arnold, Peter Changer, Peter Dineen, Mark Dowse, Kate Dyson, Jenny Galloway, Lewis George, Peter Gordon, Alan Haywood, Timothy Hick, Bill Moody, Paul Stewart, Daniel Thorndike, Janet Whiteside, Glenn Williams, Guy Williams.

Musicians

Kenneth Bache (trumpet), Kenneth Browne (trumpet), Howard Hawkes (trumpet), Arthur Soothill (percussion), Terry Veasey (trumpet), Anthony Wagstaff (percussion).

Production Staff

Director	Peter Hall
Design and Lighting	John Bury
Music	Harrison Birtwistle
Fights arranged by	Malcolm Ranson
Staff Director	Alan Cohen
Voice Coach	Jenny Patrick
Production Manager	Michael Cass Jones
Senior Stage Manager	Rosemary Beattie
Stage Manager	Courtney Bryant
Deputy Stage Manager	Lesley Walmsley
Assistant Stage Managers	Emma B. Lloyd, Brewyeen Rowland
Sound	Rob Barnard
Assistant to the Lighting Designer	Tim Bray
Production Photographs	John Haynes

For *Coriolanus* in Athens

Casting Director	Gillian Diamond
Master Carpenter	Dennis Nolan
Assistant Master Carpenter	Simon Cranidge
Chargehand	John Malaley
Chief Electrician	Andrew Torble
Property Master	John Pursey
Assistant Property Master	Simon Brazier
Armourer	John Wilkinson
Wardrobe Mistress	Catherine Moore
Assistant Wardrobe Mistress	Jilly Coram
Dresser	Maziar Razin
Sound Operator	Nic Jones
Wig Mistress	Joyce Beagarie
Deputy Wig Master	Peter Grice
Publicist	Lynne Kirwin

Coriolanus
at the National

Part One
"Th'Interpretation of the Time"

1
Rehearsals and Production Work

> Come, cousin, canst thou quake and change thy colour,
> Murder thy breath in middle of a word,
> And then again begin, and stop again,
> As if thou were distraught and mad with terror?[1]

So asks Shakespeare's most self-consciously theatrical protagonist, the master actor-manager Richard, Duke of Gloucester.[2] He is addressing his minion Buckingham, a man equally well versed in the art of skinning over corruption with the semblance of truth, and the latter answers confidently:

> Tut, I can counterfeit the deep tragedian,
> Speak, and look back, and pry on every side,
> Tremble and start at wagging of a straw,
> Intending deep suspicion. Ghastly looks
> Are at my service like enforced smiles,
> And both are ready in their offices
> At any time to grace my stratagems.[3]

By thus enveloping the conspirators' plot in dramatic terminology, Shakespeare is clearly sending up the accepted acting procedure of his day; indeed the entire canon is riddled with scenes and speeches which affectionately satirize the clichés and conventions of his profession. The pageant of the Nine Worthies in *Love's Labour's Lost*, the mechanicals' production of "Pyramus and Thisbe" in *A Midsummer Night's Dream*, Hamlet's advice to the players: all offer examples of how *not* to portray a character on the stage. The only successful piece of metatheater available for inspection would seem to be the series of playlets staged by Richard III in his bid for the throne, yet even here the text does not dictate the ingredients for his performance; we see that it is effective from the response which it elicits from the people around him. The 'correct' way to create a role remains elusive, and the actor is left asking whether there is a necessary formula for playing Shakespeare. If so, then is that formula constant, or does it vary from generation to generation? Does the text demand a certain style of delivery, and if it is not described in any given play, is it implicit in the verse form itself? Although these questions seem ideal fodder for intellectuals to argue over endlessly in the pub after a hard day's academic research, they represent very practical problems which must be confronted early in rehearsal (perhaps only to be discounted) if the production is to have any sense of cohesion or unity.

Peter Hall, director of the National Theatre's 1984–85 production of *Coriolanus,* presented his cast with a set convention for speaking the text at the very start of the rehearsal process. His years of intensive work on Shakespeare's plays have led him to conclude that there is indeed a very definite formula for delivering the text, and one which must be strictly observed before the creative process of developing the emotions and exploring the character's psyche breathes life into the bare skeleton of correct speech. Far from proving a barrier to the artistic creation of the role, Hall stresses that proper phrasing points the actor to the right interpretation of his or her lines, and thus facilitates the audience's understanding of the dialogue. Careful observance of form and structure becomes all the more vital when the text in question is as intellectually and emotionally complex as that of *Coriolanus.*[4]

The greatest obstacle for a modern actor approaching Shakespeare's drama for the first time lies in his or her probable grounding in naturalistic performance. Frequent pauses, the stressing of offbeat words and, above all, the avoidance of falling into a regular vocal rhythm are all representative of the inarticulateness of realistic speech, and are directly opposed to the stylized nature of Shakespeare's stagecraft. Any attempt to formulate a compromise between naturalistic delivery and Renaissance rhetoric can only result in a half-heartedly embarrassed performance; one must have confidence in the verse form and pursue those very rhythms which are alien to modern drama as performed in 1985, if the beauty and strength of the text are to be exploited to their full potential. *Coriolanus* was written by a man who *heard* his words as he wrote them down, and his plays are constructed with the complex orchestration of a symphony. Before the key note to one musical phrase ends, a new one begins;[5] indiscriminate use of pauses thus dissipates the audience's attention and halts the production. Although Shakespeare offers no more concrete direction to performing his works than "suit the action to the word,/the word to the action"[6] and never go over the top, the structure and phrasing of the text itself are written as notes to the actors. Rhymes, ends of lines, cues and monosyllables must be picked up, used and emphasized in order to bring out the full meaning of the lines. Hall insists that the actor's task is not to create a unique pattern of inflexion, but rather to build the overall shape of the role and its individual gear changes.

In using a compilation of the Arden edition and First Folio for *Coriolanus,* the director has ensured that the text for his production is as close as possible to the original script, despite corruptions, so that his interpretation of its structure and punctuation may be the more accurate. Far from getting out his trusty bottle of Tipp-ex and removing all trace of punctuation as soon as he determines on a script, as is sometimes the case in repertory companies, Hall holds that punctuation is not a deceptive barrier to the text, but an influencial clue to analyzing the line. A full stop means a gear change, a new beat, a shift in tone; it is the signal for variety in the coloration of a passage—a quality not shared by the semi-colon or comma. The latter often tells the actor to take what Hall calls a "sniff" at a certain rhythmic point in the line; thus the first citizen says "Let us kill him, (sniff) and we'll have corn at our own/price";[7] the slightest of pauses after the comma draws attention to both movements, while placing the emphasis on the reasons for the plebeians' intended action.[8] This specific example reinforces Hall's general observation that the weight of meaning in Shakespeare resides in the second half of the line, whose end serves as the springboard into the next one. A rush of emotion may entitle the actor to run on to the next line but never into it, or the form will be lost and the result nonsense. The text is so complex that clarity of speech must be the governing principle in performance if the audience is to follow the difficult language and dense imagery.

Clarification of obscure references and images was in fact one of the prime objectives during the first month of the rehearsal process, and proved a crucial factor in the ultimate cutting of the work. After this initial five week cycle, the director ran the play in its entirety, not only for characterization and general cohesion, but in order to determine which passages would probably not be understandable to an audience with no prior knowledge of the text.[9] Wherever an illustrative gesture was felt to be theatrically worse than a cut, the line was lost. Yet this was but one consideration in the editing of the text—the play was pruned on three counts: comprehension, repetition and weakness in performance. The servant scene which follows and comments on the new-found alliance between Coriolanus and his old enemy Aufidius never found its proper rhythm in rehearsal;

it merely slowed the action without adding the necessary comic relief, and so was cut during previews.[10] Coriolanus's scorn that the plebeians dare speak of

> side factions, and give out
> Conjectural marriages; making parties strong,
> And feebling such as stand not in their liking
> Below their cobbled shoes
>
> (1.1.192–95)

was deleted as it adds no further information to his preceding lines, which establish that they

> presume to know
> What's done i'th'Capitol: who's like to rise,
> Who thrives, and who declines.
>
> (1.1.190–92)

Brutus's outraged reaction to Coriolanus's popularity in the market place was shortened by three lines:

> Seld-shown flamens
> Do press among the popular throngs, and puff
> To win a vulgar station.
>
> (2.1.211–13)

Hall felt that the religious image would be totally inaccessible to a modern audience, yet the removal of this passage had unexpected results. As James Hayes, the actor portraying Brutus, was the first to point out, the speech as it now stands has sexist implications, as the examples held up to ridicule by the tribune—the "prattling nurse," "kitchen malkin," and "veil'd dames"—are all women.[11]

In addition to such cuts, several textual emendations were made over the course of rehearsals. "Corioles" was regularized to "Corioli," "Good den" to "Good e'en" and "lenity" to "leniency," all in the interest of comprehension, and several choric lines were divided and ascribed to specific citizens or tribunes.[12] The most significant alteration to the text, however, occurs in the rebellious citizen's response to the news of Coriolanus's impending attack on Rome. The Arden edition reads

> That we did we did for the best,
> and though we willingly consented to his banish-
> ment, yet it was against our will.
>
> (4.6.144–46)

The dark humour of the pun resides in the ambiguous use of the word "will"; although the citizen is rebuking the tribunes for merely banishing Coriolanus from the city instead of invoking the extreme sentence of death, the line can be read as a total and unjustified transference of guilt. And this becomes the sole interpretation understood by a modern audience, whose whole-hearted laughter at the vacillations of the mob destroys the tension of the scene and transforms the announcement of the apocalypse into a circus. During the previews Hall therefore exchanged "yet it was against our will" for "yet it was his death we wished for," thus reducing the ambiguous phrase to a single meaning and preserving the serious tone of the scene. Although this change does clarify the citizen's intentions, it is regrettable that the line no longer scans; seven syllables have become eight, and that small addition ends the line with a weak preposition rather than a strong noun. A problem of interpretation has thus been transformed into a structural defect.[13] Generally speaking, however, the cuts and alterations made by Hall do serve to clarify what is an exceptionally difficult text, both in its psychology and its politics, and keep the play moving at a quick and energetic pace that maintains the audience's interest throughout.

After two weeks of preliminary work on language and verse speaking, Hall began to put the show on its feet and establish a skeletal blocking which would be fleshed out later in the rehearsal period. This phase culminated in the first run-through of the production on 14 November, two weeks before the projected date for the play's first preview. In his preparatory remarks before the run, Hall told his cast that they would not be followed on text, since it was crucial at this point that they begin to live their roles, and not just repeat lines. He stressed that the main object should be to act the play, to live it and do it, to react verbally and physically, improvising whenever necessary, so that the actors might find new inspiration with which to experiment during the last ten days of rehearsal.[14] The danger in striving to be classically correct is that one can become too bound to tradition—the performances also need that energy which flows from creativity and humanity if they are not to become dry and dull. There is a necessary tension between form and the freedom of the individual; for the purposes of this first run, Hall emphasized the need for the actors to exercise their freedom.

The run was not only necessary for the cast to develop their roles in a continuous sequence from beginning to end (instead of isolating their characters at a specific moment in time as they had necessarily been doing until now), but also for the director to assess the strengths and weaknesses of the overall production. At its conclusion, Hall remarked that the level of creativity and clarity of presentation was very high; it now remained to tighten the show and concentrate on holding the text. The first half needed to be shortened by fifteen minutes, the second by eight, and all without cutting a line. The overriding concern lay in the time limit—with only the equivalent of six working days left, Hall urged the company to work quickly and to do a great deal of homework, in order to ensure that they would be ready for the first preview.

The week following this rehearsal saw the production's next run, this time in the theater and with an audience. Posters had been set up in the lobby of the National advertising an open rehearsal, so that a typical cross-section of the theater-going public might be assembled and their reactions gauged, in the hopes that their feedback would provide material for further work. There was some confusion at the play's opening: unused to dealing with an audience on stage, the "citizen" actors were unable to adequately convey the points at which they should come down to the sandpit, and when they should sit down again. As a result some people went back to the stands too early, while others remained too long on the stage. Many character, text and movement problems surfaced, especially during the first half where the stage audience's uncontrolled presence in several scenes made sightlines chaotic.

The second half of the run was much improved, largely due to putting down the house lights, so that energy became more focused on stage. Soon feeling more accustomed to the stage audience, the actors (those portraying the tribunes in particular) began to make increased use of speaking to the people in the stands, thus exploiting rather than merely tolerating their contribution to the play's action. Although the pace had been tightened by the editing of minor furniture and props, the show still went a quarter of an hour over the director's projected running time. Overlooking the inevitable technical problems, some brilliant moments began to emerge: even without the proper sound and lighting cues, Volumnia's triumph proved extremely moving, and Coriolanus's silent grasping of his mother's hand in the second persuasion scene was electric. Despite such promising developments, the run showed Hall that the production was still significantly behind schedule, both because of the complexities of the play and his own temporary absence from rehearsals due to illness. Thus the decision was made to cancel the first previews, turning 30 November into a public dress rehearsal, and delaying press night until 15 December, so that the company would gain time in which to iron out their weaknesses and the public would be treated to a polished rather than a tentative performance.

Prior to the dress run a week later, Hall announced to the audience that the show would be played as a rehearsal rather than a performance, as the actors were not yet thoroughly acquainted with the set. Certainly their task was not rendered any easier by the fact that the scaffolding had been erected in the wrong position, so that Coriolanus had difficulty in descending from his perch in 1.4, and the first citizen injured his ankle in the voices scene (2.3). Nevertheless the company's adrenalin was high—no doubt it was a relief to finally give a public performance after such an extended rehearsal period—and the audience responded sympathetically to the actors' efforts, ignoring technical slips and good-humouredly applauding McKellen's one dry, appropriately enough on the aside

> Like a dull actor now
> I have forgot my part and I am out,
> Even to a full disgrace.
>
> (5.3.40–42)

Commenting on the run before the first preview the next day, Hall described to his cast how the audience, which had started out watching a rehearsal, was gradually drawn into the action of the play, remaining completely held by the company's story-telling, especially in the first half.[15] The second act, which contains less physical action, held less well. It needed to be made more active, worried and full of tension, having reached the stage where the actors could add a greater variety of tone and not just play on the single note of doom. Early into previews Hall stressed that what the show needed now was absolute confidence, arrogance, and pride in performance; the audience's violent reactions for or against it proved that the production was both successful and controversial.

It was during the two week preview period which followed the public dress run that the show was radically restaged. Gone now were refinements to the blocking made over the past month, in favour of a complete revamping of major sequences; an audience seeing *Coriolanus* on 30 November and 15 December, the opening night, would have witnessed what amounted to two different productions. I have purposely chosen not to write a prose description of the physical changes which occurred during the rehearsal process. For those interested in the mechanics of theater, a complete rehearsal diary is included in Part Two, and significant alterations are chronicled in the analysis of the set performance which forms the core of Part One. A sample passage should serve to give a taste of the various options explored in staging the play, and a reproduction of the text on the facing page illuminates the detailed interpretation which Hall gave to his cast. One of the most difficult sequences to stage within the context of the arena setting was the domestic scene of 1.3, in which the introduction of the matrons of Rome provides a lighter interval between the declaration of war and its bloody aftermath. It is this scene which I have chosen to transcribe in full (see pages 32–41).

The public style of delivery that Hall has demanded from his cast is appropriate both to the style of the play, which was written for the open air theaters of the early seventeenth century, and to the requirements of the modern Olivier stage, built on the model of the amphitheater at Epidaurus. Both theaters allow the play's momentum to be maintained through rapid cross-cutting during scene changes, and John Bury's design for *Coriolanus* exploits this convention to its full potential, while providing the physical embodiment of the production's philosophical eclecticism.[16] Bury has constructed an amphitheatrical setting which at once localizes the action in ancient Rome and creates an atmosphere of hard political debate akin to that found in a modern United Nations or House of Commons, where the speaker is surrounded by representatives of all parties. Promenade seats stand to either side of the central sandpit and are used as secondary acting areas during those moments when the stage audience is called upon to swell the scene as the Roman mob. Up center loom the gates of Rome, the central stage image of the play. Their false wall moves inwards to transform the set into the Volscian cities of Antium and Corioli. Old and discolored posters reading "Vota DP" reinforce the political aura which permeates the play, while "Danger" notices unite with the iron scaffolding to create the sense of an ancient society in the last stages of deterioration and decay. Coriolanus's Rome and twentieth-century Europe are alike represented in this most powerful stage image.

This visual eclecticism inherent in the set has been pursued in Bury's costume design as well. Modern dress is worn by citizens and civilians, the senate sports classical robes, and the Roman ladies simple gowns; the military uniforms have a futuristic feel,[17] while Coriolanus and Aufidius strip down to primitive loincloths for their gladiatorial combat. The result is the creation of a society which exists independently of time and space—a conscious decision on the part of both director and designer to reflect the very heart of a work whose themes are universal. Instead of adhering to a consistently modern or completely Roman dress, the visual accessibility of the production allows its audience to concentrate on the more important demands of the play's language. Far from proving a radical departure from Elizabethan stagecraft, the design for both set and costumes has been executed in a style basic to the original, for the Elizabethans played in the open air with a minimum of furniture, and costumed their productions from the cross-section of articles available in stock. Again there was no unity of time or place, though the actors would largely have performed in modern (i.e., Renaissance) dress.[18]

Great care was taken, theoretically at least, to clothe the characters in the modern equivalent of their Roman/Elizabethan function: the hungry working classes thus wear tattered sweatshirts, jeans and caps, while their tribunes carry briefcases and sport turtlenecks and sweaters under their robes of office. Yet even though the design dictated the overall look of the production, it did not extend to providing its specifics. The actors portraying the citizens were told to supply their costumes from their own wardrobe, and though their garb necessarily appears comfortable and lived in, it in no way transforms them into the physical embodiment of the starving poor. "Hunger" is a word much bandied about, especially at the opening of the play, yet it issues solely from the mouths, not the souls and bodies of the rebellious plebeians. The attire of several citizens plants them firmly in the ranks of the middle class;[19] one young woman wearing a scrupulously white shirt and pressed skirt looks as though she has just graduated from one of London's better prep schools. Although it is credible that such individuals would join in a demonstration from the promptings of passionately held political beliefs, it lessens the sense of desperation depicted in Shakespeare's text and dissipates the tension of acting "in hunger for bread, not in/thirst for revenge" (1.1.23–24). A second plebeian is more appropriately clad in a black woolen cap, rough trousers and an old ripped jacket, yet he does not change his costume when appearing as the Volscian citizen whom Coriolanus encounters before the walls of Antium. Admittedly this is a lapse in continuity which will go unnoticed by an audience seeing the play for the first time, nevertheless it is indicative of the generally haphazard system of costuming the mob.

The citizens are not alone in being assigned costumes not specifically made for this production; for example, the white dress uniform worn by Titus Lartius in his civilian scenes was dug out of wardrobe on the suggestion of actor Basil Henson that Bury recy-

(text continues on page 42)

Act 1 Scene 3

Enter VOLUMNIA *and* VIRGILIA, *mother and wife to* MARTIUS.
They set them down on two low stools and sew.

Vol. I pray you, daughter, sing, or express yourself in a more comfortable sort. If my son were my husband I should freelier rejoice in that absence wherein he won honour, than in the embracements of his bed, where he would show most love. When yet he was but tender-bodied, and the only son of my womb; when youth with comeliness plucked all gaze his way; when for a day of kings' entreaties, a mother should not sell him an hour from her beholding; I, considering how honour would become such a person—that it was no better than picture-like to hang by th'wall, if renown made it not stir—was pleased to let him seek danger where he was like to find fame. To a cruel war I sent him, from whence he returned, his brows bound with oak. I tell thee, daughter, I sprang not more in joy at first hearing he was a man-child, than now in first seeing he had proved himself a man.

Vir. But had he died in the business, madam, how then?

Vol. Then his good report should have been my son, I therein would have found issue. Hear me profess sincerely: had I a dozen sons, each in my love alike, and none less dear than thine and my good Martius, I had rather had eleven die nobly for their country, than one voluptuously surfeit out of action.

Enter a Gentlewoman.

Gent. Madam, the Lady Valeria is come to visit you.

Vir. Beseech you give me leave to retire myself.

Vol. Indeed you shall not.
Methinks I hear hither your husband's drum;
See him pluck Aufidius down by th'hair,
As children from a bear, the Volsces shunning him.
Methinks I see him stamp thus, and call thus:
"Come on you cowards, you were got in fear
Though you were born in Rome." His bloody brow
With his mail'd hand then wiping, forth he goes
Like to a harvest man that's task'd to mow
Or all, or lose his hire.

24/10/84

10:30–1:00

Virgilia is revealed sewing at her stand in the center of the circle.

Volumnia enters carrying a ball of yarn, takes her shoes off at the perimeter of the circle before she steps on the sand—geisha motif.

Tone must be light, airy, domestic in the texture of the play, before the bloody scenes of war we are about to witness.

There must be a real love between Virgilia and Volumnia, but a lack of communication.
One wants to avoid all talk of blood.
For the other, blood is what it's all about and must be celebrated.

At the start of the scenes there is a sense of intimacy between the two women through their physical proximity on stage as Volumnia puts her arm round Virgilia.

Movements: Initial lightness on "I pray you, daughter, sing."
Seriousness—"To a cruel war I sent him."
Movement away to the chaise on "and the only son of my womb."
Tosses yarn on "Indeed you shall not."
Return to lighter tone in preparation for the entrance of Valeria.
Walk round the stage as Volumnia mimics her son.
Direct contact again on "bloody brow"—comforting embrace at Virgilia's distress.
Virgilia tosses yarn back on "Tell Valeria/We are fit to bid her welcome."
This gesture is a response to Volumnia who has looked to her for confirmation of her line—the action tells her it's alright.
In her comforting, Volumnia domesticates blood into witty, sensual images.
On the second running of this scene, Volumnia remains a pace away at this point, and Virgilia says her line simply, eliciting a sincere response, passes the yarn, embrace.

Worth decides to enter mending her grandson's rubber ball rather than use the clichéd ball of yarn—it can be tossed back and forth more easily and is a more unusual image.

Vir.   His bloody brow? O Jupiter, no blood!

Vol.   Away you fool! it more becomes a man
Than gilt his trophy. The breasts of Hecuba
When she did suckle Hector, look'd not lovelier
Than Hector's forehead when it spit forth blood
At Grecian sword contemning. Tell Valeria
We are fit to bid her welcome.   *Exit Gentlewoman.*

Vir.   Heavens bless my lord from fell Aufidius!

Vol.   He'll beat Aufidius' head below his knee,
And tread upon his neck.

Enter VALERIA *with an Usher, and a Gentlewoman.*

Val.   My ladies both, good day to you.

Vol.   Sweet madam.

Vir.   I am glad to see your ladyship.

Val.   How do you both? You are manifest housekeepers.
What are you sewing here? A fine spot, in good faith. How
does your little son?

Vir.   I thank your ladyship; well, good madam.

Vol.   He had rather see the swords and hear a drum, than look
upon his schoolmaster.

Val.   O' my word, the father's son! I'll swear 'tis a very pretty
boy. O' my troth, I looked upon him o' Wednesday half an
hour together: 'has such a confirmed countenance. I saw
him run after a gilded butterfly, and when he caught it, he
let it go again, and after it again, and over and over he
comes, and up again, catched it again; or whether his fall
enraged him, or how 'twas, he did so set his teeth and tear
it. Oh, I warrant how he mammocked it!

Vol.   One on's father's moods.

Val.   Indeed, la, 'tis a noble child.

Vir.   A crack, madam.

Val.   Come, lay aside your stitchery, I must have you play the
idle huswife with me this afternoon.

Vir.   No, good madam, I will not out of doors.

Val.   Not out of doors?

Vol.   She shall, she shall.

Vir.   Indeed no, by your patience; I'll not over the threshold till
my lord return from the wars.

Val.   Fie, you confine yourself most unreasonably. Come, you
must go visit the good lady that lies in.

Contrast between the intimacy of the scene to this point and the incoming voice.

Valeria: Fluttery character—chattering without giving the chance for a reply.
Prose to be played quicker than the verse.
Virgilia tries to drag it back into verse but Valeria won't let her.

Attention paid to details—Virgilia's maid must sound more pleased at her one line announcement—Valeria is to be introduced in a jolly tone.

Valeria's quick entrance completes the line "And tread upon his neck," therefore is quick and pat to break the tone.
Her quick tongue contrasts with Virgilia's simple one phrase rebuttal—no breath: "No, good madam, I will not out of doors."
Bright send-up on "You would be another Penelope."
"Come, you must go visit the *good lady that lies in*"— important moment—a friend of her station and class is about to give birth in the midst of war—Virgilia is moved by this but will not budge.
Valeria tries to pull her arm to physically move her but this has no effect.
Virgilia's strength comes from her stillness—she is the only stationary figure on the stage.
Virgilia finally achieves verse before the line about Penelope.
Valeria tries to break the tension by making her laugh.

News of Coriolanus: Volumnia is ecstatic, but for Virgilia this is mixed good and bad—all her energy is put into thinking of Coriolanus in conflict.
Virgilia is afraid at the prospect of news, for if it comes this early it must be bad—cliché that bad news travels fast.
In the area of her husband, Virgilia has no sense of humor whatsoever.
"I will obey you in everything hereafter"—Virgilia pushes Valeria away.
The last line from Valeria is delivered from the perimeter of the inner circle—her final appeal elicits a strong response from Virgilia—couched in monosyllables.

Valeria is a chatty social butterfly, but underneath is very intelligent, politically au courant, etc., as is evident from her sudden seriousness when revealing Rome's military strategy.

Vir. I will wish her speedy strength, and visit her with my prayers; but I cannot go thither.

Vol. Why, I pray you?

Vir. 'Tis not to save labour, nor that I want love.

Val. You would be another Penelope; yet they say, all the yarn she spun in Ulysses' absence did but fill Ithaca full of moths. . . . Come, you shall go with us.

Vir. No, good madam, pardon me; indeed I will not forth.

Val. In truth, la, go with me, and I'll tell you excellent news of your husband.

Vir. Oh, good madam, there can be none yet.

Val. Verily I do not jest with you. There came news from him last night.

Vir. Indeed, madam?

Val. In earnest, it's true; I heard a senator speak it. Thus it is: the Volsces have an army forth, against whom Cominius the general is gone, with one part of our Roman power. Your lord and Titus Lartius are set down before their city Corioli; they nothing doubt prevailing, and to make it brief wars. This is true on mine honour, and so, I pray, go with us.

Vir. Give me excuse, good madam, I will obey you in everything hereafter.

Vol. Let her alone, lady; as she is now, she will but disease our better mirth.

Val. In troth, I think she would. Fare you well then. Come, good sweet lady. Prithee, Virgilia, turn thy solemness out o'door, and go along with us.

Vir. No, at a word, madam; indeed I must not. I wish you much mirth.

Val. Well then, farewell.   *Exeunt.*

The fact that it was heard from a senator indicates her fundamental intelligence, as he would not have passed along such important information to a mindless chatterbox.

15/11/84

2:00–5:00

All furniture has been edited from the scene—no chaise or sewing stand.

Virgilia enters right, sits and sews, while Volumnia enters left and stands by her for a moment, then speaks to establish their relationship now that the decision has been made not to begin *in medias res* (i.e., they do not enter talking).
The image of mending the toy ball has also been cut.
Virgilia is stationary—she has decided on a course of action and will stick to it.
Volumnia watches her as though she has been like this for days, as though Virgilia has left every room she has come into.
Puts more emphasis on words than on action.

Work on speed, intensity and intimacy—a genuine warmth between the two.
"His bloody brow" . . . "O Jupiter, no blood!"—as Volumnia goes to cross behind her, Virgilia clutches at her skirt and rests her head briefly against her mother-in-law's knee.
The simplicity of the set gives added impact to the words.

On the second run of the scene the action is moved from the sand to the foot of the stairs—the tighter area better suggests the interior and avoids the problem of the ladies in jewels and formal attire sitting in the sand.
To have the women standing would lose focus from the audience in the circle as they must face down to glimpse the seated Virgilia.
Virgilia still enters first and sits down. Volumnia follows, watching, then, as she bends down to set the wool on the ground, sees the sadness on her face.
The scene is lit tight, with two corridors for the path beyond, yet there is a sightline problem with all this—the audience may still be able to see, but not comfortably—only their heads are visible

National Theatre, circle entrance. Photo by Kristina Bedford.

if they are sitting, and all three women cannot stand simultaneously.
   Tried with Volumnia bringing in cushions to sit on—this both
adds a few inches and takes them back a bit.

"Grecian sword contemning" delivered as a classical, romantic
passage.

"Beseech you give me leave to retire myself" taken as the cue for
Virgilia to rise—but then the moment of grasping Volumnia's skirt
is lost.
   Tried again sitting to preserve that moment.
   After Valeria's entrance the servant brings on two cushions for
her as well.

The atmosphere is built up and then dispelled by the brilliant
entrance of Valeria.
   As the women leave, each picks up her cushions and carries them
out.

Virgilia is not whining or game-playing, she has just made a decision and refuses to change her mind—"thanks for the invitation,
but I've made my pledge and will stick to it."
   Play her strength rather than her sadness, but allow the sadness
to peep through for variation.

Valeria journeys round the perimeter of the stage as she tells her
story—but it doesn't really work.
   "One on's father's moods"—a telling moment between the two
women.
   Valeria repeatedly begins her exit, then turns back with staccato
movements to persuade Virgilia—doesn't work.

22/11/84

10:30–2:00—back to original staging.

Image of Virgilia and Volumnia both sewing on the same shirt.
   Valeria edits the awkward journey round the stage on the butterfly story.
   She now stands stage right and physicalizes the tale through
gesture and voice without travelling at all.

Public approach to the Olivier and Lyttelton theatres. Photo by Kristina Bedford.

3/12/84

12:00–5:15

Detailed work on individual speeches, eg. the butterfly passage.

The only gesture remaining in Volumnia's main speech is on "brows bound with oak"—simplicity gives added power.

Volumnia decides to cut the cushions as they make the delivery of her lines uncomfortable.

NB. Take care to preserve a public delivery despite the private nature of the scene.

Artists' entrance. Photo by Kristina Bedford.

cle his old costume from *Strider*. The decision to make such a distinction between the soldiers' civilian and military garb came well into rehearsals. At first Coriolanus made his initial entrance in battle uniform, while the young nobility were dressed as officers in 3.2 and 4.1 and Cominius retained his general's uniform throughout. As the production now stands, the nobles are clad in finely tailored suits akin to that worn by Coriolanus himself, and Cominius wears a double-breasted overcoat and gloves in 5.1, thus reinforcing the textual suggestion that he has only just returned from his ill-fated audience with Coriolanus. Such costume changes represent a vast improvement over the original design, as they increase the visual distinction between Rome in times of peace and war.

The most spectacular costume change, however, was introduced without the prior knowledge of either director, designer, or indeed any member of the cast. Unsatisfied with his uniform for 1.1, Ian McKellen took matters into his own hands and, when given the cue for his entrance, suddenly appeared in a smart white suit and overcoat, blue shirt and black tie, hair slicked back into a ponytail, carrying his golden sword.[20] The effect was stunning. Suddenly the irony and sarcasm, that had superseded anger as the dominant motifs of his performance, made sense of his portrayal of Coriolanus as Renaissance satirist. Whether this interpretation of the role is appropriate to the man as depicted by Shakespeare in his tragedy is left to the individual to decide for him/herself. Certain it is that an audience with no prior knowledge of the text, and the stage audience in particular, finds his dramatic entrance breathtaking.

This scene marks the first point at which the audience viewing the production from promenade seats are invited to descend onto the sand to swell the ranks of the citizens. Their participation in the action is an integral part of the director's vision of the play; Hall did not wish to overburden the stage with a crew of extras, but felt that certain scenes would be enhanced by occurring within the context of a crowd. Hence the decision to construct a series of stands to either side of the inner circle, in order to house those spectators who come down onto the central playing area when so instructed by the actors. Once again Hall's apparently radical staging is in fact faithful to the spirit of the Elizabethan original, recalling as it does the theatrical tradition of providing stage seats for the aristocracy, a practice observed until Garrick's renovations in the mid-eighteenth century. The only difference in this modern production is that, far from being reserved for wealthy patrons, the promenade seats are sold at a reduced rate, thus attracting a broader cross-section of society into the theater.

This desire to incorporate the on-stage audience into the action of the play leads, however, to the practical difficulty of manipulating approximately one hundred people ignorant of the actors' choreographed moves. There is a very real danger that the principal players may be lost among the melée of nervous "extras" who know neither where to stand, nor when to move aside. Thus Bury's lighting design is comprised of general lighting states, with two follow spots for the protagonists. This allows the principal actors the freedom to move to whichever part of the stage is clear, and thus solve the problem of conjestion through simple physical improvisation. These follow spots are hung from the back of the stage at a thirty degree angle, thus heightening features and basic shapes rather than providing the more flattering light of a frontal positioning—more appropriate to a work whose thrust is starkly anti-romantic.

Not only does the lighting design compensate for the stage audience's presence in the stands, but, more importantly, it exploits this central facet of the director's vision. From the very opening of the play, Bury includes the audience into the stage picture, in the first scene totally eradicating the traditional barrier between spectator and actor through the use of a preset wash. The first lighting cue comes two minutes into the action, slowly fading down the general illumination so that the audience is subtly drawn into the play's opening. The "reality" of shifting seats and rustling programs merges smoothly into the theatrical moment, without a word of dialogue being missed. The danger of the stage audience's presence intruding on the play's private scenes is avoided by the ability to "lose" the stands by dimming the wash, never losing the hot spot on the actors on the sand.

Although the audience's active involvement was part of Hall's vision of the production from its inception, the extent of this participation was radically curtailed throughout both previews and performance. He initially blocked the spectators into the riots of 1.1 and 3.1, the triumphs in 2.1 and 5.5, the end of the voices scene (2.3), the banishment of Coriolanus (3.3), the city's response to the threat of attack on Rome (5.1), and the final assassination (5.6). The audience members' actual contribution varies according to the demands of the scene. During Volumnia's triumph, for example, they are merely called upon to stand and applaud rhythmically as the procession exits through Rome gates, while in the trial scene they are invited to come down onto the stage and become one with the citizens who have assembled to sentence Coriolanus. Yet it was found early into previews that participation by the full promenade audience could lead to an overcrowding of the stage during passages where unobstructed sightlines are crucial to the transmission of the scene. Hence came the decision to tell only the outer two stands to descend to the main playing area at the end of 2.3; the audience up center stand in position so that they add texture to the stage picture without burdening the circle below with a surplus of plebeians.

Despite this refinement to the general blocking of the audience, the self-conscious reactions of individuals embarrassed to find themselves in the public eye still led to a diffusion of tension in the dynamic of the action. This distraction was visible to the main audience in the theater and felt most acutely by those actors who play crucial scenes with the enlargened mob. Little wonder that McKellen dislikes their presence during the riot of 3.1, when his threatening charges with sword held high are met with nervous titters from individuals worried at the prospect of being caught up in the stampede.[21] Not only is this response at variance with the tone of the scene but, equally important, it disrupts the actor's concentration in performing his or her role. The debate on the relative value of the stage audience's contribution raged among critics, theatergoers and members of the company alike for over two months after the opening of *Coriolanus;* then, before a line run on 21 February, Hall announced the final alterations to his staging of the crowd. Direct audience participation was eliminated from all but three scenes—the opening riot (1.1), the trial (3.3) and the assassination (5.6)—although the spectators are still asked to stand in place and applaud rhythmically for the triumphs in 2.1 and 5.5. All participation has been removed from the voices scene (2.3) and the city's panic (5.1), where the disadvantages of reducing the ranks of the citizens to a mere six bodies is compensated for by the visual continuity of seeing those six overcome by the cataclysmic news of Coriolanus's attack on Rome, or desperately developing their strategy to prevent his acceptance of the consulship. These are both highly charged episodes whose dramatic intensity could only be diminished by audience reactions which are at best neutral and bland, and at worst distractingly inconsistent with the emotional tenor of the scene.[22]

This final reworking of the crowd sequences represents a major improvement over the previous blocking. It rids the stage of self-conscious behaviour where crowd involvement is unnecessary, yet

calls for its contribution when the presence of a realistically propor-
tioned mob, or the use of the stands in a multi-level stage picture,
compensates for the inconsistencies of its "acting." Although some
critics have condemned all notion of seating a section of the audience on stage, I firmly believe its presence to be not only accept-
able but crucial to the production. The idea of creating and
populating an arena for political debate is the very essence of Hall's
vision of the play; therefore to remove this human dimension is to
drain the life-blood of one of his central images. I state this as a fact,
for I have seen the show run in the Olivier without anyone seated
on the stage, and far from proving a visual relief, as the critics would
suggest, its actual result is to render the set disquietingly in-
complete. The audience not only contributes to the performing of
Coriolanus but, merely by watching the production from the
stands, becomes an integral part of its design.

2
Act 1

The audience's presence is perhaps most effective in the opening sequence of the play, which establishes the requisite atmosphere of uncertainty and civil discord long before the first words are spoken. A guard posted atop Rome gates patrols the city as the plebeians enter carrying union banners and placards, beckoning the people to descend from their promenade seats to join in the rebellion for corn at their own rate. As the sound of shouts and alarms punctuated by intermittent bursts of gunfire issues from speakers throughout the theater, the citizens distribute a list of their demands, spraypaint political slogans across Rome gates, and address the audience in character, telling them of the reasons for their revolt. All the ingredients of a modern demonstration are present in this single image, which translates the Renaissance riot into a recognizably twentieth-century event. As the rebel plebeians circle round their main spokesman, placards are exchanged for meat cleavers and axes, and the atmosphere of danger intensifies with the threat of immediate action. The first citizen's passion for his cause and his evident love of language render him an eloquent spokesman. He builds the pitch of feeling amongst the crowd as he incites them to communal chants of "Speak, speak," "Resolved, resolved," and "We know't, we know't" (1.1.2,5,8), whose increasing intensity feeds the further violence of his own expression. As the audience watches the originally peaceful demonstration rapidly turn into a full scale riot, it also witnesses the development of opposing factions within the group. Just as the main body moves to batter down Rome gates, the second citizen calls them back to rationally articulate their griefs against Martius. Their leader grudgingly complies, irritated at the interruption which has broken off the mutiny and destroyed the momentum he has so strenuously built up. Nevertheless he is able to recapture their former feverous excitement, and the citizens once more attack the gates.

It is into this extremely explosive situation that Menenius makes his first appearance on the scene, as he emerges through a small door in the side of the main gate and parts the people to walk downstage and address their spokesman. It is a very courageous entrance, for neither he nor the audience know how the mob will react; in their present insanity they have the potential to tear him to pieces. Nevertheless his charisma and the great love the people bear him prove sufficient to ensure his safety. Even the first citizen is forced to admit that "He's one honest enough" before hastily qualifying his praise with "would all the rest/were so!" (1.1.52–53). Plebeian faces off against patrician downstage center, each man backed by sympathetic followers, in the production's first image of political debate. Passionate outrage is confronted and quelled by the voice of reason, as Menenius addresses the plebeians like children, appeasing them with the fable of the belly. His gesture of taking off his senator's robes and assuming the story-teller's position in the sand down right intrigues the crowd which presses forward to listen, while the first citizen expresses his increasing tension by pacing back and forth as he interjects sharp, dismissive questions.

The difficulties inherent in maintaining the audience's focus throughout such an extensive passage as the fable of the belly validate Hall's concern for correct delivery of the rhetoric. The speaker must heighten his verbal relish and point the speech by hitting the alliterative opening: "There was a time, when all the body's members/Rebell'd against the belly" (1.1.95–96); stressing these key words preserves the verse form and prevents the lines from running into naturalistic prose. Both the citizens' and the theater audience's interest can be held only if Menenius energizes his delivery by discovering words and images as he goes along, enjoying his own speech even as he creates it. He dumbfounds the people with a story which, underneath all the wit and the humour, he truly believes: the body politic cannot survive without a healthy oligarchy; every body needs a belly to survive. Menenius suddenly drops the assumed persona of the belly's voice to deliver his application of the tale in a serious tone, an internal gear change signalled by his physical turn as he picks up the senatorial gown and whirls it onto his shoulders. The citizens listen and accept his moralizing; Menenius has once again pacified the rebellious mob.

It is into this atmosphere of newly restored calm that Coriolanus makes his first explosive appearance.[1] After a curt "Thanks" to Menenius's hearty greeting (1.1.163), he addresses the people in a tone of scathing sarcasm:

What's the matter, you dissentious rogues
That, rubbing the poor itch of your opinion,
Make yourselves scabs?

(1.1.163–65)

Coriolanus baits the citizens with the naive pleasure of a boy
enjoying his own rhetoric and succeeds in mastering them through
his sheer presence, although in so doing he annihilates Menenius's
hard fought achievement. As a soldier and a man of action, he is
restless when there is no war into which he may channel his
energies and here attempts to create a different kind of battle in
attacking the people. Hall has physicalized this internal movement
in stage terms by having Coriolanus walk up to specific individuals
in the crowd and delightedly watch them jump back in fear. Only
the first citizen would rather die than retreat, and must be pulled
away by his fellows. This initial business both defines Coriolanus's
antagonistic relationship with his society and offers a visual parallel
to his later violent attack on the plebeians in 3.1 and to his response
to their banishment of him in 3.3.

After tiring of this aggressive game, Coriolanus moves to join
Menenius down center to inform him of the progress of the rebellion and the concessions which the senate have granted its
leaders. He spits out the sibilant names of the new tribunes "Junius
Brutus" and "Sicinius Velutus" as though he can barely bring
himself to utter such pollution. Because this interchange is private,
it is inappropriate that the plebeians should hear of their success at
this point; the problem remains that they are still present on stage,
and a dialogue audible to the audience should realistically be audible to them. Hall solves this conundrum by having the actors turn
upstage in tableau, as though engaged in conversation with each
other and with the stage audience who swell their ranks. They are
recalled to action with the announcement that "the Volsces are in
arms" (1.1.223), and the gates open for the first time to admit the
city's political leaders, tribunes among them, to endow Coriolanus
with his commission. The latter's military status is articulated by
his fellow general Titus Lartius, who declines his gesture of invitation to go first when the patricians prepare to retire: "Follow
Cominius, we must follow you,/Right worthy your priority"
(1.1.245–46). Coriolanus puts his hands on his friend's shoulders in
a gesture of thanks, then Lartius moves to follow him out before the
exit is interrupted by the former's final explosion at the citizens.
The crowd scatters at this renewed threat, and the senate exits
through the gates with Coriolanus exulting at his small triumph,

leaving the tribunes to comment acerbically on what they have just witnessed. Brutus and Sicinius move in to confer with each other down center, as they revile the general's insolence and plan their strategy for dealing with the inflammatory situation. At present this consists solely of biding their time and seeing how he will manage his military campaign.

As Sicinius and Brutus exit through Rome gates, the outer doors swing shut to transform the scene into the Volscian city of Corioli. The stage, which has just contained the tribunes' intimate dialogue, is suddenly teeming with the enemy lords who converge from opposite ends of the playing area to take up their seats along the lowest level of the stands. The senate's (and consequently the audience's) attention is focused on the figure who stands alone down center, clad in a black coat and carrying a black baton of command similar to that given to Coriolanus in 1.1. The visual parallel is unmistakable. Even before the first senator names him, the audience knows this to be Tullus Aufidius, the "lion" whom Coriolanus is "proud to hunt" (1.1.234–35). The effect is similar to a cinematic cross-fade between a group of men in conversation to a close-up on the subject of their discussion.

In response to the senate's inquiry about Rome's activities, Aufidius pulls a letter from his glove, a gesture indicative of neurotic possession and one which mirrors Coriolanus's exchange with Menenius in 5.2. He proceeds to read his informant's communication, which conveys the best possible news for the Volscian nation: "The dearth is great,/The people mutinous" (1.2.10–11). In the midst of the general details on Rome's military strategy comes a line which is of personal interest to Aufidius; his "old enemy" Martius heads one of the powers against Corioli, and the Volscian general savours the ironic paradox that he is "of Rome worse hated than of you" (1.2.13). Thus the first scene depicting Rome's civil strife is immediately counterpointed with its verbal description from the enemy perspective. The energy and flow of the lines give a ritual sense of destiny and inevitability to the passage, while the verse slows to monosyllabic heaviness as a textual clue for the actor to take his time in relishing his deep hatred of Martius. The ceremonial leave-taking which follows is directly contrasted with the chaos of Coriolanus's departure with the Roman senate. Again ritual is the keynote of the threefold farewell which precedes Aufidius's exit through the audience. Despite their outward confidence at being able to hold Corioli, the Volscians are deeply worried at the prospect of the oncoming war, and the quiet delivery of their final salute transmits this sense of gravity to the audience.

The talk of blood and war which has so permeated the opening of the play is domesticated into witty, sensual images by the matriarchs of Roman society in the scene which follows. The first appearance of feminine presence introduces a light and airy tone to the texture of the play, though a tension yet remains in the two women's irreconcilable responses to the dangers of the battlefield. Coriolanus's gentle wife recoils from all thought of blood and war, while Volumnia holds them to be the very essence of life, and to be celebrated rather than ignored. Yet the intimate nature of the scene is difficult to preserve in the context of such a public space. Both the stage and the set seem to fight against the depiction of private discourse within its confines. Thus, when the ladies enter through the main gates and seat themselves in the sand slightly right of center, it is difficult for the audience to make the mental transition from the political arena of 1.2 to the present domestic interior. Several alternatives were explored during rehearsals to ameliorate the awkwardness of this entrance, the diary recording of which is transcribed in Chapter One.

At first the women were to be "discovered" on the set after a brief blackout, Virgilia in position at her embroidery stand, Volumnia lounging on a day-bed. Yet all furniture and internal blackouts were cut from the production before its first run on 14 October to facilitate the cross-cutting between scenes and keep the audience's attention by maintaining the play's relentless momentum. A second version had them enter from opposite ends of the stage; yet this too was found to be awkward because of congestion in the wings after the mass exit of the Volscian senate in the preceding scene. The final alternative was to move the action from the sand to the foot of the stairs. The tighter area better suggested an interior setting and avoided the problem of the ladies in jewels and formal attire sitting in the sand. Obscured sightlines, however, rendered this impossible. Although the audience was still able to see the women, it could not do so comfortably, as only their heads were visible when they sat on the stairs. To block them standing, especially with the added presence of Valeria halfway into the scene, could only be artificial and unrealistic, even with the most well-intentioned suspension of disbelief. Thus the action was restored to the center of the sandpit— the best possible solution to a difficult piece of staging.

The scene opens with the two women embroidering the sleeves of Coriolanus's dress shirt. Their physical proximity and joint labour transmit a sense of the close bond which exists between them, despite their outward lack of communication. The intimate at-

mosphere is built up, then dispelled by the sparkling entrance of
Valeria, whose chatty prose breaks through the slow formality of
her friends' verse and quickens the pace of the scene. She brightly
sends up the image of the dutiful wife with "You would be another
Penelope" (1.3.82), and seeks to entice Virgilia out of doors to
"visit the good lady that lies in" (1.3.77)—an important event, as a
member of her circle is about to give birth in the midst of war.
Virgilia is moved by the request but, like her husband, cannot be
brought to infringe her vow. Valeria takes her arm as though to
move her physically, but the gesture has no effect. Virgilia's
strength comes from her stillness, and she is the only stationary
character on stage. She does not whine or play games; she has
simply made a decision and, like Coriolanus, she is "constant"
(1.1.238).

The scene works best when the actress plays Virgilia's strength
rather than her sadness, allowing a sense of melancholy to peep
through only occasionally, to add variation to the role. Valeria's
reference to her son gives her the opportunity to play maternal
pride and affection, while the description of young Martius as "the
father's son" (1.3.57) chasing and "mammocking" butterflies brings
a moment of ironic recognition. This speech marks the introduction
of one of the play's key emblems, an image used by Cominius to
characterize the Volscians following Coriolanus:

> Against us brats, with no less confidence
> Than boys pursuing summer butterflies,
> Or butchers killing flies
>
> (4.6.94–96)

and again later by Menenius in his aphoristic explanation of Rome's
helpless plight:

> There is differency between a grub and a butterfly;
> yet your butterfly was a grub. This Martius is
> grown from man to dragon: he has wings: he's more
> than a creeping thing.
>
> (5.4.11–14)

Communication of the image must be clear and precise; it is therefore regrettable that its significance is missed in the domestic scene,
where a sense of intimacy is largely created at the expense of
audibility. This is not the fault of the actresses involved, but rather
the result of a structural defect in the theater itself. The Olivier is

notorious for its poor audibility, and James Hiley documents this problem in his book on the making of the National's 1981 production of Brecht's *Galileo*.

Communication with the audience improves at the end of the scene, with Valeria's public announcement that there is "excellent news" of Virgilia's husband (1.3.88–89). Volumnia is ecstatic, but her daughter-in-law experiences mixed emotions; she is obsessed by the thought of Coriolanus in battle, and fears that any news which arrives so early must report defeat, perhaps even his death. In addition to its expository function, this passage is crucial to the actress's characterization of Valeria. Up to this point she has been presented as a social butterfly, but the audience here catches a glimpse of the bright and politically aware woman that exists under the witty exterior. She possesses knowledge of Rome's military strategy and the fact that she has "heard a senator speak it" (1.3.94) is a testament to her fundamental intelligence, for he would not have passed such important information to a mindless chatterbox. Yet even this news cannot tempt Virgilia to quit the house. She refuses with monosyllabic firmness and moves off right, while Volumnia and Valeria exit left to celebrate the Roman success.

Even before the ladies have completed their exit, the lights go down on the sandpit and a spot hits the scaffolding right, where Coriolanus stands perched for his opening line "Yonder comes news" (1.4.1). The audience is immediately transported to the Roman camp before Corioli mentioned by Valeria in the preceding scene. The dramatic "discovery" of the warrior above plunges us into the action *in medias res* and establishes the fast-paced dynamic which is maintained throughout the battle sequences in Act 1. Soldiers fill the stage and Coriolanus descends to join them, as the messenger runs down the central aisle to deliver his report on the enemy troops: "They lie in view, but have not spoke as yet" (1.4.4). Tension fills the air in the moments that precede the full eruption of war, yet the overriding impression is one of the good humour and physical camaraderie which characterize the Roman camp. The freedom which Coriolanus experiences on the battlefield marks a complete contrast with the hatred the people bear him in Rome.

The rhythmic beating of drums and the emanation of smoke from behind Corioli's walls draw the army's attention to the gates upon which two Volscian senators stand, inviting them to battle. Suddenly the gates open to reveal the Volscian soldiers in a haze of smoke, illuminated from behind so that they appear as faceless figures, their weapons gleaming in the light. The Romans stand amazed; the surprise tactic momentarily conquers them before

Coriolanus exhorts them to attack. The blocking of this fight sequence proved to be of greater difficulty than most battle scenes in Shakespeare because of its dependence on strategic intelligence for success. Hall stressed that great care must be taken to follow the textual pointers and information given in individual lines, as this is clearly not a war that is to be won on the strength of brawn alone. At the same time the actors must not lose their sense of militaristic frenzy and pleasure in blood-sport. They must consider what Shakespeare is saying about the kind of fighting men they are and the kind of war they are engaged in, then push for the same critical reception it would have found among the audience indigenous to its time.

The fight director also met with the logistical problem of having to block the sequence with twelve actors for the Roman power and only eleven for the Volscian side; of those eleven, two are women and four musicians, yet they must initially prove the victors of the field. Thus it was decided to create the menacing tableau within Corioli gates, and to use the musicians to swell the army only during the rout. The women carry flags and utter war cries as they chase the Romans around the perimeter of the circle to the upstage walls, then disappear again into the city.

Despite the textual reference to ladders being used to beseige the city (1.4.22), fight director Malcolm Ranson opted against having the Roman soldiers scale the walls. Such an image would have reduced Corioli to the small space represented by the gates, which must form the focal, though not the sole visual point of reference if the element of spectacle is to be exploited to its full potential. Likewise, the stage picture is dramatically weakened if the Volsces "issue forth their city" (1.4.23) while the Romans are perched above their heads. The moves of the actual fight must be brief and remain a peripheral image to the gates and to Coriolanus himself, who stands in the center of the stage brandishing the Roman banner, and cursing his men as they run past in twos and threes to retreat to the safety of the trenches below. The gates slowly open inward, while hazy illumination and eerie music mystically entice the warrior to enter its confines. It is ironic that the sense of supernatural danger which proves irresistible to Coriolanus also accounts for his soldiers' lack of enthusiasm to follow him into the city. He is separated from his men by that ideal code which is the very essence of his heroism, but which remains incomprehensible to the ordinary footsoldier who follows orders rather than glory. Thus the second soldier's practical comment that the gates have shut him in "To th'pot" (1.4.47) explodes the emblem of romantic heroism we have just witnessed and reveals Coriolanus to be as isolated within the culture of the battlefield as he is in the public sphere of Roman society.

Titus Lartius, who had earlier been driven offstage right, now returns to meet with an extraordinary sight: the men whom he has last seen in the throes of battle stand lost and inactive, their general nowhere to be found. Apprised of the situation, he stands center and delivers a eulogy with sword upraised toward the gates through which Coriolanus has vanished. Lartius delivers his lines with a Germanic firmness that is appropriate both to his own characterization as a practical man of action, and to the harsh consonantal sounds of the words themselves:

> A carbuncle entire, as big as thou art,
> Were not so rich a jewel. Thou wast a soldier
> Even to Cato's wish, not fierce and terrible
> Only in strokes, but with thy grim looks and
> The thunder-like percussion of thy sounds
> Thou mad'st thine enemies shake, as if the world
> Were feverous and did tremble.
>
> (1.4.55–61)

Far from being written as a moment of melodramatic sentimentality, this is a eulogy uttered for and by a military commander, and must be spoken in appreciation of his efforts rather than in lamentation for his loss.

Almost before Lartius can conclude his speech, the gates reopen to reveal Coriolanus *"bleeding, assaulted by the enemy."* This sequence was run in several different forms before the blocking was finalized. At first the warrior opened the gates himself, shrouded in a veil of mist as he reached for the tattered flag and waved it to beckon his men. To achieve an added sense of mysticism, the sequence was revised so that the doors opened of themselves; one saw only billowing smoke, then the Roman standard, and finally the figure which the soldiers recognize to be that of Martius. Hall, however, ultimately decided to return to the original stage direction in order to allow the audience a glimpse of the solitary figure painting the city "With shunless destiny" (2.2.112), as Cominius later reports him to the senate. Thus the doors now open to reveal Coriolanus driving back two Volscian opponents. He turns to summon his troops, banner in one hand, sword in the other, and the soldiers enthusiastically rush through the gates to "fetch him off, or make remain alike" (1.4.62).

This dramatic exit flows smoothly into the opening of the following scene. Almost before Corioli gates have closed behind the attacking power, Coriolanus and Titus Lartius appear above to ceremoniously replace the Volscian flag with the Roman standard, then turn to face upstage to acknowledge the cheers of their triumphant army. Their attention is recalled to the sandpit below as the gates suddenly reopen to disgorge the looters who exultantly emerge laden with the spoils they mean to carry to Rome. Enraged at their mercenary activity, Coriolanus uses the Volscian banner as a spear to hurl down at "these movers" (1.5.4). To him war can never be spoils or reward, but only the glory of the deed itself. Two of the looters exit right as the missile hits the sand, while the third dodges left, returns, grabs the standard, and runs off right waving it delightedly. Hearing the sound of battle raging in the distance, Coriolanus ignores his friend's cautionary remonstrances and scales down the walls to arm himself with the shield conveniently dropped by the looters. He pauses downstage center, an emblem of heroic energy, before running through the audience to exit via the auditorium's main doors. Lartius then turns to his lieutenant to issue commands for holding the town; individual heroism is thus counterpointed with the mundane necessities of military life.

The scene in Cominius's camp maintains the atmosphere of heightened emotion established in the preceding battle sequences. The soldiers enter from various sides of the stage (visually foreshadowing the revelation that they have "retired" from, rather than won, the field (1.6.50) in that state of complete physical exhaustion where tempers can flare and any explosion is possible. Thus Cominius almost runs mad when he realizes that the messenger has brought false news, and that Titus Lartius has not lost the day. The necessity of playing the full stops in his opening exhortation enables the actor to give a mosaic coloring to the speech, punctuating it with gasps of desperation and exhaustion. Coriolanus enters through the audience literally a "flay'd" man (1.6.22); blood streams down his chest as he runs down the stairs and onto the stage to embrace Cominius, as the physical and sexual imagery of the verse reaches its climax:

> Oh! let me clip ye
> In arms as sound as when I woo'd; in heart
> As merry as when our nuptial day was done,
> And tapers burn'd to bedward.
>
>   (1.6.29–32)

The two men break apart and return to practical consideration of the wars after Cominius's greeting "Flower of warriors" (1.6.32). The sequence leading up to the embrace is played as a moment of absolute tenderness rather than hearty friendship, and their slowness of movement lends the gesture an air of ritual dignity and true affection. Coriolanus proceeds to tell him of Lartius's success, and Cominius at first cheers the Roman conquest along with his men, then suddenly turns with a violent explosion to draw his sword on the soldier who reported defeat; in public scenes (2.2, 3.3) Cominius experiences a tension between the public image and the private self, but here the high adrenalin which comes with intense physical exertion renders his response completely emotional, and it is Coriolanus who must force him to regain control. As Hall told the actors in rehearsal, the scene is absolutely Elizabethan;[2] the keynotes are adrenalin, exhaustion, blood and war, and they must be accentuated rather than ignored in order to exploit the full dramatic impact of its rising dynamic.

The tone suddenly becomes ominous as Cominius describes their enforced retreat and the power of the Volscian army. Just as the Roman forces are at their weakest they must face a crack lot, and above all a crack lot led by Aufidius himself. The slight pause after the comma and the repeated alliteration of "Martius, we have at *di*sad*v*antage fought,/An*d di*d retire to win our purpose" (1.6.49– 50) betrays Cominius's difficulty in finding the proper words. Yet Coriolanus thrives when pitted against impossible odds, which provide but another opportunity to test and display his superhuman prowess; and his enthusiasm for the fight infuses the exhausted soldiers with renewed courage and dedication. He delivers a brilliant oration which encapsulates the nature of his heroic identity, the importance of fame, defiance of death, and invincibility in fair fight:

> If any such be here—
> As it were sin to doubt—that love this painting
> Wherein you see me smear'd; if any fear
> Lesser his person than an ill report;
> If any think brave death outweighs bad life,
> And that his country's dearer than himself;
> Let him alone, or so many so minded,
> Wave thus to express his disposition,
> And follow Martius.
>
> (1.6.67–75)

As he speaks, he drops his sword and removes the tattered, blood-stained jacket that hangs about his shoulders;[3] he is then picked up by two soldiers, while a third waves a red banner in front of the tableau to mask the moment when he ascends the other's shoulders. Thus Coriolanus delivers the final lines from above, extending his arm in a fist salute to "express his disposition" on the first cry of "Martius," which is picked up by the warriors in a three-fold cheer. Then, waving the Roman standard passed to him, Coriolanus utters the final invocation "O me alone! Make you a sword of me!" (1.6.76) in a chilling emblem of the "thing of blood" described by Cominius in 2.2 (line 109). One might well believe his sword to be "death's stamp . . . whose every motion/Was tim'd with dying cries" (2.2.107–10), as we see him standing on the soldier's shoulders with his fist in the air, dripping with the blood of his victims, the red flag flying. Hall wisely decided to conclude the scene with this most powerful image, and consequently cut the speech which follows. Coriolanus simply descends as he rhetorically demands "If these shows be not outward, which of you/But is four Volsces?" (1.6.77–78) and rushes off to "Run reeking o'er the lives of men" (2.2.119). The soldiers barely pause for Cominius's command to "March on, my fellows" (1.6.85), as they move to follow their leader to the battlefield; and the scene ends with a burst of climactic energy.

The short sequence which follows largely fulfills the practical function of allowing Coriolanus time to accomplish his brief costume change, and to get into position for his next entrance. The problem when directing this scene lies in making such theatrical filler of dramatic interest to the audience, especially when the information transmitted is purely verbal and military, in the midst of the fast-paced action of the war. Titus Lartius and his party enter through the main gates in a clear image of conquest. Yet even though the Romans are the present victors of the siege, an air of uncertainty and imminent danger still pervades the scene, as the general cautions that "if we lose the field,/We cannot keep the town" (1.7.4–5). Seriousness of tone and clipped speech characterize the actor's delivery of his brief lines, enhancing our sense of his professionalism, and preserving the line of tension which must feed into the single combat that follows. The soldiers salute one another, and Lartius follows his guide off left to the Roman camp; his lieutenant reenters Corioli gates, which snap shut behind him. The image of the Roman high command in action has been conveyed in but a few short seconds.

The misty illumination of the upstage gates is replaced by a pool of light hitting the sand, as the enemy generals suddenly appear to either side of the circle and confront each other on the battlefield. Shakespeare offers very few textual clues for the blocking of their encounter; the stage directions read *"Here they fight, and certain Volsces come in the aid of Aufidius. Martius fights till they be driven in breathless"* (1.8.13). Four different interpretations for the visual narrative were discussed during rehearsals.[4] The two generals could enter already flanked by representatives of each army. Coriolanus could enter solo, see the Volscian power and say that he will fight with "none but thee" (1.8.1), which results in the one to one combat with Aufidius. Coriolanus and Aufidius could both enter alone looking for one another, fight, then be joined by the Volscian army seeking out their missing general. Or, finally, the Volscian soldiers could observe the battle from all four corners of the set and, when Aufidius is disarmed upstage, move in to encircle Coriolanus in the center of the sandpit. Hall decided it to be unlikely that Aufidius would endanger himself by entering solo; the army seems to enter on cue the second that he is in trouble. The presence of representatives from each power also removes the logistical problem of what to do with the banners which Coriolanus and Aufidius display on their entrance. The necessity of placing the flags in artificially arranged cornerposts is avoided by passing them to two soldiers who act as batmen. The armies then watch from their position on the shadowy perimeter as their generals fight in the brightly lit circle of sand. Although this interpretation is theatrically practical and textually justifiable, I found the earlier version of Coriolanus and Aufidius entering entirely alone more powerful; there was no elaborate preparation—just two bodies and two flags seeking combat. This image also allowed Aufidius more integrity in cursing his officers' "officious" and unvaliant intervention, and intensified his psychological journey at the end of the play, when he does resort to treachery as the sole means of annihilating his enemy.

In a demonstration given at the "Coriolanus Weekend" hosted by the National Theatre in May of 1985, fight director Malcolm Ranson described other versions of the combat discarded during the planning stages. The rationale for such a complex piece of choreography was governed first by the physical limitations of the space, which is deceptively large in appearance, for the actors' manipulation of their weapons is restricted by the audience presence on stage. There is no freedom to engage in a free-for-all brawl—the moves must be short, tight, and at a distance from the spectators if one is not to lose their trust. Secondly the fight arranger must consider the individual personalities of the characters concerned: Coriolanus and Aufidius are both proud soldiers, and there is honour in their engagement. Each can turn away with the security of knowing that he will not be stabbed in the back. Finally, the actors themselves must influence the style of the fight, if the director is not to impose moves which they cannot interpret in character, or which they are physically incapable of performing. The demands of the fight are increased by the space in which it is enacted, for the sand creates an uneven surface beneath the actors' feet (despite the gymnastic bags which line the pit to increase stability).[5] Consequently, the sand kicked into the air during the scuffle renders the weapons slippery to hold and restricts visibility.

Much thought went into the choice of the weapons to be used by the two warriors. Ranson originally planned to equip the men only with the pennanted spears which appear for the initial flourish in the finished production. The fight was to begin with an image of civilized warfare and end in a primitive scuffle with broken weapons, the warriors slowly getting closer and closer until they were down in the sand, the audience not knowing whether they were making love or fighting. However, the decision was soon made to throw out such a depiction of their love/hate relationship, because of the logistical problem of removing the spears from the sand once Aufidius's soldiers rush in to his defence, and because the actors preferred their first touch to come with the climactic embrace in 4.5. The use both of rapiers and broadswords was likewise discounted. The image they convey is inconsistant with the costuming of the company in classical robes and modern dress, and neither weapon is capable of producing the desired sound. Hence the conclusion to arm the men with military sabres and shields, as the only solution visually consistant with the rest of the production.

Once the type of weapon had been chosen, it became necessary to determine the material from which they would be constructed. As the cinema has conditioned audiences' auditory response to any stage fight, the sound made by the swords and shields became a primary consideration. The shields are constructed with secure handles for the actors to grasp, since they are used by the two warriors until the final moments of combat. Designed like a bell top, and made of heavy steel, they have a central pivot and an arm for support. The weight and strength of this weapon are crucial, for Aufidius falls to the sand and uses his shield as a fulcrum to rise and regain his balance—even a heavy one runs the risk of bending with the weight imposed. As an added safety precaution, the central

"T"-section is welded and bolted onto the inside of the shield to prevent it breaking off.

Light swords too run the risk of being brittle; therefore it was necessary to give them a certain weight to avoid breakage in performance. Because the director had chosen to amplify the battle din, thus heightening the surrealistic feel of their encounter, the use of heavy swords was also preferable. Lighter weapons would have given a tinnier sound, and the reverb board would have picked up and echoed distracting noises. The fight director considered the use of a sword knot to prevent the actors losing their weapons before the appointed time, but since Aufidius is disarmed before the end of the fight this was concluded to be impossible. It would have broken the visual continuity for one actor to be "tied" to his weapon, the other not, and would have undermined Coriolanus's fame for invincibility in fair fight. Nevertheless a sword knot for Coriolanus might have come in handy toward the beginning of the run; because of the quick change between 1.6 and 1.8, in which McKellen's body and arms are liberally coated with stage blood, the paint ran down the actor's wrists and hands, rendering the hilt slippery to hold. Coriolanus was several times the first to be disarmed (including the performance on opening night). On each occasion, however, McKellen quickly retrieved his sword, and I doubt whether the audience took the slip for anything other than a blocked move in the fight sequence.

As finally performed, the scene begins with a rush of excitement as Coriolanus and Aufidius run onto the stage, nearly naked and unarmed, wearing only primitive loincloths and carrying banners. As each man utters his first line he holds the army's standard out in front of his body, thus displaying the emblems of the Roman and Volscian nations.[6] They then turn to arm and helmet themselves for gladiatorial combat, reentering the circle at the same moment. Coriolanus is more stationary and controlled in the confrontation, while Aufidius moves with the supple and lithe quality of a young animal on "Halloa me like a hare" (1.8.7). Their lines leading up to the battle contrast with the public show of their physical preparations; they are spoken for each other alone, and in no way for the soldiers lurking in the sidelines. Coriolanus wins the battle of words as well as of swords with his taunt that "Alone I fought in your Corioli walls,/And made what work I pleas'd" (1.8.8–9), prompting Aufidius's vain boast:

> Wert thou the Hector
> That was the whip of your bragg'd progeny,

Thou shouldst not 'scape me here.

(1.8.11–13)

The actors' makeup reinforces the impression of the Roman's supremacy. The "painting" which coats Coriolanus testifies to his vaunt that " 'tis not my blood/Wherein thou seest me mask'd" (1.8.9–10), whereas the red streaming down Aufidius's chest runs in straight lines, suggesting that it issues from wounds on his own body. The epic nature of their confrontation is intensified by the use of a reverberating soundboard that magnifies and echoes both the clash of their steel blows and the vocalizations added in the second sequence, when the exhausted warriors gear up their courage and express the increasing drain on their energies. At one point before his ultimate victory, Coriolanus temporarily downs his enemy; but by exerting pressure on the former's shield, Aufidius sends him reeling by sheer force of foot. Although disarmed, Aufidius is still successful in knocking down his opponent and attempts to decapitate him by thrusting the rim of his shield into the sand. Coriolanus, however, rolls to one side and disarms him of his last remaining weapon.[7] The panting general runs to a point of safety upstage center, while the Volscian army rushes in to ambush his vanquisher. As the Romans move to counter the attack, Coriolanus waves them back in order to fight on single-handed; the two men have vowed to fight solo, and even if the Volscians are prepared to break the compact, Coriolanus refuses to become the "promise-breaker" he so despises (1.8.2). He chases the officers off left, leaving Aufidius naked and weaponless to suffer the agonies of absolute defeat. The latter moves downstage to clear away the remains of the battle, violently grabbing his shield and helmet from the sand as he curses his men, and exits trailing his sword behind him. The image of the proud warrior at the start of combat is thus powerfully transformed into an emblem of epic frustration.

Rather than plunging immediately from this potent evocation of despair into the midst of the Roman festivities, Hall and McKellen chose rather to attenuate their visual commentary on the ravages of war by incorporating the tableau of Coriolanus bloody and wounded in the moments after the battle. He puts a sling over his arm before the action begins again, then remains stage left huddled in a blanket, exhausted and angered at the prospect of hearing his little "dieted/In praises sauc'd with lies" (1.9.51–52). The scene begins as the Roman army is illuminated for the first time since taking up their position stage right in 1.8, and Cominius moves forward to congratulate the warrior on his superhuman achievement. Titus Lartius enters with his power through the audience, left, to cap the general's praise, and the soldiers advance to shake Coriolanus's hand; Hall stressed in rehearsal that this salute must be crisp and professional, evoking the feeling of a "Roman Third Reich" rather than *Henry V* or "public school hearty."8 These soldiers know and love their leader, and any performance of this scene must transmit to the audience Coriolanus's ability to cope with their demonstration of approval and affection on a masculine, jovial level. It is only back in Rome, outside his own culture of the battlefield, that his violent repulsion from public praise becomes ungovernable. Although any acclamation must of necessity be torture for Coriolanus, his men are able to control his outbursts by maintaining a light and witty tone; they give him a trumpet fanfare, the gift of a horse, a name, and even take delight in his embarrassment. Thus the transition between the agonized cry of "May these same instruments, which you profane,/Never sound more!" (1.9.41–42), to a stubborn desire to bring their hyperbolic imagery down to earth with "I have not wash'd my nose that bled" (1.9.47), and finally to grudging acceptance of praise—"when my face is fair, you shall perceive/Whether I blush or no: howbeit, I thank you" (1.9.67–68)—makes both textual and dramatic sense. The success of this passage lies in the actors' ability to find different dimensions in their lines, and thus avoid playing the same pattern twice, despite the length of the scene.

Unlike the depiction of Coriolanus in 1.1, the dramatic tension does not spring from the warrior's desire to stand in isolation from his fellows, but rather from an impossible desire to become one with them. "I have done/As you have done" (1.9.15–16), "(I) stand upon my common part with those/That have beheld the doing" (1.9.39–40)—in this scene he wants only wine, good fellowship and unity with his men; it is they who seek to separate him as their leader, their saviour and their god. Thus their bestowal of the agnomen "Coriolanus" becomes an extremely reverential, even a holy moment, as the soldiers raise their swords and stand at attention, chanting his name in choral unison to the beat of the trumpet fanfare.

During the ritual formality of that moment, Hall again stressed that the actors maintain the Germanic emphasis inherent in an absolute affirmation of physical prowess, and not lapse into the British tendency to retreat from such display with a self-deprecating smile. Thus the earlier communal cry of "Martius, Martius, Martius!" (1.9.40) is punctuated by the fascist fist salute, as the cheers are picked up and echoed by speakers throughout the theater for added texture in the celebration. "So, to our tent" (1.9.71) comes as Cominius's factual capping of Coriolanus's thanks, and provides the cue for the musicians and the main body of soldiers to exit and clear the stage. Those who remain crowd around Coriolanus as he requests his sole reward: that they "give my poor host freedom" (1.9.85). Thus a sense of physical and psychological claustrophobia combines with exhaustion to prompt his forgetting of the Volscian's name—an important moment, for it shows the audience that it is not the poverty but rather the vascillating nature of the Roman mob that renders the plebeians hateful in his eyes. Cominius is solicitous during his emotional collapse, hastening to accompany Coriolanus to his tent and to see to his wounds. The final image of the scene thus represents the hitherto isolated figure surrounded by his friends, who share in his triumph and support him in his need.

This tempered moment of victorious celebration and cameraderie is immediately cross-cut with the devastation that afflicts the Volscian party. As the Romans exit en masse stage right, the enemy soldiers appear from either side of the playing area, as though regrouping in a weakened state after their enforced retreat. Aufidius enters as we last saw him, naked, though now with the black coat draped over his shoulders, his body streaming with blood, sword trailing behind him. The despair and anger of his opening line "The town is ta'en!" (1.10.1) mingle with the quiet solemnity of the stage picture, as the ravages of war find visual expression in the wounded bodies lying strewn about their leader. Aufidius surveys the devastation, and makes the internal shift from humiliation at his powerlessness to regain the city without imposed "Condition" (1.10.3) to a personal sense of outraged pride: "Mine emulation/Hath not that honour in't it had" (1.10.12–13). This increasing withdrawal into a sense of his personal griefs is signalled by a physical move downstage away from the soldiers, to visualize the enemy in his mind's eye as he curses his defeat:

> Five times, Martius,
> I have fought with thee; so often hast thou beat me;
> And would do so, I think, should we encounter
> As often as we eat.
>
> (1.10.7–10)

His impotent frustration builds to a climactic outburst of animalistic fury, as he vows to "Wash my fierce hand in's heart" (1.10.27). He can return to a tentative, bitter form of self-control only through submerging himself once again in the overriding demands of practical action; he orders his soldiers:

> Go you to th'city;
> Learn how 'tis held, and what they are that must
> Be hostages for Rome.

(1.10.27–29)

The Volscian general strides through the audience to make his way to the cypress grove,[9] while his wounded men silently pick themselves up and exit in several directions to tend their wounds and carry out his orders.

3
Act 2

Act 2 scene 1 returns the audience to the Roman street which formed the setting for the opening of the play, thus heightening the visual juxtaposition between the city on the threshold of war and its response to the news of Coriolanus's victory. Menenius and the tribunes enter the square, now empty of the throngs which had earlier filled its perimeter, as the patrician exultantly announces that "The augurer tells me we shall have news tonight" (2.1.1) and that the omens are good, though "Not according to the prayer of the people" (2.1.3). Such an arch comment is well calculated to provoke the sensitive magistrates, who confront him from their position downstage center with his own reputation as a "per/fecter jiber for the table than a necessary bencher in/the Capitol" (2.1.80–82); Menenius, however, easily parries their verbal blows as he lounges back in his seat in the stands, right. The stage picture thus conveys a sense of the elder statesman's "humorous" disposition (2.1.46) and unflappable self-confidence, while linking the two tribunes in their isolation from Rome's aristocracy.

Their battle of wits is interrupted by the ladies' entrance through the green doors which have once again replaced Corioli gates at the end of 1.10. Menenius rushes upstage to meet them and to receive certain news of Martius's success, while the tribunes remain in their solitary position at the foot of the sand. The mingled joy and relief with which the women greet their friend brings an added lift to the scene and quickens its tempo, as each caps the other's line and Menenius poses question after question, almost before receiving an answer to the last.[1] The glee with which he demands "Is he not/ wounded? He was wont to come home wounded" (2.1.117–18) and Volumnia's staunch "Oh, he is wounded; I thank the gods for't" (2.1.120) cannot fail to meet with hearty laughter from a post-Freudian audience, which finds the image of this self-contained middle-aged mother bloodthirstily revelling in the battle scars of her son infinitely amusing. Menenius's agreement that his wounds become him if they "be not too much" (2.1.121) is delivered by actor Frederick Treves as a quiet conciliation to Virgilia's distress at their talk of blood and war. Yet the private interchange must be uttered in a public tone in order to preserve audibility for the audience, and to maintain the momentum of the scene.

Again the relentless flow of the lines seems to defy the logic of immediate response, as Volumnia momentarily ignores Menenius's inquiry whether the senate is "possessed" of this news (2.1.131) to hurry her friends to meet the procession with "Good ladies, let's go" (2.1.132). Then, as though suddenly recollecting his words, she answers with a rapid "Yes, yes, yes" (2.1.132) as they run arm in arm to take up their positions for the triumph. The talk again turns to Coriolanus's wounds as they crane to catch an early glimpse of the oncoming party. Menenius again exploits the humor of the exchange by delivering "Martius is coming home: he has more/ cause to be proud" (2.1.143–44) and "every gash was an enemy's/ grave" (2.1.154–55) over Volumnia's head to the tribunes, who stand beside, though still in isolation from them. A trumpet fanfare announces the approach of the victorious army, and the fast-paced prose suddenly moves into verse as Volumnia sets the scene for her son's victorious entrance. Her lines

> Death, that dark spirit, in's nervy arm doth lie,
> Which, being advanc'd, declines, and then men die
>
> (2.1.159–60)

are chillingly counterpointed by the sound of a single drum beat, recalling the awesome force of his deeds on the battlefield, and setting the tone for the triumphal ritual to follow.

The herald takes his position above Rome gates as the senators and nobles enter from various sides of the stage to assume a circular formation, with Volumnia, Virgilia, Valeria and Menenius at its center. Hall wanted the Roman ceremony to be "supremely vulgar,"[2] in order to heighten Coriolanus's disgust with the hollow trappings of social intercourse. Thus he originally blocked the scene with four red banners suspended from the flies, a red carpet issuing from Rome gates and running the length of the sand, and a rush of gold metallic confetti falling over Coriolanus's position at the foot of the stairs, alluding to the modern practise of hailing the conquering hero with a ticker-tape parade. However, use of the confetti during previews was found to be impractical, for there is no opportunity to clear its remains from the sandpit before the interval, and its presence proves distracting during the interior domestic and senate scenes. Hence it was cut before opening night. Hall instead chose to incorporate four extra banners within the stage picture; two drop into position near the wings, and one falls to either side of the nuntio above. They unfurl simultaneously with the company's mass entrance and the herald's announcement "Know, Rome, that all alone Martius did fight/Within Corioli gates" (2.1.161–2).

Cued by the actors, the stage audience stands and applauds rhythmically as Coriolanus, accompanied by Cominius and Titus Lartius, makes his way down the central aisle to arrive at the foot of the stage for the proclamation of his agnomen. Flags are waved to the sound of a trumpet fanfare, prompting Coriolanus's angry outburst "No more of this; it does offend my heart" (2.1.167), the first of the warrior's futile gestures to break through the offensive formality of public show.[3] Cominius recalls him to the necessary performance of the triumphal rite with "Look, sir, your mother" (2.1.168), and Coriolanus ascends the stage to kneel at her feet, attempting to release his emotion within the bosom of his family, and thereby to transform the public event into a private reunion. This Volumnia cannot allow; she raises her son to his feet as she pronounces the name which he has won "By deed-achieving honour" (2.1.172)—"Coriolanus."[4]

Now Virgilia steps forward to silently greet her husband, who enfolds her in his cloak of victory and tenderly embraces her on "My gracious silence, hail" (2.1.174). The momentum of the scene is like a whirlpool spinning in tighter and tighter circles, as Coriolanus greets mother, wife, friend and senators; it was found in rehearsal that a slow procession of one after the other to shake his hand diminished the rising dynamic. Valeria has therefore been positioned right so that she can be easily seen by Coriolanus over Menenius's shoulder as he clips his friend, before hastily moving to kiss her hand on "O my sweet lady, pardon" (2.1.179).

Volumnia's "I know not where to turn" (2.1.180) gives the cast its cue to spring into action to greet the three returning generals, and the stage is momentarily overcome with a flurry of ecstatic handshakes and embraces. This visual confusion is resolved only with Menenius's enthusiastic pronouncement "You are three/That Rome should dote on" (2.1.185–86), as the generals turn to link arms and face him centerstage. Yet the well-meaning patrician cannot resist a jibe at the two tribunes who still stand in their original position down left, and whose sour faces do indeed resemble the "crabtrees" tauntingly mentioned by Menenius, that "will not/Be grafted" to the general relish (2.1.187–88). The whole scene suddenly halts with the old man's faux pas, as the assembly turns to observe their confusion. Some find the remark silly, some offensive, but all find it eminently interesting. Coriolanus utters a dark laugh and ironically agrees "ever, ever" (2.1.191), while Cominius hurriedly signals to the herald to restore order with "Give way there, and go on" (2.1.192).

All might still be well, but Volumnia refuses to allow the ceremony to end without publicly announcing her desire that Coriolanus's military triumph also be crowned with the laurels of political office. Cominius again jumps into the breach to move the procession offstage before the explosive situation becomes irredeemable. Trumpets sound and the stage audience rhythmically applauds as Coriolanus exits upstage center, flanked by his wife and mother, and closely followed by the rest of the cast. As Rome gates close behind the patricians, the stage audience seats itself once more and the tribunes move centerstage to comment on the action, as they did in 1.1.

They now have greater cause than ever before to fear the danger of Coriolanus's power, for his victories have restored his lost favour in the eyes of the people. Just as they anticipate the end to their authority which must certainly accompany his consulship, a messenger arrives to confirm their worst forebodings. Hall gave much thought to the identity of this minor character, which remains unspecified in the text, for his own attitude to the news he bears must necessarily colour the audience's reaction as well. At one point in rehearsals he was personated as a citizen, who speaks of Coriolanus's probable election with worried aspect and scathingly describes the matrons' flinging gloves, "Ladies and maids their scarves and handkerchers" (2.1.262) in an ironic tone. Yet Hall decided that much of the dramatic tension of the following sequences would be lost if the audience is forewarned of Coriolanus's tyrannical sway by such a depiction of universal dread, and so the messenger became an aedile. Consequently his speech expresses pleasure and awe rather than anxiety. His breathless entrance through the main gates suggests that unbounded enthusiasm has prompted him to hurry directly from the end of the procession to summon the tribunes; " 'Tis thought/That Martius shall be consul" (2.1.258–59) is then delivered on one breath as the label of the scene. This alternative is preferable to the previous staging, for it adds a rich overtone of irony to the passage, as the messenger is bursting with excitement to tell that which must be the very last thing that Brutus and Sicinius desire to hear. It makes textual as well as theatrical sense, for the image which remains uppermost in the mind of the audience is that of the spectacular triumph. Coriolanus is still riding high on the crest of his victory; there is as yet no cause for any but the tribunes to experience concern.

As the tribunes exit through Rome gates, they are passed by two officers who enter to transform the arena into the Roman senate. At first they were blocked to set purple cushions along the lowest level of the stands as seats for the city's magistrates, but this was cut during rehearsals when it became evident that the time-consuming process merely slowed the pace of the scene without significantly enhancing the stage picture. Instead, they simply assist one another to roll up the triumphal carpet and bring on the stool which is positioned centerstage, enjoying their job and the conversation as they move about their business. This sequence was radically pruned before the show entered previews, in order to convey the crux of the dialogue to the audience without straining its attention span and losing the build-up to the entrance of the senate. Their discussion both serves to summarize our perception of Coriolanus thus far and, in springing from the mouths of lower officials, it characterizes the people as intelligent and articulate when not swayed by the emotional shifts of mob psychology. The slight pause between "but he seeks their hate" and its punch line "with/greater devotion than they can render it him" (2.2.18–19) provokes a hearty laugh of recognition from the audience and wins its sympathy for the speakers. They jump to attention at either side of the main gates as they hear the approach of the senate, then close the doors behind the oncoming party.

The elders listen good-humouredly to Menenius's introductory remarks, seating themselves on "Most reverend and grave elders" (2.2.42) as they prepare "to thank and to remember" Coriolanus "With honours like himself" (2.2.47–48). The image transmitted is that of magistrates assembled to conduct the everyday affairs of state, with applause and parliamentary-like demeanor to punctuate the scene. The quick assumption of their positions in the stands draws an immediate parallel with the Volscian senate in 1.2. Cominius seats himself in the upstage corner nearest the right hand door, while Menenius remains in the midst of the senators stage left, and the tribunes distance themselves by immediately moving to the outer right stands. Brutus sits ramrod straight, while Sicinius indicates his cynical response to the proceedings by lounging back against his granite seat. Despite their visual isolation from the city's elders, the tribunes remain congenial in their game-playing at the opening of the scene, scrupulously observing the decorum of board-room behaviour. Yet the fatal mixture of events—that the first day of the tribunes' power should coincide with Coriolanus's election for consul—creates an underlying tension to the scene, whose quick pace is constantly punctured by dangerous interruptions and explosions.

The senators sense the potential inflammability of the situation and try to rush through their agenda, while at the same time ensuring strict adherence to political protocol. "Leave nothing out for length" (2.2.49) is thus said for the benefit of the new tribunes who are unfamiliar with the mode of proceedings, while addressing them as "Masters o'th'people" (2.2.51) is meant to flatter them into submission. The atmosphere is as yet "all port and cigars."[5] The first eruption threatens to occur only with the unwanted and unlooked for interjection by the tribunes, as Sicinius waves a document from his portfolio to catch the senators' attention, then makes a short but carefully prepared speech reminding Coriolanus of the necessary duty of honouring the people. It is the very overelaborate politeness of the tribune's words which sparks Menenius's curt response "That's off, that's off!/I would you rather had been silent" (2.2.60–61), thus in turn increasing the tone of confrontation in Brutus's reply. The senate is surprised by Sicinius's unexpected interjection—the tribunes are not meant to speak during these proceedings, nor indeed is Coriolanus; it marks a serious breach of expectation among the establishment gathering. Yet their strong reaction to the tribunes' exchange with Menenius must also include concern at the response which it will elicit from Coriolanus; all of Rome knows the contempt in which he holds them.

It is at this point that *"Coriolanus rises, and offers to go away"* (2.2.66); until now he has remained seated on the stool which the officers had positioned centerstage in the preceding sequence. The question was raised in rehearsal as to whether or not he should face the audience during the tribunes' interchange, but the stage image was judged to be more eloquent if he were to sit facing the senate upstage, with his back to the audience and his shoulders drooping. His mood is sufficiently established by our glimpse of his face when he first enters and looks about uncomfortably, before assuming his position at the center of the arena. His words to the tribunes are delivered in the tone of one who, though deeply angered, is struggling to remain in control of his violent emotions out of the great respect which he bears the senate, thus providing variety in the pattern of his revulsion from praise and public show.[6] Moving to regain his seat at Menenius's behest, he suddenly interrupts the gesture in mid-movement as he "flies" from their words, declaring

> I had rather have one scratch my head i'th'sun
> When the alarum were struck, than idly sit
> To hear my nothings monster'd
>
> (2.2.75–77)

in a tone of mingled anger, desperation and apology, before hastily exiting through the main gates.

As in (2.1), Cominius quickly fills the shocked silence which hangs over the senate. He begins his elegiac praise of the absent warrior on a note of absolute desperation, before warming to his subject and finally entrancing his audience, which bursts into "spontaneous" applause at the description of Coriolanus when first "brow-bound with the oak" (2.2.98). A sense of mystery and awesome power permeates his evocation of Coriolanus's deeds of battle, while a sudden drop in volume on "For this last" (2.2.101) recalls the audience's attention to the mystical wonder of his feats at Corioli, building to the monosyllabic crescendo of "He was a thing of blood, whose every motion/Was tim'd with dying cries" (2.2.109–10), a terrible war-machine who "struck/Corioli like a planet" (2.2.113–14). The tribunes and senate alike are impressed with the speech, and Coriolanus reenters to the sound of their applause,[7] but it does nothing to ameliorate the political situation. The soldier must still face the repulsive duty of showing his wounds to the people.

The officers open the gates to reveal Coriolanus sweating it out with his face to the upstage wall. Perceiving that his breach of decorum has been smoothed over by his friend, he embraces Cominius in a direct echo of their elaborate greeting on the battlefield in 1.6. Coriolanus picks up the consul's robe from the stool on which Cominius has placed it at the end of his speech, and fingers it in dreaded expectation of the trial to come. Intellectually he realizes the necessity of showing his wounds to the people, but remains emotionally repulsed by the act. Menenius attempts to make light of the request, knowing all too well the violence with which his protegé will respond. After "It then remains/That you do speak to the people" (2.2.134–35), Coriolanus quickly picks up the half-line cue as though to forestall further injunction. He delivers "I do beseech you,/Let me o'erleap that custom" (2.2.135–36) and

> It is a part
> That I shall blush in acting, and might well
> Be taken from the people
>
> (2.2.144–46)

in a casual tone, as though belittling the significance of the act.[8] These lines cannot be addressed to the tribunes who stand whispering amongst themselves stage right. In part they form a public speech directed to the whole senate, but primarily they are spoken to convince his uncle Menenius on a personal level that even though the ritual itself may not be a bad one, it is a role which his retiring nature renders him wholly unable to enact. Menenius rises and moves to face him directly on "Do not stand upon't" (2.2.150); he replaces the consul's robe on the stool and passes the gown of humility from Brutus to Coriolanus. Not donning the "humble weed" becomes a constitutional point, for it is absolutely impossible to be elected in the manner Coriolanus suggests without the overthrow of all tradition. The tribunes in their turn become increasingly desperate; if the approval of the senate alone is sufficient to elect their head of state, then the people stand to lose their newly-gained power.

This scene marks a crucial stage in Shakespeare's exploration of the mythic hero, and of the crisis which results when he is transplanted from the context of his superhuman achievement to the paralytic existence of daily life within the society that has accorded him fame. In Coriolanus, Shakespeare has created an extreme example of the traditional warrior-hero posited at an extreme moment in time, when the ideals of the past can no longer be recreated as the people and their tribunes will not allow it to happen. The senate would like to approve his request, but is powerless to do so because of their historic measure of allowing the people to elect their own representatives. The tribunes in their turn do not want an empty shell of office, but rather to return the life-blood to Rome's empty ritualized ceremonies, and to embue them with a sense of actuality. As Hall concluded in rehearsals, "One hundred years ago *Coriolanus* would not be a tragedy; one hundred years from now Coriolanus would not exist."[9]

Menenius lifts Coriolanus's hand on high as he wishes him all the "joy and honour" (2.2.154) which must be anathema to his soul, and the senate exits en masse through the main gates. The officers move to clear away their props from the stage during the tribunes' worried exchange rather than after their exit, thus facilitating the transition between scenes and enabling this sequence to run smoothly into the next. The citizens enter from various sides of the stage to meet in the market square and to discuss the upcoming election. The mood is light and festive, for all appreciate Coriolanus's victories for Rome, and have agreed to grant their voices if he "do require them." The "great toe" of their earlier rebellion stubbornly insists that they may still withold their vote, but his fellow, the third citizen, good humouredly rejoins that although

We have power in ourselves to do it, . . . it is a power that we have no power to do. For, if he show us his wounds and tell us his deeds, we are to put our tongues into those wounds and speak for them.

(2.3.4–8)

The speaker clearly enjoys the wit and paradox of his own lines; and in their subsequent interchange as the second and third citizens, actors Bill Moody and Glenn Williams bring a moment of expertly handled comic relief to the hitherto uniformly serious action of the play:

> *Second Cit.* Which way do you judge my wit would fly?
> *Third Cit.* Nay, your wit will not so soon out as another man's will;
> 'tis strongly wedged up in a blockhead. . . .
> *Second Cit.* You are never without your tricks; you may, you may.
>
> (2.3.25–36)

The amused assembly gives a hearty laugh as the prankster receives a well-deserved boot in the rear. It is into this spirit of festive gaiety that Coriolanus makes his scowling appearance. The citizens eagerly crane forward to watch his approach in humble weeds from the stands above left, then themselves exit right to prepare for the encounter. Only the "great toe" remains on stage throughout, perched in the scaffolding above right.[10]

Coriolanus enters closely followed by Menenius, as though coming directly from being schooled in the proper mode of behaviour. The back of the gown of humility is threadbare, and battle-bruises are visible on his right cheek, his chest and down his throat. He clutches the garment closely about his body, as though avoiding for as long as possible the moment when he must display his scars to the people, then stands with his friend stage right, glowering ominously on the wooden stool which the citizens positioned in the center of the sand at the top of the scene. He walks around the stool in disgust at the mere thought of the humiliation which he must undergo, muttering "Think upon me? Hang 'em!/I would they would forget me" (2.3.58–59). Menenius counters with the warning "You'll mar all" (2.3.60) as he points to the stool, which Coriolanus finally mounts, then to the warrior's head, which the latter violently covers with a large-brimmed hat. Coriolanus smiles ironically, revealing a self-deprecating sense of the ridiculous figure he now cuts. Menenius exits through the audience left, conjuring his protegé to "speak to 'em . . ./In wholesome manner" (2.3.61–62), while Coriolanus calls after him in a final vent of spleen "Bid them wash their faces,/And keep their teeth clean" (2.3.62–63).

McKellen and Hall engaged in long discussions as to how Coriolanus should behave toward the various "braces" who appear before him. He cannot be angry or the citizens would immediately react against him, but he must be sufficiently peremptory to awaken their doubts. The citizens who enter are sympathetically serious in their demeanor as they greet the hero; the humour of the scene stems from Coriolanus's own barbed puns and double meanings, rather than any hammed-up piece of stage business on their part, as he caustically demands the "price o'th'consulship" (2.3.74). The citizens exchange confused looks, while the "great toe" answers from above: "The price is, to ask it kindly" (2.3.75). Alerted to the fact that he is being watched, Coriolanus sarcastically bows toward his observer in the scaffolds on "Kindly, sir, I pray let me ha't" (2.3.76) and "There's in all two worthy voices/begged" (2.3.80–81), before dismissing the two citizens with a curt "adieu" (2.3.81). They exit right even as the second brace pass by to give their voices, regretting their election of one who clearly remains unaltered in his contempt for the people, yet still unprepared to recall their vote.

Coriolanus's impotent rage and hostile mockery build in his treatment of this next couple, who stand in mute incomprehension as he delivers his request for their voices quickly yet distinctly, so that the audience may follow his line of thought even if the untutored plebeians cannot. The rapid dynamic of the speech reaches its climax on "that is, sir, I will counterfeit the bewitchment/of some popular man, and give it bountiful to the/desirers" (2.3.100–102). Then, perceiving that they remain in total ignorance of his petition, he articulates his words syllable by syllable as though speaking to autistic children: "Therefore, beseech you, I may be consul" (2.3.102); he takes off his hat and holds it out in a gesture of arrogant supplication which makes the request unmistakable. The woman reacts to his physical signal and replies "We hope to find you our friend, and therefore/give you our voices heartily" (2.3.103–4). Then, fearing Coriolanus's growing violence of expression, she drags her husband offstage right to the safety of a neighbouring street.

Alone on stage for the first time since arriving in the market place, Coriolanus delivers an angry soliloquy which marks his first moment of direct communication with the audience. McKellen plays this speech in two ways, depending on the dynamic established in the preceding sequences. At times he begins with a tone of cold arrogance on "Better it is to die, better to starve,/Than crave the hire which first we do deserve" (2.3.112–13), building the crescendo of increasing violence to its pinnacle on

> What custom wills, in all things should we do't,
> The dust on antique time would lie unswept
> And mountainous error be too highly heap'd
> For truth to o'erpeer. Rather than fool it so,
> Let the high office and the honour go
> To one that would do thus.
>
> (2.3.117–22)

Yet it is McKellen's alternate manner of delivering this soliloquy which, to me, makes most sense of the character, and above all the character when placed in this situation of having to behave with a false humility that his soul abhors. The verse comes as a sudden explosion the moment the well-meaning citizens are clear of the stage, as Coriolanus unleashes an angry torrent of long pent-up frustration. He demands of the audience, in a direct reference to the scene just witnessed,

> Why in this wolvish toge should I stand here,
> To beg of Hob and Dick that does appear
> Their needless vouches?
>
> (2.3.114–16)

He descends from the podium on "Custom calls me to't" (2.3.116) and crosses downstage to address the lines which follow to individuals in the audience, thus intensifying the line of communication which has been opened between them. This violent outburst has the calming effect of enabling Coriolanus to regain his self-control. He concludes with the perverse resolution that if he must perform a role he will do it well: "I am half through,/The one part suffer'd, the other will I do" (2.3.122–23). Thus, when the third brace enters tentatively, expecting sarcasm, they are greeted with an unlooked-for friendliness, as Coriolanus exposes how easy it is to be superficially democratic. With each repetition of the word "voices" he moves to shake the plebeians' hands,[11] remounting the stool and standing with his hat stretched out before him, as he delivers "Indeed I would be consul" (2.3.130) in a tone of meek docility wholly alien to his spirit. His friendliness completely disarms the citizens, who enthusiastically proclaim him consul and exit with celebratory applause and cheers through the wings, right. Coriolanus's caustic delivery of "Worthy voices!" (2.3.136) punctures their cheerful mood and casts an ironic resonance over all that has gone before.

Menenius now enters through the audience, left, closely followed by the two tribunes. He joyfully announces that "You have stood your limitation, and the tribunes/Endue you with the people's voice" (2.3.137–38). Coriolanus expresses amazed disbelief with "Is this done?" (2.3.140), calling upon Sicinius to admit that he has indeed fulfilled the necessary form. Assured of his election, the warrior tentatively steps down from the podium and enquires whether he may now "change these garments" (2.3.145). Menenius promptly moves to cover him with the consul's robes and Coriolanus, with a sudden wriggle of his body, drops the antipathetic gown of humility to the sand and rushes up through the stands left. He pauses at its summit to throw down his hat before disappearing offstage, followed by Menenius.

The plebeians once again assemble in the square, as a disheartened Brutus asks his fellow to "dismiss the people" (2.3.152) who have entered with the celebratory joy that characterized their last exit, and who cannot at first understand the tribunes' disapproving reaction to their choice. Only the "great toe" immediately confirms their skepticism, as he descends from the scaffolding to assert that "He flouted us downright" (2.3.158). The payoff for his continued presence onstage throughout the preceding sequence comes with his ability to now speak with the authority of an eye-witness. The second citizen prompts the assembly to consider whether anyone actually saw "His marks of merit" (2.3.162); the round of "No"s (2.3.163) reaches its climax with the final "no man saw 'em" (2.3.163), as the citizens reach their mutual realization chorically and in rhythm.

The citizens form a single unit when schooled by the tribunes in the sequence which follows, yet here still function as individuals uncertain of their situation and ignorant of Coriolanus's treatment of the others. Each thinks that someone else has seen his wounds, and they therefore accord him their voices heartily; it is only when posed the direct question that there is a mounting crescendo of "I thought you saw them." Their recognition is characterized by amazement rather than angry tension, in order to preserve the serious portrayal of the crowd and to prevent it from visually turning into an unthinking lynch mob. Thus the "great toe" plays passion for his cause rather than personal hatred of Coriolanus as the dominant motivation for his actions. His line "He's not confirm'd: we may deny him yet" (2.3.207) comes less as a statement of fact than a possibility quickly picked up by his fellow plebeians and the tribunes themselves.[12] The latter then fight to transmit an urgent sense of danger to the ambivalent multitude, and to convince them of the necessity of rescinding their vote. As the dynamic rises, the circle of citizens tightens, and they stand enrapt by the passionate words of their leaders. There is better tension and simple energy in this staging of the sequence than in an earlier version, which lacked the semi-circular formation. Yet Hall constantly stressed in rehearsal that the wall of plebeians makes audibility difficult for the audience in the stands behind. The actors must be especially careful to pronounce their lines clearly and distinctly—it is all right to assume that the citizens want to hear what the tribunes are saying, but not that they do.

The current staging of the scene also preserves an excellent sense of variety in the plebeians' reactions, as their initial self-satisfaction becomes tempered with growing doubt and is finally transformed into angry revolt. This contrast maintains the audience's attention, which is never dulled by the deadly practice of playing solely on one note. A dynamic of rising excitement concludes the scene at its climactic peak, as Brutus enthusiastically tells the assembled mob to "Lay/A fault on us, your tribunes" (2.3.224–25): "Lay" comes at the end of the line, as though to signal a blinding idea which Brutus grasps and Sicinius pursues in issuing his instructions to the citizens. Their rapid momentum is in turn picked up by the people in their choric agreement "We will so" (2.3.252), before the solo voice chimes in with "almost all/Repent in their election" (2.3.252–53). The scene gains energy as the characters catch fire from each other, then rush off in several directions to intercept the senate's procession to the Capitol.

4
Act 3

The current staging of the senate's entrance at the opening of the third act was finalized shortly before previews on 5 December. An earlier version had Rome gates open to reveal the three generals at the head of the procession, followed by the city's elders, and a musician who rhythmically beat his drum as the party advanced, temporarily halting upstage center for the report on Aufidius's activities. Yet the subsequent filling of the sandpit with the tribunes and angry plebeians trapped Titus Lartius on stage during the riot sequence, in which the text accords him neither lines nor any piece of stage business. This creates a difficulty for the actor in performing the scene, for his character as a professional soldier should logically take an active part in the defence of his friend. At first Hall had him exit after "Weapons, weapons, weapons!" (3.1.183) as though to summon the military. This solution, however, was felt to be inadequate, as the reason for his departure remains unclear and distracts from the rising dynamic of panic in the riot itself. Thus Basil Henson suggested an alternative, which Hall adopted for the final blocking of the opening. Coriolanus enters with the two generals from stage right, while the main gates swing out to reveal the Roman senate; the stage thus opens up simultaneously. After delivering a public announcement of Volscian activities and personal communication of Aufidius's whereabouts, Lartius salutes his friend, pauses as the latter shakes his hand and bids him "Welcome home" (3.1.20), then exits again stage right as though to recover after the fatiguing journey from Corioli. This solution is successful in removing the later logistical problem of his continued yet silent presence, and gets him offstage at a natural break in the dialogue.

As Coriolanus and Cominius move to join the procession, the two tribunes run down through the audience to halt their progress.[1] Sicinius's speech, "Pass no further" (3.1.24), is delivered in desperate haste while still on the move, in a tone of mingled pleasure and frantic desire to avoid further violence. This central confrontation, which occurs at the very heart of the play, encapsulates the thematic conundrum expressed in the lines:

> When two authorities are up,
> Neither supreme, how soon confusion
> May enter 'twixt the gap of both, and take
> The one by th'other.
>
> (3.1.108–11)

Coriolanus argues that the consul is the head of state, embodying the nation, and elected on the basis of prowess.[2] The office is akin to kingship without the divine right, as he must remain accountable to the senate. Yet he finds it debasing to be dependent on the "mutable, rank-scented meinie" (3.1.65) for election, and not only attacks the tribunes, but the senate as well, for giving the tribunes power to distribute corn gratis.[3] Shakespeare is in favour of a single monarch as ruler of the nation, with the proviso that he be balanced in head and heart as well as by the aristocracy and the people. Only thus will the commonwealth be a healthy organism. The tribunes express a legitimate fear that Coriolanus's anti-democratic principles will destroy the present system of government, and argue their case with passionate authority. In the same way, the senate does not wish to overthrow the tribunes, feeling that it would be regressive to return to a by-gone era in which one man won the wars, made the laws and ruled the state. Yet Coriolanus, as the absolute singular principle of the mythic hero, cannot function in any other social context—he has been conditioned from birth to be the greatest soldier that ever was, in a society where warriors are seen as heroes and put in a position to which they are totally unsuited as their reward. His entrapment is complete.[4]

Coriolanus breaks away from the senate for a face to face confrontation with the tribunes at their position up right, on "Have you not set them on?" (3.1.36) and "Have you inform'd them sithence?" (3.1.46). Neither Sicinius nor Brutus gives an answer to his questions. To halt the procession is the tribunes' goal, and evasion becomes part of their logical strategy to make Coriolanus as angry as possible. Menenius vainly attempts to calm the furious hero, while Cominius seeks to master the confrontation by signalling the drum to drown their voices, as he commands the procession to "set on" (3.1.57). The senate advances but a few paces before Coriolanus returns to the obsessive matter of the corn: "This was my speech, and I will speak't again" (3.1.61). The senators move as though to interpose themselves between the quarelling factions, but Coriolanus will not be hushed:

> They know the corn
> Was not our recompense, resting well assur'd
> They ne'er did service for't; being press'd to the war,
> Even when the navel of the state was touch'd,
> They would not thread the gates: this kind of service
> Did not deserve corn gratis.
>
> (3.1.119–24)

As he pronounces this speech, Coriolanus advances toward Brutus, and his sheer physical presence is sufficient to rout the tribune downstage. The latter stands precariously balanced at the top of the stairs until the irate warrior backs off, then, humiliated, hastily moves to rejoin Sicinius up left. Coriolanus points to the audience out front on "your herd" (3.1.32), "Must these have voices" (3.1.33) and "Hydra here" (3.1.92), calling out with his hand cupped to his mouth on "rank-scented meinie" (3.1.65) and "We did request it" (3.1.132). It is as though the audience were an extension of the citizenry standing at a distance, but whom he equally desires to provoke with his words.[5] Coriolanus punctuates his demand that

> In a better hour,
> Let what is meet be said it must be meet,
> And throw their power i'th'dust
>
> (3.1.167–69)

by scornfully throwing a handful of sand at the tribunes' feet, prompting Brutus's accusation of "Manifest treason" (3.1.170), as he summons the aedile to apprehend the offender. Just as Coriolanus's present arrest seems certain, Sicinius halts its progress so that the people may bear witness to the warrior's treachery. The stage is permeated with a thick mist of tension as, within a few moments, Coriolanus is called "traitor" (3.1.161), "treasonous" (3.1.170) and is almost arrested; the analogy drawn by Hall in rehearsal is to the queen on her way to the coronation being arrested by an ordinary citizen.[6] "Hands off" (3.1.176) thus becomes an only slightly less dangerous moment than the actual drawing of the sword.

The threat of civil arrest is in fact such an incredible proposition that the senate at first cannot take it seriously and assumes that its promise to "surety him" (3.1.176) will prove sufficient to avert all crisis. They are not worried at the prospect of a possible trial, as they believe the charge will be immediately dismissed as ridiculous. Yet Sicinius will not loose his hold on the arm of the accused, and Coriolanus responds by grabbing at the collar of his gown. The tribune overreacts, dropping to his knees and gesturing to the people to draw near, and the stage audience to come down from the stands, to witness this attack on their leader. Menenius at first remains moderate in his council: "On both sides more respect" (3.1.179);[7] however he soon loses his own control in terror of the citizens closing ranks and moving in on Coriolanus, who stands immobile at the center of the stage.

Shakespeare offers textual clues for the blocking of this sequence in the dynamic of the dialogue itself. The crowd cannot press about too soon, or Coriolanus would draw his sword at an earlier point in the action. It is enough for the mythic hero to utter a verbal threat for the people to cringe; they dare move in only when he pushes Sicinius to the ground, yet still keep their distance around the perimeter of the circle. Nor do they initially respond by screaming like a hysterical mob. First comes a united agreement to arrest. The senators' cry of "Weapons, weapons, weapons!" (3.1.183) sets off the general panic, as the threat of civil war is brought home by this call for military assistance.

Mass panic spreads about the stage like wildfire, and causes a natural division of the assembly into small groups. The senate remains in a body in the stands right, while the tribunes stand together above left, and the arena fills with people. Some are actors, some audience; all are talking about the central figure who, with the instinct of a professional soldier, stands silently in the middle of the stage to gauge the situation. He does not yet explode at the threat of a riot but, like an expert fighter, reacts with sudden calm and practicality to the atmosphere of physical violence. It is only when the aediles advance to lay hold of him that he releases the anger which has been building within him; he grabs one officer by the arm and hurls him into the other, knocking over their staves and clearing the area stage left.[8] Chaos reigns as he snatches two plebeians by the neck and uses them as a battering ram to scatter the citizens, exultantly dashing them to the ground on Menenius's agonized cry "Coriolanus, patience!" (3.1.189).

Great care was taken to orchestrate the preceding cries of "Tribunes! Patricians! Citizens! What ho!" (3.1.184); each word comes in on cue with the precision of a new musical instrument entering a symphonic movement. It was, in fact, the composer and musical director Harrison Birtwistle who coordinated these vocal passages, stressing the necessity of having confidence in the stylized presen-

tation of the sequence, and avoiding the fatal temptation of naturalistic performance.[9] Variety of delivery adds both texture and
tension to the gathering momentum of the scene: the first "Down
with him" (3.1.182) endorses the arrest, while "Weapons, weapons,
weapons" (3.1.183) comes as a cry of fear and "Tribunes" (3.1.184)
as a call for help. The action continues overtop Menenius's speech
as he appeals to Sicinius to pacify the mob, while the latter responds by further enflaming their rising fury. A heated battle of
words takes place over the heads of the assembled company, as
Cominius counters the tribunes' incitement to civil revolt from his
position at the top of the stands upstage right, with the desperate
warning:

> That is the way to lay the city flat,
> To bring the roof to the foundation,
> And bury all which yet distinctly ranges
> In heaps and piles of ruin.
>
> (3.1.202–5)

The tribunes recall the focus of both audience and plebeians to
their vantage point in the downstage left stands, as Sicinius ignores
the general's caution and asserts "This deserves death" (3.1.205).
The citizens close in on Coriolanus at the center of the stage,
chanting "Yield, Martius, yield" (3.1.213), and the aediles advance
to effect the arrest when, suddenly, the warrior causes the lynch
mob to freeze in its tracks with a gesture that is the more chilling for
the self-contained calm with which it is performed. Staring fixedly
out front, he quietly vows "No, I'll die here" (3.1.221) and draws his
sword, thus creating a perfect emblem of civil war. All movement
momentarily stops to draw focus to this central action, then the
crowd hurriedly retreats as Coriolanus walks about the stage, brandishing his sword and scornfully inviting the terrified plebeians to
"Come, try upon yourselves what you have seen me!" (3.1.223). As
the aediles and plebeians move in to arrest him with cries of "Down
with him, down with him!" (3.1.227) Coriolanus again flourishes his
sword and chases them offstage left. Then, as the remaining assembly moves to follow and attack him from the rear, he wheels about
to rout them offstage right.

His pursuit of the mob is halted only by the physical intervention
of the second senator, who draws him back. He returns downstage
center to recover his energies and gloat over his triumph: "On fair
ground/I could beat forty of them" (3.1.240–41). Menenius, who
had earlier pushed his way through the panicking crowd to motion

the tribunes to withdraw, now advances to calm the enraged warrior and tactfully entice him back to the safety of his house with the humour of his agreement "I could myself/Take up a brace o'th'best of them; yea, the two tribunes" (3.1.241–42). The stubborn Coriolanus, however, still refuses to budge. The serious, rhetorical voice of Cominius chimes in to urge the necessity of his immediate departure, epigrammatically insisting that the very foundation of Roman society is collapsing in fragments about them:

> But now 'tis odds beyond arithmetic;
> And manhood is call'd foolery when it stands
> Against a falling fabric. Will you hence
> Before the tag return?
>
> (3.1.243–46)

Coriolanus, who has resisted persuasion, cajoling, even screaming, finally gives ear to their repeated request and exits, shrugging his shoulders, through Rome gates. A moment of relieved silence follows, then is broken by the patrician's regretful condemnation "This man has marr'd his fortune" (3.1.252)—Menenius's first indication that the sympathies of the senate have altered. He hastily attempts to regain their support by defending his absent friend with "His nature is too noble for the world" (3.1.253), but himself concludes with the regretful lament "What the vengeance,/Could he not speak 'em fair?" (3.1.260–61).

The citizens rush back on stage from the left and right wings and through the audience, to search the set for the traitor,[10] while the tribunes appear from the upstage left stands, demanding:

> Where is this viper
> That would depopulate the city and
> Be every man himself?
>
> (3.1.261–63)

Sicinius hits Coriolanus in absentia with the accusation that "he hath resisted law" (3.1.265) and refuses to listen to further explanation. The crime is absolute and irredeemable, and the people demand the full sentence of death. Menenius desperately attempts to fulfil his promise to patch things up "With cloth of any colour" (3.1.251), but Sicinius remains adament in his stance of hard realism, refusing Menenius the opportunity to pacify the mob with a tale as he did in 1.1. Exile is danger, he asserts, and forgiveness means certain death (3.1.285–86). The tribunes express their high level of adrenalin by pacing back and forth as they herd the plebeians to pluck Coriolanus from his house, while Menenius stands calm and contained as he seeks to rationally persuade the multitude to judicious action:

> Now the good gods forbid
> That our renowned Rome, whose gratitude
> Towards her deserved children is enroll'd
> In Jove's own book, like an unnatural dam
> Should now eat up her own!
>
> (3.1.287–91)

As Brutus cuts short all argument with "We'll hear no more:/ Pursue him to his house, and pluck him thence" (3.1.305–6), Menenius moves into position upstage to intercept the lynch mob. He urges the tribunes to "Proceed by process" (3.1.311), in a calculated appeal to their Achilles' heel of following the letter of the law. In exchange, he will himself act as the people's officer by bringing Coriolanus to the market square, "Where he shall answer by a lawful form—/In peace—to his utmost peril" (3.1.322–23). The first senator interjects his agreement, "Noble tribunes,/It is the humane way" (3.1.323–24), as the tribunes take a short walk downstage to regroup and discuss their strategy. Finally, they grudgingly comply, with the warning that "if you bring not Martius, we'll proceed/In our first way" (3.1.330–31). The stunned citizens reluctantly drop their weapons and exit via the left and right wings, while Menenius and the senate pass through Rome gates to face the onerous task of persuading Coriolanus to stand trial by the people's court.

The timing for Volumnia's entrance in the following scene has been slightly altered from the suggestion given in the text. Instead of appearing on stage after line six and interrupting her son in mid-discussion, she passes the exiting senate to appear simultaneously with him through the main gate, thus overhearing Coriolanus's full interchange with his friends without herself being seen. He enters right, followed by the young nobility of Rome, exulting in his defiance of the people and affirming the constancy of his resolution to "still/Be thus to them" (3.2.5–6) with monosyllabic firmness. Theoretically, this entrance should transmit to the audience that Coriolanus has been abandoned by the senate and is now supported only by personal friends of the same age and class as himself. Yet the blocking for this opening sequence in no way establishes a sense of personal relationship between the four men, for the nobles stand as though lined up at attention around the right hand perimeter of the circle, while Coriolanus addresses them from his position centerstage. There is no sense of cameraderie or past history in this stage picture, which must depend on physical gesture and blocking to convey the relationship, as the young nobility are given no lines after the single "You do the nobler" (3.2.6). The only visual clue to their identity lies in their dress, for they are costumed in well-tailored suits akin to that worn by Coriolanus himself; yet I wonder whether an audience with no prior knowledge of the text would realize who these three actors are meant to portray.

Volumnia's slow and stately entrance contrasts with the impetuous force of her son's hot tirade, though each remains absolute in his or her respective stance. Coriolanus catches a glimpse of her implacable figure over his shoulder, and hastily crosses upstage to greet her. He delivers his speech

> I talk of you.
> Why did you wish me milder? Would you have me
> False to my nature?
>
> (3.2.13–15)

in a tone of mingled petulance and defiance, as though moved by an uneasy sense of guilt in being thus overheard, yet with a stubborn determination not to retract a syllable. As he speaks, he kisses his mother's cheek and holds her hand, thus foreshadowing the famous gesture at the end of the second persuasion scene (5.3), and transforming the proud warrior into a ten year old child in a potent image of domestic tyranny. In his following line, Coriolanus seeks to explain to his mother the overriding reason for his refusal to bend to the people's will. This marks the only cut from the production which, to me, detracts from the power of any passage. The accumulation of theatrical images both before and after this moment—"It is a part/That I shall blush in acting" (2.2.144–45), "You have put me now to such a part which never/I shall discharge to th'life" (3.2.105–6), "Like a dull actor now/I have forgot my part and I am out,/Even to a full disgrace" (5.3.40–42)—all express the warrior's inability to perform a role alien to his spirit. Yet here, for the only time during the course of the play, Coriolanus articulates in a single phrase the one part he *is* able to perform: "Rather say I play/The man I am" (3.2.15–16). By cutting this line, one removes the sole positive theatrical image to issue from Coriolanus's own lips, and loses the feed for Volumnia's later rebuttal "You might have been enough the man you are,/With striving less to be so" (3.2.19–20). The entire scene is concerned with the process of acting and with getting the role right. Coriolanus loathes dissimulation in any form and desires only to be "The man I am," while Volumnia insists that he be other than what she herself has created.

As Volumnia shakes her hand free to cross down right, cursing the people in her frustration, Menenius enters with certain representatives of the senate to try what the force of patrician authority can accomplish. Exchanging a look of worried collusion with Volumnia, Menenius utters his lines in a tone of rapid urgency, as he tries to impress on the stubborn warrior that he "must return and mend it" (3.2.26), or the inevitable result will be civil war. Volumnia assumes the voice of calmness and maternal reasoning, immediately distinguishing her approach from that of Menenius in the difference of her vocal tempo.

Suddenly Coriolanus appears to mellow, asking "What must I do?" (3.2.35) and "Well, what then? what then?" (3.2.36) with a smile that lulls his advisers into a false sense of security. All seems to be going well, until the violent explosion of his demand "For them? I cannot do it to the gods,/Must I then do't to them?" (3.2.38–39). The silent senators and nobles listen with tense anxiety to these various modes of attack, never forgetting the underlying desperation of the life and death crisis, despite Volumnia's attempts to make the tone milder and more motherly. Yet at the same time everyone in the scene realizes that he is present at an elaborate nursery lesson, in which the greatest fighter of the age is being scolded into submission by his mother; it is a very embarrassing as well as ironically wonderful moment. Coriolanus responds by alternately shifting his feet in the sand and swinging his sword like a pendulum, as though with the fighting man's instinct to channel his frustrated energies into physical movement, yet with his attention nonetheless keenly fixed on the speakers' words.

It is during this moment of comparative calm that Cominius makes his climactic entrance through the main gates with a terrifying and completely new piece of information: "All's in anger" (3.2.95). In his first acceptance speech, Coriolanus deliberately plays with his advisors, starting a series of false exits before returning to confront his mother, to impress upon her the gravity of her request:

> Must I go show them my unbarb'd sconce? Must I
> With my base tongue give to my noble heart
> A lie that it must bear? Well, I will do't: (false exit)
> Yet were there but this single plot to lose,
> This mould of Martius, they to dust should grind it
> And throw't against the wind. To th'market place! (false exit)

You have put me now to such a part which never
I shall discharge to the life.

(3.2.99–106)

The senators and nobles facially register alternate expressions of
relief and increasing desperation, as it becomes evident that Coriolanus's verbal acquiescence is tenuous at best. Cominius seeks to
reassure him that a successful performance is still possible, despite
his dreadful miscasting in the role of suppliant: "Come, come, we'll
prompt you" (3.2.106); yet his words of comfort elicit only a dark
laugh and ironic look from the desperate soldier.

Volumnia perceives their loosening hold on Coriolanus, and immediately tightens the maternal reins by calling him "sweet son"
(3.2.107) and bidding him perform "To have my praise" (3.2.109).
Coriolanus is stung by her betrayal of him in this scene, and decides
that his only option is to do what she says and then get out. He
resignedly concedes "Well, I must do't" (3.2.110), before launching
into a corrosively cynical description of what it means to be a
politician. As he speaks, he dashes his consul's robes to the sand in
the violence of his contempt for the duplicity inherent in public
office:

> Away my disposition, and possess me
> Some harlot's spirit! My throat of war be turn'd,
> Which choired with my drum, into a pipe
> Small as an eunuch, or the virgin voice
> That babies lull asleep! The smiles of knaves
> Tent in my cheeks, and schoolboys' tears take up
> The glasses of my sight! A beggar's tongue
> Make motion through my lips, and my arm'd knees
> Who bow'd but in my stirrup, bend like his
> That hath receiv'd an alms!

(3.2.111–20)

Coriolanus accompanies these last words with a gross exaggeration
of Volumnia's illustrative gesture on "Thy knee bussing the stones"
(3.2.75), while on "harlot's spirit" (3.2.112) he mimics her arm
movement on "perform a part/Thou hast not done before" (3.2.109–
10). She responds by turning away in disgust at the personal insult.
Then suddenly, after always having done as he was told, Coriolanus
comes to a sense of himself as an individual, and finally seeks to act
in independence of her judgment:

> I will not do't,
> Lest I surcease to honour mine own truth,

And by my body's action teach my mind
A most inherent baseness.

(3.2.120–23)

The modulation of Coriolanus's final resolution is extremely difficult to control, so that the audience will not respond with amused laughter. Experimentation in playing the scene during previews and early performances showed that the moment can only work if the actor takes a long pause, as though to summon up all his self-control, before uttering the lines. Her back still turned, Volumnia shrugs her shoulders and says with calculated indifference "At thy choice then" (3.2.123), before turning to blast her son with the full guilt treatment:

To beg of thee it is my more dishonour
Than thou of them. Come all to ruin; let
Thy mother rather feel thy pride than fear
Thy dangerous stoutness, for I mock at death
With as big heart as thou. Do as thou list.

(3.2.124–28)

Her tactics prove successful, and Coriolanus capitulates as though borne on a wave of intense fatigue. She has completely crushed his spirit and robbed him of the basic ability to care anymore. There is an element of pathos in his meek

Pray be content.
Mother, I am going to the market place:
Chide me no more

(3.2.130–32)

and the audience's inevitable laughter is now only half amusement, half shameful recognition.

Volumnia's continued indifference prompts the violence of his agonized cry "Look, I am going" (3.2.134), then, desperate to remove the barrier between them, he attempts to take her hand and to send a commendation to his wife. Volumnia, however, rejects the conciliatory appeal. She casts aside his hand and, staring coldly into his eyes, delivers her final "Do your will" (3.2.137), before turning deliberately away and exiting stage left. Coriolanus stares dumbly after her, apparently oblivious to Cominius's urgent instructions, then pulls himself together to face the ordeal ahead. Again, a series of false exits threatens to interrupt his progress to the market place, as he explodes with every mention of the key word "mildly."

Menenius, however, will not allow him to turn back, and all but pushes him through the main gates. With a final ironic "Mildly!" (3.2.145) which encapsulates all his corrosive self-loathing for the performance ahead, Coriolanus finally exits to face the people's court.

The trial in 3.3 proved another sequence which underwent massive revision during previews. The original staging had the action played out with a dual focus on Coriolanus above right, and the tribunes above left; yet this leads to something of a tennis match for the audience which has been brought down from the stands, as each side vies for its attention. Coriolanus responds to the accusation of treason by delivering "Let them pronounce the steep Tarpeian death" (3.3.88) in a tone of easy contempt rather than violent anger. He has already decided to leave the city, and thus can afford to provoke the tribunes with ironic laughter and arm movements which demonstrate to the audience the ridiculousness of the situation. Coriolanus descends from the stands only with the statement of his own banishment from the city; as he speaks, he picks out individual faces in the crowd to whom he may address each line. It is a chilling moment because the insult is made personal, the more so as it is said in a tone of ironic knowledge, cool and detached, rather than in the heat of anger. Yet this gesture of upstaging the prosecution, and thus taking control of the trial, seems much more characteristic of the theatrically flamboyant Richard II in his verbal conquest over Bolingbroke during his deposition, than the explosive tenor of Coriolanus's single-minded return to the matter of the corn, the people's cowardice, and the necessity for patrician rule. Although playing irony as the dominant note of the scene highlights unexpected passages and calls attention to the complexity of thoughts and images which had hitherto seemed straightforward, it seems to create a depth of interpretation which is not inherent in the text. Coriolanus acts and speaks from the simple strength of passionately held beliefs. He can see but a single truth, and irony implies the ability to stand back and examine a situation from many different angles. Coriolanus can never respond in this detached manner—if he could, he would probably not be at the point of banishment now. He is always an active participant in the action for he speaks in accordance with his beliefs, not only out of stubborn pride, but a highly developed sense of integrity. Thus the decision to have Coriolanus stand in stunned and contemptuous silence during his sentencing, rather than respond with mocking laughter and applause, is more consistant with the character whose rise and fall we have witnessed thus far.

As the scene now stands, the tribunes enter while the gates close on the domestic scene, and immediately move to the downstage perimeter of the circle. They pace phrenetically back and forth as they add finishing touches to their plot to further incriminate the proven traitor:

> In this point charge him home, that he affects
> Tyrannical power. If he evade us there,
> Enforce him with his envy to the people,
> And that the spoil got on the Antiates
> Was ne'er distributed.
>
> (3.3.1–5)

Each phrase comes with the driving force of a completely new idea, and the audience becomes caught up in the tribunes' excitement as they formulate their strategy before its very eyes. The aedile enters from the right wings to bring the news of Coriolanus's imminent appearance. He then hastens to exit through the audience to execute his order to "Assemble presently the people hither" (3.3.12), but is repeatedly called back by Sicinius and Brutus as they think of further refinements to their instructions:

> And when they hear me say, "It shall be so
> I'th'right and strength o'th'commons," be it either
> For death, for fine, or banishment, then let them
> If I say fine, cry "Fine," if death, cry "Death,"
> Insisting on the old prerogative
> And power i'th'truth o'th'cause.
>
> (3.3.13–18)

Once decided on a course of action they remain in a state of nervous excitement, not knowing which way the trial will go. It is not a question of simply passing sentence; they are still in need of the people's support. As Sicinius issues his final command to "Make them be strong, and ready for this hint/When we shall hap to give't them" (3.3.23–24), the aedile is already in the process of making his way up the central aisle. The rapidity of the exchange, necessitated by frequent half line cues and elisions in the verse, establishes a driving momentum which builds, then is broken by the entrance of the reluctant Coriolanus and his followers.

The tribunes move to take up their position as a unified front down left,[11] while the patricians appear through Rome gates. They pause while Coriolanus forces himself to pronounce the tactfully prepared speech which has, no doubt, been composed by the senators en route to the market place:

> Th'honour'd gods
> Keep Rome in safety, and the chairs of justice
> Supplied with worthy men, plant love among's,
> Throng our large temples with the shows of peace
> And not our streets with war.

> (3.3.33–37)

Coriolanus cannot resist an ironic tinge as he pronounces these words, so that he subtly mocks his accusors even as he humbles himself before them; yet he never formally violates the necessary decorum of the courtroom.[12] He advances to the center of the circle as Sicinius summons the plebeians with "Draw near, ye people" (3.3.39). The stage suddenly fills as they rush through the audience and from the left and right wings, motioning the stage audience to descend from the stands so that the senate may take up its position above right, and the tribunes above left. They then seat themselves around the perimeter of the sand, thus heightening Coriolanus's sense of claustrophobia, as he is completely surrounded by the common cry he later denounces. The tribunes assume a lawyer's deportment in an effort to seem tolerant, and it is in fact not they who infuriate the hero, but the well-meaning Menenius, with his patriotic speech about Coriolanus's wounds. Cominius hastily attempts to quiet him with "Well, well, no more" (3.3.57), for he knows from bitter experience that the warrior's psychological revulsion from praise will inevitably result in an outburst. As Hall pointed out in rehearsal, Cominius's desperation to calm the situation largely stems from the sequence in 2.3, when Coriolanus walked out and "left (him) for six bleeding minutes on his own"[13] to retrieve their lost ground.

This moment proves the fulcrum of the play in tragic terms. If Menenius's generous heart had not prompted him to plant his foot firmly in his mouth, Coriolanus might have been able to contain himself and so be acquitted of the charge. Instead, he breaks into a raging fury, scorning further trial and demanding immediate sentence. But first he seeks an explanation for the attack on his integrity:

> What is the matter,
> That being pass'd for consul with full voice,

> I am so dishonour'd that the very hour
> You take it off again?

> (3.3.58–61)

The confrontation reaches its climax with Coriolanus's acerbic attack on Brutus:

Cor.   What do you prate of service?
Bru.   I talk of that, that know it.
Cor.   You?

> (3.3.84–85)

At this point the people are quite prepared to invoke the full sentence of death, but the tribunes again insist on following the letter of the law. This decision in favour of merciful banishment proves a wise tactic, for if Coriolanus were to be killed, the patricians would split the country and the people would lose their power as surely as if Coriolanus were consul. The tribunes want to be seen in their own eyes, in the eyes of the patricians and in the eyes of history, as wise and clement men; and Sicinius delivers the legal indictment as though calmly reading a preestablished document. Cominius rushes down onto the stage to stop the sentencing which he knows, once read, can never be retracted, but the legalistic process proves inflexible and his own intrusion is taken as a personal outrage against the people's court. Sicinius explodes with "He's sentenc'd: no more hearing" (3.3.109) and several citizens rise in protest. All formality breaks down, as Coriolanus is no longer to be tried by process—he has condemned himself.

The people's chorus of "It shall be so"s (3.3.106) comes as much as independent votes as a mechanical echo of the tribunes' earlier command. The first "It shall be so" is said with gravity rather than hostility, and is cued by Sicinius in his preceding speech. The decision is made and assimilated, then the repetition of the phrase grows in intensity as individual voices chime in from either side of the stage, and culminates in a final choric utterance when all raise their arms in a right hand vote. Pronunciation is crisp, for impact and emphasis. Only the first citizen points to the Tarpeian rock (localized to the back top of the Olivier for continuity) on the earlier cry of "To th'rock, to th'rock with him" (3.3.75). The rest again vote silently with the extension of their hands in the air. This preserves the integrity of the people's court, and ensures that the sentencing comes not as the hysterical cry of a lynch mob, but as the affirmation of a judicial verdict. The cries become emotional only with Brutus's stirring restatement of the sentence:

> There's no more to be said but he is banish'd,
> As enemy to the people and his country.
> It shall be so!
>
> (3.3.117–19)

The citizens are accorded but two choruses of "It shall be so" (3.3.19) at this point in the text, but Hall has included three additional repetitions of the phrase, as the people jump to their feet and incite the stage audience to join in the chant and thereby assume an active role in banishing Coriolanus from the city. The moment is powerful and provocative, and the audience readily enters into the action which they have until now only passively observed. The stage is covered in a frenzy of vocal and physical movement, as the plebeians move in on the still stationary central figure to invoke the penalty without further delay.

Suddenly the hero speaks for the first time since demanding sentence a full thirty lines earlier. His explosive words stop the citizens dead in their tracks:

> You common cry of curs! whose breath I hate
> As reek o'th'rotten fens, whose loves I prize
> As the dead carcasses of unburied men
> That do corrupt my air: I banish you!
>
> (3.3.120–23)

As he curses the people in vengeful terms which he himself is fated to enact, Coriolanus walks among their ranks and addresses each phrase to individuals in the crowd, causing them to look away and transforming their violent frenzy into an aura of silent yet stubborn revolt. Delivering "Despising/For you the city, thus I turn my back" (3.3.133–34) from his position down left, he stands for a moment to survey the mob with a look of scathing contempt, then determinedly marches off through the wings, left.

Even after his exit, Coriolanus's presence hangs over the stage, as his disembodied voice booms across the auditorium: "There is a world elsewhere" (3.3.135). It is his final statement of heroic isolation and invincibility; this Coriolanus cannot rest without ensuring that he has the last word, even if it comes from offstage. At first the citizens stand in stunned silence—Coriolanus's dramatic exit has successfully deflated their triumph—but their excitement grows in intensity as the aedile calmly pronounces "The people's enemy is gone" (3.3.136) and the "great toe" joyfully picks up the cry "Our enemy is banish'd! He is gone!" (3.3.137). The sudden drop in tone which follows their high-pitched hysteria is broken by the exultation of a people united in their desire to banish their enemy from the city. They cheer, throw up their caps and embrace one another, before Sicinius curtails their ceremony by according them a still more active role in the proceedings:

> Go see him out at gates, and follow him
> As he hath follow'd you, with all despite.
> Give him deserv'd vexation.
>
> (3.3.138–40)

They rush through Rome gates to carry out his orders, motioning the stage audience to return to the stands as they go. The tribunes exit stage left under the protective guard of their aediles.

An image of organized chaos dominates the third act of the play. Scenarios are constantly set up only to be dashed to the ground as Coriolanus, in his noble attempt to pursue an honourable course, finds his absolute nature swaying back and forth between a desire to please Volumnia and his instinctive revulsion from dissimulation. The tension is heightened in this third scene as Coriolanus seeks to quell the civil discontent, yet is repeatedly confronted by words, uttered by those who wish to help him, which are innocent in themselves but bound to trigger his explosive temper. The revised staging of the trial sequence successfully dramatizes the hero's inner dichotomy. He finds himself literally caught between the opposing forces of the senate and the tribunes, and is surrounded by the people whom he despises yet who are to act as masters of his fate. The tension is the greater for the unflinching integrity with which the people and the tribunes are portrayed. This is no simple case of unjustified villainy persecuting an innocent hero, or indeed of a fascist tyrant persecuting an innocent nation—each side is painted, like Cromwell, with "warts and all." The momentum builds to fever pitch with the final eruption of the hero's curse and the joyful celebration of the people's triumph, then suddenly drops as the audience is invited to witness the devastation wrought by Coriolanus's banishment in the scenes that follow.

Sir Peter Hall in rehearsal for *Coriolanus*.

Ian McKellen as Caius Martius with Greg Hicks (Tullus Aufidius), preparing the fight sequence.

McKellen with Wendy Morgan (Virgilia).

Frederick Treves (Menenius) in rehearsal for 5.2, turned away by the Volscian guard.

Irene Worth as Volumnia.

Sir Peter Hall directing Wendy Morgan in the domestic scene (1.3).

Judith Paris (Valeria), Irene Worth, Wendy Morgan, and Sir Peter Hall working on 5.3: the women of Rome plead for their city.

Sir Peter Hall announces that the first preview has been cancelled in favor of a public dress rehearsal.

The on-stage audience joins Rome's plebeians for a pre-show public demonstration.

Menenius attempts to calm the rioters with the voice of reason: "most charitable care / Have the patricians of you" (1.1.64–65).

The "great toe" of the rebellion (Geoffrey Burridge) scoffs at Menenius' fable of the belly (1.1.95ff).

Caius Martius makes his first entrance atop the stands vacated by the stage audience, wearing the white overcoat and ponytail (1.1.162).

Volumnia imagines her son's exploits in the war against the Volsces—"See him pluck Aufidius down by th' hair"—as Virgilia sits in anguished silence (1.3.30).

Martius prepares for battle (1.4).

The Volscian army issues through Corioli gates, ominous figures backlit against a haze of smoke (1.4.22).

The gates open a second time to reveal the solitary Martius bearing the Roman standard and beckoning his men to enter the city (1.4.61).

The soldiers lift Martius on their shoulders as he exhorts them to follow him in battle (1.6.67–75).

Martius extends his arm in a fist salute, then waves the Roman standard crying "O me alone! Make you a sword of me!" (1.6.76).

Martius and Aufidius in single combat (1.8).

**Aufidius rants against his enemy, vowing to "Wash my fierce hand in's heart"
(1.10.27).**

Family and friends prepare to welcome Martius home, as a single drumbeat heralds his approach (2.1.160).

5
Act 4

At the opening of the fourth act, Coriolanus enters right with his
family and friends well before the tribunes have completed their
exit, so the audience will not assume that the climactic banishment
scene marks the end of Part One.[1] He is framed by his wife and
mother, while Cominius, Menenius and the young nobility take up
their positions around the perimeter of the circle. Again the stage
picture conveys that the senate has abandoned Coriolanus, who is
now supported only by a core of loyal friends. Grief-stricken, Volumnia crosses to an isolated position near the upstage doors and,
with upraised fists, curses the people who have banished her son:
"Now the red pestilence strike all trades in Rome,/And occupations
perish!" (4.1.13–14). Coriolanus attempts to coax her back to her
usual stoic calm, with the humorous reminder of her former boast:

> If you had been the wife of Hercules,
> Six of his labours you'd have done, and sav'd
> Your husband so much sweat.
>
> (4.1.17–19)

He scolds Virgilia like a child with "Nay, I prithee woman" (4.1.12),
wagging his finger in the air, and elicits a pained smile from both
women before turning to comfort Cominius and urge him to put a
brave face over his inner torment. Having given vent to his frustrated anger in the preceding scene, Coriolanus is clearly uncomfortable with these continued and debilitating displays of emotion,
as Virgilia persists in hanging about his neck and even his mother's
indomitable face is stained with tears. He himself is excited at the
prospect of his new-found liberation and looks forward to the soli-
tude which must accompany it. He lovingly personifies this image
of loneliness in his self-comparison:

> to a lonely dragon that his fen
> Makes fear'd and talk'd of more than seen, your son

> Will or exceed the common, or be caught
> With cautelous baits and practises.
>
> (4.1.30–33)

This is a prophetic utterance, for both events are to occur in the second part of the play. Although Coriolanus states his desire to be alone and to excel with his former superhuman invincibility, he does not know how to achieve his goal in any other context than the battlefield and so ends with the generic conclusion "I'll do well yet" (4.1.21).[2] Volumnia consciously understands this statement of his isolation to be the ultimate breach between mother and son and seeks to send Cominius, the very symbol of the city, as his escort. Thus he may take something of Rome, and of herself, with him; yet he ignores her plea and cuts short the painful farewell. He crosses left to shake hands with "My friends of noble touch" (4.1.49), then takes his wife and mother by the hand and bids them "smile" (4.1.50).[3] "I pray you, come" (4.1.50) is the cue for the young nobility to tier up and begin their exit through the audience. Cominius and Menenius follow suit as the old man utters his final words of support:

> If I could shake off but one seven years
> From these old arms and legs, by the good gods
> I'd with thee every foot.
>
> (4.1.55–57)

Coriolanus pauses downstage center, framed by the two women, again bidding them "Give me thy hand./Come" (4.1.57–58), and the solemn trio joins the procession up the central aisle of the theater. Volumnia and Virgilia halt half way up the steps and watch the retreating figure of the hero, already in position for their reentrance in the following scene. As Menenius descends to join them, the tribunes enter through Rome gates and recall the audience's attention to the action on the stage, as this sequence flows seamlessly into the next.

Sicinius and Brutus are accompanied by an aedile, whom they immediately dispatch with a threefold repetition of their command to send the people home. The audience expects the tribunes to be triumphant, excited and pleased at their victory; it is not prepared for the tone of wariness in which they discuss their tenuous situation:

> *Sic.*   . . . he's gone, and we'll no further.
> The nobility are vex'd, whom we have sided
> In his behalf.

Bru.   Now we have shown our power,
         Let us seem humbler after it is done
         Than when it was a-doing.

                                                        (4.2.1–5)

The tribunes are genuinely concerned at the continued unrest in the city, and their nervous adrenalin is heightened by the fact that they have just left a very excited crowd on the other side of Rome gates. Hence they formulate their strategy spontaneously, and the repetition in their lines comes as the result of great tension.

It is at this point that Volumnia, Virgilia and Menenius pivot round to begin their slow descent to the stage; the tribunes catch sight of the advancing party and seek to avoid them. That Coriolanus is gone is cause for satisfaction, and its recentness adds to their elation, tempered though it be. They do not wish their mood dampened by an encounter with his mother, who represents for them the very figure of retribution.[4] They at first seek to avoid her by hastening their exit toward the left aisle, but perceiving that "They have ta'en note of us" (4.2.10), they resolve to see through the unpleasant situation. Volumnia greets them with a curse as she mounts the stage. Facing right, with her hands to her brow, she attempts to control her tears—"If that I could for weeping, you should hear" (4.2.13)—then wheels about to confront them directly on "Nay, and you shall hear some" (4.2.14). As they make a motion to quit the scene, Virgilia, who has been silently leaning on Menenius's shoulder, suddenly gives vent to a passionate cry which forestalls their exit: "You shall stay too. I would I had the power/To say so to my husband" (4.2.15–16).[5]

Wendy Morgan's portrayal of Virgilia in this scene has greatly improved over the course of the run. At first she found it necessary to express her violent emotion through physical contortions, rushing toward Sicinius and Brutus and casting sand at their feet on "He'd make an end of thy posterity" (4.2.26), then throwing herself to the ground to keen and writhe for the remainder of Volumnia's exchange with the tribunes. Yet such business seemed out of keeping both with her strong and silent characterization in the production thus far, and with the audience's expectation of how the wife of Coriolanus should behave in the face of affliction. Gradually, Morgan toned down her performance, and her later depiction of the agonized woman is the more moving for its subtlety. She now depends on the force of her words to convey the violence which was inadequately expressed through movement, merely weeping silently upstage center before crossing to fall at Volumnia's feet and embrace her mother-in-law at the end of the scene. The sparsity of her stage business to this point thus lends greater power and pathos to the gesture.[6]

The tribunes' reaction to Volumnia's curse, and indeed to meeting her at all, is a mixture of embarrassment, awkwardness, effrontery at her words, and fear at her physical presence. They are, however, affected by the strength of her emotion, and seek to calm her with an expression of qualified sympathy:

> *Sic.*   I would he had continued to his country
>   As he began, and not unknit himself
>   The noble knot he made.
> *Bru.*   I would he had.

(4.2.30–32)

Volumnia is infuriated by the self-righteousness of their tone, and mockingly apes Brutus's "I would he had" (4.2.33) as anger supplants grief as the dominant note of her performance. Perceiving that rational argument will inevitably prove fruitless, Sicinius and Brutus complete their interrupted exit up the left hand aisle, leaving Volumnia centerstage to address her grief to a higher court: "I would the gods had nothing else to do/But to confirm my curses" (4.2.45–46). As she speaks, she lifts her arms toward the heavens in an appeal which is made no longer in anger, but in a moment of complete vulnerability. She has been stripped of her prophetic madness and her stoic facade; only the woman remains. This scene is a crucial one for Volumnia, as it marks her loss of power within Roman society. With the exile of her son she has been robbed of the medium through which she vicariously won the wars and ruled the state. Thus, for Volumnia, 4.2 is not a scene about what happens when she meets the tribunes, but about the personal devastation which accompanies her son's departure from Rome.

Volumnia looks down to find her daughter-in-law weeping at her feet. Confronted with the physical embodiment of her own emotion, she once again finds refuge in stoic self-control and pulls Virgilia to her feet:

> Come, let's go.
> Leave this faint puling, and lament as I do,
> In anger, Juno-like.

(4.2.51–53)

She speaks not in contempt for Virgilia's tears, but in an effort to instill in her the strength which comes from courage and anger. As the two women exit arm in arm stage right, Volumnia pulls her scarf over her head as though in mourning and utters "Come, come, come" (4.2.53) in a regular rhythm which heightens the ritualized presentation of grief. This rhythm is in turn picked up by Menenius for his rueful "Fie, fie, fie" (4.2.54), as he looks out after the retreating figures of Virgilia and Volumnia, then brings his gaze out front toward the direction in which Coriolanus vanished during the preceding scene. Thus he brings together the play's dominant images of grief and isolation for the end of Part One, as the lights come down on the figure of the aged man lamenting both the exile of a friend, and the end to an era in Roman history.

*   *   *

Just as the action of Part One begins as though *in medias res,* so too is Coriolanus already in position in the stands, left, before the audience resumes its seats after the interval.[7] He sits muffled in a trenchcoat and large-brimmed hat, passing unrecognized by the stage audience around him, and his first words provide the technical cue for the lights to dim to a spot on his figure, with secondary illumination on Antium gates to give a sense of the building whose interior lies offstage. After the fast-paced dynamic of Part One, there is an elegiac feel to this speech before the enemy town. Coriolanus is presented as the dragon searching for his fen, and the stubble on his face suggests that his obsessive quest has left him little respite for sleep or repose. Despite his fatigue, he remains ready for action and decides to pursue his entry into Antium:

> Then know me not;
> Lest that thy wives with spits, and boys with stones,
> In puny battle slay me.
>
> (4.4.4–6)

As he speaks, he adjusts the brim of his hat so that it conceals his features, and crosses upstage toward the gates.

His progress is interrupted by the entrance of a Volscian citizen, who appears from the right wings to follow the path along the upper perimeter of the circle. Coriolanus approaches to meet him left of the doors, but the Volscian continues on his way, stopping only when directly addressed on "Save you, sir" (4.4.6). He turns to point out Aufidius's house (the upstage gates), and remains standing quizzically, as though awaiting further question. Coriolanus paces, then turns to dismiss him with a curt "Farewell" (4.4.11), ending up in position in the pool of light to the right of the doors, a diminutive figure against their towering height. He delivers his final soliloquy before moving to enter Aufidius's domain. He passes through the door, pulls it to, then reenters immediately through the left hand side. As the door opens, the audience catches the faint strains of music and laughter issuing from the banquet offstage. The sound moves from speakers at the right to the left side of the auditorium, and a dim light is brought up on the sand to convey the impression of entering Aufidius's house.

As Coriolanus completes his entrance, two servants appear from the left wings and cross to the right vomitorium, whose bright illumination suggests the wine cellar where they seek the elusive Cotus. The second servingman exits down the vom, while his fellow turns to catch sight of the ragged figure standing in the center of the sand. Hall said in rehearsal that he wished to convey the impression of a mythic world, in which Zeus descends to the earth as a beggar to seek hospitality among mortal men and to punish those who refuse to accord it him.[8] Thus when the servant moves to show him the door, Coriolanus, with a fluid extension of his arm, twirls him round and sends him flying stage left. The second servant reappears from the wine cellar and, sensing the atmosphere of danger, also seeks to forcibly remove the stranger; but the latter neatly trips him with a foot behind the back leg. The comic convention has thus been established, and even as the third servant appears from the left wings to investigate the disturbance, the audience gives a knowing laugh in anticipation of the fate that awaits him.

The third servingman is presented as the mustachioed major domo of the establishment, who walks up to Coriolanus with all the mincing arrogance that comes with full confidence in the prestige of his exalted station. He addresses the intruder in a patronizing tone and is rewarded with a tweak on the ear, as Coriolanus snatches the silver trencher from his hand and uses it to slap him across the rump on "Follow your function, go, and batten on cold bits" (4.5.34).[9] The startled retainer scampers to safety stage left and bids the first servingman "tell my master/what a strange guest he has here" (4.5.35–36). He then lays hold of the second servant, who is in the process of sneaking away; with a firm point of his finger he commands his fellow to remain, lest he himself be abandoned to face the threatening stranger alone. During this exchange, Coriolanus does not respond with angry violence, but rather with a grim enjoyment of the game he is playing. He is well assured of his supremacy over the cocky menials, and physically assaults them only as a ruse to lure Aufidius out of the house.

Aufidius is escorted on stage left and remains at the perimeter of the circle, while his three servants stand together up left to witness the meeting between the two generals. His first request for the stranger's name is made in a tone of easy command; Aufidius has no need to express trepidation—he is head of the house and leader of the nation. Moreover, he carries a sword, whereas the figure before him is patently unarmed.[10] Hall pointed out in rehearsal that the actor must deliver these lines as though they were written in verse rather than prose, as the alliteration and repetition give a definite rhythm to their structure:

> Whence com'st thou? What wouldst thou? thy name?
> Why speak'st not? Speak, man: what's thy name?
>
> (4.5.54–55)

Coriolanus assumes that he will be recognized and therefore does not turn away, but directly faces his enemy as he replies:

> If, Tullus,
> Not yet thou know'st me, and, seeing me, dost not
> Think me for the man I am, necessity
> Commands me name myself.
>
> (4.5.55–58)

Aufidius's renewed inquiry takes on a tone of eager interest, as the stranger is obviously aware of his identity and, moreover, addresses him by his first name. He advances downstage, still maintaining the line of distance between them, to survey the mysterious figure from a point of vantage:

> Thou hast a grim appearance, and thy face
> Bears a command in't. Though thy tackle's torn,
> Thou show'st a noble vessel. What's thy name?
>
> (4.5.61–63)

It is only with Coriolanus's continued evasion that Aufidius loses patience and asserts with angry irritation "I know thee not! Thy name?" (4.5.65), thus preserving a variety of delivery which holds the audience's interest, and building the atmosphere of tension and suspense for the climactic revelation of Coriolanus's identity. By this point, Aufidius is quite capable of drawing his sword and executing his enemy on the spot. Hence Coriolanus's long speech is energized with a sense of urgency, as he is forced to arrest the Volscian with his words to convey the message of his intended defection. His strategy proves successful; Aufidius stands rooted in the sand as he assimilates this new information. He does not yet know that the aristocracy has turned against Coriolanus, even if he is aware that the rabble seeks his downfall. Most importantly, he does not know that Coriolanus himself has turned against Rome— the surprise must elicit a strong response from the actor.

Coriolanus then changes his line of attack and goads the hesitant Aufidius to the point of resolution.

> I will fight
> Against my canker'd country with the spleen
> Of all the underfiends. But if so be
> Thou dar'st not this, and that to prove more fortunes
> Th'art tir'd, then, in a word, I also am
> Longer to live most weary, and present
> My throat to thee and to thy ancient malice;
> Which not to cut would show thee but a fool,
> Since I have ever follow'd thee with hate,
> Drawn tuns of blood out of thy country's breast,
> And cannot live but to thy shame, unless
> It be to do thee service.
>
> (4.5.91–102)

The brief pause which ensues is electric with unspoken possibilities, for the audience cannot know how the Volscian will react to these inflammatory words. Aufidius heightens the moment of tense ambiguity by taking a step back with his hand to his sword and delivering "O Martius, Martius" (4.5.102) in a flat tone of voice, as he plays with his enemy before completing the phrase with "Each word thou hast spoke hath weeded from my heart/A root of ancient envy" (4.5.103–4). Depending on the dynamic of the preceding speech, Hicks at times draws his sword from his scabbard and places it against Coriolanus's throat, before throwing it to the sand with his acceptance of the proposed alliance. The effusive energy of his response contrasts with Coriolanus's, although psychologically unscripted, not quite spontaneous utterance, as he expresses his joy in hyperbolic images and an obsessive repetition of Coriolanus's name:

> O Martius, Martius!
> Each word thou hast spoke hath weeded from my heart
> A root of ancient envy. If Jupiter
> Should from yond cloud speak divine things
> And say " 'Tis true", I'd not believe them more
> Than thee, all-noble Martius.
>
> (4.5.102–7)

The embrace which follows was blocked in several forms before the final version was adopted for performance. Coriolanus originally knelt when offering his throat to the enemy, and Aufidius "twined" his arms about him from behind, before helping him to his feet. An alternate staging had Coriolanus advance after the initial request, so that it was he who first extended his arms; Aufidius then pulled away after the prolonged embrace to deliver the rest of his speech from a short distance. As the speech now stands, Aufidius takes a short walk round the stationary figure as he delivers

> Let me twine
> Mine arms about that body, where against
> My grained ash an hundred times hath broke,
> And scarr'd the moon with splinters.
>
> (4.5.107–10)

He gazes in exultation at Coriolanus's body, allowing the image to sink in and the dynamic to build before advancing with open arms, so that the actual embrace comes only on "Here I clip/The anvil of my sword" (4.5.110–11). Aufidius delivers a large portion of his speech while still in Coriolanus's arms, suiting the action to the word as they now contend as hotly for love as ever they did in hate. He steps back to gaze on Coriolanus once more on "but that I see thee here" (4.5.116), expressing his joy with monosyllabic emphasis, and the two warriors do not touch again until the final handshake at the end of the scene.

Aufidius announces his former purpose "Once more to hew thy target from thy brawn,/Or lose mine arm for't" (4.5.121–22)—again using hyperbolic imagery to express the intensity of his emotion, for the most a soldier can do is sacrifice his fighting arm—before offering him "Th'one half of my commission" (4.5.139). Coriolanus's half line interjection "You bless me, gods" (4.5.136), originally delivered as a quiet aside, now comes as an active realization of his good fortune, an enthusiastic climax to the news he has received. He assimilates Aufidius's words as he crosses left, as though to enter the main hall immediately, then turns round as the Volscian calls his name. Aufidius offers his hand on "A thousand welcomes!/And more a friend than e'er an enemy" (4.5.146–47), then momentarily withdraws it for the knowing irony of "Yet, Martius, that was much!" (4.5.148). The powerful tension in the tentative alliance between the two generals is finally resolved. The men shake hands warmly and exit together stage left, followed by the three bewildered servants.

As they pass out of the audience's field of vision, Antium doors once again reopen to reveal Rome gates, and a bright wash floods the stage to suggest the spacial transition from midnight revelry to the Roman market square by day. The tribunes enter right, Brutus in a turtle-necked shirt and carrying his robes of office, Sicinius in a sweater and dark glasses, as though the sun were smiling now that Coriolanus is no longer a threat.[11] Menenius, also wearing casual attire, and sporting a panama hat, joins them through the main gates. The tribunes cannot resist a self-congratulatory "I told you so" at the old man's expense; Sicinius's taunt "Your Coriolanus is not much miss'd/But with his friends" (4.6.13–14) provokes a hearty laugh from the audience, with the actor's strategic pause at the end of the first line. Menenius's "All's well" (4.6.16) is delivered in a jocular tone. He is genuinely pleased that Rome is peaceful and contented once more, despite his personal desire that Coriolanus "could have temporiz'd" (4.6.17). The image of civil concord is completed by the entrance of a family on their morning stroll. They appear left and are met by the tribunes who hurry to cultivate their popular support; Sicinius's delivery of "Live, and thrive" (4.6.23) over the head of the infant in its mother's arms provides a wonderful pictorial reference to the cliché of the politician and the baby. As the couple crosses to continue their promenade through the right wings, Brutus calls out after them "Farewell, kind neighbours. We wish'd Coriolanus/Had lov'd you as we did" (4.6.24–25). Yet the line is primarily directed as a further dig at Menenius, and is spoken with a knowing look over his shoulder at the patrician. The tribunes move in on his position centerstage to convince him of his friend's arrogance, but Menenius refuses to listen, offering a mild rebuke on "I think not so" (4.6.33). Their complacent analysis of the soldier's manifold defects is cut short by the arrival of the aedile, with the devastating news of Coriolanus's defection to the enemy camp.

Confusion suddenly fills the stage, a complete visual contrast to the earlier contentment and lyrical atmosphere. The aedile tentatively begins a false exit after "Go see this rumourer whipp'd" (4.6.48), as though uncertain how to proceed; then with the messenger's confirmation of his cataclysmic news, he again moves to fulfil the tribune's command to "Go whip him 'fore the people's eyes" (4.6.61), when he is interrupted by a further report. The stage, which had formerly been characterized by a languid tranquility, is suddenly flooded from all directions by a stream of aediles, who enter one after the other in rapid succession, to build the momentum of the scene and intensify the atmosphere of doom hanging

over the city. The first messenger descends through the left stands
to the upper lip of the stage, while the second pauses halfway down
the stands, right, to deliver his tidings, then hurriedly retraces his
steps to disappear once again above. Cominius, accompanied by
certain members of the senate, makes his climactic entrance
through the main gates and immediately crosses downstage to
accuse the tribunes face to face. Menenius's constant interruptions
increase the scene's already rapid momentum, and build the suspense prior to the final statement of Rome's certain devastation:

Com. O, you have made good work.
Men.   What news? What news?
Com. You have holp to ravish your own daughters, and
       To melt the city leads upon your pates,
       To see your wives dishonour'd to your noses—
Men. What's the news? What's the news?
Com. Your temples burned in their cement, and
       Your franchises, whereon you stood, confin'd
       Into an auger's bore.
Men.   Pray now, your news?—
       You have made fair work, I fear me.—Pray, your news?
                                                   (4.6.81–89)

Cominius cuts short Menenius's digressive questioning "If Martius
should be join'd wi'th'Volscians" (4.6.90) with a monosyllabic
firmness that banishes all hope: "If!/He is their god" (4.6.90–91).

   The tribunes stand huddled together right of center, breaking
their silence only with the outrage of the aristocracy denying their
share in the general blame. Sicinius explodes on "Say not we
brought it" (4.6.121) and utters a darkly ironic laugh in response to
Menenius's rebuke "How? Was't we? We lov'd him" (4.6.122), as
the senators conveniently forget their own abandonment of Coriolanus. As the citizens rush to fill the stage,[12] terrified at the
rumour of the approaching holocaust, Menenius turns the full force
of his anger in their direction, describing them in terms of vehement
contempt that might issue from Coriolanus's own lips:

              You are they
       That made the air unwholesome when you cast
       Your stinking greasy caps in hooting at
       Coriolanus' exile. Now he's coming,
       And not a hair upon a soldier's head
       Which will not prove a whip.
                                                   (4.6.130–35)

They stand rooted and listening, betraying as much shame-faced guilt as defensive anger at the patrician's words. They assimilate the rebuke, then deal with their despair by sheepishly asserting their innocence and turning against the hapless tribunes: "When I said banish him, I said 'twas pity" (4.6.141). The round of "And so did I"s which follows (4.6.142–43) grows in conviction, building to the "great toe"'s direct accusation "That we did we did for the best,/ and though we willingly consented to his banish-/ment, yet it was his death we wished for" (4.6.144–46). Despite the revision of the line,[13] the audience still responds with scornful laughter to the vacillations of the mob, and the patricians encapsulate this sense of disgust in their stunned looks at the assembled citizens. Menenius breaks their tense silence as he asks Cominius to go up with him to the Capitol. The general pauses, then hits the monosyllables of his reply "O, ay, what else?" (4.6.149) in a tone of weary despair which conveys the futility of all defensive action. With a final contemptuous glance at the "clusters," the patricians exit through Rome gates, leaving Sicinius and Brutus to dismiss the people home. Their subdued exit through the right wings contrasts with the desperate energy of their initial approach, and the scene ends on a note of solemn tension as the tribunes cross upstage to follow the senate to the Capitol.

As they exit, the black gates close behind their retreating figures to transport the audience back to the Volscian camp, where we hear the report of Coriolanus's progress as head of the enemy army. Aufidius enters left, and immediately strides across the sand to take up his position downstage center. The Volscian lieutenant appears simultaneously from the right wings to join his leader and reply to the brooding question: "Do they still fly to th'Roman?" (4.7.1). As the general bitterly describes the proud invincibility of his nemesis, his lieutenant silently retreats to his final position right of center, thus leaving Aufidius to deliver his analysis of Coriolanus's fortunes in the form of a soliloquy, facing front. The Arden edition of the play reports a controversy in readers' and spectators' responses to this passage. Coleridge writes:

> I have always thought this, in itself so beautiful speech, the least explicable from the mood and full intention of the speaker of any in the whole works of Shakespeare, I cherish the hope that I am mistaken, and that, becoming wiser, I shall discover some profound excellence in that in which I now appear to detect an imperfection. (Arden edition of *Coriolanus*, p. 273)

Philip Brockbank, the editor, concurs, adding that

> A strain of self-communing soliloquy in the speech, yielding peculiar shifts and ambiguities, makes it an unexpected passage of dialogue between commander and lieutenant. (Ibid., p. 273)

Rehearsals proved the validity of Brockbank's concerned remark. When delivered to the lieutenant as an extended answer to his inquiry "think you he'll carry Rome?" (4.7.27), the speech fell flat. Its length and purely rhetorical function threatened to tax the audience's attention span, while providing insufficient motivation for the actor's continued impassioned delivery. The energy of the lines stems from their obsessively inward-looking resentment; they only made sense when Hicks began to deliver the speech out front from his isolated position at the foot of the stage, as though the lieutenant's question had unleashed a stream of consciousness which is verbally expressed for himself alone. As Brockbank suggests, he is indeed communing with himself, and his analysis of Coriolanus's character takes the form of spoken thought. Thus Hicks begins on a reflective note, which builds in intensity to his passionate vow of personal vengeance: "One fire drives out one fire; one nail, one nail;/ Rights by rights falter, strengths by strengths do fail" (4.7.54–55). Suddenly recollecting the presence of an observer, he curtly bids him "Come, let's away" (4.7.56), as though annoyed at being thus overheard. Aufidius then pauses for a brief yet determined restatement of his oath: "When Caius, Rome is thine,/ Thou art poor'st of all: then shortly art thou mine" (4.7.56–57).

6
Act 5

As Aufidius and his lieutenant exit up the central aisle of the theater at the end of the fourth act, the audience returns its focus to the main stage where Roman tribunes and senators assemble to discuss their proposed embassy to Coriolanus. Menenius enters right, slightly in advance of the others, refusing their request to try his powers of persuasion with a wave of his hand on "No, I'll not go" (5.1.1). The official party is followed by a small brace of plebeians, who stand behind their leaders and listen with worried concentration, then move in with a look of silent pleading as the patrician shows signs of melting:[1]

> I'll undertake't.
> I think he'll hear me. . . .
> He was not taken well; he had not din'd:
> . . . Therefore I'll watch him
> Till he be dieted to my request,
> And then I'll set upon him.
>
> (5.1.47–58)

By thus choosing to incorporate the citizens into the scene as the "others" ambiguously referred to in the stage directions, Hall has ensured that the full gamut of Roman society is represented on stage. Patrician, plebeian, soldier, senator, tribune—all unite to present a consolidated front before the impending attack, while at the same time creating a varied stage picture of differing facial responses.

Brutus gives voice to the people's speaking looks as he takes a step forward to encourage Menenius with "You know the very road into his kindness,/And cannot lose your way" (5.1.59–60). The patrician takes this line as his cue to begin his assent up the central aisle of the auditorium, delivering his final speech on the move:

> Good faith, I'll prove him,
> Speed how it will. I shall ere long have knowledge
> Of my success.
>
> (5.1.60–62)

As he exits, Cominius takes over his central position at the top of the stairs to foretell the failure of Menenius's embassy, hitting his monosyllabic prophesy "So that all hope is vain" (5.1.70) with a staccato emphasis that drives home the dismal certainty of Rome's destruction. The plebeians advance with renewed hope when he reveals that "his noble mother and his wife . . . mean to solicit him/ For mercy to his country" (5.1.171–73) before exiting right, while the senatorial party passes once again through Rome gates.

The action cross-fades back to the Volscian camp, as two guards enter from opposite sides of the stage and give a brief nod of recognition when they converge at the center of the circle. Menenius begins his climb up the stairs, appearing from the left aisle, and the soldiers immediately jump forward with pikes outstretched to halt his progress:

> *First Watch.*   Stay! Whence are you?
> *Second Watch.*   Stand, and go back.
>
> (5.2.1)

Menenius waves his hand as though to brush away their extended weapons, and compliments their efficiency with "You guard like men" (5.2.2). His affability contrasts with their threatening brusqueness, before he too adopts a tone of gentle authority, hitting the alliteration on "(I) come/To speak with Coriolanus" (5.2.3–4); this vocal stress is demanded by the structure of the verse and adds weight to his simple statement. The guards once again arrest his progress onto the stage, prodding him with their spears and humorously playing with him as they create a series of appositions in answer to his straightforward remarks: "You *may not* pass; you *must* return" (5.2.5) and "Be it so, go back: the virtue of your name/ Is not here passable" (5.2.12–13).

The guards attack Menenius as an insignificant old man and despise him as a Roman. As Hall said in rehearsal, "all Romans are sensuous hedonistic piss-artists, as far as they are concerned."[2] The first watch, played by Lewis George, is contemptuous and sadistic; he enjoys patronizing the defenceless old man, and his tone shifts from cool sarcasm to cruel threat as he commands the statesman's retreat:

> Faith, sir, if you had told as many lies in
> his behalf as you have uttered words in your own,
> you should not pass here; no, though it were as
> virtuous to lie as to live chastely. Therefore go back.
>
> (5.2.24–27)

Menenius suddenly alters his strategy and takes a step downstage to enquire "Has he dined, canst thou tell? For I would not speak with him till after dinner" (5.2.33–34), iterating his words to Cominius in the preceding scene (5.1.50–58). The Volscian watch cannot at first believe that the representative of stoic Rome should thus prove a self-confessed epicure, and drop their pikes to the sand to ask in amazement "You are a Roman, are you?" (5.2.35).

Menenius seeks to align himself with the object of his quest, saying "I am as thy general is" (5.2.36), but is met with an explosion of indignant rage, as the first guard circles him downstage to cathartically release the violence which has been building within him:

> Then you should hate Rome, as he does.
> Can you, when you have pushed out your gates the
> very defender of them, and, in a violent popular
> ignorance, given your enemy your shield, think to
> front his revenges with the easy groans of old women,
> the virginal palms of your daughters, or with the
> palsied intercession of such a decayed dotant as you
> seem to be? Can you think to blow out the intended
> fire your city is ready to flame in, with such weak
> breath as this?
>
> (5.2.37–46)

Thus the scene makes the transition to a new tempo of speech. The fun and the game-playing are over; aggressions surface and the pace quickens. Menenius's futile attempt to regain control of the situation is cut short as the Volscian again picks up on his verbal inaccuracy, this time in anger rather than in scorn:

> *Men.*   Sirrah, if thy captain knew I were here, he would use me
>   with estimation.
> *First Watch.* Come, my captain knows you not.
> *Men.*   I mean thy general.
>
> (5.2.50–53)

The guards finally succeed in prodding Menenius back down the stairs, the upstage gate is pushed open, and the newly-allied leaders advance to investigate the disturbance.

This is the first time that the audience witnesses for itself the transformation in Coriolanus described by the Romans in 5.1. He appears in the black Volscian uniform, his back straight, his stance firm, his answers to Menenius brief phrases in verbal contrast to his former explosive outpourings: "What's the matter?" (5.2.58) and

"Away!" (5.2.78). His mask is firmly in place, and it is one which inspires respect and fear within his new troops; at the first sign of his approach the guards split to stand at attention at opposite sides of the circle. Aufidius remains up center while Coriolanus comes downstage to face Menenius. The scene's vivid momentum is broken by his slow and deliberate disavowel of friendship, spoken as much to convince himself as his old mentor:

> Wife, mother, child, I know not. My affairs
> Are servanted to others. Though I owe
> My revenge properly, my remission lies
> In Volscian breasts. . . . Therefore be gone.
>
> (5.2.80–85)

Although cold control is the keynote for McKellen's playing of the scene, a brief moment of emotion is allowed to break through:

> Yet, for I lov'd thee,
> Take this along; I writ it for thy sake,
> And would have sent it.
>
> (5.2.87–89)

His letter to Menenius represents the grief behind the mask.[3]

It is a fatal gesture to thus transmit the document in Aufidius's presence, for it betrays the fact that he is in communication with the enemy camp. His integrity, however, will not allow him to wound the old man with an untempered rejection. Menenius responds joyously, but Coriolanus again retreats with the warning "Another word, Menenius,/I will not hear thee speak" (5.2.89–90), then turns to Aufidius for confirmation of his constant resolution. As the guards once again move in on the Roman to taunt him with the failure of his mission, "Now, sir, is your name Menenius?" (5.2.93), the two generals cross upstage; they do not complete their exit, but stand frozen in a tableau facing the gates. Menenius retraces his path up the right aisle, as the guards provide a final summary of the interchange:

> *First Watch.*   A noble fellow, I warrant him.
> *Second Watch.* The worthy fellow is our general: he's the rock, the oak not to be wind-shaken.
>
> (5.2.107–9)

Thus the scene, begun with a loud command, ends on a note of silent musing.

As the guards split to exit up the right and left aisles of the theater, Coriolanus and Aufidius pivot to commence the following sequence. The sentries' cries of "Pass, pass" echo from opposite ends of the auditorium,[4] announcing the arrival of the embassy which climbs the stairs right of the stage; the Roman ladies are already in position across the center of the sand as Coriolanus interprets their tableau for the audience, down right:

> My wife comes foremost; then the honour'd mould
> Wherein this trunk was fram'd, and in her hand
> The grandchild to her blood.
>
> (5.3.22–24)

He is genuinely shaken by this sight of the family he has foresaken, and with a great effort channels his energies into a desperate restatement of his resolution to maintain his isolated stance:

> Let the Volsces
> Plough Rome and harrow Italy; I'll never
> Be such a gosling to obey instinct, but stand
> As if a man were author of himself
> And knew no other kin.
>
> (5.3.33–37)

Virgilia's greeting "My lord and husband!" (5.3.37) cuts off his monologue to the audience; he momentarily abandons his stoic control to embrace her, and to kneel to receive his mother's blessing. She accords it him, then participates in his inversion of Nature's cycle by sinking her own knee "i'th'earth":

> Whilst, with no softer cushion than the flint,
> I kneel before thee, and unproperly
> Show duty as mistaken all this while
> Between the child and parent.
>
> (5.3.53–56)

This is the first in a series of "unnatural" images presented in this scene, which illustrate how the hero's breach of natural law extends to the world around him in a pathetic fallacy of universal proportions: a mother is depicted on her knees to her son, Rome on its knees to a traitor; a mother kills her son with a blow that must prove most mortal to him—the mother who should give life, brings death. Volumnia notes her continued power over Coriolanus and expresses her consciousness that all is going well, as he raises her

o her feet: "Thou art my warrior:/I holp to frame thee" (5.3.62–63).
She calls Coriolanus's attention to the silent figure of Valeria, who
stands to his left, and he greets her with words of poetic beauty that
bear witness to the internal growth which has taken place within
he formerly inarticulate soldier:

> The noble sister of Publicola,
> The moon of Rome, chaste as the icicle
> That's curdied by the frost from purest snow
> And hangs on Dian's temple! Dear Valeria!
>
> (5.3.64–67)

The image is precise, referring to particular icicles on a specific
temple, and betrays the intensity of Coriolanus's emotion. He
misses Rome and finds in Valeria the physical embodiment of its
great virtue.

Coriolanus now turns to embrace his son. The vulnerable wit of
his blessing contrasts with the formal wit of his interchange with
Volumnia:

> The god of soldiers,
> With the consent of supreme Jove, inform
> Thy thoughts with nobleness, that thou mayst prove
> To shame unvulnerable, and stick i'th'wars
> Like a great sea-mark standing every flaw
> And saving those that eye thee!
>
> (5.3.70–75)

As he speaks, he puts the child on his shoulders, and the young
Martius extends his arm in an echo of his father's fist salute,
reinforcing our sense of Nature's inexorable, cyclical pattern. Coriolanus has shown that despite his outward defection he is still his
mother's son. He kneels to Volumnia, kisses Virgilia, greets Valeria
and blesses young Martius—he keeps melting, and it takes a supreme effort of will for him to realign himself with Aufidius stage
right, as he refuses to grant the only thing they have to ask:

> Do not bid me
> Dismiss my soldiers, or capitulate
> Again with Rome's mechanics. . . . Desire not
> T'allay my rages and revenges with
> Your colder reasons.
>
> (5.3.81–86)

Volumnia moves to join the virgins of Rome at their position left
of center as she begins her argument of persuasion, calling attention
to the physical devastation which betrays "what life/We have led
since thy exile" (5.3.95–96). Coriolanus listens in silence, moving to
seat himself in the sand down right with Aufidius at his shoulder
for he will "Hear nought from Rome in private" (5.3.93). Perceiving
that her rhetoric cannot sway him, Volumnia advances to confront
him directly with her bared wrist. She vows that she will kill herself
rather than see him destroy his native city:

> thou shalt no sooner
> March to assault thy country than to tread—
> Trust to't, thou shalt not—on thy mother's womb
> That brought thee to this world.
>
> (5.3.122–25)

Virgilia's and young Martius's affirmation of her oath overwhelm
the seemingly implaccable warrior. He rises as though to physically
brush away his debilitating leniency, and crosses with Aufidiu
further right. Volumnia breaks away from the Roman contingent to
pursue her son and arrest his departure with "Nay, go not from u
thus" (5.3.131), bowing before the Volscian commander to mak
her request for peaceful reconciliation between the warring nations
She appeals to Coriolanus's personal loyalty and integrity, to hi
name and fame, then abandons all vocal persuasion for the creatio
of a more powerful visual emblem, as the Roman virgins prostrat
themselves in the sand before his new position down left:[5]

> Down ladies: let us shame him with our knees.
> To his surname Coriolanus longs more pride
> Than pity to our prayers. Down! an end:
> This is the last.
>
> (5.3.169–72)

The women first kneel in the sand, then drop even further down
in supplication, lying absolutely flat, middle-eastern fashion. It i
initially a very slow, formal and dignified action; the attitude o
begging comes only with the final obeisance.[6] Perceiving that he
strategy has proven fruitless, Volumnia cues the ladies to rise an
to begin their cross stage right. She moves with them, then, sud
denly catching sight of her grandson who mimics their gesture o
supplication, calls upon Coriolanus to witness the moving sight:

> Nay, behold's,
> This boy that cannot tell what he would have,

> But kneels, and holds up hands for fellowship,
> Does reason our petition with more strength
> Than thou hast to deny't.
>
> (5.3.173–77)

When Coriolanus still proves adament, Virgilia gathers up young Martius and Volumnia once again beckons the procession forward with "Come, let us go" (5.3.177), before interrupting her own exit for a final attack on her son. She crosses to confront him face to face:

> This fellow had a Volscian to his mother;
> His wife is in Corioli, and his child
> Like him by chance.
>
> (5.3.178–80)[7]

Throughout the scene, even when reunited with his child, Coriolanus has assumed his fundamental invulnerability to their arguments. Now he is confronted with the image of having a Volscian as his mother and of both himself and his son being bastards; although he has just stated his desire to stand without any kin, he is destroyed the moment the consequences of that resolution are articulated for him by Volumnia. She looks him in the eye, then deliberately turns away in a powerful gesture of maternal rejection. Coriolanus literally clutches at her retreating figure, and *"Holds her by the hand silent"* (5.3.183).[8] Still turned away, Volumnia straightens her back, and the expression on her face shows her knowledge that she has triumphed. The moment is electric. Slowly she turns and the two face each other once more as Coriolanus utters "O mother, mother!/What have you done?" (5.3.183–84) in the tone of an agonized child. There is no apology, just a moving statement of the knowledge that in giving life to Rome, Volumnia has robbed him of his own:

> You have won a happy victory to Rome;
> But for your son, believe it, O, believe it,
> Most dangerously you have with him prevail'd,
> If not most mortal to him.
>
> (5.3.186–89)

As he speaks, he squeezes her hand in rhythm to the lines to drive the point home. Suddenly he breaks away and crosses right, uttering an active acceptance of his fate: "But let it come" (5.3.189). His movement away from his mother comes as a step towards death. He no longer feels himself in competition with Aufidius, for he has metaphorically renounced his part in the material world. Still, he seeks to preserve his alliance with the Volscian, asserting that "though I cannot make true wars,/I'll frame convenient peace" (5.3.190–91). He moves upstage to physically position himself once more beside Aufidius, and obsessively repeats his name in a desperate cry for confirmation of his integrity:

> Now, good Aufidius,
> Were you in my stead, would you have heard
> A mother less? or granted less, Aufidius?
>
> (5.3.191–93)

He does not catch the coldly ironic tone of the reply, but blindly seeks to summon up his shattered control with the self-deprecating humour of "And sir, it is no little thing to make/Mine eyes to sweat compassion" (5.3.195–96). Coriolanus then moves to gather his family about him stage left, comforting them after the devastating revelation "I'll not to Rome" (5.3.198). Aufidius crosses downstage to deliver his aside, which comes as the statement of a narrative fact, rather than a commentary on the scene he has just witnessed:

> I am glad thou hast set thy mercy and thy honour
> At difference in thee. Out of that I'll work
> Myself a former fortune.
>
> (5.3.200–202)

The first line is focused on Coriolanus, the second on the audience, as he prophecies the warrior's imminent downfall. Coriolanus beckons him to join with his family in a farewell drink offstage, "Come, enter with us" (5.3.206), and the assembly moves in a unified body to exit through the Volscian gates.

The blocking for this exit was not firmly set during rehearsals. Any one of a series of alternatives may be performed depending on the dynamic of a given night: Coriolanus may be either framed or followed by his wife and mother; Aufidius at one point offered his arm to Volumnia,[9] but usually exits at Coriolanus's side, indicating his continued though superficial support of the Roman general. More interesting is the version which has young Martius framed by his father and Aufidius. The audience is left to decide for itself whether he will be nurtured under Volscian tutelage. A final alternative has Coriolanus move to embrace his son, but the child runs away to the safety of his mother's arms, lending added pathos to Coriolanus's softly ironic congratulation of the women:

Ladies, you deserve
To have a temple built you. All the swords
In Italy and her confederate arms
Could not have made this peace.

(5.3.206–9)

As the party exits, Rome gates once again move into place to
transform the scene back to the city which remains ignorant of its
salvation. Menenius and Sicinius were originally blocked to enter
above left and deliver their dialogue while sitting in the stands, but
this staging was felt to be too static after the mounting tension of the
preceding sequence, and so was revised before the first preview.
They now enter from the left wings to remain standing in the circle,
left of center. Sicinius carries a flask of brandy, and his slurred
speech suggests that the two men have been out drinking together,
thus projecting an image of unity in adversity; and Menenius's
constant refrain of "I told you so" is much more gentle here than
earlier in the play. He hits the harsh consonants of his opening line
"See you yond coign o'th'Capitol, yond cornerstone" (5.4.1) for
total emphasis on the repeated alliteration of the "c" sound, before
the scene moves fully into prose.[10] There is a complete contrast
between the exchange we have witnessed in 5.2 and the way in
which it is described. Menenius's account creates a myth rather
than an accurate rendering of the event:

He
sits in his state as a thing made for Alexander.
What he bids be done is finished with his bidding.
He wants nothing of a god but eternity, and a heaven
to throne in.

(5.4.21–25)[11]

The messenger of death enters right to report the attack on
Brutus, while the messenger of good tidings is revealed through the
main gates, rolling out a red carpet in preparation for Volumnia's
triumphal procession into Rome. Sicinius's initial response to the
second aedile entering hard on the heels of "They'll give him death
by inches" (5.4.40) indicates his trepidation. The red carpet might
after all be for Coriolanus—he has no way of knowing to the
contrary. He crawls from his kneeling position in the sand[12] to
pursue the messenger with "What's the news?" (5.4.40), and is met
with the enthusiastic reply "Good news, good news! The ladies
have prevail'd,/The Volscians are dislodg'd, and Martius gone"
(5.4.41–42).[13] The sound of "trumpets, sackbuts, psalteries and

fifes,/Tabors and cymbals and the shouting Romans" (5.4.50–51)
issues from speakers at the back of the theater to announce the
arrival of the triumphal procession,[14] and the scene which began on
a note of grim solemnity is suddenly transformed into a joyful
celebration.

The wounded Brutus joins his fellow tribune from the right
wings, as the stage fills with political representatives who come to
greet Volumnia, and the audience in the stands is motioned to rise
and applaud rhythmically as the women of Rome slowly make their
way down the central aisle of the theater. The perimeter around
which the senators align themselves remains in semi-darkness.
Only the center of the circle is brightly illuminated for Volumnia to
receive the adoration of the multitude. A single drum beats while
the first senator appears atop Rome gates to announce:

> Behold our patroness, the life of Rome!
> Call all your tribes together, praise the gods,
> And make triumphant fires. Strew flowers before them;
> Unshout the noise that banish'd Martius;
> Repeal him with the welcome of his mother:
> Cry, "Welcome, ladies, welcome!"
>
> (5.5.1–6)

Volumnia's triumph is truly a stunning piece of stagecraft. Standing
at the center of the circle, surrounded by the city she has saved, she
spreads her arms wide, fighting back her tears as she turns to accept
its expression of joy and thanksgiving. Her facial expression bears
witness to the conflicting emotions of public triumph and personal
grief at war within her, creating a visual culmination to the persuasion scene of 5.3. As she completes her turn, the stage audience is
once again instructed to applaud rhythmically, and the procession
exits through Rome gates, the image of general celebration human-
ized by Sicinius's simple gesture of wrapping the injured Brutus in
his cloak of office.

The Volscian doors snap shut behind the exiting party to effect
the final scene change of the production, and to transport the
audience from Rome's festivity to a dark world of treason and
conspiracy. Aufidius enters left to dispatch his attendant through
the upstage gates with a letter to the Volscian senate, while the
three assassins descend from their positions in the right and left
stands to converge around the figure of their leader downstage
center. One by one, they urge Aufidius to cut short his enemy's

reign, and the general works himself into a frenzied resolution to accept their counsel:

> There was it:
> For which my sinews shall be stretch'd upon him;
> At a few drops of women's rheum, which are
> As cheap as lies, he sold the blood and labour
> Of our great action. Therefore shall he die,
> And I'll renew me in his fall.
>
> (5.6.44–49)

Their exchange is interrupted by the sound of Coriolanus's approach, and the conspirators scatter as the senate appears through Corioli gates. At the same time, the citizens enter from the wings, beckoning the outer stands to descend and swell their numbers.

Coriolanus runs down the central aisle, carrying the Volscian standard and followed by a single attendant, to be met with the enthusiastic cheers and applause of the people who rush to shake hands with the returning hero. His entrance provides a complete contrast both to Aufidius's reception into the city—

> Your native town you enter'd like a post,
> And had no welcome home; but he returns
> Splitting the air with noise
>
> (5.6.50–52)

—and to his own encounters with the citizens of Rome. Now he is treated as a popular hero, and for the first time performs the role with distinction. He acknowledges the whistles, cheers and throwing of gold confetti with an easy satisfaction as he runs a triumphal lap around the circle, then takes up his position downstage center. He addresses his first lines out front to the main audience, as though they were an extension of the Volscian multitude:

> Hail lords, I am return'd your soldier,
> No more infected with my country's love
> Than when I parted hence, but still subsisting
> Under your great command.
>
> (5.6.71–74)

Coriolanus then turns upstage to pass the treaty into the hands of the assembled senate. Aufidius puts a sudden end to the celebratory acclamation, as he commands from his perch on the right ledge of the gates:

> Read it not, noble lords;
> But tell the traitor in the highest degree
> He hath abus'd your powers.
>
> (5.6.84–86)

Unprepared for this attack from his supposed ally, Coriolanus at first responds in a tone of bewildered incomprehension, which grows in intensity to an explosion of angry violence when he is addressed by his *cognomen* "Martius" (5.6.87). Aufidius descends from the stands as he provokes his enemy to further words of self-incrimination:

> Ay, Martius, Caius Martius! Dost thou think
> I'll grace thee with that robbery, thy stol'n name
> Coriolanus, in Corioli?
>
> (5.6.88–90)[15]

The two warriors face off against each other at opposite ends of the ring. This betrayal by his only remaining connection in the mortal world proves too much for the hero's psychic and physical stamina. McKellen accords his lines "Measureless liar, thou hast made my heart/Too great for what contains it" (5.6.103–4) a literal interpretation, as he clutches his hand to his breast and staggers in the sand before mastering the pain which has momentarily overwhelmed him. Aufidius has stripped him of his title, his status and his honour, reducing the lone warrior to a mere boy; the violence of his resulting grief and anger causes his heart to crack. Thus McKellen pronounces his subsequent lines with slurred speech, as he duplicates the physical symptoms of the heart attack which becomes the key image for the play's conclusion.

Coriolanus fights back the pain and the emotion welling up inside him to bid the senate "thrust the lie unto him" (5.6.110), but Aufidius's sadistic taunt "thou boy of tears" (5.6.101) proves more than his heroic integrity can bear. He verbally attacks the Volscian nation before the lords can intercede. His inner conflict stems from the paradox with which he was confronted in 5.3. Throughout his life he has fought to be absolutely what he is and has never temporized; now he is emotionally involved with the treaty of Rome and has, in fact, performed exactly what Aufidius accuses him of now trying to cover up. The treaty marks the first point at which Coriolanus acts out of character and he knows it. He knows too that the taunt "boy of tears" is a direct reference to his drops of "compassion" (5.3.196) shed at Volumnia's supplication. It is thus the very truth of Aufidius's insult that prompts Coriolanus to plunge headlong into the enemy's trap. He finally realizes that one who changes allegiance, no matter what the moral or political reasons, is a traitor; there is no escape but death.

Coriolanus stands centerstage to deliver an angry boast of his former invasion and conquest of the Volscian nation:

> Cut me to pieces, Volsces, men and lads,
> Stain all your edges on me. Boy! False hound!
> If you have writ your annals true, 'tis there,
> That like an eagle in a dove-cote, I
> Flutter'd your Volscians in Corioli!
> Alone I did it. Boy!
>
> (5.6.111–16)[16]

During this speech, he tears off his Volscian uniform in an effort to get back to the primitive warrior of Act 1, where real heroism was possible. The gesture, however, proves futile; his heart is broken and he is completely disillusioned. The human circle around Coriolanus tightens as individuals in the crowd accuse him of his war crimes, throw sand at his feet, and point their fingers in a gesture of threatening accusation. The Volscian senators react in the same manner as their counterparts in Rome; they do not want a public confrontation in the streets, and so cry out:

> Peace, ho! no outrage, peace!
> . . . His last offences to us
> Shall have judicious hearing. Stand, Aufidius,
> And trouble not the peace.
>
> (5.6.123–27)

Pain and rage blind the hero to the possibility of rational defence. He summons the last vestiges of his fading strength to draw his sword and utter the insult which finally provokes the Volscian to give the signal for his assassination:

> O that I had him,
> With six Aufidiuses, or more, his tribe,
> To use my lawful sword.
>
> (5.6.127–29)

As he concludes the vaunt, he lunges toward his treacherous enemy but the conspirators put a sudden end to this last, vain attack.

The blocking of the assassination sequence was completely altered during the week which preceded the first preview. Hall wanted above all to undercut any image of romantic heroism, insisting that Coriolanus's end must be ugly and very rapid. Fight director Malcolm Ranson originally had the three conspirators converge on the central figure from opposing corners of the playing area. The first cut him across the stomach, the second slashed him at waist-height from behind, while the third slit the back of his throat. His spinal column cut, Coriolanus's head fell forward and he collapsed like a broken puppet; there can be no "noble corse" after such an execution, just a bloody trunk. This, however, gave rise to the practical problem of cheating a run on a half-naked body, a piece of stage business which must appear completely artificial to the stage audience which stands in close proximity to the action. Because Coriolanus is positioned alone in the focal center of the sandpit, it would be discordant with his past fame as a great soldier for three men to run at him from a distance and overpower him. Thus it became necessary to rethink the staging of the assassination.

Hall felt that the play's already well-established eclecticism justified the modernization of this sequence. Hence he has armed the conspirators with pistols and a rifle, positioning one man on the left ledge of Corioli gates, and the other two in the slips at opposite ends of the theater. As Coriolanus makes his ill-fated run on Aufidius, they brutally gun him down in a powerful emblematic explosion of the heroic myth. This also intensifies the disintegration of the protagonist's power; as McKellen, who originally proposed this blocking, said at a seminar given as part of the "Coriolanus Weekend" in May, 1985, "You feel the old Coriolanus would have caught the bullets in his teeth." It is only unfortunate for the continuity of the production that no guns are seen earlier in its action, but the dilemma of how to stage these final moments arose too late in rehearsal to introduce modern weapons into earlier sequences, and so prepare the audience for their use. The only concession possible was to include rifle fire in the sound tape used to suggest the citizen's revolt in 1.1.

The ending works dramatically, and yet might have been even more effective had the theater not run into bureaucratic red tape from the Greater London Council. Guns on stage using blank wadding and flame can fire up to (and sometimes even beyond) nine yards, and must be cleared by the fire brigade for safety to actors and audience alike. The fire brigade cleared the weapons for *Coriolanus,* but the G.L.C. stepped in with the objection that the gunfire comes as a surprise, and might cause someone in the audience to have a heart attack. When the theater countered with the argument that unexpected explosions constantly occur in the cinema and are transmitted in stereophonic sound without censorship, the answer was "No, it's completely different—you have a live audience here!" As a compromise, the armorer investigated accessible lower charged blanks and settled on short 2.2s; in addition, the theater erected a notice in the lobby warning the audience of the use of gunfire, thus avoiding untoward surprise, but unfortunately weakening the dramatic effect.

Though something of an auditory shock, there are no visual horrors to the assassination: because Coriolanus is shot from a great distance (the ledge of the gates and the slips at opposite ends of the theater), no individual actor is sufficiently close to transfer blood to the body of the hero.[17] Even had McKellen not made the decision to strip off his Volscian uniform, the expense of making a second costume which must be cleaned between each performance would have been extreme. The issue was thus reduced to a choice between the impact of an unexpected explosion or a continuation of the visual theme of blood. As it now stands, with emphasis on auditory rather than visual effect, the assassination is a clear, stark dramatic moment. The image of the hero's corpse lying within the empty circle, bloodless though it be, movingly encapsulates the barbaric violence and impossible "absoluteness" which lie at the heart of the play.

After Coriolanus's body falls to the sand, Aufidius rushes to stand in triumph on the corpse of his dead enemy,[18] descending only after his first expression of self-justification:

> My lords, when you shall know (as in this rage,
> Provok'd by him, you cannot) the great danger
> Which this man's life did owe you, you'll rejoice
> That he is thus cut off.
>
> (5.6.135–38)[19]

The stage is covered in a flurry of chaotic movement as citizens rush in panic across the circle, and one man runs to physically remove Aufidius from the body, before being restrained by the Volscian aediles. Women scream, and the senate moves forward to express its shock at the act of desecration which Aufidius has committed:

First Lord.   O Tullus!
Second Lord. Thou hast done a deed whereat valour will weep.

Third Lord.   Tread not upon him. Masters all, be quiet!
                 Put up your swords.

(5.6.131–34)

They refuse to allow Aufidius the opportunity to justify himself.
First it is time to honour the dead, and "mourn you for him"
(5.6.142) is addressed directly to the warrior, rather than uttered as
a command to the general multitude. Thus rebuked, Aufidius loses
mastery of his social mask; he moves from vitriolic loathing to
intense grief as he realizes the full consequences of his act. His
hatred for Coriolanus has always been personal, one individual's
envy for another, and the removal of that object means that the
greatest part of his own life is dead with him—there is to be no more
fighting, no more hunting the lion on the battlefield. Thus "My rage
is gone,/And I am struck with sorrow" (5.6.146–47) conveys a
profound sense of emptiness and desolation.

As Aufidius issues his commands for the noble burial of his
enemy, five officers advance to serve as pall-bearers for the funeral
procession. They ceremoniously lift the body and carry it in state
around the outer perimeter of the circle, fully presenting this final
emblem of human and heroic waste to the audience, before exiting
silently through Corioli gates. Piercing music and a high pitched
whine build to ear-shattering intensity, to be cut off only with the
climactic crash of the gates slamming shut. The tragic cycle is
complete.

7
Ian McKellen on *Coriolanus*

On 26 August 1985, the day after the closing of "Coriolanus," I spoke with Ian McKellen about his approach to the leading role, first asking what had attracted him to the character, and whether its differences from other major Shakespearean roles rendered it more difficult than his celebrated Macbeth of the late seventies.

Well, I suppose the simplest answer to the first part of that question is that you can't play Coriolanus unless you're believably the young man of action who singlehandedly goes into battle—and not only does Coriolanus do that, he's seen to do it. Unusual in that you never see Macbeth accomplishing his great feats that are talked about in the first scene on the battlefield. But Coriolanus has to fight, so you have to believe that you are convincing, and for that you have to be able to do the run, so I thought that if I didn't do it soon I probably wouldn't do it at all. If there's anything innately difficult in the role of Coriolanus, I think that is a difficulty—to be convincing doing the fight, and for that you need a lot of energy.

There is an innate difficulty in the part, because most of Shakespeare's heroes are attractive to a modern audience when they come to the theater, and I think Coriolanus has very few redeeming features. Modern audiences can't see why they should love him or why they should like him. They might listen to his views and understand that in certain circumstances they are relevant, relevant to society, but I think in the end whether Shakespeare takes sides or not, he does see Coriolanus as a dinosaur as far as his political views are concerned. And clearly Rome is in a state of flux; it's shifting its ground with the granting of suffrage to the people. There are the tribunes, which Coriolanus alone opposes, publicly opposes. Those tribunes are there to stay, so Coriolanus is just going to have to be silenced either by exile or death, it doesn't really matter. I mean that's as far as the problem is concerned. So it is a difficulty to get the audience's sympathy.

Now he is the title of the play. Well, Shakespeare's not awfully good at titling his plays: Romeo is not a better part than Juliet, perhaps a worse part, really. The play should be *Juliet and Romeo;* it should be called *Cleopatra and Antony.* It's called *Coriolanus.* And there are certain expectations, I think, on the audience's behalf. A quality of many of Shakespeare's main parts is that they have to share their views with the audience through soliloquies. Well, there aren't many in this play; there are only about two or three. So clearly Shakespeare doesn't want Coriolanus to have that special appeal. It isn't a play about Coriolanus at all, as I said. John Osborne's title is a much better one: *A Place Calling Itself Rome.* So that's the problem. The audience is expecting something from it which the play is not designed to provide.[1] And if you strain too much in that way you risk losing the spirit of the play.

This production consciously keeps a very even keel between the right wing versus left wing political parties. There's often a problem in producing "Coriolanus" in balancing the conflicting elements of the play—the last production that I saw in Canada was criticized for making it too much a family piece and underemphasizing the politics. Did you find it a difficult balance to maintain in this production?

Not really, no. The family element is very strong, and the domestic scenes are really the easiest scenes of the play because they're just between two or three people. But it's just a behind the scenes insight as to how a powerful family goes about making up its image—it's all those discussions between the royal family about how we're going to appear in public. That's really basically what the argument's about. Coriolanus, whatever his views, which may not be attractive, does have that integrity of "I can only be what I am," which his mother, who is the arch-politician, no doubt about it, wants him to suppress, and play up to the people. That's what a politician has to do; that's how you get your votes. And Coriolanus can only say "I just have to be what I am," and she says "it's easy; you'll get away with it and they'll love you; and don't be so stupid." But he doesn't want to be a politician; he wants to be a man of truth. The family scenes, the relationship between Coriolanus and his mother, are intimately related to, really are another aspect of the main theme, which is how does a society govern itself. It's about the nature of politics.

Did you find the relationship with Aufidius to be more problematic, because I have heard both you and Greg Hicks say that you had difficulties with the scene outside Antium, for example, working on the actual embrace in 4.5?

I think it's very tempting to play that scene in a hugely theatrical way and get the audience interested in their psychological entanglement; and I don't think it really gets you anywhere. I think it's better if you simply work on Coriolanus's sense of Aufidius—and he never stops thinking about him all the way through the play. It's at the center of the play; you don't have to push it. If you push it, I think you get away from the main point of the play. It doesn't really worry me that that scene isn't dead on target.

It just seemed that it was one of the scenes that was improvised around most frequently—I've seen several different versions in performance.

Yes, well, I think that would have happened whether we'd had a firm direction, or line on it, or not. There doesn't seem to be a lot of mileage in saying that the thing with Coriolanus is that he's gay—he seems to be extremely happily married and to be very much in love with his wife, and certainly happy with his son. So I think the relationship between his nature and his hate for Aufidius is ostensibly in the words; they don't need any bolstering up. So it didn't worry me in the end that that scene wasn't stronger stated.

And having played Aufidius before, I remembered that scene as being a highspot of the previous production, but that was under a director who was extremely interested in Coriolanus's psychology. So what I'm saying is that I don't think that's the major interest of the play.

You said in an interview at one point that it was a scene that you liked to "play jazz" with, which is something you also do with Irene Worth as Volumnia in the domestic scenes, to keep them fresh.[2]

Well, not so much to keep them fresh—it's just the way she likes to work, and I like it as well. It's just a different style of playing. Crucially Irene and I always played the same basic form of relationship; it was just the subtle adjustments.

Did you have many rerehearsals when Yvonne Bryceland took over the role?

No, very few. She was called on her own, but I wasn't in for that many.

Do you find that the casting change has at all affected your performance in the domestic scenes?

No, I don't think it has, but I don't see in what Yvonne does something strongly different from what Irene did to make me re-think those scenes. I just find it a bit unsettling to be playing them with somebody else. Yvonne's strengths are characteristics which I don't think are particularly Volumnia's: they have to do with kind-liness and gentleness, which I don't think are particularly Volum-nia's traits.

One of the main preoccupations in the first month of rehearsals was the verse-speaking, teaching the company the basic rules of Peter Hall's approach. Did you find that frustrating, because both you and Irene Worth were already quite experienced in that tech-nique of delivering the text?

It was, I think, a pity that that kind of work hadn't happened before rehearsals, because too much time was spent on it, of course. But if you cast a play with people who aren't used to blank verse—Peter Hall had to give them a quick course so that they were all at the same level.[3]

Another thing about the verse-speaking: early on in rehearsals Peter Hall said that although it seemed an authoritarian approach to the text, sticking to the basic rules of delivery, it would actually liberate the actor once you'd mastered them, and there seemed to be varying opinions as to whether or not this were in fact the case.

Not for me, no. I agree with Peter. I think Shakespeare's verse is giving keys and clues and instructions to the actor and director. It tells you how you should say the line—not just where the stress in the line should come, but where the stress of meaning in the sentence leads you. When you examine that, what the basic rules of blank verse tell you, then it does give you an indication of how to say the line, how to get into the next line; I do think it's necessary to clear verse-speaking.

It's a very tricky question indeed. The technique of playing Shakespeare is extremely difficult. The actors are asked to use their imagination to fill out the basic structure of the role, using the verse, and not distort the structure of the play. But there are limits in abilities and a limit in the time factor. There's a limit to what you can do, so one area of the play is often better realized than the rest, and you call upon the audience to use their imaginations. Often a very effective production is one that casts a strong light on one area, instead of bringing out the whole.

What did you yourself find to be the most difficult element of Coriolanus's character to deal with when you came to approach the role? I remember that you came to his anger quite late in rehearsal.

Yes, I guess I wasn't very good casting for that side of the part; it took me a long time to come to terms with it. I think during rehearsals I—there didn't seem to be much time to try different things, and Peter's being ill at the last moment was a setback for me. Because that's when Peter would have come in very strongly and made specific demands on the basis of the work that had been done to that point.

And what about the other central characteristic of his pride? Scholars have either criticized or condemned Coriolanus on the basis of an overwhelming pride which they feel to be completely negative; yet it seems intimately linked to his integrity, and this response doesn't fully account for his reaction to his military reward.

It's very pleasurable and very silly at the same time. Coriolanus is not one to be blackmailed. He doesn't need to get honours for his performance on the battlefield. Praise is not what he wants, though he does accept it.

But he accepts only as much as he feels to be appropriate: a new name, fame, and his fellow general's horse.

And the consulship. And when you accept an award you become an accomplice—you are no longer a free man. He wants the status and he wants the power, but he doesn't want the responsibility. It's a very interesting part of his psychology, but I don't really think it's what the play is about; it's just another example of how public figures relate to their positions. The play is about the city, and really the central character who understands what you can do and how you can act in relation to the state is Volumnia, who originally, of course, used to be played by a man.

In rehearsal Peter Hall directed Coriolanus's capitulation in the second persuasion scene to come with Volumnia's denunciation and attack on his legitimacy. But in performance it seemed as though the point of crisis really comes when he catches sight of his son on his knees. How do you approach the playing of that moment?

He is under tremendous pressure in that scene. First of all, his family is his enemy now; but in the end he does give in. He's having to measure up to his past, with Aufidius watching. And he's confronted with his son whom he adores, and who he himself was twenty years ago. I think it is the sight of his son, the sight of that child, that ultimately sways him; and then it's added to Volumnia's words. He can't bear it—he needs the support of his mother. So it's really a combination of the two. But the future of the play is in the little boy.

Returning to your earlier point about the audience's attitude to Coriolanus; it responds differently to this play because, as you say, one can't fully sympathize or identify with the titular character. There isn't the same process as in other Shakespeare plays, and yet people go to the theater expecting to have that bond.

Well, I don't know what it does to an audience emotionally, but I suspect the audience goes away having learned not to be so dogmatic about news and about politics and about politicians. I think if I saw our production, I would be rather relieved that life was going to be a bit simpler now, without Coriolanus. However, how long Aufidius is going to keep the peace is another matter.

It seemed to me when I saw the play for the first time that whether or not one sympathized with the character, the sense of loss was as complete as in the other tragedies because of the energy that he has, and because even if it is impossible to live within the state and to try to rule the state as he does, peaceably, he does at least try to live in accordance with his integrity, which is a great deal more than can be said of the other characters involved.

Yes, and you can say that perhaps of people with whom you have no sympathy at all, like dictators. But Coriolanus doesn't really seem to have any strongly thought-out view of the state which he is passionately defending—he's just passionately defending his class, and Rome, as a fighting machine. Well, it then becomes a question of how aggressive society should be, and can lead to all sorts of questions as to whether Switzerland is a happier country to live in than some great fighting nation. And there are no easy answers. A really intelligent director, who came to see it the other day, said to me he thought that nations keep throwing up Coriolanuses and then not being able to cope with them and not knowing what to do. And then, suddenly, there's a need for a great heroic war-leader, and if the nation's lucky it produces one, and then it throws him out—in the way that Churchill was despised and despised and despised and ignored, then brought into the service of this country during the Second World War; and when the need of the war was over, was rejected by it. It's the same situation with Coriolanus and Rome.

Because you've worked on two different productions, could you talk a little more about the difference in approach that was taken in each. You said, for one thing, that in the first there was more emphasis on the psychology of the character, and that that was perhaps not as satisfying.

Well, Tyrone Guthrie, who directed that, thought the crucial balancing axis of the play was the relationship between Aufidius and Coriolanus.

Rather than Volumnia and Coriolanus.

Rather than Volumnia, although she's a large part of that, certainly. And he thought that (the relationship with Aufidius) was, crudely, a homosexual relationship; but, well, it's there, and it was very nice for me playing Aufidius.

But not as satisfying in the long run.

Well I don't know; I can't remember. It's a long time ago, and there's still the problem that if you're in a play you never see it. Guthrie hated figures of authority, even though he was one himself, and so there was an awful lot of ironic laughter at the expense of the patricians. And Menenius was played as a more crucial figure than in our production, I think, as someone who has a strong sense of humour—a rather bumbling figure really. The long speech of Cominius to the senate about Coriolanus was a man who had written and was reading a speech out and kept losing his place; papers kept falling down off the lectern. That was very much Guthrie's view of state speeches of that sort.[4] It was more, I don't know . . . Guthrie was always on about people's failings in this play. On the whole I think I prefer Peter Hall's approach to this production, which was to look for people's strengths: the right that those tribunes have on their side, the genuine problems of the people, Coriolanus's own remarkable character, Cominius's kindness and strength. On the whole I think that's much more true to the spirit of the play.

8
Greg Hicks on *Coriolanus*

On 3 September 1985, between rehearsals for "The Real Inspector Hound/Critic" double bill, I spoke with Greg Hicks about the development of his character, Tullus Aufidius, and the special challenges of playing a Shakespearean role.

The thing I believe most firmly about Shakespeare, and in a way Peter Hall is very supportive of this and lets you do it, is that you can only find these parts by the process of actually playing them. Rehearsing them is actually not as useful. It has to be done because you have to know where to come on and go off, and you have to have some idea of where your character is going, but I know that the people I have really, really watched in Shakespearean roles have found the role eventually by virtue of playing it—if they are good actors. And by good actors I mean if they are very responsive to the text, and if they do certain things which I think you need to do if you're going to be a good classical actor, which is principally to have an emotional and physical instrument that is able to respond and allow the language to live in a way that is unexpected. So each time you do a role out there you never, I mean *I* never set myself a brief; I never think "Ah, that's the character." I always allow myself another door to throw open. I mean, having watched *Coriolanus,* it's quite clear that there are loads of things I'd changed since rehearsals. I didn't decide to do them, I found myself doing them actually while I was playing it. I might have monitored it as I was doing it and thought to myself, as actors do, "Ah, this is interesting; this is how it should have been played," or maybe "this isn't how it should have been played." I mean, for example, that development at the end of the play about dropping my sword (a piece of stage business in 4.5). I suddenly realized that it was a wonderful symbol of my impotency, or the end of the game between us, or the end of the duel between us; or it was a symbol of the throwing down of my whole raison d'être, and I thought "Hmm, that's quite useful."

That moment works much better now than it used to. But the embrace (in 4.5) changed significantly as well.

Oh, unbelievably. I can't even remember how it was at first. Well, I can remember that black costume I was given, and the very first piece of blocking was Ian and me "twining" from behind, which I felt was very contrived and I never really liked doing it. But that's the one scene that remains a total dissatisfaction for me. I still don't think I've cracked it. I don't think Ian and I work very well together in it—not really. No, it doesn't feel good. I don't like the way I handle him particularly, and I don't particularly like the way he handles me.

He also mentions that as the one scene that hasn't been cracked.

But you see he found something fantastically useful, only very much later on in the run. I felt that one of the problems about that passage is that Ian didn't successfully set up his own speech before I spoke, so that it was all slightly flat. And he started to do something towards the end of the run which was really useful for me, so that it used to go:

Auf. I know thee not! Thy name?
Cor. My name is Caius Martius, who hath done
To thee particularly, and to all the Volsces,
Great hurt and mischief: thereto witness may
My surname . . .

(4.5.65–69)

and then he used to leave this terrific pause, and he used to bellow "Coriolanus"; and it was a shock for me, because there was a time when he just used to say (the same speech said flatly). And I know why he did it: because he felt that the man was exhausted and psychologically not within himself and all that, and tired. But anyway, it's those kind of crucial moments that you never find in rehearsal, ever. I've never known a major moment to be found truly in rehearsals. It's always found in the process of playing.

And these rehearsals were quite slow at first. When they really picked up was during the previews, but then there was such a rush to get it on stage that exhaustion began to set in.

That's right. It seemed to be like wading through mud for a while, although I personally had a strong instinct about how to play Aufidius from the word go. How *I* would play it, not how *to* play it. Barry Rutter (an actor with the NT company) said to me when he knew that I was going to play the part, "Well, what you must do, you particularly must do as an actor, is to learn how to stand still in this part. Because if you start leaping and jumping around," like I usually do, "it won't work." And I think the one thing that I had in my head when I started was that this man stands still—a lot. And I think I carried that through pretty well to the final performance. Which, of course, we haven't done yet because we have two more to go in Greece. But the subtleties and the ambiguities of the character I also knew were there. I always had a kind of yen for them.

Then it was a role that you were very interested in playing?

Oh yes. I was absolutely thrilled when Peter asked me to play it. Because I think it's a really interesting part. It's a very difficult part, and in many ways it's a difficult part to deal with practically because of that long gap. I mean, that is very tricky. He has a lot of long gaps before he comes on and does something else, and I found that quite taxing. I mean, the last time we see him (in 1.10) he's covered in blood and has sworn vengeance. The next time we see him (in 4.5) he's in a totally different situation, but there's a huge gap between those two events, and I found it quite difficult to learn how to deal with it. I always used to listen to the play. I never used to do anything divorced from the play.

That growl, you see, that came in that bloody scene (1.10)—that was something that I found in performance, although I always used to deliver "would I/Wash my fierce hand in's heart" (1.10.26–27), fiercely, but that breathing thing became bigger. And I didn't decide to do it, but having done it I thought "Well, actually this is rather good because he's referred to as a lion." And it came across. When I did that growl for the first time a number of people came up and said "Mmm, that's wonderful; that's a wonderful moment. It was like an animal." And I thought "an animal—a lion—that's wonderful. Well, maybe I'll make it sound more like a lion next time I do it." And of course I began to do it several times instead of just once. In many ways what I'm saying is slightly irresponsible in terms of the process of acting, because really you can't say to an audience "Well, I'm awfully sorry you're seeing it on the first night, but, boy, you'd better wait and come back and see it in sixty performances' time." Because actually the show is the show, and it has to be there on the first night, but it never is. I mean, Ian's performance has changed beyond measure since the first night. For example, he used to do this terrible thing at the end about flapping his arms on "like an eagle in a dove-cote" (5.6.114). And then over a period of time he started to just turn around and really whap it at me, all that stuff about "Boy" and "I did it," and I thought "Yeah, that's what he must do."

The one thing that the production had on opening night was a tremendous energy level, even if the ingredients weren't all there.

Oh yes, it had an amazing energy level.

It was quite an unexpected evening after the slowness of rehearsals during Peter Hall's illness, and having to delay the press night.

The ingredients which were sustaining it are in the play itself, which is a magnificent piece of work, and the acting in the main, which is good. I think the set is great. I think it's one of the best sets that I've worked on apart from *The Oresteia* and apart from *Malfi*.

One thing about the set, though. Having seen it both with the audience there and without the audience—because I know that you don't like its involvement on stage¹—the design really doesn't work without them at least sitting there.

I know. I realize that. No, it wouldn't work within the context of the set, it just wouldn't, unless we'd completely redesigned the whole concept of it, and done a great kind of Passolini thing with visual pictures of two citizens in white up there, and a sick Roman soldier down there. I mean, if it were done like Philip Prowse would have made it look, it might have worked. But yes, it just would have looked like an empty space. But I do think it's bad for the citizens. I've always thought that it took away from their function as actors; I've always thought that. Those citizens disappear, apart from the first citizen, and even he disappears a little in that kind of melée of normal people. By normal people I mean the public. And I've always felt that it didn't give the actors playing the citizens a chance to really sharpen up what they felt, or thought, or how they could structure their performances. I think the citizen area of the play is a very generalized area. I don't like it very much. Not really. I love what David and Jim do (as the tribunes), but I don't particularly like what the citizens do. And it's not their problem—they just find themselves in that position.

They're having to cope with different reactions every night.

Well, it's not defined, is it? I mean the director hasn't made an opinion about what kind of citizens they are. Are they poor? Or are they just mouthing? Are they justifiably angry? And what do they look like? How are they dressed? I mean, some of them are dressed in the most ridiculous things. Kate (Dyson), who's now taken over from Sarah (Mortimer), she looks like somebody who's stepped out of a lift at Harrod's. It's just ridiculous. Now that's alright if that's what you intend, if that's what you want to say, but I'm not sure whether that's what Peter did mean to say. Or maybe he did. In any case, I think Peter has accidentally created a kind of anonymity for those citizens which is actually rather condemning. It makes them appear . . . as they do anyway in the play a bit. I mean, they do appear a bit of a prattish group. The first citizen doesn't, but most of them do appear to be absolute prats, idiots, fools—wayward, fickle, easily swayed.

So do you think that Peter Hall's concern for pointing out the genuine problems of the people was really channelled into the tribunes, and not into the crowd?

Yes, I do think that's true, yes. I think certain decisions were made about character which sprang directly from the play, which is always good. You know, the play led the way. I mean, there is no way Ian could continue really instinctively doing that business on "an eagle in a dovecote"—the text eventually would have to make him do it: "Alone *I* did it." "Don't call *me* a boy." I mean, for me with Aufidius, I think all the way along my ear's been pretty finely tuned to what the text is trying to tell me. For example, you see, I wouldn't choose to play that last speech as just a piece of political "Oh well, I'd better say something nice." It's quite clear that something happens to that man in that last speech. It's written in these short bursting sentences: "Take him up" (5.6.147), "Trail your steel pikes" (5.6.150). You could translate it another way, I suppose, but anyway, I choose to play it the way I play it, which works for some and not for others. I think I'm pretty close to how I would quintessentially like to play the part.

But as you said, that's something that happened during the actual performances.

Oh yes. I had certain lines on it. Stand still. And I felt a certain sympathy about him. I didn't think he was a shit, just a shit. I thought there was something much more than that. I remember writing on my script early on in rehearsals "A good man gone wrong." That's how I thought of myself. I mean, good in terms of the ethics of the play—courageous, valiant, honest, noble—gone wrong, just been beaten one too many times. He knew he was second best, and he just couldn't stand it anymore. Well, he says "My valour's poison'd" (1.10.17). And it's quite clear that Aufidius is no mean force; he's a pretty reckonable man. He's the second best, otherwise Coriolanus wouldn't even bother. I also decided he was a loner, that there was something lonely about him. And I had this whole story in my head during the big capitulation scene that in fact his wife had died, and that his mother had died, and in fact he didn't have any family at all, so watching Coriolanus mix with his family was a big deal for him, and made him fearfully bitter. The homosexuality of the man, if that's what you can call it,—the sexuality of the man—I found that rather difficult to place in re- hearsals, especially in that scene outside Antium. I never felt I was free to experiment with Ian at all, either to be overtly sexual or to be very cold. It was always rather generalized. And it took me a long time to . . . I mean I think there is a sexuality about their rela- tionship which is quite clearly transmitted into the language: you know, "Let me twine/Mine arms about that body" (4.5.107–8) and all that stuff. There's a lot of homosexual imagery in that, or transferred sexuality one could call it. But I still haven't quite decided in that moment where I hug him . . . I mean, there were performances when the hug was just a full-blooded hug, and there were performances when it was more than that, when it was kind of a dangerous thing, a destructive thing and a sexy thing. And I haven't really made up my mind about that. I mean, I'm an entirely instinctive actor, and I won't do anything unless it feels right. Sometimes I take the sword out and throw it down, sometimes I don't.

So it depends on the build-up of that particular night.

It depends what the build-up of the scene is like. I can't set it completely unless it's absolutely marked down. You see, in Philip Prowse's production of *Malfi,* very little changes, because it was all absolutely part and parcel of the visual image. Now in a way that has its joy, because you know where you're going every time you do it, and what you have to do is try to recreate it. On the other hand, you can never really experiment. Now, part of the joy of working with Peter is that you can try anything. I mean, Ian has done some absolutely outrageous things and I have too. All that stuff with the sword, it was never in Peter's conception.

But he didn't have so much a clear visual image of the play beyond the amphitheatrical setting—it was more thematic.

Yes, I think he had a thematic feeling about the play, but certainly no visual feeling at all.

Did you find that to be a drawback in rehearsals, or did it give you more freedom for exploration?

No, I think it was a drawback. And as a matter of fact I absolutely jumped at the chance to work with Philip Prowse, because I was just hungry for someone with a clear vision of how something should be. I wouldn't like to work like that every time, but after *Coriolanus* it was so refreshing to have someone say "You come on here, and you go off there, and that's the way I want it to look; and the feeling of this scene is that, not that." Now I think there are misjudgements in this production of *Malfi*, but they're misjudgements which in a funny kind of way I kind of quite respect, because they come from a vision. Whereas Peter, I think, has successfully trusted his actors. I mean, he trusts me as an actor, he knows I'm going to do something; he knows Ian's going to do something; he knows David Ryall's going to do something. He knows we're all going to do something.

So rather than having a visual image in mind, he had a lock on the textual interpretation of the play.

Yes. He knew we were going to do some good work.

How did you feel about his theory of verse-speaking?

Well, I respect it, you see, because I worked with him on *The Oresteia,* and I rather like the constraint of those rules; I rather like them. Now, whether I stick to them or not is another matter. I mean, in that scene with the lieutenant (4.7), I'm pretty close to exactly how it's written. And I'm rather pleased with the way that scene's managed to hold up throughout the run, because it's a fucking difficult scene; it's totally complex. And that speech is a fucker; it really is a difficult speech. And I know that in most of the performances, bar, you know, ten, the audience follows it. I chose to stand still, and I chose to follow absolutely how it's written, and the punctuation marks, and I think it works.

There's one thing that really interested me about that scene: it's one of those passages that has caused a great deal of academic controversy, because it seems absolutely incredible that a general would talk to his lieutenant in such a way. But then you began to deliver it as a soliloquy, out front, as though his questions had made you think about the situation and you were mulling it over in your own mind, and it works extremely well. But before that, when you were talking directly to him, it seemed somehow wrong. Was that a conscious change, or did it come about instinctively?

Yes, it felt right to play to the audience. There's that wonderful line—and in fact one night I found myself turning around, which is one thing I don't like doing in a production very much because it's tricky when you've not got much to say and it's complex, to turn your back on that audience—it's that really complicated line, it's almost unintelligible, about

> And power, unto itself most commendable,
> Hath not a tomb so evident as a chair
>
> (4.7.51–52)

—like a public place where it's talked about. And it felt very public to do that. Yes, my instinct did lead me to get off trying to play it realistically as a convention with the lieutenant. Although what the lieutenant says is very important, because it's the catalyst for the way Aufidius replies. And I used to very much like the way Nigel (le Vaillant) used to play it, because there was a kind of rather acidic concern. Tim (Hick)[2] is a very generous actor, but he hasn't got the edge that Nigel had, but he has the concern. And also he's quite good because he just kind of stands there and is modest really, whereas Nigel used to demand attention, which may have been wrong for the scene.

I hate the shooting at the end of the play. Although I've made it work for me, in my own head. I've got my own story now about what happens, but it's taken a long time to find that story. I just now try to think of it as a moment of impotency rather than anything else. You know, they do it, and it's clinical, and it's quick, and it's not full-blooded, and it's not what I wanted to do, but it's what I knew I'd do when I say "I'll potch at him some way" (1.10.15). I mean the word "potch" is a very interesting word, because it implies something that's really, you know, in the back, getting someone in the back. When we first did it I hated it, because I just felt it gave me no chance to follow through to "My rage is gone,/ And I am struck with sorrow" (5.6.146–47). I've had to kind of do a circuitous route, really. You see, there's another example of something technically difficult. It's only been very recently that I've started to really blow on

> My lords, when you shall know (as in this rage,
> Provok'd by him, you cannot) the great danger
> Which this man's life did owe you, you'll *REJOICE*
> That he is thus cut off.
>
> (5.6.135–38)

I used to have to really go on that ("rejoice") in order to set up "My rage is gone." Before, I used to take the rage into the rest of the speech (same speech quoted)—just recently it's come out, when I've gone "You will *rejoice* that he is thus cut off"—and then I pause, and then the feeling of sadness has begun to creep into the previous lines, so that it doesn't come out of the blue. I haven't made up my mind about that; it still doesn't feel quite right. Bill Moody (an actor in the *Coriolanus* company) says to me that he always thinks that it's best when I don't split the line, because I tend to split that line up a lot: "My rage is gone,/And I—uh, uh,—am struck with sorrow." I mean, I do a terrible cheat on it.

To get the transition.

Yeah, it's a fucking difficult transition. It's a difficult transition for a 1985 audience, because it just sounds contrived. I guess for a Shakespearean audience, they would have bought it. You know, a man does this, and then he says that. But I think our emotions tend to meander into each other. You think someone's crazy if he suddenly swings between anger and grief. I do it a bit just before I say "Take him up"; I sometimes have a terrible danger of saying "Take him up" (sad monotone)—you probably can't hear it on stage, but I do it mentally.

It is a difficult moment, and I've seen it cheated in another way, which was to take a purely cold, political approach in addressing the other senators—as if to say "Well, I'm not really struck with sorrow, but I'm going to say it to keep the peace." But that's a cheat on the character himself, because it diminishes the relationship that he's had with this man.

And I don't think that it's as interesting for the actor to play it that way. Maybe if it is just coldly clinical, then there's no weight to the final sentiment about Coriolanus. And the play does actually end with a statement of remembrance for this strangely wayward, great man. Now, if it's just a cold, clinical statement, then the audience isn't going to really follow along—I mean, I do that thing where I can't continue the sentence, because the line ends with "he," doesn't it (5.6.150): "Though in this city he . . ."—like that, because it allows the actor to do that. "Though in this city he—he— (struggles to go on)"—you can fight for the next line, which implies something about your state, and something about the man you're talking about.

Then in this case the interpretation of the verse lines which Peter Hall insisted on—

Really works, yes. Because if you hadn't had that pointed out to you, that in fact the last word of that line is "he," you might miss it, and it allows you to discover something emotional from the verse.

That was a very interesting way to approach the text, because although it does constrain you technically, it is liberating for characterization.

Yes, well, for example, it gave me the idea to play those two lines in that particular way. I mean, if I hadn't been told that, I might have just said:

> Though in this city he
> Hath widow'd and unchilded many a one,
> Which to this hour bewail the injury,
> Yet he shall have a noble memory.
>
> (5.6.150–53)

(Said strung together.) But because I know so much about line endings now, it allowed me to explore what happens between "he" and "hath," that maybe what happens between "he" and "hath" is that Aufidius can't get the words together. And that's an interesting psychological journey for him. So yes, there were certain decisions I took, but most of them came from doing it, rather than deciding to do it.

The actual assassination—did you prefer the original blocking: slash across the back, thrust to the stomach, and slit to the back of the throat, which was even more anti-Romantic than the gunfire?

I think it was better. I think if they really analyzed it, most of the people in the audience who'd seen it would probably say "Well, I did feel the plugs being pulled a little," because you aren't even aware where it's come from, it's just over so fast. However, one critic writes that "Oh, how marvellous that they chose to do this cold, clinical kind of airport-tarmac assassination," and how right that was, because it sums up the whole kind of world which Coriolanus in fact couldn't deal with, which is the quick replacement of people who don't fit in with the political situation. And I can see that. But that was never really an intention. I think if it was really an intention, well, then we would have played it, but it's not really one thing or the other.

I suppose because the decision came so late in rehearsal, the whole concept was never fully integrated into the production, except for a few moments of gunfire on the opening sound tape.

I think it's good, though, that I don't do it, and I think I would have gone along with that even if we had stuck to the knife thing. I mean, I liked the idea that Aufidius never actually got to do it himself.

So the first direct contact he has with Coriolanus's person occurs when he stands on the hero's corpse, then serves as pallbearer in the play's final ironic emblem of human waste.

9
The Athens Remounting

The closing of *Coriolanus* in the Olivier Theatre on 26 August 1985 was not to be the company's final performance of Shakespeare's tragedy: it had been decided in the autumn of 1984 that the National would tour one of its productions to the annual Arts Festival at the Herod Atticus Theatre in Athens. The play a masterwork of English literature, written by the country's most celebrated dramatist, the production a critically acclaimed success with an actor of international renown in the leading role, *Coriolanus* was a strong choice both to represent British theater and to draw audiences that would pack the house. The stage at Herotheo (or its antique equivalent) is in fact the only venue that could accommodate the physical demands of the production. It would be impossible to tour *Coriolanus* to Europe or North America because of the prohibitive expense of recreating the set, the impossibility of transporting the bulk of the scaffolding, gates, and false stage that surrounds the sandpit, and the rarity of open stages in Western theaters. The impact of Bury's design would be radically diminished were *Coriolanus* to be mounted à la pros arch. Yet the ancient stadium in Athens is itself the equivalent of the Rome that Bury had created for the Olivier Theatre. Because of the production's already amphitheatrical setting, the full auditorium became one with the stage, and the company had the privilege of performing in a building whose very structure dates back to the general temporal setting of the play. The practical suitability of touring *Coriolanus* was self-evident.

Although the set itself was rebuilt in Athens, it was necessary to transport the three tons of sand used to fill the central pit, as it was of a quality only to be found in certain areas of northern Greece. Thus a week before the company itself arrived, the requisite thirty bags were flown across the Atlantic. The same number of bags were brought back to England after the production, but they contained a mere five hundredweight, the balance being left behind to be distributed over Athens's beaches, thus saving unnecessary labor on the return journey. Although the sandpit and false stage remain an exact visual duplicate of the London original, some alterations to the set were made in order to accommodate the very different physical demands of the Greek amphitheater. Much of the scaffolding was cut, as were the political slogans and danger notices that lined the walls, and it was decided to reduce the number of stands on stage to two, although there was an increased number of benches (at a lesser angle of incline) extending to the back of the stage. The most significant alteration lay in the construction of the gates that form the focal center of the set. Because the open air theater does not offer the same backstage mechanical resources as the Olivier, it was impossible to differentiate between the cities of Rome and Corioli/Antium through the use of two sets of alternating doors; hence one set of gates, built from blond wood and operated manually by NT stage hands, served for both.[1] Spacial transitions were thus visually suggested only through costume and textual reference. Yet there was no point at which the physical localization of any given scene was unclear.

The evening of Wednesday, the 18th of September, saw the cast and crew of *Coriolanus* fly into Athens to prepare for their weekend engagement. A hectic schedule lay ahead of the company: they were to fit two rehearsals, two official receptions, and two performances into the three days preceding their departure on Sunday morning. Although the actors were able to get a good night's sleep before the morning's 8:00 rehearsal call, it was necessary for the production staff to work until 3:00 A.M. to erect the newly constructed segments of the set. The next day's rehearsal scheduled four hours' work in the morning (the afternoon sun being too hot to work under with any degree of comfort) and concentrated on adjusting the blocking of entrances and exits to suit the demands of the amphitheater, with projection exercises to prepare the actors for the arduous task of vocally filling a space five times the size of the Olivier. Unaccustomed to the necessity of projecting at such a distance, many problems of vocal and breathing technique which remain camouflaged in the smaller houses of Western theaters were exposed, and many despaired of meeting the challenge. The larger part of the company, many of them younger actors, were forced to shout in order to make themselves heard at the back top of the amphitheater, thus running the risk of straining their vocal chords for the performances, and so the decision was made to mike the front of the stage. Although this somewhat alleviated the problem, it did not entirely eradicate it, and produced a distracting echo whenever the actors stood on certain sections of the stage.

At twelve noon rehearsals finished for the day. Again, though the actors were free to relax and tour the city, the production staff was forced to return to the theater that night to reassemble the set, which had been dismounted for the evening's performance by the Washington Symphony Orchestra, and then light the production. Breaking at 6:30 the following morning, they were able to catch but a brief hour's sleep before the next 8:00 A.M. call. On this second and final day of rehearsals, Hall rehearsed the crowd scenes, and finished with a quick cue-to-cue run for the benefit of the technical staff. Yet there remained insufficient time in which to do a full dress/tech rehearsal, or even a line run, which accounts for the several lighting errors (including a blackout with actors struggling to keep the scene moving on a dark stage), and many textual inaccuracies which peppered the performances. As on the previous day, rehearsals broke at 12:00 so that the company might attend a reception held in their honor at the British Embassy, before returning to the theater at the half for that evening's first performance. The pressure under which they had been working and the uncertainty of an unknown audience and a daunting space led to a higher level of adrenalin than the production had ever known both on- and back-stage, as the cast assembled in small groups for a moment of nervous relaxation, smoking a cigarette, having a quick cup of tea, or flipping through the program.

The latter indeed held an unexpected surprise: of all the production photographs that could have been reprinted, one was chosen from the final scene and pictured Coriolanus stripped to the waist, uttering his last words, with the figure of Brian Kent as the Volscian lord looming hazy and ghostlike behind him. The reason that this seemingly innocuous photograph produced such an electric impact is that Mr. Kent died of lung cancer some months before the end of the London run, and his friends in the cast had been discussing only weeks before how strange it would be to perform in Athens when they had so clearly envisaged him being among their number. In a very extraordinary way, he was.

By 9:15 P.M. the audience, six-thousand strong, had taken their seats in the Herod Atticus Theatre, and the actors were positioned in the wings ready for their beginners' call. The citizens entered first to bring the stage audience down from the stands and establish the initial image of civilian revolt, which opens the show. From the very first moments of performance—the interchange between the first and second citizens—it was evident that a fundamental new philosophy of playing had become operative: the actors were treating the on-stage audience much more as though they were already committed members of the rebellion, and directing their lines out to the main auditorium, facing front and cheating lines on the diagonal whenever they were addressed to fellow actors. The scene appropriately became more public than ever before, and there was a greater degree of physical freedom than was seen on the London stage. The performances had finally opened up.

Nor was the audience presence on stage felt to be visually distracting—even Greg Hicks, the company's most vocal advocate for its removal, agreed that it significantly enhanced the overall look of the production. The reason: a brief rehearsal prior to the performance. The seats had been sold long in advance, and the short run limited the number of people involved. Thus it was feasible to invite the on-stage audience to a short segment of that afternoon's rehearsal to brief them on the nature of the plebeian roles they would be called upon to assume, and the type of apparel that would be appropriate to the stage picture. Largely clad in jeans or loose-fitting skirts and sweatshirts, they did in fact look the part of the average citizenry they were meant to portray. No longer was there the intrusive presence of briefcases, business suits and evening wear to which both critics and cast members quite rightly objected. And having received more explicit instructions than was possible in the brief moments before the Olivier performances, there were no nervous titters or facial muggings. The stage audience joined in the communal chants with conviction, cheered the comments made by the leader of their rebellion, and muttered under their breath at the second citizen's attempt to defend Coriolanus. Certainly it was an exciting evening to be among the audience in the stands, if only for the unique experience of standing on the stage with Rome gates looming up on one side, its blond wood catching the light and making a shining contrast to the ebony of the night sky which roofed the vast stone structure, with the majestic presence of the Acropolis presiding over the scene. The sight of this ancient ruin lit up in the distance moved actors as well as audience. Hicks commented after the company's return to London that each time he looked up it shone a different colour; just at the moment when he stood on the body of his dead rival, the Acropolis was illuminated by a red beam of light. The excellencies of the production aside, it was more than worth the price of a ticket to *Coriolanus* for the moving experience of witnessing the natural glories of its setting. One was not in a theater personating Rome in 494 B.C.—one was there.

The stunning quality of the space more than offset the absence of certain technical effects which enhanced the London version of

Hall's production; because the extent of the scaffolding had been curtailed, it was impossible for McKellen to utter his first words in 1.3 from above right; and the absence of fly-space necessitated the cutting of the suspended banners from the triumphal march in 2.1. The assassination was reblocked from stage right to stage left so that Aufidius could perch himself on the pole ladder, which extended the length of Rome walls. Fully expecting Coriolanus to meet his demise on the opposite side of the stage, I found myself directly in the line of fire, and had the conspirators been armed with real bullets I would be a dead woman today. Because of the vast space of the amphitheater, entrances and exits which were originally made from the back of the Olivier Theatre were put forward to the middle of Herotheo's auditorium, yet it was even more visually exciting to see the soldiers, musicians and standard-bearers enter through the audience, first horizontally from opposite ends of the theater, then converging at the center, and finally linking up to descend in single file to the foot of the stage. An impressive sight indeed, and one that took careful timing in rehearsal to coordinate with the text.

It was apparent from the performance that not only had the physical business of entrances and exits been fine-tuned, but the delivery of lines had been given a new and fresh timing as well. I have already mentioned that the first scene was characterized by a more open style of playing and a freer physicality; the same may be said of the voices sequence of 2.3 and the servant interlude preceding Coriolanus's alliance with Aufidius in 4.5. The playing of the "common folk" was big and out front;[2] suddenly the comedy of the scenes took off and the appreciative audience roared with laughter—as they inevitably did to a wholly serious line earlier in the play:

> They choose their magistrate,
> And such a one as he, who puts his "shall,"
> His popular "shall," against a graver bench
> Than ever frown'd in Greece.
>
> (3.1.103–6)

Though they frowned in verse, they smiled in fact.

The audiences which the *Coriolanus* company received in Athens were by far the most responsive of the run. Completely unselfconscious about their presence in the theater, they ate, smoked, snapped photos, and yet remained totally held by the action of the play, registering their involvement through the warmth of their laughter, and the held intensity of their silence—and the actors drew still further energy from their voiced appreciation. The Athens audience was in fact instrumental in creating the most moving moment of the evening: the reception with which it greeted the company when Rome gates slammed shut at the end of the play. To call it merely warm or generous would be an understatement: a standing ovation for the full company, with cheers and the stamping of feet for principals Yvonne Bryceland and Ian McKellen. The continued applause after their general exit was so strong and per-sistant that it brought out the company for a second curtain call, with another thunderous welcome for McKellen, which reached its climax when Peter Hall came down from the director's box to join his cast on stage and take a well deserved bow. The reception on the show's second and final night was as stunning. I was glad to have a seat on the stage stands at that moment, for although I did not have the main audience's objective perspective on the production, I did share the company's view of their reception: a sea of people on their feet in a circle extending all around the stage, the clamour of their shouts and applause almost deafening in intensity, the brightly lit Acropolis towering in the distance. One could not but feel emo-tionally engaged in the moment, and thrill to the sight of such enthusiastic appreciation. Few companies can have experienced such a rich and immediate reward for their many months of hard, and often unacknowledged work, as did the cast of *Coriolanus* during those five minutes on the Friday and Saturday nights. And the reviews published in the Athens press on the days which fol-lowed reflected this public acclaim. Certainly the production as performed in Athens deserved the high praise accorded it: adrena-lin increased by the prospect of facing an unknown space, the excitement of performing on tour in a foreign country, nine months of playing the text and refining the moves—all the ingredients were present to make those two performances the best given by the company during its long run. It is only to be regretted that the London audiences were not treated to its equivalent.

There was another major factor that was crucial to the success of the NT tour and was operative only in Athens: the emergence of a strong company spirit. *Coriolanus* went into rehearsal when the National began to realize the projected structural revisions which split the actors and production staff into five distinct companies under the leadership of five different directors. Although ostensibly under the banner of Peter Hall's group, many of the performers were streamed into Ian McKellen's or Richard Eyre's and David Hare's new companies, while others had contracts that terminated at the end of the *Coriolanus* run. Thus the only contact the actors had with one another after the opening night was either on stage or in the dressing rooms if they happened to share with members of the same production. Nor were the rehearsals themselves of a kind to promote company feeling; such spirit is usually engendered by the director, who in this case was ill, and even temporarily absent during the ten week period of preparation. Little wonder then that the dominating atmosphere was one of insecurity and fragmentation until the week of previews, when the director called his cast for long hours' work on the massive restaging of key sequences, to make up for lost time. Thus it was only at the production's second opening in Athens that the company came together once again with the confidence that they were performing in an acknowledged hit; and the physical facts of the tour—that they flew over together, stayed in the same hotel, rehearsed together and holidayed together, schedules permitting,—created that feeling of unity which had been missing for a great part of the run. It is that strong company spirit that gave the Athens performances their added spark.

10
Conclusion

What audiences of *Coriolanus* carry away with them from the theater of course largely depends on the reasons for their presence in the first place. If they come purely to be entertained, then there is no doubt that they receive their money's worth: the story is presented with a simple clarity which makes an exceedingly difficult text accessible to those with no prior knowledge of the play. Should anyone find him or herself unable to follow the logic of the verse, it will largely be due to accoustical problems within the theater itself, rather than to the actors' delivery of the lines. Hall's painstaking insistence during the ten-week rehearsal period on the actors' following the natural rhythm of the language has ensured that the Renaissance verse flows with the ease of modern English, and it is this clarity of presentation which forms the basic strength of his production.

Effective too is his creation of a series of visual emblems to reinforce the imagery which bombards the spectators' audial sense. Not only is this technique necessary for communication with an audience rooted in a primarily visually-oriented culture, but it is also faithful to the very essence of Shakespeare's stagecraft. As a poet, Shakespeare would have been heavily influenced by the emblem books which were so popular in the fifteenth and sixteenth centuries; these consisted of a series of illustrative engravings with an aphoristic caption, often in Latin, followed by a verbal interpretation of the emblem above. Shakespeare's plays are riddled with such moments: when Richard III appears before the Mayor of London to accept the crown, he presents himself as the very emblem of piety, with all the symbolic trappings of bishops and rosaries that such an entrance would demand, and Buckingham interprets the visual picture for his audience:

> Two props of virtue for a Christian Prince,
> To stay him from the fall of vanity;
> And, see, a book of prayer in his hand—
> True ornaments to know a holy man.[1]

As the product of Shakespeare's later and more experienced pen, the emblems presented in *Coriolanus* are accorded a more subtle yet organic position in the work as a whole. Gone now is the literal interpretation by a supposedly objective observer; instead the playwright creates a series of stage pictures and tableaux which both stem from and further motivate the movement of the verse. It is these symbolic moments that lend the production much of its great power; few could easily forget the emblems of childhood, maidenhood, matrimony, and motherhood prostrating themselves in the sand before the husband/father/friend, the mingled triumph and despair of Volumnia's welcome back to Rome, or the crashing finality of the Volscian gates closing for the last time behind the hero's corpse, the sand littered with his uniform and helmet as the only remnants of his towering yet troubled existence. Hall has also created a series of symbolic tableaux where none are explicitly called for by the text, such as the emblem of Coriolanus as the "thing of blood" perched on the soldier's shoulders with fist upraised and banner flying in 1.6 and the image of the people's court trying the heroic defendant in 3.3. These images invariably work hand in hand with the text to supplement the information conveyed through the lines; and when the Renaissance images are translated into their modern equivalents, as in the tribunal which presents the senators and tribunes as attorneys for the defense and prosecution of Coriolanus, or indeed the rapid gunfire which mockingly cuts short the hero's final demand for single combat, they remain faithful to the spirit and essence of the original. The transitions between stage pictures are also effected with seemingly effortless precision. Image flows smoothly into image, and scene into scene, for the creation of a self-contained and harmonious whole.

My one serious criticism of this production, however, arises from this wholeness: it is almost too neatly packaged and too easily presented, strange as that may sound. This is above all a highly intellectual staging of the play, and consciously so, yet it seems as though in adopting this approach much of the 'blood and guts' of the drama have been lost. *Coriolanus* is an earthy play about the confrontations between the illiterate masses and a non-thinking man of action, and between violent warriors on the field of battle, set in the primitive days before Rome became a republic. It is a play, too, in which the major transitions within the hero occur either offstage or during moments of silence; Coriolanus literally makes his decision to join forces with the Volsces during the interval. Likewise, his final capitulation in saving Rome is signalled by the impulsive clutching at his mother's retreating figure; a long pause ensues in which he *"Holds her by the hand silent"* (5.3.182) before repeatedly murmuring:

> O mother, mother!
> What have you done? Behold, the heavens do ope,
> The gods look down, and this unnatural scene
> They laugh at. O my mother, mother! O!
>
> (5.3.182–85)

He takes action, then resigns himself to the consequences of that action; he cannot rationally explain his decision, for it was made on a purely emotional level. It is thus appropriate that Coriolanus has been accorded the least soliloquies of any Shakespearean lead, for such verbal proficiency requires an articulacy and rhetorical skill alien to his simple nature. Of the two soliloquies he is given, the first is uttered as a violent—and again emotional—reaction against the necessity of humbling himself before plebeians who are not worthy to clean his military boots (2.3.111–23), and the second merely makes a calm statement of his resolution to form an alliance with his old enemy Aufidius. It contains none of the fundamental questioning of existence of a Hamlet, nor anything of Lear's realization of man's bare essence. Coriolanus's intellectual powers can lead him to no more inspired conclusion than if friends "fast sworn" can "break out/To bitterest enmity: so fellest foes" may "grow dear friends" (4.4.12–21).

Menenius encapsulates his psychological makeup when he says "His heart's his mouth:/What his breast forges, that his tongue must vent" (3.1.255–56). This single phrase brilliantly sums up the essence of Shakespeare's last tragic hero—it is what Coriolanus's breast and not what his mind forges that governs his behavior. His relationship with his wife is likewise based on the heart rather than the head; Virgilia is his "gracious silence" (2.1.174). As the only virtually silent character in the play, she embodies the spirit of truth in a society where to speak is to lie, and where words are used for dissimulation rather than communication. Again one returns to the theatrical imagery at the heart of the play; Coriolanus can perform but one role: "The man I am" (3.2.16). No society can contain such a pure form of integrity, and so the hero is exiled and finally destroyed to preserve the fabric of Roman and Volscian nations alike.

Just as the production itself offers a primarily intellectual interpretation of the tale, so too is McKellen's Coriolanus an articulate and intelligent hero. It is of course vital to the unity of any show that the central figure prove a concise embodiment of its form and style, and McKellen's powerful, clearly delivered performance does just that. From his first entrance in 1.1, he brings to the stage a towering energy that flows through his words and gestures with an apparently effortless ease, and which is consistently sustained right to the final moments of the tragic action. Yet his power, like that of the production, is often too neat and well-bred. Not in the domestic scenes—his transformation from proud warrior to spoilt child provides wonderful and universal moments of filial disintegration—nor even in the battle scenes in Act 1, when he takes on a city single handed and scorns the subsequent praise of his men. I speak primarily of his reaction to the vacillating multitude in Rome, and to the necessity for dissimulation in public life.

Mention has already been made in the chronicle of the National's *Coriolanus* that irony is the keynote of McKellen's performance in these scenes and the reason why the decision seems to me an inappropriate one. There is no doubt that his portrayal is theatrically effective and consistent with the thrust of the production, yet it is hard to believe that the man as written by Shakespeare would have the self-possession to deliver "There is a world elsewhere" (3.3.135) from offstage, rather than blast the plebeians face to face with a full unleashing of titanic anger, or that he would disintegrate into the "boy of tears" scathingly described by Aufidius in 5.6 (1.101). This line refers to his capitulation to his mother's will in 5.3 rather than to his behavior before the Volscian senate. Likewise, his literal playing of Coriolanus's line "thou hast made my heart/Too great for what contains it" (5.6.103–4) as though the hero's violent emotion had caused him to be stricken with a heart attack, weakens his stature in the moments leading up to the assassination. It is an interesting choice, and lends unexpected pathos to his later vain attack on his enemy despite the great pain under which he is laboring; yet it casts a darkly ironic hue over the Volscian lord's interjection:

> Peace, ho! no outrage, peace!
> The man is noble, and his fame folds in
> This orb o'th'earth.
>
> (5.6.123–25)

The figure to whom he refers stands huddled beside him, his body ravaged by physical pain and tears of passion—a complete opposite to the mythic warrior his words describe. There is no reason, however, to interpret these lines as anything other than a straight-forward restatement of the hero's identity. The word "noble" and its acronyms are applied to Coriolanus at least thirty times during the course of the play, by patrician and plebeian alike, and frequently recur throughout his own vocabulary. Even his enemies, though they deplore his proud and arrogant nature, are forced to admit to his inherent nobility, thus conveying this characteristic to the audience as an uncontestable fact.

Coriolanus's nobility largely resides in his unflinching dedication to the preservation of his pure integrity. Even if this ultimately proves an impossible goal, it is because the superhuman hero is human after all. He discovers that there are indeed times when "Great nature cries, 'Deny not'" (5.3.33), that it is impossible to disobey instinct and stand "As if a man were author of himself/And knew no other kin" (5.3.36–37). The audience is left to enquire of itself whether pure integrity is ever to be consistent with fallible humanity, or whether the demands of personal loyalty and love supersede a worthy aspiration toward Polonius's precept "to thine own self be true."[2] One need not agree with the autocratic principles that lie at the heart of Coriolanus's integrity, or indeed condone the manner in which he expresses them; but one must appreciate his unflinching dedication to the pursuit of honor and excellence.

It is this unresolvable dichotomy within the audience's response to the hero, rather than the complexity of the man himself, that embues the tragedy with its great power and fascination. We are left in the paradoxical position of admiring the nobility of his aspiration without necessarily admiring the aspiration itself. Thus, it would be stronger to play Coriolanus's final moments as an unabashedly absolute statement of his name and fame, rather than cloud the issue by portraying the physical symptoms of a heart attack, visually interesting though it be. It would also heighten the harsh irony of the play's conclusion, which demonstrates the futility of romantic heroism in this new age of pragmatic reason. Were Coriolanus strong and determined in his attack on Aufidius, the rapid gunfire which suddenly cuts him down would have still more impact. As the scene now stands, it seems that even if the conspirators do not kill him, his weak heart will give out before he has completed his run across the sand.

After criticizing McKellen for offering too civilized a portrayal of Coriolanus, I must add that no other interpretation would be consistent with the style of the overall production. Any depiction of primitive heroism and barbaric violence in a world peopled by characters in business suits and academic gowns would prove jarring at best. Both the performance and the design concept work and fulfil the director's aims in producing the play; my tempered response comes as the result of specific preconceptions about the play, formulated long before attending the first rehearsal. Despite these reservations, I remain enthusiastic about the high calibre of acting, directing and design, which marry to create a visually stunning and well-crafted production.

Although the play's central character must prove the driving impetus and energy for the work, no show can prove successful without strong performances in its secondary roles as well, and McKellen is fortunate in being supported by a uniformly excellent cast. Daniel Thorndike and Geoffrey Burridge, as the First Volscian Senator and First Roman Citizen, stand out among the minor players to create memorable characters from apparently negligible roles in the text. Their fellow actors in the crowd scenes supply varied and unique responses that transform a potentially unified mob into a collection of distinct individuals. Although visually presented as an inseparable team, the people's tribunes are also endowed by the actors who portray them with opposing characteristics. James Hayes plays Brutus as a blunt and fiery-tempered man of fierce convictions, while David Ryall's Sicinius represents the more equivocal brand of politician, who delights in the protocol of public office. Their foil among the nobility is Menenius, elder statesman and mentor to Coriolanus, played by Frederick Treves as a self-contented "humorous" patrician, whose easy-going nature ideally suits him for the role of mediator between Rome's social orders. His understudy Daniel Thorndike, who took over the role while Treves was suffering from a back injury, heightened the sense of intimacy with Coriolanus, presenting Menenius more in the light of surrogate father than supportive friend, thus increasing the personal devastation of his rejection by "my son Coriolanus" (5.2.62).

Aside from Menenius and the but briefly seen 'young nobility,' the protagonist's closest relationships have been formed with his fellow generals, and represent the cameraderie of the battlefield, of men united in their bid to fight a common foe. Although John Savident was not an obvious casting choice for Cominius, he was perhaps the quickest to take direction and is most effective in the senate scene of 2.2, with his climactic delivery of the famous oration on Coriolanus's deeds of war. As Titus Lartius, Basil Henson likewise turns in a strong performance; it is only to be regretted that the director vetoed his mock suggestion to perform the role on crutches, thus visually heightening his verbal response to Coriolanus's question "What, art thou stiff? Stand'st out?" (1.1.240):

> No, Caius Martius,
> I'll lean upon one crutch, and fight with t'other,
> Ere stay behind this business.
>
>   (1.1.240–42)

The characters whose opposing claims on the hero result in his ultimate destruction must be, and are, portrayed as the physical embodiments of their respective nations. Irene Worth plays Volumnia as a woman with a will of iron, who can calmly state her preference for her son's noble death over continued ignoble existence as she embroiders the sleeve of his shirt, or delightedly discuss the gaping wounds he may show to the people while awaiting his triumphal reentry into Rome. Although she is capable of seeming the "innocent flower" while acting "the serpent under't,"[3] she shares something of Coriolanus's simplicity of character, and remains stubbornly blind to the impossibility of her request that he act contrary to the manner in which she herself has framed him. She comes to a partial understanding of the consequences of her maternal breach with Coriolanus only when confronted with his image clad in the enemy uniform. Her pleas for the salvation of her city come with a tearful urgency that springs from desperation rather than sentimental weakness and, despite her deep emotion, she is able to summon the full force of her rhetorical skill to plead her case for the defence of Rome:

> If it were so that our request did tend
> To save the Romans, thereby to destroy
> The Volsces whom you serve, you might condemn us
> As poisonous of your honour. No, our suit
> Is that you reconcile them: while the Volsces
> May say, 'This mercy we have show'd', the Romans,
> 'This we receiv'd'; and each in either side
> Give the all-hail to thee, and cry, 'Be bless'd
> For making up this peace!'
>
>   (5.3.132–40)

As she speaks, she literally and metaphorically bows before the equal claims of Aufidius, and exchanges a look with the Volscian leader which contains as much eager curiosity as pleading, when she finds herself for the first time in the presence of the enemy she has long pictured only in her mind's eye. From the end of June, the role of Volumnia was taken over by Yvonne Bryceland, who turns in an accomplished and varied performance despite entering the production quite late into its run. Although lacking something of

Worth's stature of presence, she nevertheless attacks the role with great power and integrity, lending even greater subtlety of approach to the mother's manipulation of her son in the play's persuasion scenes.

In his role as Tullus Aufidius, Greg Hicks captures the animalistic violence that lurks under the skin of the most rational of military strategists. His calm assessments of both his own initial defeat and the reasons for Coriolanus's later banishment from Rome are punctuated by angry outbursts expressing the strength of his obsessive hatred for Martius. Hicks's performance transmits to the audience the primitive nature of the tribal warfare in which he is engaged and of the nation which he leads—a necessary infusion of violence in a production which presents Rome as a civilized society rather than a tribe under the rule (or consulship) of a seasoned warrior. While Hicks was temporarily off due to a leg injury sustained while performing the final scene, the role of Aufidius was taken on by his understudy Guy Williams. Williams toned down the overt animalism of Hicks's interpretation, to present the Volscian as a man whose outward control thinly veils the ever-growing hatred that is fully unleashed only in the vicious taunts preceding the assassination. His obsession is the more powerful for the obvious energy channeled into his fight for self-mastery. In addition, the rising intensity of his emotions to fever pitch in 5.6 gives a sense of continuity to a character who remains offstage for the central one and a half hours of the production. Effective, too, was Williams's handling of the transition between rage and grief in his final speech; he pronounced the lines with a simple sincerity that preserved the tone of desolation for the play's finale.

In addition to seeing the principal cast in performance, I was also able to attend several understudy rehearsals, including a full run with the alternate cast. The National is fortunate in having resources within the building to provide a talented understudy company whose performances, although necessarily different from the main cast, are often as interesting. I have already mentioned the simple directness of Williams's Aufidius, and Thorndike's fatherly Menenius; also noteworthy is the deceptive softness which Janet Whiteside brings to the role of Coriolanus's mother. This Volumnia does not rule her son with a rod of iron, but rather with a gentle firmness that makes the withdrawal of her approbation in the persuasion scenes even more soul-destroying. When playing their understudy roles of Virgilia and Valeria, actresses Jenny Galloway and Sarah Mortimer convey a sense of real intimacy and affection between the two women. This Valeria is as much the friend of

Coriolanus's wife as she is of his mother, a relationship which remains unclear in the principals' performance. Galloway, who regularly plays Virgilia on the Olivier stage when Wendy Morgan is scheduled to appear in the Lyttelton as *Martine,* is also successful in infusing her character with an added strength and dignity appropriate to the wife of a warrior who cannot tolerate violent displays of emotion. Her stillness during the encounter with the tribunes in 4.2 lends great pathos to the woman's silent suffering. In the role of her husband, Nigel le Vaillant captures Coriolanus's single-minded energy and obsessive, passionately held beliefs, setting the warrior at an impossible distance from the representatives—both military and political—of his own society in Rome. Thus the principal company of *Coriolanus* turns in polished, intelligent, and clearly delivered performances, while the understudy cast, though necessarily less experienced, makes up for any lack of "technique" with its grasp of the simple raw energy at the heart of the play.

Excellently performed and stunningly presented, the National Theatre's production of *Coriolanus* well deserves the critical and popular acclaim which it has enjoyed since its opening on 15 December 1984. Hall took a risk in not imposing an attention-grabbing yet ultimately superficial conceptual gimick on his production. Instead, he has allowed the play to exist in all its contradictions and complexities, without offering a simple solution to the philosophical issues raised and explored, yet never fully resolved, within the context of the drama. It is a courageous decision to make in the 1980s, when audiences have become accustomed by the comfortable medium of television to being spoon-fed self-contained, neatly tied-up, story lines in short half-hour or hour segments; yet it is the most theatrically rewarding for the spectator. In remaining faithful to the text and allowing the play to speak for itself, Hall has created a work whose appeal will stand the test of time, for it is not limited to one country or one era in history. Like its design, the production is timeless and universal. It is a demanding play to watch as well as to perform, for the audience is constantly called upon to assist the actors with its unflagging concentration, to repeatedly readjust its evaluations as the social debate rages between patricians and plebeians, and to accept the contradictions within individuals without passing judgement on their actions until all the facts have been presented. Yet this difficulty is in fact the essential beauty of Shakespeare's final tragedy; as Peter Brook writes in *The Empty Space,*

> The power of Shakespeare's plays is that they present man simultaneously in all his aspects: touch for touch, we can identify and with-

draw. A primitive situation disturbs us in our subconscious; our intelligence watches, comments, philosophizes. . . . We identify emotionally, subjectively—and yet at one and the same time we evaluate politically, objectively in relation to society.[4]

There are no easy answers, just a truthful account of the human struggle for life and for integrity.

Crowned with the oaken garland, Martius takes up his position for the triumph between fellow generals Titus Lartius (Basil Henson), and Cominius (John Savident) (2.1.161).

Banners unfurl from the flies as the hero is rewarded with the proclamation of his new agnomen "Coriolanus" (2.1.161–65).

Coriolanus embraces his wife, enfolding her in the cloak of victory (2.1.174).

Cominius offers a powerful evocation of Coriolanus' deeds in war to the Roman senate, as he recommends his friend for the consulship (2.2.82–122).

The people's tribunes Sicinius (David Ryall) and Brutus (James Hayes) express concern at the possibility of Coriolanus' election (2.2.155–60).

Wearing the cloak of humility, Coriolanus pays the "price o'th'consulship" as he begs the people's voices (2.3.74).

Goaded by their tribunes, the citizens "Repent in their election" (2.3.253), and resolve to deny Coriolanus the consulship.

The Roman senators enter through the main gates to receive news of Aufidius and the Volsces (3.1.1).

Coriolanus stands immobile at the center of the stage as the tribunes charge him with treason, demanding a sentence of death (3.1.205–12).

The people flee in terror as Coriolanus brandishes his sword: "Come, try upon yourselves what you have seen me!" (3.1.223).

Menenius attempts to calm the angry mob, and bids the tribunes "Proceed by process" (3.1.311) or risk the outbreak of civil war.

Volumnia commands her son to humble himself before the Roman court (3.2).

Aufidius's servingmen (Bill Moody, Paul Stewart, and Peter Gordon) discuss his alliance with the now-banished Coriolanus (4.5.149ff). This sequence was cut in performance.

As Coriolanus utters a blessing for his son (Tod Welling) he lifts the boy onto his shoulders and young Martius extends his arm, echoing the fist salute (5.3.75).

The Roman women prostrate themselves before the would-be destroyer of their city (5.3.171).

The final tableau of supplication, with Aufidius watching in silence at the perimeter of the circle (5.3.172).

As Volumnia moves to lead the women from Antium, Coriolanus clutches at her retreating figure and "Holds her by the hand silent" (5.3.182).

Aufidius and the conspirators (Guy Williams, Peter Gordon, and Desmond Adams)
plot the assassination of Coriolanus (5.6.10ff).

Aufidius stands on the corpse of his enemy and bids the Volscian senate "rejoice /
that he is thus cut off" (5.6.137–38).

Part Two
"The Swelling Scene"

Rehearsal Index

Diary of the Rehearsal Process

24/10/84

10:30–1:00

Three weeks into rehearsal—stage of beginning to block the show.

Text: Combination of the Arden edition and First Folio.

Olivier Theatre—rounded open stage with four branches for entrances and exits; arena staging.

Set for 1.3: Round inner circle filled with sand.
  Chaise longue and stand with sewing on it.
  Cushions on the benches for the audience shaped like stone slabs.
  Modern dress.

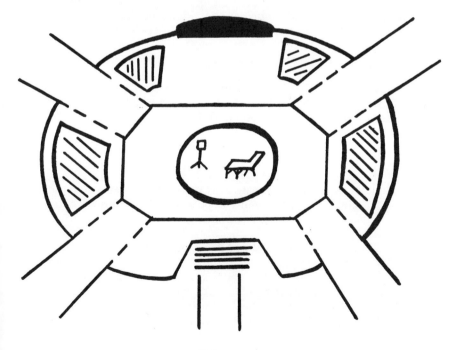

I.3

Virgilia is revealed sewing at her stand in the centre of the circle.

Volumnia enters carrying a ball of yarn, takes her shoes off at the perimeter of the circle before she steps on the sand—geisha motif.

Tone must be light, airy, domestic in the texture of the play—before the bloody scenes of war we are about to witness.

There must be a real love between Virgilia and Volumnia, but a lack of communication.
One wants to avoid all talk of blood.
For the other, blood is what it's all about and must be celebrated.

At the start of the scene there is a sense of intimacy between the two women through their physical proximity on stage, as Volumnia puts her arm around Virgilia.

Movements: Initial lightness on "I pray you, daughter, sing."
Seriousness—"To a cruel war I sent him."
Movement away to the chaise on "and the only son of my womb."
Tosses yarn on "Indeed you shall not."
Marks return to lighter tone in preparation for the entrance of Valeria.
Walk round stage in triumph as she mimics her son.
Direct contact again on "bloody brow"—comforting embrace at Virgilia's distress.
Virgilia tosses yarn back on "Tell Valeria/We are fit to bid her welcome."
Gesture is a response to Volumnia who has looked to her for confirmation of her line—action tells her it's alright. In her comforting, Volumnia domesticates blood into witty, sensual images.
On the second running of this scene Volumnia remains a pace away at this point and Virgilia says her line simply, eliciting a sincere response, passes the yarn, embrace.

Worth decides to enter mending her grandson's rubber ball, rather than to use the clichéd ball of yarn—it can be tossed back and forth more easily and is a more unusual image.

Contrast between the intimacy of the scene to this point and the incoming voice.

Valeria: Fluttery character—chattering without giving chance for a reply.
Prose to be played quicker than the verse.
Virgilia tries to drag it back into verse, but Valeria won't let her.

Attention paid to details—Virgilia's maid must sound more pleased at her one-line announcement—Valeria to be introduced in a jolly tone.

Valeria's quick entrance completes the line "And tread upon his neck," therefore is quick and pat to break the tone.

Her quick tongue contrasts with Virgilia's simple one-phrase rebuttal— no breath—"No, good madam, I will not out of doors."

Bright send-up on "You would be another Penelope."

"Come, you must go visit the *good lady that lies in*"—important moment—a friend of her station and class is about to give birth in the midst of war—Virgilia is moved by this but will not budge.

Valeria tries to pull her arm to physically move her but has no effect.

Virgilia's strength comes from her stillness—she is the only stationary figure on stage.

Virgilia finally achieves verse before the line about Penelope.

Valeria tries to break the tension by making her laugh.

News of Coriolanus: Volumnia is ecstatic, but for Virgilia this is mixed good and bad—all her energy is put into thinking of Coriolanus in conflict.

Virgilia is afraid at the prospect of news, for if it comes this early it must be bad—cliché bad news travels fast. In the area of her husband Virgilia has no sense of humour whatsoever.

"I will obey you in everything hereafter"—Virgilia pushes Valeria away. The last line from Valeria is delivered from the perimeter of the inner circle—her final appeal elicits a strong response from Virgilia—couched in monosyllables.

Valeria is a chatty social butterfly, but underneath is very intelligent, politically au courant etc., as is displayed in her sudden seriousness in revealing Rome's military strategy—the fact that it was heard from a senator indicates her fundamental intelligence, as he would not have passed along such important information to a mindless chatterbox.

I.2

Aufidius and the senators enter up on the stands, Aufidius forward, one behind right, the rest left—entrance from above gives a feeling of power.

The stage is suddenly teeming with Volscian lords as the senators converge from opposite ends of the playing area.

Tullus Aufidius enters first—close-up on the figure that the previous scene was talking about, so that he is immediately recognizable to the audience.

He is centrestage at the "Aufidius" of the first speech.

Four men on his left, two on his right to break the sense of symmetry.

Breath before "Till one can do no more" to give emphasis—heavy on monosyllables—then all the senators together on "The gods assist you!"

Letter of news tucked down Aufidius's shirt—indicative of neurotic possession.

"The dearth is great,/The people mutinous"—best possible news for the Volscians.

Aufidius enjoys the paradox that the Roman leader is worse hated than himself.

The tight grouping on the stage indicates the sense of unity and secrecy in establishing the war strategy—solemnity and a sense of dignity.

"Till when/They needs *must* show themselves"—again heavy on monosyllables—keep selves veiled until they must be seen.

Energy and flow of the lines give a ritual sense of destiny, of the inevitable.
    Verse slows down to relish the deep hatred of Martius.

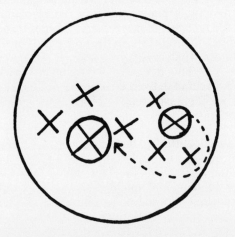

Ceremonial leavetaking—three-fold farewell, last time in unison.
    Aufidius exits centre and his lieutenant takes a step forward on the final farewell for the tableau finale. The Volscians are deeply afraid about the oncoming war and about Coriolanus—very quiet note on the final farewell to transmit that sense of gravity.

I.10

"The town is ta'en!"—despair and anger mingled with quiet solemnity on the stage picture—ravages of war emblematized in the wounded soldiers.

Now the Volscians enter on a level to reflect their weakened state, and from the sides as though regrouping after an enforced retreat.

Obsession with the other civilization as well as with the other man: "I would I were a Roman" parallels Coriolanus's later "I would I were a Volscian."

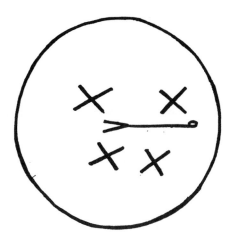

Moment of silent humanity among soldiers as they tend their wounds, mop brows etc., and put blanket under the head of the figure lying on the ground.

"Or wrath or craft may get him"—quiet response to come in right on cue with "He's the devil."

Aufidius kneels front centre on "Wash my fierce hand in's heart."
    Uses the sand and throws it to the ground in the intensity of his hatred.
    Loathing—mere contact with Coriolanus means conquest.

Muted rage breaks forth with the hollow comfort of being returned the city on "Condition"—humiliation at his powerlessness.
    Outraged pride: "Mine emulation/Hath not that honour in't it had."
    Return to bitter self-control—return to practicality of *action*.

On second running, the decision that it is stronger for Aufidius to begin upstage centre on "The town is ta'en" and move down on "Five times, Martius" after the picture of defeat is established.

2:00–5:30

Costumes: Menenius—black suit, sharp tie, carnation, senator's robes
    overtop.
    Coriolanus—armour, the complete soldier.
    Eclectic use of the Roman image.

4.2

The tribunes' meeting with Volumnia and Virgilia after the banishment.

Audience expects the tribunes to be triumphant, excited and pleased; it does not expect this tone of wariness, of a situation that could get out of hand.

In the previous scene we have seen Cominius finally back off, leaving Coriolanus with his father figure Menenius, but the most important image is that of Coriolanus coming in with the young nobility—the senate is worried and has backed off.

It is a time of new men making new rules—a sense of experimentation— seeing how things will go.

Tribunes are genuinely concerned and want to be respected members of the community.
    See themselves as up against a Hitler figure and as therefore morally justified in their actions.
    Though he is in a minority class, Coriolanus is backed by the power of the army—when he draws his sword it is the image of civil war unleashed.

Nerves—threefold repetition of "Bid them home."
    Excitement of having won.
    The aedile does not bid them home on the first command because he too is an interested party and wants to hear more.
    They have just left a very excited crowd outside, therefore their nervous adrenalin is flowing and they come up with their strategy spontaneously.

Two tribunes develop opposing characterizations: Brutus is blunt and fiery-tempered, while Sicinius is more equivocal, delighting in protocol— nice balance.

The two enter left and see Volumnia approaching down the centre aisle through the audience—figure of retribution—they want to turn and run away but are forced to brave it out.

Volumnia and Virgilia are still watching Coriolanus leave at the start of the scene, then pivot to return to the stage.

Volumnia walks around right, Virgilia left, so the two women herd the tribunes into a corner and surround them.
    Virgilia is "motivated" to do her cross by wanting to stand aside and distance herself from what is happening.

Volumnia: "Was not a man my father"—cross centrestage.
"Than thou hast spoken words"—come upstage centre—almost divinely appointed figure of authority.
"Nay, but thou shalt stay too"—come downstage, pace up and down.

Menenius: "Come, come, peace!"—advances to entreat Volumnia as she breaks down.

The tribunes are affected by Volumnia's emotion—they are sorry, but her son did bugger things up and therefore they were justified—a tone of self-righteousness which is infuriating to Volumnia.

Tribunes begin to advance, but stagger back with the vehemence of Volumnia's aping retort "I would he had," as anger breaks through grief as the dominant emotion.

Tribunes are upset at the violent display of emotion and deal with it by displaying irritation—"you can't blame us—it was your bloody son and you brought him up."
"my son"—anger still dominant.
"This lady's husband"—grief breaks through again.
"I would the gods . . ."—arms up in an appeal to the heavens—on second run decision to change the arm movement—not an appeal in anger but in a moment of complete vulnerability and the gods take no notice of her.

No disdain for Virgilia's "faint puling"—rather picks her up, collects her and seeks to infuse her with courage and anger.

Cross and exit right, Menenius left.
Volumnia leads Virgilia off hand in hand.
Cannot have tears, even in front of Menenius—must have anger, must have Juno.

Volumnia would have been considered "unwomanly" in the Shakespearean world picture.
Shakespeare was always fascinated by women who break away from the norm.

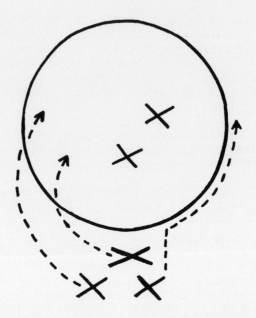

"Good man, the wounds that he does bear for Rome!" directed to Menenius, which motivates his "Come, come, peace!"—don't cry in front of them.

The stage can barely contain her violent emotions of grief and anger.

Menenius's "Fie, fie, fie!"—no exit—lights down on his solitary figure as he first looks out after the exit of Virgilia and Volumnia, and then out in the direction in which Coriolanus vanished at the end of the preceding scene, bringing the two images together for the end of part I.

Front of stage

tribunes

Virgilia crying

Menenius

Volumnia

as the central figure of retribution in front of Rome gates

On the second run Volumnia no longer leads Virgilia off, but the two go
out side by side, Volumnia only slightly in advance of her daughter-in-law.

1.1

Menenius's first entrance—bravery as the keynote.
    The mob are battering at Rome gate—it is therefore a very courageous
entrance for Menenius to walk through them, as they have the potential
to tear him to pieces—they don't, and this establishes his character.

"Malicious" as the leitmotif which Menenius picks up—more pejorative
to us.

"I shall *tell* you a pretty *tale*"—verse achieved through stress.
    Becomes prose if one says "*I* shall tell you a pretty *tale*" and runs on to
the end of the line.
    Verbal relish in the fable of the belly.
    Tone as though addressing children.
    Pointing the speech: "all the *bo*dy's members/Re*bel*led against the
belly"—keep to the verse form—do not run into prose.

5.2

Two members of the watch meeting on their patrols—one left, one right,
converge at the centre and sit down—on the second run decision not to sit
down but to cross each other and nod as they pass.
    Menenius joins them from down centre.
    Pikes held out to preserve distance between the Roman statesman and
the Volscian guards.

"I am an officer of state"—moves as though to go past them as a matter of
course.
    Not expecting to be stopped.
    Loud and threatening on "Stand and go back," big pause, then tone of
joy and affability in Menenius's "You guard like men."
    Alliteration on "*c*ome/To speak with *C*oriolanus"—stress demanded by
the structure of the verse.
    Joke in apposition to the response to his weighty remark—"You may not
pass; you must return"—monosyllables drive home—patronising tone.
    "Good my friends"—reply must be immediate to keep up the mo-
mentum.

Wit again with "the virtue of your name/Is not here passable."
    Playing with him on the basis of every word he says.
    Menenius's "I tell thee, *fellow*" betrays a new touch of irony in his tone.
    Guards look at each other—now the whole scene goes into prose, as

what Menenius is saying begins to sink in—transition to a new tempo of speech.

The fun is over and aggressions surface and the pace quickens.

"Therefore go back"—guard's rudeness prompts a dangerous tone from the Roman on "Prithee, fellow, remember my name is Menenius."

Coriolanus enters through the gates, hand in hand with Aufidius.

Aufidius remains up centre, while Coriolanus comes down to face Menenius.

Vivid momentum broken by the slow and deliberate speech by Coriolanus—deliberate disavowal of friendship.

National Theatre, Thames view. Photo by Kristina Bedford.

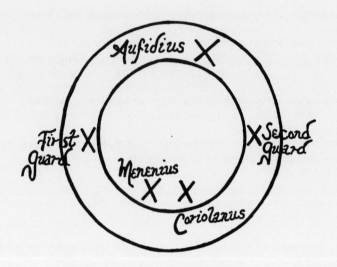

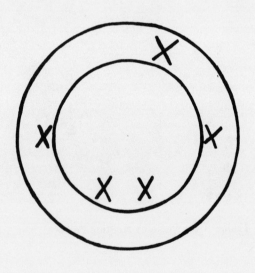

After his exit the guards close in to taunt Menenius.

Scene begun with a loud command ends in silence.
  Last line preserves the musing tone: "he's the rock, the oak not to be wind-shaken"—take time in saying it.

Coriolanus's letter to Menenius: the grief behind the mask.
  Some emotion shows through—otherwise the keynote of the scene is cold control.

Second run: At the start Menenius walks right through the pikes.
  The guards back up and cross pikes to forcibly stop him.
  " 'tis well"—Menenius moves on the caesura.
  Play up the ridiculousness of the situation—an unattended old man from the enemy camp expects admittance to the general.
  Just before the entrance of Coriolanus the scene turns very ugly.

"What's the matter?"—causes the guards to split, stand at attention at opposite sides of the circle, and indicate Menenius—fear of their leader.

Coriolanus has written the letter, not knowing that Menenius is coming.
  Foolish to give it in front of Aufidius—it shows he is in communication with the enemy camp.
  Internal struggle—should he give the letter or not—finally makes the fatal gesture.
  Slips his old friend something to make the wound a bit better—Menenius responds joyously, but Coriolanus retreats again emotionally and warns him not to start anything.
  Because of his stupid, wonderful integrity, he reveals to Aufidius that he is communicating with the Romans.

25/10/84

10:30–1:30

I.5

Volscian gates open to reveal Roman looters entering up centre to move left round the perimeter with their cart of spoils.

Coriolanus and Lartius stand atop the city gates commenting on the action.
  Look down and see the looters at the sound of a trumpet blast.

Noises off: Sound of fighting but unclear who is winning.
  Generals then appear above to plant the standard of victory.

Logic of scene 5 emerges from the previous episode—go back to clarify.

1.4

Gesture for the town made by one man running in to plant the standard in the sand before Corioli gates, followed by the soldiers' entrance.
  Change: Coriolanus should be making the gesture.

Soldiers fill the stage, Coriolanus centre, see bearers of news approaching down the centre aisle.

Good humour and physical camaraderie—freedom in war as a great contrast to the hatred which the people bear him in Rome.

Soldiers enter two by two and spread out to fill the stage.

Coriolanus's superhuman/superheroic code expects others to live up to his ideal, and he demands to be followed only by the bravest.

Look at Corioli gates and turn when Coriolanus sees the messenger.

The previous scene establishes that the troops are already outside Corioli and will make it brief wars, therefore the troops could creep up in the dark of the set change and appear suddenly.

The summons cannot be given until Cominius's letter, as they could be the filling in the sandwich if Aufidius returns.

Soldiers now enter from both sides—fast dynamic if enter separately.
  "They lie in view, but have not spoke as yet": tension before eruption.
  "To help our fielded friends": move back to face Corioli gates, Coriolanus in the centre.
  Volscian appears above—excitement and awareness of being caught in the middle.
  Coriolanus waves the standard and addresses the Volscian—drum beat.

Daring move on the Volscians' part to open the gates and attack.
  The Romans stand amazed—surprise tactic momentarily conquers them.
  Romans advance, but are beaten back to the trenches.
  Volsces at the upper edge of the circle, Coriolanus centre, cursing as the Romans ring the stage down below.
  Romans beat the Volsces back, gates wide open, Coriolanus centre of gates.
  In first encounter gates shut with the Volsces outside.
  In second encounter the gates open again to admit the Volscian soldiers.
  Coriolanus enters and the gates shut him inside.

Fighting remains a peripheral image to the gates and to Coriolanus.

As the Volsces retreat, the gates open inward rather than outward, also motivating the soldiers' lack of enthusiasm to follow Coriolanus as the gap is so small.

Titus Lartius, who had early been driven off upstage right, now enters into an extraordinary situation—soldiers just standing silent.

Gates open revealing Coriolanus, soldiers enter, gates shut.

I.5

Spoilers appear furtive and professional.

Coriolanus crosses down centre and out—pause as Lartius watches him go.

Siege image—bring ladders to start with, but do not use them to take the city.

Problem in staging the fight—12 Romans against 11 Volscians of whom 2 are women and 4 musicians.

Necessary that the verbal preparation does not bear the weight down.

Perhaps the means of getting Lartius offstage when he should be involved in the fight is to give him a sword but no shield, so that he can be beaten off—otherwise why is he not in the front line?

Set as a broken down old amphitheatre with modern wooden scaffolding as though to patch it up, and actors in modern dress because of the audience involvement.
   Audience called upon to enact the crowd—stand up for ceremonial scenes and ring the stage at the assassination of Coriolanus.

3:00–4:30

I.I

Open with spray painting slogans across Rome gates.

Rebel plebeians circle round the main spokesman—go to break down the gate when they are interrupted by a figure on the dais, left.

Menenius enters through a door in the left gate and parts the people.
   First citizen right, Menenius left, each backed by sympathetic plebs.

"crammed with grain"—first citizen circles Menenius.
Menenius sits left to deliver the fable of the belly.
First citizen—tension—paces up and down, back and forth.
"How apply you this?"—Menenius picks himself up.

Martius appears above left and scatters all to the right perimeter.
First citizen dragged back to face him.
Menenius and second citizen remain left.
Second citizen slowly walks right to rejoin his fellows.
Messenger enters down centre followed by senators.

Problem: The reason behind the incredible difficulty of the fight scenes is that unlike the battles in many of the other plays it depends on STRATEGY.
Great care must be taken not to ignore the textual pointers and information given in individual lines.
Brawn and strength are not enough.
Need to portray a sense of strategic intelligence.

I.7

Lartius: "if we lose the field,/We cannot keep the town."—seriousness and tension in the pause highlight the line.
Enter through the central gates.
Image clear: "Hence; and shut your gates upon's."
Gates start to shut before they are passed through.
Titus Lartius and four soldiers watch until a split second before the gates snap shut, then turn about and exit downstage centre.

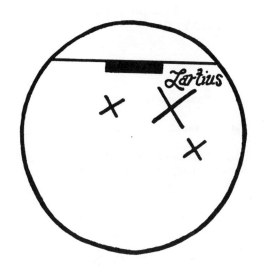

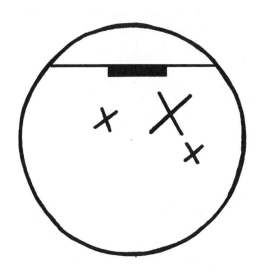

Quite a grim little scene—anticipation of imminent danger.
Guider exits just in front of Titus Lartius to lead the way, always on the
lookout for anything looking Volscian.

5.3

Volumnia enters down centre, Coriolanus left.

First reading neutral in chairs facing one another.

The first part of the scene is about the fact that he will not see her.
Tribute to Valeria—sign of how much he has changed—great poetry
from a formerly inarticulate soldier.
The image is extremely precise—particular icicles on the temple.
He has been missing Rome, and she represents it in a concrete image.
He is homesick.

Half-line pause as she embraces her son before he greets his wife, then
shuts him out.
Coriolanus: I hate Rome but I still love you.
Volumnia: direct reply—No darling, I am Rome, as much as those you
hate.
Silences enormous—key word "noble" in the heroic sense. Volumnia
therefore breaks up "nobleman" into its component parts.
Coriolanus gives the answer of a child—some sense of rejection—"O
mother, mother!/What have you done?"—not an apology.
Movement away from them all—step towards death.
No longer in competition with Tullus Aufidius—out of this world.

Unnatural: Mother on knees to her son.
Rome on its knees to a traitor.
Mother killing her son, as the blow must be most mortal to him.
Mother that should give life brings death.

Coriolanus is able to say a line to Volumnia and a line to Aufidius, as he
has already begun his journey to the other realm—the scene becomes
formal, ritualized.
"O mother! wife!"—he has finished with them and gives them no
chance to react—"I'll not to Rome"—just shatters them.

Difficulty in the question as to whether Volumnia should embrace Coriolanus, as his eyes have been sweating "compassion"—it would not take
much to make him melt.

Volumnia says nothing from this point on, as there is nothing more to say.

Instead of an embrace on "O mother! wife!" there is the colder, more formal bow of leave-taking—emotional, intimate, private moment.
It is the last time he will see his family and he knows that.
Possibility that he lies to spare his mother further pain—will he come to Rome?—"Ay, by and by"—but first let's have a little drink before you go and I'll join you later.

Constant mosaic pattern of differing impressions:
Coriolanus in the city: set up to dislike him.
Coriolanus in war: wins our sympathy.

30/10/84

10:30–1:00

2.1

Nuntio is positioned above left with his staff, cast in a circular formation.

Coriolanus enters down centre to greet his family.

Front view of the foyer entrance. Photo by Kristina Bedford.

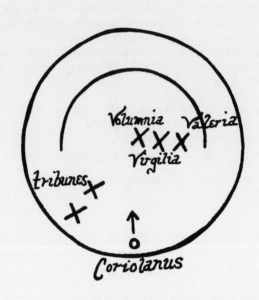

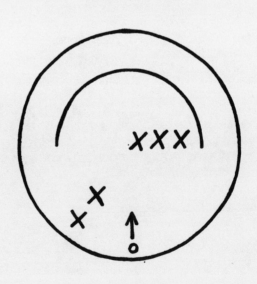

Volumnia comes down and, when Virgilia follows her, goes up right.
The dynamic of the scene is like a whirlpool spinning in tighter circles as Coriolanus greets mother, wife, friend, generals, therefore a slow procession of one after the other to shake hands cannot work.
Valeria moves from left to right so that she can be easily visible to Coriolanus over Menenius's shoulder as he embraces him.

Private events happening in the context of a public arena.

"Pray now, no more."—emotion to be released in the bosom of his family.
Volumnia then begins to make it public.
Cast moves off in several directions to greet the returning generals Coriolanus, Titus Lartius, and Cominius.
Picture of the three generals together as Menenius breaks down centre to give voice to his sentiments and the lightness of the joke.

Tribunes stand silent down left, not participating in the festivities.
Joke about the tribunes—more humorous, better—only Coriolanus is serious with his line "Menenius, ever, ever." Cominius gives the signal for the nuntio to cover Coriolanus's distraction.

Volumnia dramatizes the situation, so Coriolanus deliberately makes it personal rather than military.

Coriolanus exits to a flourish upstage centre flanked by Volumnia left and Virgilia right.
Then followed by Cominius left and Titus Lartius right.

Initial revulsion from the ceremony is brought to a peak by the climax of the rhythmic clapping—then he is brought to his mother and drops to his knees.
Again exit to the rhythmic hand clapping, turning into applause and broken by the outburst of the tribunes remaining on stage, Brutus right, Sicinius left.

The tribunes converge downstage centre as they move into the plot of his downfall.
Messenger then enters from up centre and breaks between them to deliver the news of Coriolanus's welcome.

Perhaps as a contrast to the building of the applause the scene should begin at a very low pitch and build from there.

Technique of breathing with the verse and phrasing with the end line.
Hammer in with "I never saw the like."

2.2

Opens with two officers speaking of Coriolanus: "he's vengeance proud, and loves not the common people."—building dynamic to keep the scene exciting, though its purpose is largely to pass on information.

Care must be taken with the phrasing to clarify as much as possible.

The elders seat themselves around the dais on the cushions put out by the officers during the preceding interchange.

The National's upper terrace. Photo by Kristina Bedford.

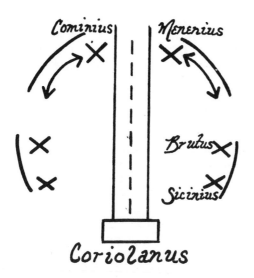

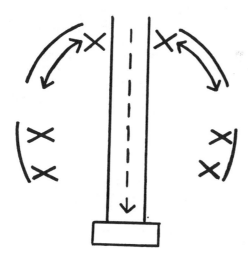

Cominius sits centre right and Menenius centre left.
Coriolanus moves centrestage and sits on the stool.
Image of people seated, conducting everyday business.
Two tribunes seated slightly apart and down left.

Switch in the stage picture—it is better not to have both generals sitting so
near the doorway—Menenius now takes up his position the third in from
the doors.

At the first entrance the senators speak in a group, listening to Menenius,
while the tribunes go to their seats, thus separating themselves visually
from the others.
    In their speeches, however, the tribunes are very congenial in their
    game-playing.
    Sicinius and Brutus are the first to stand on his line.
    Applause and parliamentary-like demeanour punctuate the scene.

Something is apparently going wrong as early as the tribunes' first input,
though Cominius is invited to speak and does so to bridge the awkward
gap.
    Therefore he should be standing rather than sitting.

The clear image should be the meeting of the establishment with a whole
series of unwanted interruptions—quick tempo necessary.
    Initial flattery of the tribunes by the senate.
    Tribunes make their case for the people with real authority.

Desperate attempt to save the day after Coriolanus's outburst.
    Cominius delivers his speech standing up centre but walks down to the
    tribunes on "counter-pois'd"—implication as he walks past the tribunes
    that 'if the cap fits, wear it.' Desperation in Cominius to make it all
    right, then warms to his subject and entrances his audience.
    As he speaks he walks up and down among the senate.
    Absolute desperation and rapidity of delivery in his bid to save Cor-
    iolanus.

On the next run of the speech the explosion now comes from a stationary
position up centre, and Cominius merely looks at the tribunes on "coun-
ter-pois'd."
    "For this last . . ."—sudden drop in volume as the feats described are
    so extraordinary.
    Change of tone before "as weeds before/A vessel under sail," as he
    chronicles the wonder of it all.
    Humour in language on "The common muck of the world"—he has won
    his audience round and therefore can afford the humour.
    Quiet tone describing his nobility and total lack of covetousness—
    extraordinary.

Tribunes are impressed by the speech, but it does nothing to ameliorate the political situation.

Coriolanus reenters to applause, but this only makes his trap the worse—now what?—he must show his wounds to the people.

Watch for the break in the verse at the end of the line for the natural dynamic in phrasing "the people/Must have their voices."

As the gates open, Coriolanus is revealed outside sitting and sweating as though for an interview—central image.

Coriolanus intellectually knows that he must show his wounds to the people, but he is emotionally repulsed from the act.
>   Menenius makes light of the request, as he knows the violence with which Coriolanus will react.
>   After "speak to the people" Coriolanus must move quickly into "I do beseech you," as though forestalling that negative reaction.
>   Coriolanus wants to avoid going on public display—it is not necessarily a bad ritual, but he will be bad in enacting it.

Menenius rises and goes to him on "Do not stand upon't"—not donning the gown of humility becomes a *constitutional* point.
>   It is absolutely impossible to become consul in this way without the complete overthrow of all tradition.
>   The tribunes are desperate—if the senate's approval alone is sufficient, then the people will lose their power.

Mythic personage of the *REAL HERO*.
>   In Coriolanus we have an extreme example posited at an extreme moment in time when the past can never be returned to, as the people and their tribunes will not allow it. The senate would like to say alright but cannot, due to the historic measure of giving the people power in elected representatives.
>   The tribunes in their turn do not want an empty shell of power but to put some blood back into Rome's empty ritualized ceremonies and imbue them with a sense of actuality.

NB. 100 years ago *Coriolanus* would not be a tragedy.
>   100 years from now Coriolanus would not exist.

31/10/84

2:30–5:30

3.1

Coriolanus confronts the plebeians about the corn.
Plebeians surround Coriolanus centre—on "Triton of the minnows" sits down centre.

Play about confrontation—what happens when "two authorities are up/ Neither supreme"—it is at this point that chaos can set in—the case for Coriolanus.
If Coriolanus had left his case here he could have won, but he goes back to the obsessive bloody corn.

The consul is the head of state, embodying the state.
For the purposes of this play there is only one and not a triumvirate.
Elected like the president on the basis of prowess.
Coriolanus finds it debasing to be dependent on the tribunes for election.
In Shakespeare's mind a consul is king but without divine right, as he is accountable to the senate.
Coriolanus not only attacks the tribunes but also the senate for giving the tribunes power to distribute the corn gratis.

Sicinius hits on the word *"traitor"*—the first time the word is mentioned.
The consul is answerable to the senate and answerable to the people, but if you put a bloody fascist in you've had it, as he will grab power.

Separate beats in Coriolanus's speech addressed to many individuals and as words within that must be uttered—Coriolanus must be centred and strong.
Culmination in the drawing of the sword as the emblem of civil war.

Shakespeare is in favour of kings, but they must be *balanced* within themselves as well as by the aristocracy and the people.
Head and heart in a balanced relationship, so that the commonwealth too may be healthy.

The tribunes fear that Coriolanus will wreck what is good with the present system and in that sense are not revolutionary.
The senate in the same way do not want to overthrow the tribunes.
It would be regressive to go back to a time when one man won the wars, ruled the state, etc.
Coriolanus was conditioned to be the best soldier that ever was in a

society where warriors were seen as heroes and put in a position to
which they were totally unsuited as their reward.

The aediles enter—there is almost an arrest happening right now, but
Sicinius halts it—so that the people may see the result.
 Within a few moments Coriolanus is called "traitor," "treasonous" and
is almost arrested.
 It is as though the queen on her way to the coronation were arrested by
an ordinary citizen—"hands off" is therefore as dangerous a moment as
the actual drawing of the sword.
 "On both sides more respect"—Menenius is moderate at first, but soon
loses his own control in terror of the citizens closing ranks and moving
in.

Some kind of violent gesture must occur to motivate "Help, ye citizens!"
 Half nelson?
 Coriolanus grabs him by both arms and chaos ensues?
 Or are the tribunes just so terrified at the vocal threat that they over-
react?
 The mob does not start out at fever pitch—the anger develops with the
scene.

Coriolanus is a very dangerous figure in the centre, around whom all else
move in.

Shakespeare has set up the audience response to the mob by what has
been said in the preceding scene.
 The crowd cannot press about too soon, as Coriolanus would draw his
sword earlier.
 It is enough for the mythic hero to say "fuck off" for the others to
cringe.
 They dare move in only when he pushes Sicinius to the dirt and he calls
them, but they must still keep their distance around the perimeter of the
circle.
 "Seize him, aediles!" as the cue to move in.
 Cannot scream like a mob yet—first comes the agreement to arrest.
 Cry of "Weapons, weapons, weapons!"—now a sense of civil war and
danger if weapons will be brought out—cry sets everyone off—panic.

Senate sticks to one area of the stage and sticks together, tribunes stand
together.
 Panic brings about a natural division into groups.
 Mass panic spreading like wildfire.
 Coriolanus as a soldier stands watching to understand—does not get
passionate—good soldiers do the opposite—physical violence brings
them back to reality.

Senate go up above right, the tribunes take up their position above left.
The arena fills with people, some actors, some audience, all talking
about the central figure still standing in the middle of the stage.
Repeatedly try to bring about civil arrest.

Coriolanus draws his sword—all draw back immediately and flinch as he
walks about brandishing it.
In mutiny the aediles, tribunes and people all come in to arrest him.
He flourishes the sword and all are bloody gone within seconds.
Preserve Coriolanus as a really dangerous power source with people
bustling about at a distance, as they dare not go near him.
Central image of the bull in the ring.

"On both sides more respect."—after the tribune has been hit to the
ground.
Menenius must wait for the line until after the mass entrance, or this key
notion of the play will be thrown away.

The aediles are at first quick and sharp in their reactions, as they are just
policemen doing their job—matter of fact in their attitude.

Individual cries are activated by individual meanings.
"Down with him"—endorsing the arrest.
"Weapons"—cry of fear.
"Tribunes"—cry for help.
Beat of stillness after "Weapons" for the implication to sink in, then
reaction.
Continual buzz underneath the main dialogue as they wait for the
tribunes to speak—atmosphere of intense danger must persist until
Sicinius actually makes his pronouncement.

Sudden turning on "This deserves death."—move in again, provoking the
drawing of the sword.
Menenius fights his way through the crowd to get the tribunes to
withdraw, as Coriolanus rushes stage right to chase those farthest away.
The rest of the mob closes in behind him, then are chased off left, as he
wheels about to pursue them.
Pushes the audience back to their stands.
With this mass exit the tempo is intense—earth shattering situation—
Time has stopped.
Coriolanus is in his element—"could have killed all of 'em."

"One time will owe another."—things slightly calmed down.
Half line joke.

Coriolanus is having the time of his life and is also excusing himself with
"what's the problem?"

Now the serious voice strikes in—Cominius saying that the fabric of Rome is collapsing all about them—epigrammatic—rhetorical voice representing the Homeric world.

Sicinius really hits Coriolanus in absentia—"he hath resisted law"—absolutely incredible—he's broken the law and NO we don't want to talk, we've come to throw him down the rock—lynch mob incited.
    Coriolanus wants to "depopulate the city and/Be every man himself"—the ultimate form of megalomania.

Menenius is desperate to patch things up by whatever means, but Sicinius will not budge from his stance of hard realism—exile is danger and forgiveness means the people's certain death.
    That Rome "Should now eat up her own"—half line pause taken—textual clue that something therefore happens.

Scene ends on a note of quiet threat.
    The whole scene is a huge hot event—10 days that shook the world.

At the beginning of the scene Coriolanus and the senate enter in a group up centre and are forestalled by Brutus down right and Sicinius down left.

1/11/84

10:30–1:00

3.2

Volumnia enters up centre, Coriolanus with the young nobility from the right.
    Volumnia enters in state, slowly as she is highly pissed off.
    Contrast with Coriolanus's hot tirade.
    Menenius and senators come in up centre to convince him to apologize.

Suddenly we see Coriolanus with new fellows of the same class and the same age.
    He is arrogant in his absoluteness—there is no question of backing down, and they are supportive of his stance. Then comes the worm—why will his mother not support him in this?

Volumnia is crisp in her refusal to go along with him.

The costume of the young nobility must reflect their connection with Coriolanus in visual terms—perhaps they should wear swords if he carries one in this scene.

It is terribly important to maintain the domestic juxtaposition.
Coriolanus feels he is treated like a child and is under terrible pressure—his wife is kept away from him.
Feels he is totally in control and he's not.

Coriolanus walks up centre to meet his mother—petulance on "Why did you wish me milder?" but gesture of submission in the kissing of her cheek.
The senate give her no elaborate greeting, just a nod of acknowledgment.

There must be more initial firmness in Coriolanus's entrance to contrast with his attitude to Volumnia.
Fearful image of the criminal at the top of rock Tarpeian.
They will make it higher and higher so one cannot even see the bottom.
Slows for impact of the monosyllables on "yet will I still/Be thus to them."
"You do the nobler"—then the line about his mother comes out of nowhere.

Menenius comes in to say that he must return and mend it when he thinks he has already dealt with the situation.

The whole scene is about acting and getting the role right—Coriolanus hates to act and wants only to be "The man I am."
Volumnia asks him to be other than what she has created.

"Ay, and burn too"—prophetic and the beginning of their estrangement.
Volumnia apparently talks him down—it is unbelievable that she who has reared him to be the man he is can say this.
Coriolanus lies sprawled across the daybed as she crosses around to convince him.
Minor note of peace before the entrance of Cominius with the news that the situation has now gone beyond all this.
Collusion in the looks exchanged between Menenius and Volumnia, as they use reason to sway Coriolanus.

ANGER—Tumult, revolution, change.
Operative word repeated throughout the scene.

"You have put me now to such a part which never/I shall discharge to the life."—he is completely miscast in the role, and success is impossible.
But he will go—therefore the "Away my disposition" speech.
Terribly ironic speech on what it means to be a politician.
Lets off energy physically by hitting his knee with his fist.

The second "Do as thou list" before Volumnia exits left includes a mo-

nent of look and touch between mother and son when she knows she has
won.

Coriolanus mimics her silly mountebank gesture, Volumnia turns away
in disgust.

Prompts the violence in his cry "Look, I am going."

Absolute agony inside as she rejects him—he keeps some distance,
hurt.

Blocking: Coriolanus lies on the day bed with the nobility behind his left
shoulder.

The senators are stationed to his right, Volumnia circles about.

Coriolanus rises to follow Volumnia with his eyes after her exit, but is
recalled to the present by Cominius.

Seeks to reconcile his nature to the task ahead by the matter of fact
gestures of arranging his collar and preparing his dress for the physical
ordeal of meeting the people.

This is one scene where Coriolanus can be completely different from the
expectations inherent in the image of his name.

3.3

All the public are brought down into the arena for the first time since the
opening.

The tribunes enter with supporters—image of a solid mass of people as
Coriolanus comes in to play the scene "mildly."

All meet in the middle, one aedile coming down from the top.

First the tribunes arrive down centre wondering what the hell is happening.

"Tyrannical power"—complete and total megalomania.

Tremendous unbridled energy of Brutus released in his pacing.

Aedile goes out down centre.

Coriolanus enters coming down over the back stall from above right,
then stands on the upper level to deliver his first speech.

The mass of people converge in the centre of the circle.

The tribunes sit in the stands, left, but on a lower level than Coriolanus.

Coriolanus: "What is the matter . . ."—sense of a public demonstration.

They are saying what a good fellow he is, and Coriolanus is saying more
than is necessary, as always.

He breaks through the people to face the tribunes directly on this
question.

On the second run he says this to the people above but on a lower level.

Most of what he says before his climactic outburst on "Traitor?" are
little bubblings out, warnings of what is to come.

Sudden complete change to the ominousness of "To th'rock."
He is talking now to the people and deliberately ignoring the tribunes.
Therefore stress is "Answer to *us.*"

2:00–5:30

3.3

On his first entrance Coriolanus just looks at the crowd to gain his balance.
He had expected to walk into a riot, instead he sees a square full of people.

Old psychological problem of Coriolanus—he is doing quite well, as he promised Volumnia, until they begin to praise him—then instinctive repulsion.

The people stand amazed at his absolutely unbelievable response to Brutus's speech: "I am content."—it does not matter whether they are pro or con.
"Lo, citizens, he says he is content."—i.e., to be judged by the people's voices—end of the movement.
Pause, then he goes back to Act II and the oration of his merits.
Coriolanus reacts with "I can't bear this"—humiliated by praise.
Cominius sees this and also wants Menenius to shut up—last time Coriolanus walked out and left him for six bleeding minutes on his own.

Twenty different people have twenty different answers—no unity in a crowd.
It is a complex unit shifting from minute to minute.
They have just come from the scene where he drew his sword and pursued them—most would find him a dangerous bloody fascist.

It is this repulsion from praise which initiates Coriolanus's "What is the matter."
Keeping his integrity safe—proper moment as he asks the crowd why they have done what they have done to him.
Bursts through and goes mad as he is called a traitor.

The people want to kill him, the tribunes want to follow point of law.
Brutus wants to be able to say death *BUT* clemency.
Wise tactic for him to do so on behalf of the people.
If they were to kill Coriolanus the patricians would split the country.
They want to be seen in their own eyes, in the patricians' eyes and in the eyes of history to be wise and clement men.

The confrontation reaches its peak on "What do you prate of service?" "I talk of that, that know it." "You?"

Sicinius goes on with the legal indictment, as though reading a pre-established document.

Cominius jumps up on the stands left and moves upstage, but cannot stop the law, and the people heed the reading of the document—the legalistic process is inflexible and unstoppable.

The aediles are not to be seen as secret police having to protect the tribunes from the people, but stand behind and above—the common people's justice of the peace.

The tribunes need to gain the people's approval and convince them to kill the man, then appear whiter than white in offering mercy.

"He is sentenced and that's it"—Sicinius comes down with the aediles as though to dismiss their suit.

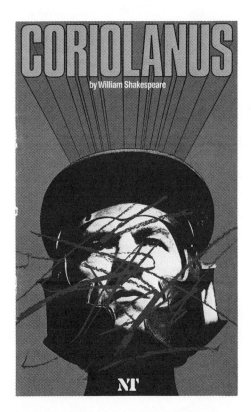

Front cover of the production program.

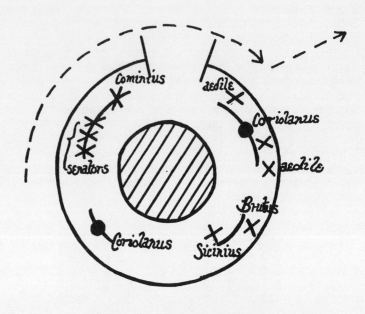

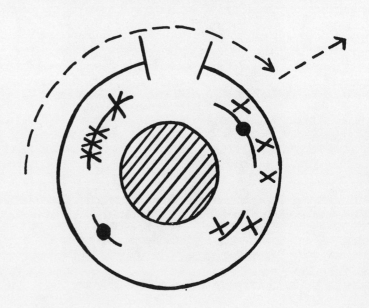

"You common cry of curs"—Cominius and Menenius have egg on their faces, as Coriolanus makes a burning emotional speech which does nothing to stop the great legalistic flow of rhetoric.

Then the aediles come forward to arrest him.

The people shout "It shall be so, it shall be so!" as Coriolanus takes up his position in the stands right.

Cominius speaks in a desperate attempt to stop the aediles in their tracks.

Coriolanus runs over and, above the top of the gates, delivers "You common cry of curs!" then jumps over the back of the stalls and disappears.

"The people's enemy is gone"—official statement, quite quiet but meets with a yell of pleasure from the multitude who throw up their caps.

On the shouting the audience is moved back to their places.

The festivities are interrupted by Sicinius saying 'now don't go home, see him out at gates and send him off with just vexations.'

Stops them going off down centre and reroutes them through the gates up centre.

All exit except the two aediles who go ceremoniously down the steps (down centre) having done their jobs.

They are followed by the tribunes looking very relieved.

"You common cry of curs" is delivered still from the stalls right up until "That won you without blows"—this time comes down and exits through the gate.

After running Act 3 for basic text and blocking, go over the words and lines missed or misquoted—absolutely crucial to be word-perfect.

Menenius gets to Sicinius by saying in 3.1 "Proceed by process"—what may be seen to bring him round is an appeal to the law.

Cominius—desperate sincerity and openness—this means more than wife and children.

Extremely difficult section of the play and it must be made real.

Basic difficulty in the portrayal of the tribunes and to what degree the people trust them at what point in the play.

Swaying back and forth, yet there is a fundamental unity in manipulation.

3.1: "And throw their power i'th'dust"—Coriolanus literally kicks the dust under his feet in the face of the tribunes.

3.2: Between the final two "mildly"s Coriolanus takes off his sword and tosses it on the daybed as the physical emblem of his speech.

3.3: "There is a world elsewhere!"—said with his back to the people, as he hesitates before taking his first step out on his own.
  Banishment of Rome—sudden drop on "thus I turn my back."

The image of organized chaos dominates the staging of the third act of the play—Coriolanus in his noble attempt to act an honorable course finds his absolute nature swaying back and forth between his desire to please Volumnia and his natural revulsion from playing roles he knows to be alien to his nature—constant set up of scenarios crushed to the ground.
  Tension between Coriolanus's attempts to quell the discontent and the words uttered by those who wish to help him, innocent in themselves but bound to trigger him off.

2/11/84

10:30–1:00

4.1

All enter right in a unified body, Coriolanus framed by Volumnia (right) and Virgilia (left) with Cominius, Menenius and the young nobility around the perimeter.
  Volumnia crosses to an isolated position, absolutely grief-stricken but like a stoic will try to rise above it.

Coriolanus wants to be alone but does not know how to achieve this in any context other than the battlefield—Coriolanus loves the image of loneliness personified in the dragon and his fen—image often identified with him throughout the play.
  Excited about his liberation and leaving the city.

Volumnia consciously understands that this is the ultimate breach between mother and son and wants Cominius to go with him as the symbol of Rome, so that he will have something of Rome and of herself with him.

The young nobility are grief-stricken and must indicate so physically.

The nightmare of the scene is embodied in Virgilia's wailing on stage.
  Loss of son, husband, adopted son, greatest protegé, friend.
  Virgilia hangs about his neck at their entrance, and he is clearly uncomfortable.

Coriolanus wants to run away and get rid of this debilitating display of emotion.
Same reaction to Volumnia's tears—"Where is your ancient courage."
"Nay, I prithee woman"—reprimand to Virgilia's violent emotion, indeed he reprimands most things said to him in this scene.
Volumnia cannot bear the line "The beast/With many heads butts me away."
"Now the red pestilence . . ."—Volumnia runs to the gates and bangs against its walls.
Coriolanus is appalled at this unlooked for anarchic image.

Volumnia, Virgilia, Menenius and Cominius—these people all owned him in some way and projected him into something that he is not.

Virgilia is a very emotional woman all through the play, but here is the first time that Volumnia's violent emotion bursts through her tight control.
Coriolanus addresses very different lines to each woman—Virgilia he absorbs and deals with as though it were a situation he is well used to. He projects his frustration onto his response to Volumnia.

"My friends of noble touch"—the young nobility move in to shake his hand.
Very emotional and genuinely heroic moment, as he wants to put a smiling face on grief before the multitude and leave with a happy image of Rome.

Virgilia—honest and fulfilled emotion, and that is what love is about.

Coriolanus at this point looks forward to being alone, being a dragon, and does not want anyone to accompany him.
Having given vent to his grief he wants to put a brave face over it.
Image of Cominius utterly sagging, something a soldier just does not do, and Coriolanus is moved to say "Droop not"—world turned upside down.

Coriolanus goes out into the world but the world does not want him, and as he cannot go back to Rome the only alternative is Antium.

2:00–5:30

4.2

The tribunes are very frightened at the unrest in the city.
They don't want the rabble running about in chaos and the nobility vexed.
Brutus has been a hot-head and is now desperately trying to cool it.

They want a celebration, but the nobility are too upset to make it possible.

Coriolanus left Rome with no senators, only the nobility, Cominius and Menenius—the tribunes want to placate them and get back to the status quo.

When they see Volumnia coming, part of the reason they don't want to meet her is her alliance to madness and chaos.

That Coriolanus is gone is cause for satisfaction, and its recentness adds an extra elation—they do not want their mood dampened by the threatened encounter.
>   The tribunes enter from up centre while Coriolanus and company exited down centre, so the energy for their entrance actually comes from watching them leave.

Volumnia enters with a curse for the tribunes; Virgilia collapses at the top of the stairs down centre; Menenius goes to raise her, but is interrupted by Volumnia's violent outburst and Virgilia remains on the ground.
>   Virgilia's outburst stops the tribunes exiting left.

The tribunes' reaction to Volumnia's curse and indeed to meeting her at all is a mixture of embarrassment, awkwardness and effrontery at what she is saying, and fear at her physical presence.
>   The figure of Retribution is embodied in Volumnia until the point of the vulnerability of her plea that the gods should listen to her, then we are back to Volumnia the woman. Retribution—as a madwoman on her entrance she delivers her prophecy—set up as the equivalent of Cassandra or the witches in *Macbeth*.

The tribunes' first leave-taking is attempted with dignity, not as though running away.
>   If Volumnia addresses them they will stay, but it is not pleasant to meet someone not in their right wits.

It is a crucial scene for Volumnia, as it marks her loss of power.
>   NB. For Volumnia it is not a scene about what happens when she meets the tribunes, but what happens when her son goes.

4.4

Coriolanus enters up centre outside the gates of Antium—he is disguised and muffled so that we do not recognize him at first.

The great banquet is talked of as a well known fact.

Coriolanus is under great tension—he is making up his mind as to whether he should go on with it when he realizes that he is able to go unrecognized.

The scene is kept light from the point of view of the Volscian citizen. The tension is caught up by the suddenness of "Save you, sir," as the citizen enters hard on the end of his soliloquy.

4·5

As he is stopped by the servants, Coriolanus neatly trips the first by catching him with his foot behind the back leg.

Banquet—the servants are hot, sweaty and flustered to begin with, then after the first encounter are very nervous about the presence of Coriolanus.
Comic formation of the three trapped servants, left.
Coriolanus takes the third serving man by the ear and boots him offstage.

Tullus Aufidius comes on with the second serving man, left.
Coriolanus is stationed on the right perimeter of the circle, Aufidius left, so that they face each other with the distance of the sand between them.
Aufidius ultimately leads him off by the hand, left.

The real issue is that Coriolanus purposely trips up the serving men outrageously as a ruse to get Aufidius out of the house—when he trips the third servant, who is at the top of the domestic triangle, nothing is left but to get the boss.
The third servant is the most innocent in his assumed invulnerability due to his slightly higher station.

The first servant enters left and crosses right to look for Cotus, then on his way back to the house is tripped by Coriolanus and runs left to confer with the second servant, who approaches, is tripped in his turn, and repeats the process with the third servant.

Try the same segment again with the difference of Coriolanus being seated.
Coriolanus grabs a bottle of wine from the returning Cotus, who turns to face him when he hears the chink.
Image of the old beggar man coming in and sitting down near the hearth.
Cotus sees the hand coming out to trip him and jumps aside the first time.
Coriolanus remains seated until the line before the revelation of his identity to Aufidius—then turns to face him to give him the chance to recognize his old enemy.

Embrace—Aufidius begins to move on "clip" and actually embraces him on "Contend."

The sexuality of the speech is accentuated through the movement.

I.I

Menenius cuts through a dangerous mob and copes by telling the fable of the belly.

He assumes the storyteller's position sitting on the ground right.

Paint the speech by hitting key words—enjoyment and energy in his use of language.

"all the *body's* members/Re*bell*'d against the *belly*."

"The belly answer'd"—pause—deliberate technique to awake the interest of his audience and to enflame the first citizen's question.

The first citizen does not want to hear the moral, only the belly's answer.

Comedy in the schoolmaster's answer "Your most grave belly . . ."

Sense of Menenius discovering words and images as he goes along and enjoying it tremendously.

Menenius is very wise, canny and witty.

Histrionic ability when he takes the stage and makes speeches.

Known to be a "humorous patrician"—the key to his character.

In Elizabethan medicine the court was the heart.

The belly is quite a deliberate senior and not rash—can be characterized.

Menenius suddenly gets very serious as he explicates the tale and points out the parallel with the rebels and the senators.

Dreadfulness of Rome and her rats at the point of battle.

He dumfounds the people with the story that underneath the wit and the humour he truly believes.

The body politic cannot survive without a healthy oligarchy.

Everybody needs a belly to survive.

4.2

This is not only a scene about Volumnia meeting the tribunes and about what happens to her with the banishment of her son, it is a scene about *DEATH,* since Coriolanus's exile means that he will never return to Rome alive.

3/11/84

10:30–12:00

2.3

In the voices scene Coriolanus stands on a stool wearing the gown and cap of humility—incapable of movement.
It is absolute anathema to him to "mountebank" the love of the people who enter by twos and threes.
Surliness growing out of complete embarrassment to asking.
Pathos of his request to the tribunes "May I change these garments?"

Brutus's delivery of Coriolanus's lineage—wonderful comic parody.

3.1

Great contrast in Coriolanus, whom we last saw wearing the humble weeds—he now appears in his military guise, preparing yet again to do battle with Aufidius, and is stopped in his tracks by the tribunes withdrawing the people's voices.

3.2

This time when Coriolanus says "Look, I am going" he edits the mockery on "mountebank" and delivers the line quietly instead of shouting it.

3.3

On "thus I turn my back./There is a world elsewhere!" Coriolanus exits through the audience rather than through the gates on stage.

General Notes on the First Day in the Theatre

The full space of the theatre can now be exploited—no longer limited to the rehearsal room mock-up—can take advantage of the full potential of certain positions on the actual stage.
Diagonal entrances are very powerful.
In mass scenes the actual positions are not crucial as long as one concentrates and listens—the looseness of the mob concentrating makes wonderful shapes.

The whole staging strategy is right—the audience will work.

Text, however, is dreadful—inaccurate and not known.
Punctuation is lost so one can't understand what is said.
Half-line cues are forgotten or given a naturalistic rhythm.

No give and take among actors in the general panic.
The text is so difficult to follow intellectually and emotionally that one needs the correct form to convey it to the audience without being boring.

The text is not naturalistic or pausal as it was written for outdoor theatres.

The lines are attention grabbing—before the key note to a musical phrase ends a new one begins—like film editing directing focus.
Not enough attention is being grabbed in these half-line pauses.
Too much time is given to the pause which halts the production.
Needs a great deal of homework done on the text.
A good week of work lost today.
The play's words and *structure* are not known.

Go now to the truths of the character and the truths of the emotion.
No more time for grammar and structure or will get behind.

The text used for this production is as close as possible to the original despite corruptions.
Full stop means a gear change—a new beat, a change in tone—gives colour for variety—not true for the semicolon or the comma.
Do not pause at the end of a line, but mark it by a slight change in tone.
Earn time to rush onto the next line in a rush of emotion, but only in the last line as the text is so complex.
If one goes for emotion first the form will be lost and the result nonsense.
Shouting makes a gabble of the lines—go for clarity—can speak quietly and fast.

Indeed the whole play must go flatly and quickly.
The stage and the design concept both allow for actual cross-cutting in scene changes.

The production is stunning, but the danger is in the textual form.
The style is there if we grab it.
The centre is right, Coriolanus is right, need all else to follow for unity.

This is one of the most difficult texts to do.
The rhythm in the prose is almost more marked than the verse.
Verse: quick, colloquial, represents real speech.
Prose: for common people, for rational argument; very rhythmical, like John Donne's sermons.

3.1.15–17: ". . . that he would pawn his fortunes
　　　　　To hopeless restitution, so he might
　　　　　Be call'd your vanquisher."

Right interpretation through phrasing.
"Might" at the end of the line is a subtle indication of the word's importance.

The play was written by a man who *heard* as he wrote.
Thus inflexion is not the actor's task—rather to find the shape and gear changes.
Shakespeare wrote the structure and phrasing as notes to the actors.
Half-lines *always* take the cue and begin before the last line has ended.
The weight of meaning in the second half of the line and the end is the springboard to the beginning of the next line—one can run on but not in.
Rhymes: Use them, do not ignore them.
Ends of lines: Use them, do not ignore them.
Cues: Take them, do not ignore them.
Monosyllables: Not quick delivery but find how to spread them out and emphasize each word.

In late Shakespeare "and," "but" and " 'til" are often placed at the end of the line, cuing the actor to search for the next word.
Not 'and—here it is.'
But 'and—how can I say it.'

The rapidity of the rehearsal process and the physical structures of the open air theatres necessitated the inclusion of such clues to the actors for their preparation of the text.
The actor then added a creative emotional sense to the rightness of how to play the line.

Quickness should come from taking up the cues rather than the speed of delivery.
Work for intensity not speed.

5/11/84

11:00–1:00

4.5

Try the opening sequence having edited the business of Coriolanus tripping the servants—he now threatens them with his vocal and physical presence.
Fear in the air, no one knows where, but only feels its presence.
Also edit the stealing of the wine etc., so that when all say later that he spun them round it becomes story-telling exaggeration.

In stage time he only says "I have deserv'd no better entertainment/In being Coriolanus," but in real time the servant goes in to warn the others.

We are in the mythic world of Zeus disguised as a beggar seeking hospitality.

The third servant comes in and stops in his tracks, awed.
"batten on cold bits"—the point at which he kicks the third servant.
Explosion of violence at the end which they fear all the way through.
The violence is real and it scares the shit out of them.
The third servant has circled the outside of the perimeter warily.

A different dynamic is tried with Aufidius entering from above—but wrong.
He needs to be established as one just entering from a banquet with no knowledge of who it is who disturbs him. Aufidius's first line is perfectly normal.
"Why speak'st not?"—second line slightly stronger, though not heavily significant.

Coriolanus calls him by his first name "Tullus"—this elicits a strong reaction.
"Under the canopy"—such a weird image that he must play up the weirdness of it.
The servant tries to lighten the situation with the joke about "daws," but is insulted and advances due to the impertinence, then backs off again at "Thou prat'st and prat'st."

Aufidius: "Thou hast a grim appearance"—circles somewhat downstage to observe Coriolanus from a point of vantage. When called "Tullus" he stops in his tracks—shift in dynamic.

At the end of his long speech and before "Martius, Martius," Coriolanus moves centre to draw both the focus and Aufidius himself toward him.
Coriolanus appears to be goading Aufidius on to cut his throat, calling him "fool" and saying that his very life is a shame to him.
Possibility of Aufidius putting the sword to his throat in a sudden lunge forward to surprise Coriolanus—cut as it is not right.
Still need to find a way to equalize Aufidius, as the audience will guess his reaction of conciliation if he remains stationary left.

Coriolanus seems to just accept all offered him quite matter-of-factly.

Aufidius: "A thousand welcomes"—Aufidius offers his hand, Coriolanus goes to grasp it, but it is momentarily withdrawn for "Yet, Martius, that was much," then it is shaken warmly.

Tremendous tension in the tentative advance and alliance between the two generals.

The response to the throat offering is almost sexual.
Aufidius turns to Coriolanus after he repeats his name, on "Each word."
The minute he pronounces the name "Martius," it could be the last ten seconds of his life—controlling emotion in the Stoic mean.
Yet in the speech which follows, Coriolanus becomes more and more daring—he does not excuse anything, he just says "I hate them, I want to join you and if not then kill me."
Not quite plain speech—corrosive, ironic edge to it.
Coriolanus uses clipped speech as he says what he planned to.
What he says is not scripted but not spontaneous, thus it contrasts with the effusive energy of Aufidius's response.

Aufidius: Continual mounting irritation waiting for the name.
Containment contrasts with emotional improvisation.
"most absolute sir" versus "generous host."

4.6

Citizen picnics up left with her child, Menenius enters and sits with her.
A couple with their infant enter left and cross to greet the tribunes.
Shows the complete contrast of Rome in times of war and peace.

Tribunes are talking right of centre when the messenger enters right with news of the attack—now confusion fills the stage—the complete visual opposite to the earlier contentment and lyrical atmosphere.
Second messenger enters up centre to corroborate.
Third messenger and Cominius join him.
Menenius, Cominius and the messengers exit up centre.
Citizens cross and exit conferring amongst themselves.

After the tribunes' controlled calmness comes Sicinius's absolute explosion on "Nor I."

Need even more sunshine at the opening of the scene.

Implication that the tribunes enter already talking about him.
Sicinius can gloat about Coriolanus's supposed "friends"—dig on "blush," as Coriolanus has turned against the patricians—in the previous scene he called them "dastard nobles."
Pause of self-satisfaction on "We stood to't in good time."
Menenius's entrance is no threat—they see him all the time now.
Menenius's "All's well" can be hearty, as he is happy that Rome is happy, but it might have been much better if he could have temporized.

"I hear nothing"—the tribunes are surprised—'we thought you were a friend'—but "His mother and his wife/Hear nothing from him."
Exterior public face put on for the tribunes.

Brutus says to the citizen couple "We wish'd Coriolanus/Had lov'd you as we did" for Menenius's benefit, and both tribunes now move in to convince him of his friend's faults and arrogance, but Menenius refuses to listen.
Rebuke on "I think not so."

The first messenger speaks hard on the last word of the tribunes' self-congratulation.

Guilt in the tribunes—they want to talk about other things, but Coriolanus's name keeps creeping back, and the nobles who also dumped him are now seeking to shift their share of the blame and guilt completely onto the tribunes.

The messengers give their separate pieces of information in separate beats.
   i) The Volscians
   ii) Have entered Roman territory
   iii) War has been declared
   iv) 'tis Aufidius.

6/11/84

2:00–5:30

5.4

Menenius and Sicinius enter above left and sit in the stands.

"See you yond coign o'th'Capitol, yond cornerstone?"—total emphasis in the repeated alliteration of the "c" sound before the speech goes into prose.

The two men are not falling out here, instead we have the image of unity in adversity.
Sicinius is a lonely figure in this scene—Brutus is being haled up and down, and he no longer wants to be associated with being a tribune of the people.
He has respect for Menenius's age and experience throughout the play.

Games are played between the verse and the prose to build up and break the tension.
Some characters prevent and some cannot achieve verse.

Menenius's constant repetition of "this is your fault" is much more gentle in this scene than earlier in the play—sense that they are all in the same boat.
Two people absolutely on opposite sides of the fence are now together and are completely lost.
There is not much for Sicinius to say, therefore he says very little.

Imagistic inversion of Alexander, as he sits in state to destroy the civilization which created him and therefore not realizing his full Alexandrian potential by fighting *for* Rome—power of Greek emulation.

The prose in this sequence includes an enormous amount of alliteration—this must be leaned on a little.

The messenger of death enters right.

The messenger of good tidings is revealed through the gate rolling out the red carpet in preparation for Volumnia's triumph through Rome.
Sicinius's initial response to the second messenger coming hard on the heels of "death by inches" must indicate his trepidation.
The red carpet could after all be for Coriolanus—there is no way of knowing.
Brutus enters wounded right.

5.3

The procession ends with the child—a real reunion.
All seems wonderful at this point.
"I holp to frame thee"—Volumnia kisses her son's hands.
The formal wit of Coriolanus's speech to Volumnia contrasts with the vulnerable wit of comparing his son to a "great sea-mark."

Aufidius stands on the perimeter right, Virgilia further down, right.
Rome's virgins are lined up with Valeria at their head, centre.

Coriolanus isolates himself down left.
He and Volumnia are emotionally one, except when they talk about this one issue, where they are poles apart.
Volumnia exhibits anger at his implacability.

Focus on the virgins of Rome and on Volumnia as she stands with them to deliver her long speech of persuasion.
"Destroying Rome means destroying me and I won't stand for it—I'll kill myself first."

"Aufidius, and you Volsces, mark"—Coriolanus sits down right with Aufidius standing behind him listening.

The women first kneel in the sand, then go even further down in obeisance.
Lie absolutely flat on the ground, middle-eastern fashion.
Volumnia is always saying "behold's," look at us, but she cannot get
Coriolanus to catch her eye.
"Nay, behold's" is the exception—he cannot keep his glance away.
Virgilia helps Volumnia to her feet on "This fellow had a Volscian to his
mother"—she gets up and goes to exit.
She will never know that he looked at her at this point because her face
was in the sand.
The kneeling is at first a very slow, formal, deliberate, dignified action.
Begging comes only with the final obeisance.
"Yet give us our dispatch"—her final cry— 'tell us to go if you can say
nothing else, kill us if you can do nothing else.'

Throughout the scene, even when shown his child, Coriolanus thinks he is
safe.
Until she comes right up to him at this point and calls him bastard.
Volumnia breaks away from the exiting women to run to him.
Coriolanus is split open by the image of having a Volscian to his mother,
of himself being a bastard and of his son also being a bastard.

Coriolanus has just stated his desire to stand without any kin, yet the
moment this is articulated for him by Volumnia he is destroyed.

Aufidius and Coriolanus meet centrestage.
Then Coriolanus gathers his family about him down left.

Aufidius first comments on Coriolanus's behaviour, then on narrative
fact—he will work himself a "former fortune."
Thus the first line is focused on Coriolanus, the second on the audience.
Leap of reality as he muses to himself.
Walks downstage to deliver these lines to the audience, then turns to
look at Coriolanus.
Coriolanus leads off his wife and mother, then the ladies follow two by
two—slight gap, then Aufidius turns and follows.

5.2–4—three scenes run together for the first time.

5.2: Menenius must sell it much more.

Getting a flow to the scenes—emotion and characterization continually
improving now that the lines are down.

7/11/84

4:00–5:30

5.6

Volscian citizens line the perimeter of the stage, Aufidius is placed above right in the stands—descends on "Coriolanus, in Corioli."
   Half-line pause as Coriolanus turns in reaction to his name.
   Half-line pause after "powers"—dramatic reversal.
   "boy of tears"—Coriolanus begins to be aware of the danger of the ring.

Aufidius and Coriolanus face each other in the ring, Aufidius right, Coriolanus left.
   "thou boy of tears"—hit the monosyllables—Aufidius sees right through him in his reaction.
   Coriolanus is indescribably hurt by this man saying this.
   "'Boy!' O slave!"—outburst of emotion, then pulls himself together in his address to the Volscian lords.
   Aufidius should not be so still—they are like two caged animals facing off against each other.
   Sadistic release building in Aufidius which will provoke Coriolanus's final speech.

Paradox, as all his life Coriolanus has been absolutely what he is and never temporized—now he is emotionally involved with the treaty of Rome and has done exactly what Aufidius says he is now trying to cover up, and he is covering up well for the first time—the ultimate irony.
   The treaty is the first point where he does act out of character and he knows it: "O mother, mother!/What have you done?"
   And he has wept—"boy of tears" is a reminder of that.
   Having accepted that, with bravado he can die.
   Now instead of delivering "boy of tears" as a taunt, Aufidius delivers it as a fact.

Coriolanus turns to the Volscian lords—"why don't you stop him, why don't you help me," but they do nothing.
   Suddenly makes a tremendous statement of death.

Aufidius's game is to get Coriolanus to stand in the centre and say 'I killed all your fucking people'—he is a double traitor.
   A traitor but no longer a boy.

The Volscian senate does the same thing as the Roman senate—they don't want a public confrontation in the streets—"trouble not the peace"—it can all be discussed in private later.

Coriolanus experiences a journey to such complete despair that he says "alright, go ahead and kill me"—he does not even want to fight—"Cut me to pieces, Volsces, men and lads,/Stain all your edges on me."
> This is not the death of a hero, but the death of one who has lost his soul.
> If he changes sides, no matter what the moral and political reasons, he is a traitor and is now called so before the Volscian state.
> There is no escape but death.

"O that I had him,/With six Aufidiuses, or more, his tribe,/To use my lawful sword"—finally comes up with the insult which makes Aufidius want to kill him.
> Aufidius does not do so personally, the conspirators move in.
> Aufidius attempts to get the senate to join in, but can't.
> Coriolanus is armed but throws down his sword.

Aufidius stands with both feet on the dead body of Coriolanus, then retreats at the public outcry and must quickly justify himself and justify the emblem.
> Aufidius's final speech is a mess—his character just can't get it together in rhyme and regularity until the last line.
> Some conflict between the senators in the background.
> Orders for the funeral and mourning.
> Rebuke to make the best of it.

Did Coriolanus die well?—no.
> Did he die to help anything?—no.
> Did his death achieve anything?—nothing.
> Coriolanus was a man who was too true to himself, with too much integrity and too much wrapped up in it.

Aufidius's mask is completely off at the end—first vitriolic, then sad that he has killed him—absolute bleakness of the ending as everybody is in the wrong.

Coriolanus is the tragedy of a man totally without hypocrisy and corruption.
> Celebration of integrity—says what he thinks and does what he believes.
> Then one must ask whether one really should 'to thine own self be true.'

The senate don't want to discuss reasons at this moment, just justifications.
> First it is time to honour the dead.

Aufidius's hatred for Coriolanus was always personal—the individual envy of an individual, therefore once he is removed his reaction too must be personal—the greatest part of his life is dead with him—there is no more

fighting, no more hunting—"My rage is gone,/And I am struck with sorrow" displays a profound emptiness.
   Being struck with sorrow is an active, not a passive emotion and must be fully experienced.
   His rage is gone and now something dreadful is happening—what to do.

"Tear him to pieces!" is to be continued as a violent undercurrent to the list of those he killed, right up to the senator's speech.

The senators are attempting to pacify the crowd and therefore don't see the conspirators as they move in—they pull out their swords in rapid succession 1, 2, 3.
   The conspirators then ironically act as the pallbearers.

8/11/84

2:00–5:30

2.2

Two officers come in to arrange the cushions for the senate scene.
   Enjoying the job and the conversation.
   Help each other roll up the carpet and bring on the stool.

The doors open and all enter—the senate take their place on the cushions, leaving Coriolanus centrestage sitting uncomfortably on the stool.
   "Most reverend and grave elders" as the cue to sit.

After the battle, all the scenes for Coriolanus are about being told to do something.
   He gets to the brink and then is almost physically sick.
   He wants them to stop treating him like a boy, and Menenius is the worst.

"Masters o'th'people"—meant to and succeeds in flattering the tribunes.
   The atmosphere of the entrance is 'all port and cigars.'

Question as to whether Coriolanus should face the audience or not.
   The stage image is more eloquent if he sits facing the senate with his back to the audience and shoulders drooping.
   We see his face when he first enters and looks about uncomfortably— this sets up the mood sufficiently.
   The gates later open to reveal the lone figure seated and waiting to be recalled.

"It is a part/That I shall blush in acting"—cannot be addressed to the tribunes, as they are whispering amongst themselves—in part it is a public speech addressed to the whole senate, but primarily it is to convince his uncle Menenius on a personal level.

Menenius lifts Coriolanus's hand on high as he wishes him all the "joy and honour" which is anathema to his soul.

The tribunes are left alone on stage for their final exchange.

Leave a beat until the gates shut for full formality.

2.3

When Menenius comes on to collect Coriolanus after he has 'stood his limitation,' he brings with him the consul's robe to clothe Coriolanus in after the antipathetic gown of humility.

Sicinius cannot be too bad a loser and has to admit that Coriolanus has actually fulfilled the form.

"Is this done?"—initial disbelief—when assured, Coriolanus tentatively gets down from the podium.

Coriolanus stands down right, the tribunes down left. Menenius moves right to robe him.

On the second run Coriolanus has gone on begging and now sits on the podium as they enter—he asks if he can change his robes, the tribunes agree and Menenius covers him.

As he leaves, Coriolanus sheds the gown and cap of humility behind him.

3.1

"At Antium *lives* he?"—Aufidius has opted out—disdain.

Ominousness of "sword to sword."

The tribunes now enter on this scene in desperate haste to halt the troops in their tracks—not only pleasure but a desire to avoid violence.

Good act—they have successfully incensed the multitude and now have wound up Coriolanus as well.

"Nor yoke with him for tribune." "Let's be calm."—rises from Coriolanus's upraised fist to physically attack the tribune who has insulted him.

The body of senators follows Coriolanus wherever he walks on stage to prevent a possible outbreak of violence.

"Being press'd to the war"—crosses to Titus Lartius.

Now the intervention of the tribunes actually splits up the senate physically on stage.

"Traitor" when first uttered is the key word that sets him off, as the tribune makes his announcement to the people.
The senators must get in his way and listen rather than give him room to speak—it is so incredible that a civil arrest should be in progress, that the senate should not take it so seriously at first.
"We'll surety him"—they are not afraid of a possible trial, as they believe the charge will immediately be discharged as ridiculous.

Coriolanus grabs Sicinius by the collar of his gown—the tribune overreacts, dropping to his knees and gesturing to the people to draw near and see this attack of their leader.

"What the vengeance,/Could he not speak 'em fair?"—not so much to ask.
Despair speaking through these lines—pleading tone.

12/11/84

11:00–1:00

I . I

Fine tuning and working for passion in the crowd scenes.

First fulsome, then grudging praise for Menenius—"would all the rest were so!"
It is then Menenius who goes into verse.

Timing cues by end lines, commas etc.—when one earns the run on to the next line.
Approach to the text is like the orchestration of a symphony, with each instrument or voice coming in on cue with the proper phrasing and intonation.

First citizen must work on his physical presence to make him less self-confident and assured and more neurotic—from straight posture to hunched back.

Dominance in the sheer physical presence of Coriolanus—immediate dissipation of crowd unity, as they recognize in this figure something dangerous.
The entrance of the man with his sword transforms one mob into many individuals scattered in different directions.

Opening to be played at a much higher level—bigger.
Citizens enter with placards and banners.
First citizen displays irritation—he has just got the crowd organized and is now stopped in the heat of passion.
Developing faction within the crowd—some against, some for Coriolanus.

NB. Introduction of sound to the rehearsals—the mob uprising on the other side of the city.

The citizens are already on their way out to mutiny when the second citizen speaks and draws them back.
"The other side o'th'city is risen"—wonderful to have reinforcements—instills added confidence.
"what we intend to *do,* which now we'll show 'em in *deeds*," "They say poor suitors have *strong breaths:* they shall know we have *strong arms* too"—enjoy the balance.
Menenius seeks to propitiate him—touch on the shoulder.
First citizen reacts violently as he starts away.

To introduce the subject at hand, Menenius needs to hit the alliterative opening of "all the *b*ody's members/Re*b*ell'd against the *b*elly."
"The belly answer'd"—deliberate pause provoking the impatient prodding of the first citizen.
The belly answered "With a kind of smile"—provokes laughter first at, then for him, as he gradually wins them round.
Transition as he puts on an assumed voice for the belly's reply to elaborate the dignity of the interpretation about the senate.
Gear change signalled by his physical turn, as he picks up his senatorial cloak and whirls it onto his shoulders.
No one in the crowd dares say anything.
Imperative for Menenius to catch their eye individually.

Use of improvisation to crack the scene with Menenius and the fable of the belly, and to find the titanic anger with which Coriolanus first enters on stage.
Kicks the cushions from the stalls and adds lines passing through his mind in reaction to the citizens.

Coriolanus loves coming out to bait the crowd and actually does master them, although he undoes all of Menenius's work.

There is a journey for each of the citizens during Coriolanus's speech.

One can't play any scene in Shakespeare on the basis that we've seen this many times before—we must approach it from the point of view that we have never seen Coriolanus, awful as he has been, quite as monstrous as he is now.

At this point he is still a boy enjoying his own rhetoric—his first really personal expression comes with "The moon of Rome."

The crowd cannot react on "Five tribunes," but must wait until the end of the phrase.

No matter how unnatural the need for audibility from Coriolanus.

Coriolanus is restless when he doesn't have a war into which he may channel his energies and here tries to create a different kind of battle in baiting the people.

At this point McKellen still varies between a full-blown performance and a neutral quick delivery.

It works better if Coriolanus doesn't physically attack the people, but likes walking up to them individually to see if his mere physical presence will make them jump back—need more contrast between individual reactions.

The first citizen is the only one who would rather die than retreat, therefore he is pulled away by his fellows.

13/11/84

1:00–1:30 and 2:30–5:00

I.6

All the warriors in Cominius's camp are in a state of complete and total physical exhaustion where tempers can flare and any explosion is possible—Cominius almost runs mad when he realizes that the messenger is wrong and that Titus Lartius's troops have not lost the day.

Physical and sexual imagery builds to its climactic statement in the sexual speech "when our nuptial day was done."

Coriolanus runs in down the centre aisle and round the perimeter of the stage, ending up centre—the soldiers form two lines through the centre of which Coriolanus walks to embrace Cominius down centre.

Pause before the entrance into the news of Titus Lartius.

Necessity of playing the full stops for Cominius, giving a mosaic colouring to the speech and the opportunity for gasps of desperation and exhaustion.

Inversion of metre on "tribunes for them!" to give added emphasis in outrage.

Martius enters as a "flay'd" man—Cominius sees him out centre, then all turn their heads gradually right to follow his progress before the entrance.
Need more concern on "How is't with Titus Lartius?"
See-saw of emotions—high adrenalin, exhaustion, blood, war, physical exertion.

The scene is absolutely Elizabethan—very emotional, stiff upper-lip.
In public scenes there is a tension for Cominius between the public image and the private self, but to Coriolanus there is no barrier to telling the absolute truth.
Coriolanus enters as a man smothered in blood—wants to find Aufidius—solo and absolutely superhuman.

Now try clipping the sequence with Coriolanus continuing in the circle to the mid-left point and Cominius turning to face him mid-right, both coming in to meet one another in the centre of the circle.
"Flower of warriors"—really play the moment of absolute tenderness, not as heartiness—hold the moment before going on.
Slowness of movement leading up to the climax of the embrace.
Lose the cheer from the soldiers as the two come together, as it is no longer appropriate and actually dissipates the tension.
Love and friendship between two warriors.
Now edit the second lap around the circle to keep it tight—much better as it edits a piece of unmotivated stage movement.

Sudden explosion from Cominius to punish the messenger, which the rest find funny.
The messenger is pushed to the ground by a fellow soldier.
Cominius draws, but Coriolanus stops him and picks the man up.
"in the name of Rome"—punctuated by the clash of shields between Coriolanus and one of the foot soldiers.

Transition from "But how prevail'd you?" and subsequent monosyllables to "Martius" as a sudden explosion to stop him, then headline "did retire to win our purpose."
Building in the speech about the enemy—very dangerous moment— when at their weakest they are up against a crack lot, and above all a crack lot led by Aufidius himself.

"D" sounds repeated on "*d*isadvantage fought" and "*d*id retire"—indicates how difficult it is for Cominius to find the words.

There are many different colorations in this scene which must be found and played.
"beseech you," "fought," "friends" etc.—climactic pauses in the speech requesting leave to go after Aufidius.

On the victory cry of "Martius," the soldiers raise him on their shoulders so that he is above on "O me alone! Make you a sword of me!" which is given to Coriolanus, rather than the communal shout which is indicated in the text—then down.
Need the momentary image only.
The soldiers put down their arms and move on the first "Martius," then repeat the name three times in a climactic cheer.
On "Wave thus to express his disposition" they mirror the gesture.
Only point in the play with a fascist gesture.
Force in the arm coming out and into the fist at the end.
Small moments between Coriolanus and each of the soldiers are included to build up the relationship between the general and his men—he saves one, comforts another, bangs shields with a third and stands on the shoulders of the fourth.

Now return to the theme of spoil which will be of more importance in the next scene—"If these shows be not outward."

1.8

Logistical problems with the fight—if Coriolanus holds the banner in his right hand and the shield in his left, then he is upstaged by it as it is downstage of him, whereas Aufidius's right is upstage.
Problem of placing the banners in artificially arranged cornerposts is avoided by passing them instead to the two soldiers who act as batmen.
In turn superseded by holding the standards out in front of the body rather than diagonally out to the side, to fully display the emblem.

Need to find separate moments for passing the banners, fixing foot, choosing ground and drawing the swords.
"Fix thy foot"—cue to pass the banner and step in the circle.
Physical delight in battle—they are 'not Hitler and Churchill'—it should be very sexy.
" 'scape me here"—cue to draw the sword.

The soldiers on the sidelines must be actually watching as each general is fighting for them.

Development in the fight between Aufidius and Coriolanus:
At one point before his ultimate victory Coriolanus downs Aufidius, but by exerting pressure on the former's shield by force of foot Aufidius sends him back.
Once disarmed, Aufidius still succeeds in knocking down his enemy and attempts to decapitate him by thrusting down the rim of his shield into the sand, but Coriolanus rolls to one side and disarms him of the shield as well.

Completely humiliated, Aufidius stands naked and weaponless while Coriolanus defeats his four men.

The only alternative would be for Aufidius to make his initial entrance solo, but it is unlikely that he would risk himself in this way.

Different interpretations for the story of the fight:
  i) Two generals enter with representatives of each army.
  ii) Coriolanus enters solo, sees the Volscian power and says he will fight "with none but thee," which results in the one to one combat with Aufidius.
  iii) Coriolanus and Aufidius both enter solo looking for one another, fight, then are joined by the Volscian power looking for their missing general.
  Yet the army seems to enter on cue the second that Aufidius is in trouble.
  Now Coriolanus and Aufidius enter with only one man each to whom they pass the banner, then fight solo.
  The fight is very taxing—after two or three runs the actors are exhausted.
  First run of the fight with helmet and plumes—need to rehearse not only for the physical distraction, but also for audibility.
  iv) When Aufidius is disarmed the Volscians run on from all four corners of the stage and, while Aufidius picks up his dropped sword upstage centre, they close in on Coriolanus in the middle.
  Decision to fight in extremely bright light with Aufidius lurking in the shadows.

On a subsequent run both generals again enter with their armies.
  Coriolanus is more stationary in the confrontation.
  Aufidius is more supple and harelike—"Holloa me like a hare."
  Their lines leading up to the battle are said for each other alone and in no way for the soldiers on the sidelines.
  Coriolanus wins the battle of words as well as of swords in his taunt about "Corioli walls"—provokes Aufidius's reference to Hector.
  Though the lines are private, the change in dress is largely public show—preparation for gladiatorial combat, helmets, etc.—this story ends on "Within these three hours."

On the next run the two men enter without any such preparation—just two bodies and two flags seeking combat.
  They arm and helmet themselves with the armies lurking in the background, then they hit the sand at the same time.
  The image is clean, theatrical, powerful and specific.

As the Romans rush in to counter the Volscian attack, Coriolanus waves them back to fight on single-handed.

They have made a bargain to fight solo, and even if the Volscians are
prepared to break it, Coriolanus is not.
Coriolanus chases the Volscian army out left, the Roman army follows
and Aufidius is left up centre.
Epic sense of frustration as Aufidius curses his own men.

Change: The Romans do not follow Coriolanus, but retreat into the shadows.
The final image must be that of Coriolanus single-handedly driving off
the four men.

Aufidius comes down to pick up his shield and helmet.
Clearing up the last remains of the battle.
Grabs them from the ground on "you have sham'd me/In your con-
demned seconds" in this ultimate image of humiliation.
When he appears in his next scene he is still carrying his sword and
shield as he trails them on the ground.
"The town is ta'en"—absolute devastation as they have lost everything.
He rips his helmet off, grabs his sword with a scraping motion from the
ground, then crosses for his shield.

1.9

The Romans are positioned down right, Coriolanus comes on left with a
sling, and Titus Lartius finally enters from down centre.
The two troops then meet one another right, while the three generals
encounter left.
The meeting of the troops must be brief, as they are fascinated by what
is going on between their leaders.
The choric lines must be absolutely clear and on the beat as it is not
"realistic" for groups to speak in unison.
It is a twentieth century convention to speak unison lines individually.

At first Coriolanus laughs off Cominius's hyperbolic praise, but gets tense
with its continuance by Titus Lartius.
The joke about his mother elicits a great laugh all round.
"I have done/As you have done, that's what I can"—moment of seriousness and affection with his soldiers.

The whole purpose of the scene is that after the battle all want to praise
him.
He has saved their bloody necks and they know what he is like—they
will not let him get away with avoiding their praise and therefore sound
the trumpets.
It is a very light scene for the rest, agony for Coriolanus.
The scene shows how on a very masculine, jovial level Coriolanus can

handle it; later in Rome, outside his own culture of the battlefield, he can't deal with the public demonstration of praise.
Witty and affectionately teasing—one mustn't play the same scene twice—these people can handle him.
Only for Coriolanus himself does it approach playing the same scene twice, as he will always experience praise as torture to some degree— thus he says he must go change, he must "go wash."
The soldiers can handle him in this situation, but not in Rome, in public.
Sense of being in the locker room after a football match.

They give him a trumpet fanfare, the gift of a horse, a name, they even find delight in his embarrassment.
Coriolanus keeps saying that he is just one of the rest of them, but is completely embarrassed when on "Martius, Martius, Martius" they all pull him into the centre, form a circle around him, applaud and blow the trumpets.

"So, to our tent"—factual capping of Coriolanus's half-line cue.
Fulsome praise again in the line on writing to Rome.
All exit down centre, while Titus Lartius's party go back to Corioli up centre.

Coriolanus wants wine, good fellowship and unity with his men, but they want to separate him off as their leader, their saviour and their god.

It is a difficult scene because of its length, therefore one must make it ripple with different dimensions and preserve its humour—this is largely the responsibility of the actor playing Cominius.

Coriolanus enters, fixing his sling and dressing himself.

Titus Lartius's exit cannot occur after the forgetting of the name of Coriolanus's Volscian host, or all the juice will go out of the scene.
Wait until the two armies break for sudden exhaustion to hit with the forgetting of the name.
The response in Cominius must be very supportive—"it doesn't matter, you'll remember it," as he coaxes him to his tent.

I.10

Aufidius enters as last we saw him, naked and trailing his sword and shield.
The ultimate image of impotence and the rage that arises from this complete frustration.

14/11/84

First Run Through at 2:00

Director's Preparatory Remarks

The run will not be followed on text—it is better at this point to live it than just to repeat lines.

The object is to act the play, live it and do it—improvise, react verbally and physically—be free, not set and bound and dutiful, but find new inspiration to act on the last ten days of rehearsal so that the play is yours and not for dry academics.

The danger is that one must be classically correct, but it also needs energy coming from creativity and humanity so that it will not be deadly dull.
Tension between form and freedom of the individual—need freedom.

Shakespeare must be like a well cut film in the articulations between scenes—he wrote for open air theatres where actors possessed the space and lived it, then left the stage for others to transform that space.
Thus it is better to enter earlier than necessary for this run.

1.1: The plebs no longer stand on the risers but within the circle.

1.3: The scene between Volumnia and Virgilia has lost some of its sense of intimacy—lost the business of Volumnia's embracing her daughter-in-law at the preposterousness of "At Grecian sword contemning."

1.4: The Volscians beat back the Romans with war cries and banners.
Sound of metal clashing in the background during Coriolanus's speech.
The soldiers run singly and in pairs to hide in the trenches.

1.5: Edit the cart in the scavenger scene.
Instead props are scattered about the stage.

2.1: Some problems with cues in the triumph scene.
The rhythmic handclapping twice came in too soon.

2.2: Lost the sense of Cominius desperately patching up a desperate situation in the senate scene.

5.6: Aufidius turns over the body of his dead rival to stare at his face, thus motivating "My rage is gone . . ."

Director's Concluding Remarks

The level of creativity and clarity of presentation were very strong.

This play is the most difficult from the point of view of learning and holding the text—the major problem now lies in the time limit—there are only six days more work left—must work quickly and do homework to make the show tight.
  The first part should be 1:45 and the second one hour, whereas it now stands at two hours and 1:08.

The citizens are beginning to operate, but the military still needs proper presentation, posture etc., but trust is developing within the group.

15/11/84

11:00–1:00

3.2

Edit the day-bed for Coriolanus to lie on—the nobles remain grouped left, yet listening—Coriolanus is very aware of them as he paces back and forth.

Cut from "I would dissemble with my nature" to "in honour."

"You must return and mend it"—tends to settle a bit and lose the situation.
  Need to preserve the urgency.

"There's no remedy"—cue for the nobles to back off.
  Coriolanus sees this, feels isolated and turns to face his advisor.
  The half-line cues in this scene keep the energy going and must be picked up immediately or the dynamic is lost.

Coriolanus's relationship with his mother at the end of the scene has stretched and stretched and stretched, and now has finally snapped.
  Thus when he turns his back on Rome in the next scene, he largely turns his back on something in this very room.
  The strong tension between the two needs to be even greater.

The senators are basically telling him that he must go tell lies.
  Coriolanus: "I cannot do so—even to the gods."
  Volumnia: "But they're not lies, darling"—makes it all right.
  Menenius: Urgency, rushing his lines—"You've got to do it or it's civil war."

Volumnia: Calmness and maternal reasoning—immediate differentiation from Menenius, as their tempos are so different.

At the start Coriolanus now meets Volumnia with the nobles at his shoulder—more visually grouped with them, and edits the kiss.
More anger and boasting on his entrance—makes more sense.
"What must I do? . . . Well, what then? what then?"—at first Coriolanus comes on strong, then appears to mellow and is all smiles, so that they are lulled into a false security—then crushes it on "I cannot do it to the gods."
All seems to be going well, then a sudden explosion.
"yet will I still/Be thus to them"—draws his sword and gestures with it—he and the chief noble touch swords, then he sheathes it again at Volumnia's entrance.
"you may salve so"—the point is still crucially dangerous—it will not make up for everything but may gain back some lost ground.

The scene must be intense with anxiety for the senators, even if Volumnia is making it milder and more motherly because she knows him better and now to manage him.
Underneath it is still life and death.
Many approaches are taken—it is not a unified, concerted attack.
"I am in this/Your wife, your son, these senators, the nobles"—Volumnia is very intimate.
Menenius interrupts to get on with it, an approach that Coriolanus turns away from, and Volumnia must get back to where she was before the interruption.
Coriolanus takes her hand in a foreshadowing of the final gesture.
The senators are all smiles—"Why don't you be more like your mother"—and Coriolanus is desperate because he does not want to be like her in this.

To get to the necessary emotional level, McKellen improvises and articulates his character's internal response to each line said to him in a low whisper.

Though Menenius and Volumnia are in cahoots, their approaches are different and Menenius is content that it should be so.

Everyone in the scene is present at a nursery lesson in which the greatest fighter of the age is being scolded by his mother—very embarrassing as well as ironically wonderful.
Menenius—pardons "free/As words to little purpose"—very jovial tone as he makes his little joke.

Cominius enters with a terrifying and completely new piece of information: "All's in anger!"

In his first acceptance speech Coriolanus is playing with his advisors, therefore there must be ups and downs in the response of the others on stage.

Menenius has gone out and stopped the revolution and the lynch mob by convincing the tribunes to go by due process of the law, which can only come about if Coriolanus goes back—otherwise all is in broil again.

Coriolanus is convinced less by them than by his mother, but is stung by betrayal of him in this scene—the only thing to be done is to go and do what she says and then get out.
   Suddenly after always doing what he is told, Coriolanus comes to a sense of himself as an individual and acts for himself.
   Gives a deeper resonance to "mountebank their loves."
   Volumnia turns away from him and he seeks to remove the barrier between them with the commendation to his wife.
   She turns her back because she sees in Coriolanus's speech a horrible mockery of her "buss the stones" philosophy.
   He screams at her to look at him, then retracts and tries to be nice to her but is rejected—final blow with "Do your will."

Volumnia: "Rome will be destroyed, civilization will be destroyed, and we have a spoiled baby on our hands."

Cominius turns away embarrassed, he can't watch this, whereas Menenius is more accustomed to such scenes.

After his acquiescence, Coriolanus goes to exit before receiving a commendation from his mother, but cannot leave Volumnia feeling this way.
   He comes back and paces nervously around her, then kisses her at the end of his line in a gesture of reconciliation, which makes her rejection the more devastating for him.

4.5

Reinstating the turning about of the first servant by Coriolanus to give a sense of continuity when it is reported afterwards.
   Puts a hand on the top of his head, twirls him round and pushes him away—doesn't work—edit.

Coriolanus trips the second servant between "Are you so brave!" and "I'll have you talked with anon."
   The first servant becomes increasingly worried at Coriolanus's silence—he is obviously a foreigner who cannot (or worse—chooses not to) speak their language—very suspicious.
   The attack on the first servant is restored again, but with more care to its positioning.

It makes sense textually—he is not frightened at first, there is no serious threat—Coriolanus just looks like a down-and-out—but the fact remains that he should not be there.

2:00–5:00

1.3

All furniture has been edited from this scene as well.

Virgilia enters right, sits and sews, while Volumnia enters left and stands by her for a moment, then speaks to establish their relationship now that the decision has been made not to begin *in medias res* (i.e. they do not enter talking).

The image of mending the toy ball has also been cut.

Virgilia is stationary—she has decided on a course of action.

Volumnia watches her as though she had been like this for days, as though Virgilia has left every room she has come into.

Puts more emphasis on the words than on action.

Work on speed, intensity and intimacy—a genuine warmth between the two.

"His bloody brow" . . . "O Jupiter, no blood!"—as Volumnia goes to cross behind her, Virgilia clutches at her skirt and rests her head briefly against her mother-in-law's knee.

The simplicity of the set gives added impact to the words.

On the second run of the scene the action is moved from the sand to the foot of the stairs—the tighter area better suggests the interior and avoids the problem of the ladies in jewels and formal attire sitting in the sand.

To have the women standing would lose focus from the audience in the circle, as they must face down to glimpse the seated Virgilia.

Virgilia still enters first and sits down, Volumnia follows, watching, then as she bends down to set the wool on the ground sees the sadness on her face.

The scene is lit tight, with two corridors for the path beyond, yet there is a sightline problem with all this—the audience may still be able to see, but not comfortably—only their heads are visible if they are sitting, and all three women cannot stand simultaneously.

Tried with Volumnia bringing in cushions to sit on—this both adds a few inches and takes them back a bit.

"Grecian sword contemning" delivered as a classical, romantic passage.

"Beseech you, give me leave to retire myself" taken as the cue for Virgilia—but then the moment of grasping Volumnia's skirt is lost.

Tried again sitting to preserve that moment.

After Valeria's entrance the servant brings on two cushions for her as well.

The atmosphere is built up and then dispelled by the brilliant entrance of Valeria.
As the women leave, each picks up her cushions and carries them out.

Virgilia is not whining or game playing, she has just made a decision and refuses to change her mind—"thanks for the invitation, but I've made my pledge and will stick to it."
Play her strength rather than her sadness, but allow the sadness to peep through for variation.

Valeria journeys round the perimeter of the circle as she tells her story—but it doesn't really work.
"One on's father's moods"—a telling moment between the two women.
Valeria repeatedly begins her exit, then turns back with staccato movements to persuade Virgilia—doesn't really work.

4.2

The scene is brought further upstage because of sightlines.
The tribunes then play the scene as though they are trying to exit down rather than upstage to avoid unmotivated footwork.
Virgilia now enters leaning on Menenius.

Problem with the tribunes constantly trying to leave, as repetition can make the image farcical—results in bringing the action back downstage.
Volumnia sits—a source of fascination motivating their remaining onstage to watch and listen to her.

The tribunes state a desire for improvisational exercises in which they start at the backdrop and keep moving to exit downstage, so that Volumnia has to work to keep them onstage and keep their attention.
Never followed through.

5.4

Role reversal—Menenius is now very bitter and Sicinius milder.

There is a complete contrast between what actually happened and the way in which it is described—Menenius's account creates a myth rather than an accurate rendering of the real event—he paints a big picture.

"What's the news?"—as the messenger passes Sicinius's shoulder the tribune speaks.
The messenger goes back up to brush and adjust the carpet.
Image of Sicinius chasing him along the carpet to thrust his thanks upon him is quite nice—the news takes him completely by surprise.

A city in panic suddenly turns into a giant party, but Sicinius and Menenius have been "lurking" and talking, and the whole thing has been settled without them.

3.1

Building on the titanic rage with which the citizens must enter in their search for Coriolanus.

Menenius is stationary, but Sicinius and Brutus express their high adrenalin by pacing and attempting to herd the plebs to pluck Coriolanus from his house.

19/11/84

11:00–12:30

2.3

Coriolanus should begin with a hint of tartness in his treatment of the first two voices, which they pick up and comment on.

This mockery should build to the point of explosion at the end of the scene.

The citizens need to assume a choric delivery and become a group when the tribunes come in, but here still function as individuals uncertain of the situation, each ignorant of Coriolanus's treatment of the others.

Their proclamation of his consulship must be celebratory.

Each citizen thinks that the others have seen his wounds and therefore accord him their voices wholeheartedly.

Then when the tribunes pose the question of who has actually seen the wounds, there is a mounting crescendo of 'I thought you saw them.' 'No, I thought you saw them.'—'Do you mean to say nobody saw them? Then why the fuck did you vote him consul?'

The "great toe" watches the whole procedure from above in the scaffolding right and sees the citizens make downright asses of themselves.

The payoff is that he is able to say from direct knowledge that "He flouted us downright."

"He's not confirm'd: we may deny him yet"—given added significance by the half-line pause.

At the start of the scene Coriolanus is their hero—the second citizen sets up their enthusiastic reception of him.

The gates open to reveal Coriolanus with Menenius—signals that we will witness his first request for voices, and the tableau with Menenius indicates that he just comes from being schooled in the proper mode of behaviour.

"Here he comes, and in the gown of humility"—all crane eagerly to watch his approach before they exit.

Coriolanus exchanges ironic by-play with the "great toe" on "Kindly, sir" and "There's in all two worthy voices begged," which are both directed above.

Coriolanus walks around the stool before mounting it, as though to put off the indignity until the last possible moment.

He seems, however, too meek in his final request—loses the ironic resonance in his obsessive repetition of the word "voices."

5:00–6:00

4.2

The downstage positioning of the tribunes puts them at a disadvantage.

Handle the comic repetition of their exit by having them change their direction from downstage centre to down left.

20/11/84

10:30–1:00

1.6

Rehearsal of the acrobatic sequence on "Make you a sword of me!"
Practice for ease of movement.
Change from a jump up onto his shoulders, as it is too awkward.
Walk up on a third soldier's back, using the flag for balance.
The image of Coriolanus aloft is extremely strong, therefore he will deliver the full speech from this position, waving the flag and delivering the lines to a fixed point in the audience, as though it represented his full army.
Throws the flag down, then dismounts—the soldiers stand ready with his sword and shield, so that he can ram them on his arms in another strong image.

3.1

"Seize him, aediles!"—horrific moment—should be a gesture everyone sees—leading to a startling resistance which must be forceful without being violent.

Coriolanus throws one aedile into the other, knocking over their staffs and clearing the area stage left—similar moment to the serving man scene.

Decision to choreograph the crowd for the riot and threatened civil war.

5.6

"Stain all your edges on me"—Coriolanus bares his breast.

For the actual murder the rapidity of the blows makes his death completely unheroic.
First a stone palmed to his head stuns Coriolanus.
He is then cut across the stomach, the back (at waist height) and the back of the throat.
Changed to stomach, turn to the left, slash through the side, turn back forward, slit the back of the throat.
No romantic, idealized gestures, just wham and he's dead.
The spinal column is cut, his head falls forward and he collapses like a puppet.
There is no "noble corse" after this execution, but a bloody trunk after chopping up the meat.
No drawing of the sword—move right into the slashing.
Edit the stone and change the timing for the beginning of the assassination.
The cutting of the throat is still not working—change to a slash across the stomach—no, a stab into the stomach.
Still not nasty enough—needs more hatred and ugliness.

21/11/84

1:00–1:45

2.1

The only thing in Volumnia's initial speech which Coriolanus takes offence to is being addressed as "Coriolanus."

His greeting to the Roman ladies is public yet tactful.

His greeting to Menenius indicates that he is on home ground again, yet a sense of uneasiness recurs with the oscillation among the senators.

The scene ends on a strong note of welcome—the occasion is public and joyful after he sees his mother and wife etc.
Exasperation at the end of a long journey.

Then the public welcome becomes endurable as it is transformed into a private event.
Puts an end to the first movement with "Pray now, no more."

Transition on "And live you yet?"—the crowd has remained still until now—at this point they move to congratulate him, and Volumnia moves about as stage-manager.
"You are three/That Rome should dote on"—they stand centre.
"Menenius, ever, ever"—tight pause covered by Cominius's gesture to restart the proceedings.

The incident with the tribunes sparks Volumnia's introduction of the subject of the consulship—her lines are public, though Coriolanus attempts to make them private.

When he first greets Volumnia, Coriolanus kneels as though to stop the tickertape parade and "Nay, my good soldier, up" is Volumnia's irritated attempt to get him moving again.

1.8

No vocalizations in the first part of the fight—gear change comes with the first knock-down—people who know what they are doing don't need to make sounds to frighten their opponents.

On the large moves after the knock-down the actors can make sounds reflecting the increasing drain on their energy.
Vocalization of breathing to gear up their courage and reflect tiredness.

2.3

Problem with the drive of the scene—winds down midway through the tribunes' explanation.
After "He's not confirm'd: we may deny him yet."
The solution is that this statement is only a possibility, not a certainty.
The mob has let them down before, therefore the tribunes must fight to convince an ambivalent multitude and put across an urgent sense of danger.

More contrast needed between coming on pleased with themselves to growing doubt and angry revolt—develop the holiday/festival mood as they prepare to give their voices.

Question of how Coriolanus behaves when begging their voices—he cannot be angry or the citizens would react against him, but he must be peremptory to awaken their doubts.

Coriolanus enters and walks about in psychological preparation to mount the stool.

"You'll mar all"—Coriolanus kicks off his shoes and puts on his hat before Menenius completes the line.

"adieu!"—turns his back on the plebeians.

When the second brace enter, Coriolanus turns his back again, so that he now faces front—more sense that the action is anathema to him.

His soliloquy is a sudden explosion and release of anger, then in a perverse way he decides that if he must do it, he will do it well.

Thus when they enter expecting sarcasm, they meet with nice treatment.

He exposes how easy it is to be democratic.

The second lot feel that something is clearly amiss, the first experience a niggling doubt, and the third an unexpected friendliness.

In the second brace the woman does not really understand the irony in his speech—she is confused by his language—Coriolanus takes off his hat and bows, and she reacts to his physical signal.

Thus we establish a much more divided populace when the tribunes get to them.

Problem with running into a dead end with the "great toe" perched aloft.

After the initial acknowledgement there is nowhere to go with it.

The rhythm already established is that of people coming in, playing a scene, and leaving, so perhaps it would not be disruptive if he came down.

This time Coriolanus plays the scene as though he cannot place where the voice is coming from—he just has the sense that he has been overheard and is therefore much angrier with the second brace.

On his soliloquy Coriolanus now comes down off the podium and walks right downstage to address the audience—explosion, then the decision to return when "moe voices" enter.

Deliberately walks up to the stool.

Each time he comes to a new phrase or repetition of the word "voices," he addresses it to an individual citizen and shakes his or her hand—completely disarms them.

"Indeed I would be consul"—mounts the podium again, hat in hand.

On his exit he tosses the hat over his shoulder.

At the opening of the scene, the citizen sitting on the stool takes a pebble out of his shoe, then remains seated until the "blockhead" joke.

Coriolanus puts on his hat on a signal from Menenius.

Edits turning his back on the citizens.

"And 'twere to give again"—signal for the descent of the great toe.

Coriolanus speaks so quickly to the second brace that there is no way they could follow it.

This time he addresses the woman last instead of first, therefore their staging is inverted from left to right—addresses battle lines to the man. On the last "your voices!" Coriolanus stretches to shake hands with a citizen who stands behind the rest—they enthusiastically proclaim him consul and applaud rhythmically as they go out.

After they have gone and the sound has died down he ironically dismisses their "Worthy voices!"

3.1

Timing worked out for the organized chaos of the riot scene—who will scream what and where everyone should run.

The women scream "Patricians," the patricians scream "Tribunes," the aediles cry "Brutus," and Brutus cries "Coriolanus."

All shout for peace to be heard.

The climactic moment occurs when Menenius falls to the ground and delivers his lines in confusion.

22/11/84

10:30–2:00

First Run in the Theatre with an Audience

Some confusion in the opening—the audience was not clear on when to sit down again—some went back to the stands, some came down again.

Massive crowd on stage—inseparable from the actors in the opening sequence, but the sightlines were somewhat chaotic.

On Coriolanus's first entrance, the first row can only see his head.

The senators sitting on the stands in 1.2 are almost indistinguishable from the people.

Image of Virgilia and Volumnia both sewing on the same shirt.

Valeria edits the awkward journey round the stage on the butterfly story. She now stands right and physicalizes the tale through gesture and voice without travelling at all.

Awkward transitions between scenes—especially between domestic and military.

Edit Coriolanus making the full speech atop the soldier's shoulders.

Cut once again to "Make you a sword of me!"

Trenches created by the soldiers coming down to the lip of the stage and crouching near the audience.

Awkward business with the ladder when called for and then being removed without being used.

All sorts of character, text and movement problems surfacing—trouble with the fight.

In "The town is ta'en" Aufidius loses the sense of total exhaustion and plays the scene only for anger once again.

In Cominius's speech in praise of Coriolanus he has lost the sense of having to desperately cover up and save the situation.
    Therefore the scene has also lost some sense of dramatic tension.

In the voices scene it is really difficult to believe that Coriolanus could bring himself to kiss the peasant woman.

The tribunes convey a mixture of elation and concern, as they prevent Coriolanus from proceeding to the market-place.

The newly-blocked riot sequence is still muddy—the audience does not know what to do and is terrified.
    Menenius forgot to fall to the ground.
    There are large gaps left on stage.
    "You common cry of curs" is still not cracked yet.

3:00–4:30

The second half with the audience is much improved, largely due to the putting down of the house lights—energy is much more focused on stage.

The tribunes make more use of speaking to the people in the stands.

The audience is actively involved and listening—when Coriolanus draws his sword and runs toward the stands one woman sat down terrified and covered her face with her hands.
    The crowd participation is, however, largely cut from 3.1—they are no longer brought right down into the circle.

Two brilliant moments emerged:
    i) Volumnia's triumph: even without the proper sound and lighting it is an extremely moving moment, as all form a circle with her in the centre—she spreads her arms wide, fighting back her emotion, and turns to receive the crowd's adoration.
    ii) The persuasion: Volumnia walks right up to Coriolanus to deliver her

final lines, turns and begins to walk away when Coriolanus silently grabs
her hand to pull her back.
Volumnia, still turned away, straightens her back and the expression on
her face shows her knowledge that she has triumphed.
Pause—she turns and they look at each other, then he finally gives his
line.
The moment is absolutely electric.

The ending was scotched, however, as Aufidius had trouble finding the
sense of his lines and gave up trying to inflect them properly—he also
didn't stand in triumph over the body of Coriolanus.

The decision was made to cancel the first previews, turning Friday night
into a public dress rehearsal and delaying press night until December 15,
so that the show, which is extremely promising but hopelessly behind
schedule, will not suffer from the delay due to Peter Hall's illness.

Some cast desperation surfacing, particularly among Aufidius and Coriolanus, who still voice violent disagreement over the use of the crowds on
stage.

Very productive rehearsal because of the feedback from the first audience
on stage.

26/11/84

2:00–6:00

Introduction of the sound cues.
    An extremely slow going process to get the timing right—particularly in
    the intricate changes of the first act.
    Worked to the end of Act II.

7:00–11:00

TECHNICAL REHEARSAL

Largely cue to cue to save time, but again the process is extremely slow.
    Finished only to the end of Act 1.
    Lighting designed and sound added.

Some moments are wonderful—for example, the sound of metallic reverberation superimposed over the single combat sequence.

Idea to have Virgilia onstage during the fight, as though she is seeing it all in her mind—added strength and presence, but is it really appropriate? She is seated in the stands right with her sewing.

The sightlines require that the ladies are put further upstage for the sewing scene—they sit on the sand, Volumnia on cushions, centre right.

One entrance which has never before been run with the set is Menenius's initial appearance to quiet the citizens—he comes through a small door within the left gate, and so appears to slip in rather than to enter imposingly through Rome gates.
Therefore lose some sense of his stature and bravery.

The metallic brass and syncopated rhythms of the musical score are wonderful.

The major problems of this run of Act I were that the gates were not operating to speed—Rome gates are manual and therefore fine, but the Volsce doors refused to move quickly, therefore entrances and exits could not be timed to speed.

27/11/84

11:00–6:00

TECHNICAL REHEARSAL

Things moved along much swifter today because of less complicated changes in the second half and the fact that the doors were working to speed.
Because of this efficiency, spirits were generally much improved.

7:00–10:45

SECOND TECH

Returning to the beginning of the play to run through the action slowly with full lighting and sound, and for directorial changes and fine tuning.

1.1: Brilliant entrance by McKellen in a white suit, white coat and sunglasses.
Made sense of Coriolanus as a Renaissance satirist (but is this true to text?).
Gives grounding for the ironic humour in his speeches.
Costume emendation noted and accepted.
Decision to take the metal plating off the military costumes and dis-

tinguish Coriolanus and Aufidius by a shiny band around the collar—
great improvement.
Though the audience watches the private interchange between Coriolanus and Menenius, it must be inaudible to the plebeians—therefore
they face upstage as though talking amongst themselves and not listening.

1.3: Decision made to move Volumnia from Virgilia's left to sitting on
cushions right, slightly right of centre, in the midst of the sandpit.
She delivers her speech about Martius from this seated position as well.
When Valeria enters, Virgilia stands until "A crack, madam" to dis-
tinguish herself from the others—by now Valeria is kneeling.
Virgilia then stands again only on her final refusal to join the two
women—as Valeria exits left she takes her position in the stands right—
a spot lights her simultaneously with the fighting.

1.4: Decision to have Coriolanus's first entrance come suddenly from the
scaffolding above—spot to hit him on "Yonder comes news."
The soldier replies from the back of the audience to give some sense of
distance.
Coriolanus then climbs down to speak with Titus Lartius.
The rest of the rehearsal is spent timing the battle with the lights,
smoke, and the movement of the doors.

28/11/84

11:00–10:45

SECOND TECH

1.4: Beginning again from the battle sequence.
Decision to have a less mechanically timed attack once Coriolanus has
delivered his final lines, in favour of having the army standing with
poised swords followed by a chaotic sudden charge, as the two armies
come together from either side.
Then a general rout—the fliers do not enter the gates at all, but stand in
the shadows of the door and run in pairs back to the Roman trenches, as
Coriolanus flourishes his banner.
The lighting and music make Corioli walls enticing to the soldier before
the gates shut him in—decision to have him go unrecognized by his men
when the gates reopen until the moment when he waves the tattered
flag.
Slow motion opening of the gates to give an added sense of mysticism.

1.5: Coriolanus and Titus Lartius climb to the top of the gates and

ceremoniously replace the Volscian flag with their Roman standard.
The Volscian banner is then used as a spear to throw down at the looters.
One looter then picks it up, while another drops Coriolanus's shield.
Coriolanus climbs down the side of the wall, grabs his shield and runs off to meet Cominius.

1.6: The scene with Cominius is entirely transposed—the messenger and Coriolanus both enter left instead of right.
This leads to one major complication: the emblematic embrace of the two generals is now awkward, as the shield is on the wrong side of Coriolanus's body in terms of visibility—hence he must make one entire lap of the perimeter instead of the present half lap—the result seems a bit contrived.
Work on the sense of shame, as Cominius has left the field before becoming victor of it.
Work on "Make you a sword of me!"—Coriolanus is now picked up by two soldiers after he drops his arms, and is put on the back of a third man.
He puts up his fist for the first cry of "Martius," then as the soldiers pick up the refrain the standard bearer waves the red flag in front to mask the moment when Coriolanus mounts the other's shoulders.
After he dismounts, Coriolanus picks up his arms again and exits to find Aufidius.
Before he gets on the soldier's shoulders, he removes his shirt on "this painting/Wherein you see me smear'd," so that he is already half stripped when he meets his enemy.

1.8: Stripping on stage is too awkward with the bootstraps, lacing, etc.—difficult to fit with the words.
Therefore decision to enter already stripped.

1.9: Decision to incorporate the emblem of Coriolanus bloody and wounded in the moment after the battle.
Puts a sling over his arm before the action begins, with Cominius moving forward.
Coriolanus now remains right, huddled in a blanket, exhausted and angered at the concept of hearing his actions "dieted/In praises sauc'd with lies."
Excellent use of the trumpets to punctuate each cry of "Martius."
The scene was played once with Coriolanus drinking throughout—but edited.
Coriolanus plays the forgetting of his host's name as arising from the fuss made to fulfill his one request, but it does not read that way.
Exits downing the bottle of wine—typical of him as the man in the white coat.

2.1: Coriolanus enters above—rhythmic handclapping punctuates his descent.

Takes off the laurel on "Pray now, no more"—gives it to Volumnia, who crowns him herself as she forces him to stand up—nice moment.

29/11/84

11:00–10:45

SECOND TECH

2.2: Two officers enter to lay the purple cushions along the lower level of the stands for the senators, but this time, as in 1.9, the blocking is reversed so that the tribunes are now seated right—to catch the attention of the first senator, Sicinius waves a document from his portfolio.

Gesture of distancing himself, as Sicinius throws his cushion to the ground and lounges back in his seat.

After their exit the officers clear away the cushions and stool, as the scene merges with that of the voices.

2.3: Timing the entrances and exits of the citizens so that they are not bumping into each other.

The first citizen exits between the first and second braces. Menenius and the tribunes enter through the audience left. The third citizen then carries off the stool, shoes, etc.

3.1: Timing the entrance through the main doors.

All enter together and are stopped by the tribunes who return down the centre aisle.

Constant troubles with the doors.

Timing the elaborate riot scene to keep it from being muddy—also vocal orchestration for clarity.

3.2: Volumnia does not come through the inner door but through the main gate, which opens fully to let her pass. She enters simultaneously with Coriolanus and the nobles, so that she witnesses their interchange without herself being seen.

Timing the false exits so that they do not end up too far upstage too soon.

3.3: Went quicker as there was nothing to time with the doors.

The action is played out with a dual focus on Coriolanus above right and the tribunes above left.

Coriolanus comes down only on "You common cry of curs" and delivers "There is a world elsewhere" offstage after his exit.

Timing the citizens' exit and getting the audience back in their places for the intimate scene to follow—avoid a traffic jam in the wings.
Sudden dropping of tone after the high pitched excitement of the lynch mob—followed by the exultation of a people unanimous in their desire to banish their enemy from the city.

4.2: Timing the exit so that Volumnia and Virgilia are ready to reenter.
Only Menenius goes to the top of the stairs with Coriolanus and Cominius, then jogs back down to meet the ladies.
Virgilia no longer stands at the foot of the stairs for this scene, but up centre crying silently and expressing her grief through physical contortions.
Throws herself in the sand at the tribunes, then hugs Volumnia's knees before she is raised to exit.

4.4: Timing Coriolanus's speech before Antium—goes through the door right and reenters immediately left—as the second door opens we hear sounds from the banquet—sound moves from the right to the left speaker, so that we have the impression of entering Aufidius's house.
One servant drums a platter, a second drinks, while the third tells the story.

30/11/84

11:00–5:15

SECOND TECH

4:5: Work on the comedy between the servants—when Coriolanus enters he pushes his hand into the first servant's face, trips the second and tweaks the ear of the third.
The third servant tells the first to fetch his master, then grabs the second so that he will not be left alone with the threatening stranger.
Lights from the vomitorium right establish the convention of the cellar where the servants call for Cotus.
Nice build-up to the disclosure of the name.
Change of costume for Coriolanus to a red sweatshirt and jeans.
Removal of the cloak on the final revelation.
Aufidius embraces him from behind—more sexual in its overtones.

4.6: Cut the woman and child picnicking behind the tribunes.
Sicinius enters in a sweater and sunglasses, as though the sun is smiling now that Coriolanus is no longer a threat.
Menenius enters wearing a panama hat and casual attire.
Cut the stupid caps on the aediles who bring the news.

5.1: The crowd stands back worried, then moves in to help convince
Menenius—silent pleading as he shows signs of melting.
Same process repeats itself after his exit, as they move in on Cominius at
the revelation that the Roman ladies will try to intercede on Rome's
behalf.

5.2: Increase the sense of threat.
The guards thrust forward their pikes as they cannot believe he thinks to
push past, then prod him back each time he tries to move forward.
Finally after "Has he dined" they put down their pikes as they cannot
believe what they are hearing, then threaten him again before Cor-
iolanus enters.
Then they hasten to stand at attention on opposite sides of the circle.
The guards cruelly taunt Menenius as they move in to frame him.
The false exit of Coriolanus and Aufidius at this point is indicated by a
tableau of their backs as they stand frozen facing the gates.

5.6: Briefly run through with quieter guns due to GLC regulations.
Aufidius crouches on the ledge above wearing his black coat.
On "To use my lawful sword," Coriolanus goes to rush and kill him with
his sword, but three assassins from above (on either side of the stalls
and on the ledge left of centre) betray the uselessness of such action as
they shoot him in cold blood.
Four soldiers pick up the body and circle the stage to present the
emblem to the audience and exit through the central doors which close.
The citizens exit slowly on either side.

5.3: Repetition of the scene now with the boy playing Young Martius.
Find a way to cue him to give his line.
On the blessing his father puts him on his shoulders and he repeats the
fist salute to reinforce the sense of Nature's cyclical pattern.
Decision to explore in rehearsal the gesture of Coriolanus presenting his
son to Aufidius before returning him to his wife to care for (adopted in
performance).
Final timing of catching Volumnia's hand.
"Nay, behold's" motivated by seeing the child kneel—
Volumnia turns around to see why Virgilia is not following her, then
delivers the line.

7:15–11:00

FIRST DRESS REHEARSAL—OPEN TO THE PUBLIC (stage seat)

The director made the announcement that the show will be played as a
rehearsal rather than a performance, as the actors are not yet thoroughly
acquainted with the set.

1.1: The audience is invited down to mill about on the sand—organized as a real demonstration with picketers, spray painting "Corn at our own price" on Rome gates, and distributing a list of demands.
The stage audience feels in the thick of things—told the story of the belly with immediacy, and one was equally startled by Coriolanus's first dramatic entrance.

1.3: Problems with bolts backstage led to distracting noises during the quiet domestic scene.

1.4: The scaffolding was put up in the wrong position, with the result that Coriolanus had difficulty in descending from his perch, and the first citizen injured his ankle in the voices scene (2.3).
The battle is stagy from the point of view of the stage audience, as it is close enough to see the mechanics of the blocking, and the actors are not yet comfortable enough with it to do it at speed.
Trouble with the doors, so that Coriolanus had to double back and reopen them when he appears as a bloody emblem beckoning his soldiers to enter.

1.5: The Volscian flag broke during the ceremony of exchange, therefore McKellen stopped the performance to give the stage manager a note on it—good as it reminded the audience that this was a rehearsal and not a real performance.

1.8: Quite gripping, especially in the second half, but Coriolanus dried once and so had to backtrack before going on.

1.9: Coriolanus pours wine over his head as well as drinking it at the end of the scene—a bit over the top.

2.1: Virgilia no longer stands in the middle of the stairs, isolated, as she waits for her husband's return.
This time Coriolanus did not remove the laurels to present to Volumnia, and "Oh!" in response to "your mother" was stagy and so provoked laughter.

2.2: Coriolanus omitted the business of knocking over the stool—made no difference to the audience, but it adds a nice sense of tension when Menenius must move to right it and Cominius deliver his oration while standing beside it.

2.3: Ironic humour really beginning to emerge.
Comedy in unlooked for places.

3.1: Audience was not brought down to the very perimeter of the circle, therefore there was not the same sense of immediate danger when Coriolanus drew his sword.

Real sense of elation on "I could beat forty of them."

3.3: Developing the irony of Coriolanus's response to the scene, and the tenuous control which he is struggling to maintain—ironic humour on " 'tis true, I ought so."

From the point of view of the audience on stage this dialogue between the tribunes and Coriolanus becomes something of a tennis match as they vie for focus.

"You common cry of curs"—picking out individual faces in the crowd to address each line—chilling as the insult becomes personal, the more so as it is said in a tone of ironic knowledge—cool and detached, not in the heat of anger (but is this true to the character even if it is theatrically effective?).

Coriolanus walks offstage before the delivery of "There is a world elsewhere!" which echoes on after his absence.

The audience at first took this to be the interval, as the next scene was not begun soon enough—momentary confusion.

INTERVAL

4.5: Aufidius's scenes are all off tonight, especially in the second half—there is almost no attempt to make any kind of emotional connection with the role.

"thy name" passages quite empty.

5.2: Menenius's meeting with the two guards was marred by his forgetting the lines.

5.3: The child echoing the fascist fist on his father's shoulders is quite effective.

Volumnia is, however, rather self-indulgent in rhetoric and gesture.

The catching of the hand on "O mother, mother" worked wonderfully. The second "Aufidius?" is delivered as a plea for confirmation—moving desperation.

5.5: Volumnia's triumph was very effective, though the lighting was too bright round the perimeter.

5.6: The gunshot was effective, as was the final image of carrying off the body, but the ending was marred by Aufidius's incompetent handling of the final speeches—he seemed to withdraw completely and not even make an attempt.

1/12/84

1:00–5:15

Director's Notes

Eclecticism—the play is about then and now, but it is specifically Elizabethan in verbal expression, speech, story-telling, textual clarity and image patterns.

The audience on stage is completely held but restless—therefore there cannot be any but completely earned pauses.

Need to lose another 15 minutes without cutting a line—it now runs 3:50.

The audience started watching a rehearsal and were sucked into the play—the first half held in the narrative with the clarity of story-telling, but the second half held less well as the action went out of it—it cannot be passive or lachrymose—it needs to be active, worried, full of tension.

The second half in rehearsal has been sparkier than the first, but with the first showing to an audience a reversal occurred.

1.1: Weave in and out of the crowd more.
The sound of gunfire over the speakers was too much like war rather than civil unrest.
Menenius was too isolated during the fable of the belly—the actors should not sit down to listen, as the stage audience will follow their example—it is enough if two plebeians sit down on the steps.

1.1/1.2: The first scene transmits the Roman problems—war, unrest, etc.—and the second gives them from the Volscian point of view.
A baton of command similar to that of Aufidius in scene 2 must be given Coriolanus in the first scene to make the parallel perfectly clear.

1.2: Too pausy last night.

1.3: The scene is true but slightly too private—this is a public play in a public space and therefore the intimacy needs a public quality to it.
Question of levels—slightly under volume.
The butterfly speech must be set up more—slight inaudibility.
With the first audiences the psychological response of the actors is always to play it slightly over or under volume.

1.4: Cut Virgilia in the battlefield—good.
The battle must be tighter—stage right is routed slower than stage left.

The exit for Coriolanus after "Make you a sword of me" must be immediate if he is to have enough time for the costume change.
Need a seal on the centre of the doors, as one can see people backstage.

2.1: "humorous patrician"—Menenius faces too much upstage—need to command the house.
"Give way there, and go on"—gesture with the staff to draw focus to the speaker.

2.2: The stool in the senate scene must be turned over when Coriolanus refuses to sit down.

2.3: "Bid them wash their faces/And keep their teeth clean"—deliver as one phrase for one big laugh rather than two small ones.
"the tribunes/Endue you with the people's voice"—cannot be hushed—big news.
The consul's gown must be used to wrap around Coriolanus—not an anonymous garment.
Therefore in the senate scene Coriolanus should only be given the gown of humility, and the consul's robe should be entrusted to the tribunes in exchange for the humble weeds.
Move the scaffolding slightly, as Coriolanus and the first citizen had difficulty of access.

3.1: The people were not brought down on "Help, ye citizens!"
—problem as the scene is already well underway, so there is no time to get the crowd to the edge of the circle—problem with large bags by the seats on stage.
Counterpointing on "Noble tribunes" and "Noble Menenius."

4.1: Counterpointing on "what is like me *formerly*" "that's *worthily*" to point out the irony of the situation.

1.9: The blood on Coriolanus runs in dried and caked layers—underneath he really is a "thing of blood"—it is the blood of others which he is covered in, whereas Aufidius has fresh blood streaming from his own wounds—imbalance visually pointed out.

4.6: Menenius must edit the hat taken off to the public on his entrance.
"You have made fair work!"—the staging went haywire.

5.3: The entrance of Aufidius and the soldiers feels arbitrary—need a clearer sense of purpose.

5.5: Need applause on Volumnia's triumphal exit.

5.6: Applause for Coriolanus by the Volscian senate.

Wonderful cry before "Measureless liar."
Need to technically rehearse the timing of Aufidius standing on Coriolanus's body and "My rage is gone."

1.1: Tightening the blocking of the citizens and focusing to whom Menenius can play in the belly speech—citizens standing to either side.

1.5: Coriolanus appears above and waves the Roman flag—loose cheer finished by a brief trumpet call and followed immediately by the entrance of the looters.
Titus Lartius takes down the Volscian standard, which Coriolanus uses to throw down at the looters.
Big cheer as the looters enter.
Overlap of trumpet, then dialogue.

1.6: "Make you a sword of me!"—Coriolanus runs off while the other soldiers pick up his gear and follow.

2.2: Instead of handing the consul's robe to the tribunes, it is left on the purple stool.

FIRST PREVIEW (production seat)

The lighting board blew one hour before the performance.

Improved generally over the dress rehearsal—quicker pace—lost nine minutes on the first half and six minutes on the second, but individually lines were weaker.

Menenius lost half a scene and broke blocking—gave Brutus the consul's robes, then took them back as he remembered the rehearsal decision.

Coriolanus—"baby's voice virgins lull to sleep" and "as if a molehill should be bowed to by Olympus"—inversions from the text.

Some door and sound cues late.

The crowd involvement was effective and better organized, with the beginning of the play signalled by the distribution of the weapons.

On the fable of the belly there was more sense of listening to the story, with the occasional citizen seated on the steps.

The Volscian senate entered on time—no problem with the quick change.

The battle is more effective with Virgilia edited from the sidelines.

The scaffolding was fixed so that there was no problem for Coriolanus's descent.

The battle with the sound and smoke promises to be very effective, but individually is still camp.

Coriolanus appearing within the gates of Corioli is also effective with the doors functioning properly now (he wears a helmet during this sequence so that there will be no need to wash the stage blood from his hair between 1.9 and 2.1).

Yet, one soldier barely made it through the doors before they shut, provoking laughter from the audience.

When Coriolanus scaled down the walls to rejoin Cominius the descent was still awkward, as he is not yet accustomed to the set.

The single combat with Aufidius is quite good, though the latter is still hesitant about the sequence of the shield in the sand.

The emblem of Coriolanus bloodstained and tired, putting on the sling in the spotlight with the Roman army faintly illuminated stage right, is excellent.

No laugh now on forgetting the name of the Volscian host.

Coriolanus exits drinking as usual—no more pouring of wine over his head.

The triumph was extremely effective—the nuntio was placed back on top of Rome gates, instead of delivering his lines from in the slips as last night.

Coriolanus takes off the laurel wreath again—not on "Pray now, no more" as in rehearsal, but just before he presents it to Volumnia—she places it firmly over his brow on "Nay, my good soldier, up," then he gives it to Virgilia.

Coriolanus wraps his wife in his robes as he kisses her.

The senate scene was quite effective with the knocking over of the stool, but it rolled over twice, exposing its back to the audience—this needs to be upholstered as well.

Increasing irony in his response to the citizens in the voices scene—more anger toward the second brace preparing for the explosion on "Better it is to die."

Coriolanus is naked under the gown of humility—distracting if he keeps flashing the audience, as it provokes nervous titters.

Concentration broken in 3.1, as Menenius dried badly, necessitating a prompt from the SM, and leading to further fluffing of lines.

Volumnia is still depending too heavily on vocal technique in the first persuasion scene—no real communication is happening yet.

Wonderful irony on "Mildly!" now that the anger in the previous scene is developing.

The audience was this time brought down to the perimeter of the circle during 3.1—good involvement—when Coriolanus brandishes his sword there was an excellent sense of immediate physical danger.

Wonderful sense of ironic control at the beginning of the banishment scene, parallelling that of the voices sequence, so that even as Coriolanus humbles himself he mocks his accusers—one can almost see his knuckles turning white on " 'tis true, I ought so."

Irony is the keynote of the whole scene—at Sicinius's accusation Coriolanus explodes in a fit of violent laughter and motions with his hands, as though to say "give it to me, give it to me"—decision to come down before the "common cry of curs" speech—quiet sarcasm of delivery makes sense with this build-up.

The entrance in 4.1 comes hard on the heels of the banishment scene to prevent the audience thinking it the interval.

Again humour in the resolution to be stoic in the Hercules image and "smile."

Gesture to taste the salt of Menenius's tears on that line.

Her performance in 4.2 transmits the sense that Virgilia really has not yet cracked her role—she has not found the strength in or of silence.

Virgilia turns in circles and rushes to throw herself in the sand—it really does not work—looks arbitrary and mechanical—it is not how one feels the wife of Coriolanus would behave.

INTERVAL

Aufidius stresses the sexuality of the scene more in the embrace.

The servants in the sequence after Coriolanus's exit are generally weaker, however.

Again there is no real connection in Volumnia's second persuasion scene, whereas there is greater emotion than ever before from Coriolanus—he begins to melt as early as the sight of Virgilia's doves' eyes and must struggle to keep control.

Coriolanus tries to physically align himself with Aufidius by standing next to him as he says he will not give the only thing they have to ask.

The moment of capitulation was rendered stagy as Volumnia obviously put her hand for him to grasp.

"I dare be sworn you were"—less emotionally convincing than last night.

Volumnia's triumph was again extremely effective—more and more sense of personal triumph conflicting with personal grief—rhythmic handclapping good, but some of the cast still have trouble keeping to the rhythm.

McKellen was working more on the final image of Coriolanus as the "eagle in a dovecote" and therefore exaggerated more the arm movement—a bit over the top.

When shot, Coriolanus went down with a final raising of his arm in the fist salute.

Aufidius's response to the assassination was better—more coldly political, but he still hasn't cracked "My rage is gone."

Aufidius's barking of "Assist" was good, and the final emblem of presenting the corpse quite chilling.

3/12/84

12:00–5:15

1.3: Detailed work on individual speeches, e.g. the butterfly passage.
Volumnia cuts the cushions, as they make delivery of her lines uncomfortable.
The only gesture remaining in Volumnia's speech is on "brows bound with oak."

5.3: Aufidius and Coriolanus enter together, Coriolanus obviously in command, as it is he who is given the lines about taking Rome.
Emphasis on how *"plainly"* he has "borne this business."

They go to make a false exit when they hear the sound cue on "Pass."
Ladies' entrance retimed so that they are already mounting the stage on
"My wife comes foremost."
Reblocked so that Coriolanus is stage left on "doves' eyes."
Virgilia's curtsey does not come after the pause, but to catch his eye.
On "melt" Coriolanus crosses to his position stage right.
Coriolanus's monologue ends as though cut off by his wife's greeting,
then eye contact is caught again for Volumnia's bow.

5.5: The announcer for Volumnia's triumph is placed on top of Rome gates
instead of in the slips.
Cut the sound of cheers, as it is too naturalistic—keep only the trumpets.
Get the stage audience to applaud for her exit.

5.4: The dialogue between Menenius and Sicinius no longer takes place
sitting on the stairs up left, but standing in the circle left of centre.
Sicinius now delivers the scene as though slightly pissed—as though
Menenius and Sicinius have been out drinking together—opponents
brought together during a time of crisis.

5.5: The lighting has been fixed for Volumnia's triumph, so that the
perimeter is darkened and only the centre of the circle illuminated.

General Notes

1.1: "Caius Martius is chief enemy to the people" "We know't, we
know't"—sloppy.

1.9: On the choric cries of "Martius!" the soldiers should flock around
Coriolanus, and put their swords down only after "I will go wash," as
though waiting for a further reply.

2.3: No man saw Coriolanus's wounds—lost the moment of recognition—
the round of "No"s can go quicker until the climactic "no man saw
'em."
It is a "mutual realization," but chorically and in rhythm—the choral
rhythm must be amazed rather than tense.
Menenius exits with the gown of humility—he pauses at the steps to see
whether the tribunes are coming with him.

1.2: "Cominius, Martius your old enemy"—no pause—"Martius" is what
is important.

1.4: The wager and the news—need a pause for the news to sink in
because the physical distance between Coriolanus and the messenger is
so great—therefore pause before "So, the good horse is mine."

Coriolanus then gives a gesture to refrain the trumpeter from summoning the town.

1.6: "Who's yonder"—catch cue and tempo—"That does appear as he were flay'd."
Massive gear shift, then "thunder from a tabor" is taken out to the audience.
Remove the cheer after "holding Corioli in the name of Rome"—the reaction is so hard and specific that it detracts from the end of the speech.
Subsequent decision to keep the cheer and cut the "greyhound" passage.
Dislike the soldier's cross to wrap the blanket round Coriolanus's shoulders, therefore it is given to another soldier who enters stage left.

1.10: "hostages for Rome"—overwhelming bitterness.

2.1: "Not a drop of/allaying Tiber in't"—play with the line more.
"I cannot call you Lycurguses"—deliver as more of an insult.
Virgilia and Valeria must say "Nay, 'tis true" together—choric lines do not sound silly if they are beautifully done, but lose impact if done in a half-heartedly naturalistic fashion.
Not enough of a build to "Pow, wow," therefore the line doesn't work—Virgilia is too downbeat—she needs to express more joy.
Wounds—Menenius and Volumnia must cap each other and be very up for "Now it's twenty-seven."
The citizens must in general be more argumentative and coloured about Coriolanus.

2.2: "Speak, good Cominius"—cut the applause from the senators.
Coriolanus picks up the consul's robes and holds them in his arms before being told that he must ask for the people's voices, then swaps it with the tribunes for the gown of humility.

Go tonight for as much tightening as possible—it needs public playing and the eradication of what is unclear—cut all pauses not filled by action or strong movement.

To allow empty air to enter between words is totally inappropriate to this space and to the style of the play.

5.6: At his entrance the crowds rush to shake hands with and kiss Coriolanus—great contrast to Aufidius's reception into the city.
Volsces rush to march behind the banner—they flock to him and he likes it.
"Tear me to pieces"—Coriolanus moves to tear off his uniform and

therefore remove the very symbol of being a Volsce.

McKellen is in a quandary over how to act the final moments—Coriolanus has indeed sold all for a "twist of rotten silk," is sucking up to the nobles, sucking up to the people, and is in desperate agony to recapture that nobility *he had*—not has, but had.

He is at sea—nobody loves him, nobody cares for him—how to act it? Cut the fascist gesture at the assassination.

"Put up your swords"—the point at which Aufidius gets off the body with an extra little kick.

Chaos until "My rage is gone."

Aufidius must convey more sense of desperately trying to save the situation and cover up his treachery—the appeal to the senate and "My rage is gone" must be full of respect, as must be the orders for the funeral march.

5.3: "I holp to frame thee"—the ladies think all is going well—Coriolanus feels as though the world has turned completely upside down.

Coriolanus is still his mother's son—thus he kneels to Volumnia, kisses Virgilia, greets Valeria and blesses young Martius—he keeps melting and it takes a supreme effort to align himself with Aufidius.

Move young Martius kneeling from stage right to stage left, so that on "Are suitors to you" Virgilia can rise and align herself with the Roman contingent, and the ladies again become one unit.

Instead of giving the child back to Virgilia, Coriolanus puts him down left near Volumnia, and Virgilia crosses back to stand with them.

When Coriolanus sits down right, Aufidius crosses to stand behind his shoulder.

At the end of her speech Volumnia really has convinced Coriolanus that war is wrong—she really cuts his balls off.

"Nay, go not from us thus"—Volumnia crosses between Aufidius and Coriolanus so that she speaks to both about the reconcilement of the Volscians and the Romans.

Volumnia no longer holds out her grandson's hands in supplication as she prostrates herself in the sand due to the new blocking.

"This fellow had a Volscian to his mother;/His wife is in Corioli, and his child/Like him by chance"—each line elicits a groan as she hits home below the belt—transitional rehearsal stage as the actor vocalizes his internal emotion.

Virgilia has all this time been holding the child in her arms, and as her son kneels she stands behind him.

On the next run of the scene Volumnia crosses to Coriolanus on "This fellow had a Volscian to his mother," rather than "Yet give us our dispatch."

Aufidius embraces Coriolanus on "I dare be sworn you were"—seems an inappropriate gesture.

"I am glad thou hast set thy mercy and thy honour/At difference in thee"—less as commentary and more as the telling of a narrative fact. There should be no touching, kissing, holding of hands etc.—no elaborate farewell scene, only having a quiet little drink together offstage.

SECOND PREVIEW (production seat)

Problem with the Volscian doors—the left side did not shut on time, then remained ajar.

Better tension in Aufidius's first scene.

The domestic scene is improved with the editing of Volumnia's gestures—just simple sewing—fine without the cushions, seems less contrived.

This time Virgilia sat down again directly after Valeria's entrance—she was generally less weepy and more contentedly firm—much improved.

The gates were late in "clapping to" to shut Coriolanus in Corioli.

The blood was over the top in the fight scene and the execution of the single combat was a mess.

Aufidius was much better on "I would I were a Roman"—like a caged animal—he spat out "hostages for Rome" as though it were entirely antipathetic to his soul.

Menenius was playing more with the puns in his scene with the tribunes and exhibited much more joy and animation at the news of "Martius coming home."

Again humour in the mother wishing him wounded—much better momentum.

During the triumph Coriolanus did not remove the laurels but moved to kiss Volumnia's hands.

A bit sluggish in the general congratulations.

Lost momentum in the set-up for the senate scene.

Red tassel added to the consul's stool.

Kept the long embrace with Cominius when Coriolanus enters to hear the senate's decision which was added last night—a direct echo of their embrace on the battlefield in 1.6.

Coriolanus's fingering of the consul's gown when told that he must speak to the people is effective.

"Therefore, beseech you, I may be consul"—articulated syllable by syllable to the uncomprehending second brace, who have been entirely confused by the rapid delivery of the first part of the speech.

"Better it is to die"—starts off quietly, as on Friday night, then builds to climax.

Coriolanus kneels for "Indeed I would be consul" and waves to the plebeians as they go off—adds to the irony of "Worthy voices!" but doesn't seem completely in character.

Wonderful dynamic to Coriolanus's interrupted progress to the market-place—the anger is developing—the audience has the sense of what will trigger him off, yet there is great variety to his outbursts.

Volumnia is still stagy in her gestures during the first persuasion scene—physically it needs to be simplified, though vocally it is now more interesting.

On "harlot's spirit" Coriolanus physically writhes, as the concept of what he must do is anathema to his soul.

One really gets the sense tonight that Volumnia's chiding transforms this grown man into a ten year old boy.

Coriolanus does not listen to Cominius at first, as he is completely engaged and preoccupied with looking in the direction in which Volumnia has just exited.

Coriolanus develops the mockery in his initial mild aspect to the tribunes, provoking a big laugh from the audience on "plant love among's."

"Let them pronounce the steep Tarpeian death"—again Coriolanus is laid back and dares the tribunes on with ironic laughter as he has already decided to leave—with his arm movements he demonstrates to the audience how ridiculous it all is.

Kept last night's gesture of patting the child citizen's head as he exits.

Virgilia is still too violent in her expressions of grief before the tribunes.

The final emblem of the first half shows an old man and woman standing in the centre with a keening girl at their feet in the sand—all the starkness of an image from Greek tragedy.

INTERVAL

Coriolanus does not walk through the audience in his disguise but is revealed seated at the bottom of the stands stage left, wearing a trench coat and hat.

The naming sequence with Aufidius is greatly improved, although there can be further growth if the latter starts out with less accusation in his tone.

Aufidius really hisses "O Martius, Martius" and utters a prolonged sigh as he clips Coriolanus from behind while holding both his hands—more sexual—held the audience completely rapt in attention, so that the comic interlude of the servants comes as a blessed relief.

A smaller letter was given to Menenius in 5.2 to indicate its personal rather than political nature.

The moment of capitulation was the best it has ever been—long pause before "O mother, mother"—real sense of emotional connection.

Volumnia stands silently looking at her son as though not understanding his words when he says that he'll "not to Rome."

Coriolanus leans on her and pumps her arm rhythmically to her chest on "most mortal to him."

The second naming of "Aufidius" comes as a cry from the heart, a desperate appeal—meets with a cold tone on "I was mov'd withal," then the embrace comes from Coriolanus on "I dare be sworn you were" and Aufidius politically goes along with it.

Aufidius offers his arm to Volumnia after Coriolanus appeals to him to enter with them, then on "Could not have made this peace" Coriolanus puts up his arm in the fist salute (never repeated after this performance).

Menenius and Sicinius both enter drunk with a flask of brandy as a prop.

After Volumnia's triumphal exit, Sicinius drapes his gown around the injured Brutus.

The clutching of the heart on "Measureless liar" seems over the top, as McKellen has not yet found the truth of the scene.

Coriolanus tears off his clothes to reveal his scarred body in the loincloth which he wore in the fight with Aufidius—but he could not get his boots and pants off in time, so that the moment became ridiculous—good idea but needs fine tuning if it is going to work—"The man is noble" became deeply silly.

"My rage is gone" was not properly set up and so provoked snickers from the audience.

The pallbearers carry out the body still holding on to the sword.

The houselights are no longer brought up during the final exit—the theatre remains in darkness, piercing music, then silence after the doors shut— excellent conclusion.

4/12/84

12:00–5:15

2.1: Menenius's scene with the tribunes is bringing out greater clarity, as the actors are finding the natural rhythm of the language.
Menenius keeps standing in the middle of the circle and crosses to sit only on "humorous patrician."

4.5: On entering Aufidius's house Coriolanus opens the door, pauses to hold it there and hear the music, then reenters directly without a pause backstage.
Cut the lines with the third serving man about serving his master/ mistress, as the half joke does not quite work.
Cut the serving man episode at the end of the scene.

4.4: For the "goodly city" soliloquy, until the entrance of the Volscian citizen, Coriolanus stands stage left.
Light the doors and walls to give the sense of the building.
A spot reveals Coriolanus sitting in the stands left—the citizen enters walking along the upstage perimeter of the pavement.
The interchange brings Coriolanus to the gates of Aufidius's house— only this upper area of the stage is lit.
Coriolanus stands slightly off-centre—a diminutive figure against the hugeness of the door.

4.5: Aufidius comes down centre for "Martius," then shifts his weight and brings "Jupiter" out front, and moves in to Coriolanus to "twine" from above—the actual embrace comes on "clip."
A long look is exchanged between the two, then Aufidius helps him to his feet—not because he needs help, but because Aufidius doesn't want him to kneel at his feet anymore.
Help him up before "Mars" rather than on the line—stronger.
Move in to Coriolanus before the exit—"O come, go in."

4.6: Sicinius barks out "Martius" as though to say 'what has *he* got to do with it?'

New tonal movement—from complacency to doom.

Need complacency to make the transition to panic the more potent.

Image of the politicians and the baby—the first "Good e'en" is directed to the head of the little family, the second "Good e'en" is to the whole group including the infant.

More focus on Menenius on "We wish'd Coriolanus/Had lov'd you as we did"—the line is delivered for his benefit and is now spoken down centre instead of following the citizens to their point of exit.

5.6: Coriolanus shakes hands with the citizens—playing the popular part well.

On "Traitor!" Coriolanus does not yet stand up but pivots on his knees, so that he faces the audience.

On "Measureless liar" he writhes to his feet as though literally close to a heart attack.

Aufidius strips him of his title and status and honour—reduces the lone warrior to a mere boy—literally makes his heart break.

Coriolanus comes back to his old self to some degree and so boasts that he has invaded and destroyed their country—he tries to rid himself of the Volscian uniform and get back to the primitive warrior of Act I when real heroism was possible, but it is now impossible, as his heart is broken and he is totally disillusioned.

As the citizens individually accuse him of his war crimes they point their arms and move in—the human circle around Coriolanus tightens constantly.

Coriolanus runs to attack with his sword, but is shot down by the three conspirators—parallels Aufidius's escape in the battle.

Aufidius taunts him so he will draw the sword.

Here Coriolanus's silence between the accusation and the senators' defence is not due to his transfiction by Aufidius or by escaping into his own world, but stripping down and preparing for battle.

Decision for Aufidius to stand fully on the dead body, rather than to plant one foot on the corpse, which is stronger as it solves the balance problem—to an Elizabethan audience this would have been a horrifying and degrading image, but it means fuck all to a modern audience—it needs the added enormity of Aufidius's full weight.

Aufidius can use the Volscian banner to balance himself—the banner Coriolanus brought in and has been showing off.

"My rage is gone"—pause—"And I am struck with sorrow"—delivered behind the body centre with the banner in his hand—effective.

The sword is left in the sand.

The chaos at Coriolanus's death is achieved through movement rather than voice.

Add the mysterious wailing sound on the final exit.

General Notes

3.3: Get some of the audience to stand with their backs to the perimeter of the downstage circle—they will move out of the way as it develops anyway.

3.1: Menenius's "Could he not speak 'em fair" is to the audience and is very big.

3.3: The Tarpeian rock is the back top of the Olivier—localize the spot to give a graphic sense to the image, the feeling of the rock brooding over Rome like a hangman's gallows.
The "No"s in response to "He consul!" must be sharper and bolder.
Must seat the audience again as some get stranded.

3.1: When Coriolanus drives off the people with drawn sword, he should not wait so long before reentering for the second lot on "Down with him."

3.2: "Do your will"—Volumnia's cross is already started, turn, deliver the line, then exit.

5.5: Get the audience to clap during Volumnia's triumph.

Last night's performance was more assured than Saturday—comfortable but Mondayish.

Be proud and excited about what is going on, though it still needs refinement.

The piece is working on a political level, on a personal level, and on a dialectical level, and is having a great effect on the audience.

Still a problem in part 2—chase everything that is optimistic, courageous, quick, normal and active—choose that to add greater variety and do not only play doom.

What the production needs overall now is absolute confidence, arrogance and pride in what you are doing—this is what it is and the audience can like it or lump it.

The production is successful and controversial—people are either violently for or against it.

The triumph for Coriolanus in 2.1 will be played with tickertape and banners—gold metallic confetti will fall to his position on the steps and four red banners will be suspended from the flies—confetti tonight and the banners will be added tomorrow, as they have not yet been rehearsed to fly smoothly.

THIRD PREVIEW (box)

Problem with audience control—the stage audience went back to their seats at the beginning of the dialogue and had to be brought down again.

One audience member was so into it that he raised his arms and cheered with the crowd.

Coriolanus scrapped the sunglasses on his first entrance.

Increasing sarcasm in Coriolanus's repetition of the slogans coined by the citizens.

Timing was off on the entrance of the Volscian senators—not in unison—and the "Farewell"s were messy.

Domestic scene generally slow.

Virgilia is more cheerful again but vocally weaker, then lost it—pouting too much.

Valeria also lost energy so that her humour fell flat.

Doors late to reveal Martius in Corioli.

Coriolanus's blood no longer over the top in 1.6.

The flag dropped on "Make you a sword of me," almost hitting the audience.

Single combat: Last night Aufidius lost the last movement of the first sequence, then added it to the first move of the second sequence—this should have been Coriolanus's first move, and they ran to attack each other—very dangerous. The fight then ended in the wrong position to begin the third movement, so they repeated the second before proceeding, and the fight was ten moves too long. Tonight Coriolanus was disarmed within the first ten seconds—delay as he retrieved his sword—then in the second sequence his shield missed that of Aufidius, then when Aufidius went to attack him with his own shield he dropped it, and the fight ended early.

Aufidius's last scene in part I was worse than last night—more monotonal.

"I am attended at the cypress grove"—delivered with reference to his wounds, therefore the attendance is medical.

The transition between "Now it's twenty-seven" and "every gash was an enemy's grave" was botched.

Again Coriolanus did not present his laurels to Volumnia.

"Your hand, and yours"—Coriolanus holds out his hand to his mother first and wife second.

In the senate scene Coriolanus does not sit a second time but kicks the stool over immediately when in the midst of the movement.

The props for the senate scene are now cleared away during the tribunes' dialogue rather than after their exit.

During the voices scene Coriolanus enters barefoot, without his sandals, so that there is less to clear at the end.

Cut the syllable by syllable delivery of "Therefore, beseech you, I may be consul" to the second brace.

Explosion again on "Better it is to die"—the words seem to burst forth with greater intensity than last night.

Coriolanus did not kneel on "Indeed I would be consul" with the third brace—instead he stood on the stool again and took off his hat—better!

Loss of momentum at the opening of the market-place scene.

During the first persuasion scene Coriolanus kissed his mother's cheek on "Let go" and remained holding her hand until the entrance of the senators.

"Well, what then? what then?"—Coriolanus swings his sword back and forth like a pendulum, as though his attention were distracted, whereas it is keenly fixed on their words—taps his head with the sword on "unbarb'd sconce."

Return to the exaggerated gesture on "all the trades in Rome," then his final capitulation is due to intense tiredness—he just doesn't care anymore.

"Noble lady! / Come, go with us"—Menenius addressed the wrong person in asking Volumnia to accompany them to the market place.

Lost some of the biting anger and irony in the banishment scene, especially on "Say then: 'tis true, I ought so."

Explosion on "You!" (prate of service) and "Let them pronounce."

The irony of the banishment is all the more clear with the litter of the triumph still onstage.

Coriolanus adds applause to the laughter as Sicinius banishes him.

Some members of the audience were moved to join with the crowd in the cheers at Coriolanus's banishment.

Audience again thought it was the interval after the end of 3.3.

"Nay, I prithee woman"—said to Virgilia as though scolding a child, waving his finger in the air.

"I'll do well yet"—gave the fist salute.

"they/Stand in their ancient strength"—Sicinius writing a note for the aedile.

Virgilia is still over the top in this scene with her grief, and Volumnia with her rhetoric—Virgilia screams as she throws herself in the sand—doesn't work.

INTERVAL

Coriolanus outside Antium—five o'clock shadow added to the disguise.

The reworked version of his entering Aufidius's house works much better.

More self-laughter on "Appear not like a guest" and "I have deserv'd no better."

The servants are more arrogant in their initial treatment of him.

Coriolanus kneels in the sand for the first part of the encounter.

The servant scene works better in its shortened form, but still drags—the servants really haven't established their relationship with one another.

Sicinius cut the sunglasses from his entrance in 4.6.

Menenius and Cominius exit together, whereas last night Menenius forgot and left early.

"As if a man were author of himself"—new determination, truly struggling with himself—almost in tears after kissing his wife.

Holds Volumnia's hands as she bows to him and brings her to her feet again.

"Nay, behold's"—the direct result of Volumnia's turning from her exit to catch sight of young Martius kneeling of his own accord in an affecting tableau.

Virgilia, with her back to Volumnia, finally turns to see why she does not follow her out after "then I'll speak a little."

"most mortal to him"—again Coriolanus pumps his mother's arm as though pushing a sword into her breast.

Edit the embrace on "I dare be sworn you were"—less emotional, more run on.

Menenius is more angry with Sicinius in the following scene.

The aedile picks up the fainting Sicinius to make room for the carpet, and puts him down downstage centre near the messenger.

Less initial anger from Coriolanus on "Traitor!" and more amazement at being called "Martius."

"Measureless liar" delivered as he crumbles from the pain of his heart attack, then cries out at being called "boy of tears."

Again develops the physical emblem of the eagle.

"Boy!"—a collapse rather than a cry—he is almost falling down for the rest of the scene—as though remaining on his feet through a supreme act of will.

Coriolanus only strips to the waist before his futile attack—much better.

Aufidius in tears for "I am struck with sorrow," then suppresses them with deliberation as he issues his commands for the funeral—cold as ice.

5/12/84

12:00–5:15

3.1: Change the entrance so that Coriolanus, Cominius and Titus Lartius enter right—laughter and a false exit ll. 10–11, before the report on Aufidius.
Coriolanus swings round for "Spoke he of me?"
"I wish I had a cause to seek him there" delivered as they join the senate before the gates up centre—more emotional tone.
"Shall remain!"—the turning point of the scene.
Sicinius never answers their questions—to stop the procession is the tribunes' goal and not answering is their logical strategy, part of their ploy to get Coriolanus as angry as possible.
"tongues o'th'common mouth"—provokes a laugh from the senate.
Tighten up the movement of the phalanx.

2.1: Change to the proper red carpet and four banners suspended from the flies.
The scene falls apart as Menenius puts his foot in it—the audience does not understand his faux pas.
The whole scene halts on "crabtrees"—some find it silly, some funny, some offensive, and *all* interesting.
The three that Rome "should dote on" turn around after, rather than before the line to create the emblem.
Suddenly the triumph becomes a real patricians' party, making rude jokes about the tribunes, etc.
At the moment we are missing Volumnia's public announcement that he will be consul—all must respond to it.
NB. Criticism given concerning the production's condescension to the working classes as stupid and mindless, and the tribunes as needing justification for trying to represent the people.
The citizens must not be played comically—anyone is easily swayed unless speaking from deep political passion. Had not originally wanted to play the tribunes strongly, as they are not intended to be presented as villains, but now there is the danger of them coming off as tentative fools.

2.3: The gravity of the voices scene is going.
Coriolanus can play the scene for comedy, but not the citizens.
The crowd as a crowd behaves foolishly, but individuals are sympathetic.

1.1: At their initial entrance the actors must come in with anger, with hunger, and talk to the audience as the people they are during the play. Be as serious, as tense and as real as possible from the first moments of the play and not chat up the audience. Do not play the citizens as dolts but play up their innocence—make complete decisions about your characters, families, difficulties, etc., and DO NOT KNOW WHAT IS GOING TO HAPPEN.

4.6: The citizens are giving the tribunes too easy a time when faced with the holocaust.
If they are rooted and listening it works better than to act up a storm to indicate their reactions when given no lines—then it falls apart.
At the moment the plebeians are being judged as vacillating even before the action of the play begins.
The tribunes are now explaining what they are doing so much that they are losing the passion for doing it.

1.1: The initial embarrassment of the stage audience is working for, not against the actors, as during any riot there is a key group of movers and a large body of those who don't know why they are there or what is going on.
But the audience needs to be involved even more.

3.1: Timing the chaotic cries during the riot—add a tone of desperation.
The cues are not naturalistic—the actors must have confidence in the stylized presentation.
The action continues overtop of Menenius's speech.
Menenius appeals to Sicinius to quiet the mob, whereas he actually inflames them—"You are at point to lose your liberties."
"Coriolanus, patience!"—he dashes two plebeians to the ground.
"That is the way to lay the city flat"—Cominius now delivers this speech above right, no longer a step lower than the tribunes left.
To get Coriolanus to leave the stage they try persuasion, they try cajoling, they try screaming—keep the variety in approach.
On the citizens' reentrance at "That would depopulate the city" lose the canned riot in favour of live cries of "Traitor, traitor!"
Give Menenius a hard time—cannot allow him to pacify the mob with a tale as he did earlier—Menenius must desperately fight for Coriolanus's life.

1.8: Fight rehearsal to fine tune the moves and bring them to speed.
Vocalize and exaggerate bodily movement so that the sword becomes subsidiary.

FOURTH PREVIEW (production seat)

Coriolanus emphasises sarcasm and irony as opposed to violent anger in the first scene.

Virgilia remains weepy during the domestic scene—a moment of irony on "A crack."

"Make you a sword of me"—still awkward throwing the standard.

The fight is impressive with the added sound and reverberation, though there are still errors made—the actors' movements are tentative, hence it seems more stylized than real—again Aufidius lost his shield early.

"A bribe to pay my sword"—violent explosion of anger.

"May these same instruments, which you profane,/Never sound more"—instead of staying still, Coriolanus paces centre and back.

"Wash my fierce hand in's heart"—explosion of primitive wrath and hatred from Aufidius, punctuated by heavy breathing and grunts.

Line problems during Volumnia's and Menenius's interchange in 2.1—again no tonal transition between "Now it's twenty-seven" and "each gash was an enemy's grave."

The carpet was unrolled twisted—problem rearranging it.

Banners impressive and the tickertape well timed.

Sicinius's "Doubt not/The commoners, for whom we stand" contains more violent indignation.

The messenger to the tribunes no longer enters as an aedile but as a citizen.

Preparation for the senate scene slow, though the mechanics are smoother.

Cominius's oration had less energy than usual.

The stool broke as it was carried out.

Coriolanus takes a walk round the stool before mounting it in the voices scene, as though delaying the moment as long as possible.

"here comes a brace" delivered when the citizens are already in position.

Citizens generally played down as a result of this afternoon's letter.

Coriolanus remains on the stool during his soliloquy until "Custom calls me to't."

Coriolanus kisses the ladies' hands and kneels—again seems out of character.

"When he hath power to crush"—a citizen turns his back in shame, leading Brutus to tap him on the shoulder and deliver the rest of the speech directly to him—greater communication.

One citizen holds out her hand to Sicinius, but he grunts and refuses to shake it—he needs redirection as he is too angry and surly with the plebeians whom he is supposed to represent—needs more of the passion of Brutus.

In 3.1 Coriolanus almost made a false entrance while the tribunes were still on stage after the citizens' exit.

Drum beats in the background behind the gates through which the senate will issue.

The generals join the procession at the reentrance of the tribunes—the new blocking is better, as it gets Titus Lartius offstage before the riot.

On "Triton of the minnows" Sicinius remains left rather than moving to the stairs.

Coriolanus remains up centre, then chases Brutus to the stairs—the latter waits till he backs off, then rejoins Sicinius.

"That love the fundamental part of state"—impassioned delivery from the stands right.

"it must be meet"—Coriolanus moves to confront the tribunes, but the senate put themselves between them to prevent it.

The riot is smoother though still needs refinement.

The split staging works much better with Cominius above right and the tribunes above left.

More anger on "I could beat forty of them" and less enjoyment at the boast.

Again the kiss and handholding by Coriolanus in the first persuasion scene.

Coriolanus laughs on "take in a town with gentle words" and again on "we'll prompt you."

The transition on "I will not do't" was better modulated, so that the audience did not find it amusing—pause as though to summon up all his control.

The aediles are dressed in more European-style duffel coats—no longer leather.

"What do you prate of service?"—less ironic, more a violent explosion.

Again laughter and applause at Sicinius—Coriolanus upstages the tribunes by thus taking control of the trial—mocks Sicinius's gesture of throwing his arm in the air.

The four "It shall be so"s really get the audience going and provide a nice juxtaposition with the "common cry of curs" speech.

"In anger, Juno-like"—much stronger.

"Come, come, come!" and "Fie, fie, fie!" delivered in rhythm—much improved.

INTERVAL

Much better communication in the servant scene—they dust the sand off each other after they fall, though the second part still does not work.

During the latter part of Aufidius's final speech, Coriolanus walks left before being called back to shake his hand, so that there is less of a walk for the exit.

Sicinius gives a violent "Ha" in response to Menenius's "We lov'd him."

In the tribunes' persuasion of Menenius in 5.1 Cominius wears an overcoat and gloves, as though he has just returned from his audience with Coriolanus.

The doors were slow to open to let Coriolanus out to meet Menenius, so McKellen was forced to kick them open—then they did not close again to make sense of the tableau before the gates.

Aufidius's Volscian guards no longer remain in the left and right stands, but position themselves near the wings.

Less melting on "gosling" and more scorn at such behaviour—Coriolanus melts only on "That's my brave boy!"

Volumnia always kneels too late to make sense of Coriolanus's line.

Very sharp on "Speak to me, son" and "Nay, behold's" was less motivated.

Mechanics of catching the hand obvious.

"Aufidius" again delivered as a plea, but said facing Volumnia.

Coriolanus does not wait for his mother and wife, but exits with his arm in the air, beckoning—Virgilia catches up to exit with her hand on his back.

Sicinius was drunker than last night—no longer kneels on "The gods be good unto us."

Ringing of bells added to the sound cue on Volumnia's triumph.

Drum beat during the first senator's speech.

Timing off on "Traitor? How now!" as Aufidius jumped the gun with his speech.

Eagle image subtler tonight, but Coriolanus still bursts into tears on his last "Boy!" so that he does literally become a "boy of tears."

Once on Coriolanus's body, Aufidius puts up his arm in his enemy's fist salute.

"My rage is gone" transmitted less of a breakdown, though the final speech was better.

Coriolanus's sword is picked up and carried in the funeral procession—only the helmet and gloves remain lying in the sand as mute reminders of the tragic action.

6/12/84

12:00–5:15

"Put him to choler straight"—build to this as the climactic statement at the opening of 3.3.

4.5: Retiming the exit of Coriolanus and Aufidius as the new conclusion to the scene, since the second serving man episode is cut.

4.2: Edit Virgilia's run across the stage at the tribunes—her line transmits the outburst that used to be expressed physically.

4.1: Cut Coriolanus's elaborate farewell to each group individually—retained only for his wife and mother.
"I pray you, come"—cue for the young nobility to exit.
Menenius's speech is spoken on the way down the stairs so that the end of the scene moves faster.

"I'd with thee every foot"—Menenius and Cominius exit—all go out in stages.

5.3: Timing the "Olympus" bow—Coriolanus speaks to the audience, turns, and the second he meets her eyes Volumnia bows—it should be a bigger moment for Coriolanus than Volumnia.

5.4: The aedile comes in too laid back with the news that World War III has just started—the speech needs energizing with a sense of desperation.
The first citizen must be less obstreperous and surly—more passion for his cause.

5.3: At the end of the supplication scene Aufidius remains up centre until his aside.
Scene tried with the ladies only going to their knees, but it works better with the muslim-like prostration and so it is kept.
Coriolanus exits with Aufidius and is followed by the ladies.
Suggestion made by McKellen that after "by and by" he take his son's hand and present him to Aufidius, and that they exit framing the child, but this was vetoed on the basis that it is a scene about the ladies (adopted, however, for certain performances).

2.1: More joy when the ladies meet Menenius—added lift and speed up the tempo.
Hit "true" each time for the payoff on "True? pow, wow!" or the line will fall flat.
"Has he disciplined Aufidius soundly?"—personal question, but needs a public delivery for the benefit of the audience.

1.9: The soldiers must mob Coriolanus and love him—they are not about to let him get away unpraised—rugger club atmosphere.
Titus Lartius's party no longer enters down the centre aisle but through the audience left—the soldiers stand behind Lartius without greeting the others until "Hadst thou beheld."
Soldiers get into position after the handshake to be ready for the cries of "Martius"—they only shake Coriolanus's hand and not each other's.
The bestowal of the agnomen must be a reverential moment.
Leave the trumpets and swords up until after "I will go wash," otherwise the move becomes messy and distracting—drop the swords on "wash" and sheathe them on "face is fair."
Added sound cue for three cheers of "Martius" with the final cry to issue from speakers all round the auditorium for added texture in the celebration.

5.2: Command all your vocal strength to master the Olivier.

The guards must attack Menenius as a weedy old man and despise him as a Roman—all Romans are sensuous hedonistic piss-artists as far as they are concerned.

The first watch is contemptuous and sadistic—he enjoys pushing this little old man around.

Cut part of the interchange between Menenius and the second guard for speed and momentum—keep the rhythms flowing between characters—complete the other's pattern rather than your own.

Tighten up the threatening with the spears.

Too much over-enunciation to stress the point—no need to do so.

General Notes

Take "sniffs" at the end of certain rhythmic lines—e.g., "Let us kill him, (sniff) and we'll have corn at our own price."

1.1: mob chants—"Speak, speak" "Resolved, resolved" "We know't, we know't"—need greater intensity—build the pitch of feeling amongst the crowd and feed the great toe to be even more violent—really build the meeting into a riot.

"in hunger for bread, not in/thirst for *revenge*"—a pejorative, Machiavellian word, therefore needs emphasis.

Recording of "Corn, corn, corn" shouted in the background for the sound cue on "The other side o'th'city is risen."

Menenius must smile to all sides of the auditorium rather than just one corner.

The first citizen is starting to find strength from individual words and is therefore losing the basic flow and going over the top—let it run.

"Bemock the modest moon"—up on "moon," so that Sicinius's rising tone indicates the image more.

1.2: Rearrange the cue for the stage right Volscian senators, so that all enter in unison.

2.2: "To Coriolanus come all joy (sniff) and honour."

2.3: Cut Brutus's "Censorinus" speech.

3.3: Move the senate as a block to upstage right—stronger position during the "common cry of curs" speech.

The extra "It shall be so"s worked so well that a fifth is added.

Pause after "There is a world elsewhere," then soft on the first "The people's enemy is gone" and grow in pitch from there.

No hoots and cheers as the crowd runs off, as Coriolanus's exit deflates their triumph, but Sicinius gives them a more active role—"see him out at gates," the victory is yours.

4.4: Brutus needs more strength to get the plebeians home, as he is worried that the crowd is completely out of control.

2.2: Cut the cushions in the senate scene to keep the pace fast.

FIFTH PREVIEW (production seat)

More anger on "flatter/Beneath abhorring"—punctuated by holding out his sword at them, then back to his sarcastic/ironic tone.

Instead of his usual white suit, Coriolanus wears white pants and a white sweatshirt.

Spits out the names of the tribunes—"*Sicinius* Velutu*s*."

Slip on the doors—the left Volscian gate closed early.

Domestic scene is flat.

More contented strength in Virgilia's refusal to go out of doors.

Coriolanus fell off the soldier's shoulders and the recording of "Martius" was mistimed with the live cheering.

The fight was better acted, but Aufidius missed the foot to Coriolanus's shield to push him away.

Instead of throwing sand with his foot, Coriolanus hit his sword against Aufidius's shield.

Better timing on Aufidius losing his shield (now he wears black knee and arm pads).

Aufidius screams less and conveys more animal intensity on "you have sham'd me."

Coriolanus falls against the steps and into a sitting position on "Never sound more."

New black and red flag for "The town is ta'en."

Sword forgotten on stage after 1.10.

Menenius stuttering on his lines with the tribunes.

Problem with the Volscian door—right side did not open properly for Rome.

"Oh no, no, no"—the point where Virgilia puts her hand on Menenius's back, and remains touching him when he turns to her for "if it be not too much."

"Yes, yes, yes"—the three women run hand in hand down centre to meet Coriolanus.

Wonderful punctuation with the drums on "and then men die."

"Nay, my good soldier, up"—Coriolanus kisses her hands.

Volumnia blew her blocking, so she was caught between the three that Rome should love to dote on.

The sour look on Sicinius's face was perfect for the crabtree joke.

The messenger to the tribunes was a happy bearer of news when he appeared as an aedile, but now as a citizen he delivers the lines with a worried aspect.

The second officer in the senate scene was off—still too slow despite the cut of the cushions.

"and might well/Be taken from the people"—more casual delivery, as though it really wouldn't mean so much.

Transition to the voices scene much smoother without the removal of the cushions.

As last night, the citizens are more serious and less comic, and the "great toe" is less angry and more passionate.

Coriolanus delivers his first lines in the voices scene upstage right of the stool rather than down centre, so there is no walk needed to mount the podium.

Coriolanus shakes hands with the first brace.

Cold smile on "common in my love."

No explosion on "Better it is to die"—said with cold arrogance and stays on the stool—comes down on "I am half through" and kneels after "Indeed I would be consul."

First citizen remains on stage during Menenius's and the tribunes' entrance.

No flashing on Coriolanus's exit—he leaves still wearing the hat.

"Will you dismiss the people?"—as they are already visible on stage—this earlier entrance makes more sense.

At the end of the voices scene a scatter of glitter accidentally fell from the flies.

"He's not confirm'd"—less deliberate at first—more as though trying out an idea—now Sicinius is too angry with them.

Dead space after the tribunes' exit before Coriolanus, Cominius and Titus Lartius enter.

Titus Lartius then exits immediately after he is welcomed home, so that there is no awkward exit during the riot scene.

Coriolanus points with his sword to the audience on "herd," "these" and "Hydra here."

"rank-scented meinie" and "We did request it" called out front with his hand cupped to his mouth, as though the audience were an extension of the citizenry standing at a distance, but whom he equally wishes to provoke with his words.

A bit over the top with the amount of pointing to senators, tribunes and audience, even though it does clarify who is being referred to by the complex pronouns.

"corn gratis"—Coriolanus touches Brutus on the nose with his sword to humiliate him.

Distracting sound disturbance over the speakers.

The riot is still muddy—the sides are full but the circle is empty—stagy.

Edit "Aye" after "The people are the city."

Menenius still delivers his lines from behind Coriolanus—visibility poor.

The sound disturbance is gone only by the first persuasion scene.

On Menenius's line "I would put mine armour on" Coriolanus laughs.

Volumnia is flat during this scene.

Coriolanus doubles over at the desperate ludicrousness of "we'll prompt you."

"I will not do't"—pause to keep the transition from being comic.

"Do your will"—more automatic turning away from Coriolanus's last line—no pause to make it appear a conscious decision.

Coriolanus is generally less angry and more sarcastic tonight.

"How! Traitor?" and "fires i'th'lowest hell"—no explosion, flatter.

The explosion comes from the point of "What do you prate of service."

Again sarcastic laughter and indicates Sicinius to the audience with his arm—the personal anger between Coriolanus and Sicinius is growing more organic.

Again on "Thy tears are salter than a younger man's"—tastes his tears.

"To say so to my husband"—Virgilia staggers several paces towards the point of Coriolanus's exit, then collapses right—on "He'd make an end of thy posterity" she is writhing on the ground.

INTERVAL

When Coriolanus kneels, he at first recoils from Aufidius's embrace.

Aufidius puts out his hand to Coriolanus's face, but the latter instinctively turns it away, only to look up wonderingly at "the maid I married."

"You bless me, gods!"—for the first time this becomes an enthusiastic climax to the news he has received—we see him take it in as he crosses left to turn around on the name "Martius."

Sicinius enters carrying a sweater and jogging onstage.

"yet it was against our will"—the first citizen is sheepish rather than accusatory.

The end of the scene is less violent and more solemn.

Coriolanus and Aufidius push open the gates to check on the disturbance and go back through the door to stand in tableau.

"Pass, pass"—from the right rather than the back of the theatre, due to the new position of the women by this point in the scene.

"Best of my flesh"—tender.

"do not say/For that 'Forgive our Romans' "—violently shakes her from him, then kisses her even more passionately.

When Coriolanus kneels to Volumnia, he puts his head to the sand.

Volumnia still kneels too late for Coriolanus's line.

Edit the stabbing gesture on "most mortal to him."

During the assassination scene Aufidius hides behind the corner of the ledge before assuming his usual crouching position.

Coriolanus displays the treaty to the audience as well as to the senate.

"Cut me to pieces"—not as an explosion but as a man who just can't care anymore.

He is literally a broken boy of tears at the end—playing up the heart attack.

Coriolanus did not make his usual run before the shots—once wounded he makes his futile attempt, then drops the sword.

After Aufidius gets off the body, one foot remains on the corpse for a time.

"My rage is gone"—flat but quiet—not cracked yet—the separation between each subsequent order is very controlled.

7/12/84

SIXTH PREVIEW (box)

Change in the set—barbed wire around the sides and tattered political posters on decayed brick—VOTA DP—on the left wall a slab has been put up reading "danger."

The first citizen shows more self-satisfaction and love of language—more variety in tone rather than playing the single line of anger in his response to the fable of the belly—"It was an answer"—more concession and therefore a greater juxtaposition with his impatience at the interpretation.

Coriolanus is back to the white suit and blue shirt on his first entrance.

"Nay, let them follow"—Coriolanus does not threaten them with his sword hilt again, but vocally.

Aufidius pulls his letter out of his glove—a copy of Coriolanus's note to Menenius—he is off vocally during this scene.

Audibility problem for Valeria.

Virgilia remains seated throughout and gets up on "I will not forth."

Change in the apparition of Coriolanus—he no longer opens the door himself and then reaches for the flag—the gates open of themselves, we see the smoke, then the tattered flag and finally the figure which is recognized on "Oh, 'tis Martius."

In 1.6 Cominius is already looking in the right direction for Coriolanus—cut the turning of the heads to follow the warrior's progress.

During the fight Coriolanus goes back to kicking the sand with his foot rather than hitting sword against shield.

The fight is generally much better executed and acted.

Aufidius cries out as Coriolanus defeats his men.

The red flag in 1.9 is now covered in blood.

The swords are drawn more slowly on the naming—more ritualistic.

The blanket wrapped around Coriolanus is now tattered and bloody.

Better modulation on forgetting the host's name—no laughter from the audience.

"The town is ta'en"—delivered as a question rather than a much hated fact—the scene is less biting and more thoughtful.

"you talk of pride"—Menenius dried.

Timing off for the ladies' entrance—lines!

Menenius skipped the section reporting Coriolanus's combat with Aufidius and the preliminary to their discussion of his wounds.

Carpet carelessly unrolled for the triumph scene—twisted.

During the triumph it is as though Volumnia resents the intrusion of her son's greeting his wife.

"newly nam'd"—Coriolanus kisses Volumnia's hand.

The messenger to the tribunes is no longer a citizen but an aedile—consequently he expresses pleasure and awe rather than anxiety.

The preparation for the senate scene is still very slow.

Coriolanus is more humble in expressing his dislike for having his nothings monstered before the senate because of his respect for their authority, even if he cannot sit through the ceremony—his explosion is directed to the people.

Coriolanus omitted to sit down again and push over the stool.

Late opening on the doors to reveal Coriolanus.

Sicinius no longer lounges during the senate scene, as it seemed too arrogant.

In the voices scene the citizens are presented more seriously and sympathetically—all the humour comes from Coriolanus.

No handshake with the first brace.

The second brace enter before the previous exit is completed and are not spatially separated—they stand arm in arm.

The first citizen exits with the second brace—less disruptive.

The citizens are now well onstage before "Will you dismiss the people?"

Part of the audience is to be brought down for the rest of this scene, but an error in communication led to them all descending, rather than just the outside two stands.

The citizens no longer betray angry movement in this scene—they are stationary as they stand in a semi-circle, enrapt in the passionate words of the tribunes—better in rehearsal—now it has lost energy and audibility.

The end of the voices scene is dragging—Sicinius is not energized, only Brutus has passion (the Censorinus speech is cut after "The noble house o'th'Martians").

"He's not confirm'd"—less anger and more discovery—this is not a scene about Martius, but a scene about the people's discovering that they have a voice.

Now the senators are revealed at the same time as the three generals, so that the stage opens up simultaneously.

Again on "rank-scented meinie" Coriolanus cups his hand to his mouth to call out, so that the main body of the audience is appealed to.

Shortly after this point Coriolanus completely lost his text, though he covered well by improvising blank verse.

"That love the fundamental part of state" and "A noble life before a long"—passionately hit.

Sicinius is weak during this scene—too slow and lacks energy—when he is loud he is over the top.

Coriolanus laughs on Menenius's boast "I could myself/Take up a brace o'th'best of them."

The young nobility are no longer in military garb but sharp suits with T-shirts underneath—more similar to Coriolanus's own dress.

During the first persuasion scene Coriolanus elaborately plants his feet in the sand, as though to channel all his frustration into fidgeting.

"I prithee woman"—said with more tenderness, almost kissing Virgilia.

The young nobility did not tier up early enough.

Virgilia's writhing really does not work, and Volumnia is over the top.

INTERVAL

Coriolanus missed "Save you, sir," and the sound cue was late on the door opening—also missed "I have deserv'd no better entertainment/In being Coriolanus."

Much more emphasis on the revelation of his name—"Coriolanus" is spelled out syllable by syllable.

Cut Aufidius's arrested gesture of his hand to Coriolanus's face on "the maid I married."

Again "You bless me, gods" is delivered more as an active realization than a quiet aside.

After Cominius's exit Sicinius takes the child's hand as he comforts the people.

Cominius vocalizes a staccato effect on the delivery of his news to drive the point home.

The Roman ladies are already mounting the stage on "Pass, pass."

Coriolanus's kiss with Virgilia is much more sexual—hand to bum.

The "O mother, mother" speech was wonderful tonight—some of the violence has returned on "most mortal to him"—not pumping her arm but squeezing it down to the rhythm of the lines.

Between "I dare be sworn you were" and "And sir" there is a pause as Coriolanus fights to regain control.

Sicinius sits before "The gods be good unto us."

"I am return'd your soldier" delivered to the audience as the Volscian people.

The lighting is better on Aufidius—less strident.

Playing up the heart attack so that the final boast is a last desperate attempt to regain mastery—the taunt "boy of tears" literally causes his heart to crack.

The citizens throw sand on their accusations—he begins his run before the shots.

New timing on carrying out the corpse—music and a high pitched tone come over the speakers and are cut off by the final clash of the gates—complete emptiness.

8/12/84

SEVENTH PREVIEW (back aisle seat)

The domestic scene was more low key but still too slow.

The battle was very good but the single combat was off.

"Make you a sword of me!"—this passage was brilliant tonight.

Titus Lartius in 1.7 gave a greater sense of being a worried military strategist.

There is no blood on the costumes in "The town is ta'en," but a soldier lying prostrate on the ground holds a bloody kerchief to his stomach.

More obsessive hatred in Aufidius.

The scene leading up to the triumph is much more energized.

"The gods grant them true"—more up—the punch lines make sense.

Lines generally more secure.

Cut the "Oh!" after "Look, sir, your mother"—no laugh.

No holding of hands on "Nay, my good soldier, up," nor does he kiss Volumnia.

Again Coriolanus is much more respectful in the senate scene—cut kicking over the stool.

Nothing really new is happening here, but the show is running much more smoothly and more comfortably.

Lighting problems during Cominius's speech.

The lights should gradually come down to add a sense of mystery and awe to Coriolanus's deeds, then come up again for Coriolanus's entrance.

In the voices scene Coriolanus kicks the stool into place before stepping on it.

The back of his gown of humility is threadbare and battle bruises are evident on his right cheek, his chest and down his throat.

Coriolanus turns his back on the first brace on "adieu."

Nods his head mockingly up and down as he takes off his hat to the second brace.

The soliloquy is still not cracked yet.

The crowd control is better—only the outer sides are brought down.

There is generally more energy throughout this sequence.

The tribunes enter later so that there is more sense of frantic desperation on "Pass no further," which is cried out while they are running down the steps.

"O good but most unwise patricians: why,/You grave but reckless senators"—more disappointed disbelief rather than violent anger when addressing the senators, and hatred and violence on "corn" and "people"—more variety in mood and truth to character.

The riot is much more energized and desperate in tone, as the senators try to convince Coriolanus to go home and leave the field.

Coriolanus toned down the obvious irony of "plant love among's," so that there is more possibility for growth as the scene is more subtle.

During the Sicinius speech Coriolanus stands in stunned and contemptuous silence rather than responding with laughter and applause.

Bigger on "I banish you."

Sicinius throws up a handful of the leftover gold spangles from the triumph in an ironic visual reference to that scene.

Virgilia is better in her expression of grief in 4.1, but is still over the top with the tribunes.

INTERVAL

Sicinius jogs on empty handed—Brutus follows carrying his sweater.

Again Sicinius takes the child's hand on "These are a side."

One side of the Volscian door is now set to be pushed open by Coriolanus to investigate the disturbance made by Menenius.

Cut the tableau as Coriolanus and Aufidius exit fully during the guard sequence.

After placing his son on his shoulders, Coriolanus keeps him in his arms for a few moments before putting him down for the "Your knee, sirrah" sequence.

The persuasion scene is particularly effective tonight.

Sicinius cut the entrance drinking from the brandy bottle and cut the faint to preserve the serious tone of the scene.

Coriolanus cries out on "boy of tears" as though he has been stabbed through the heart, and there are tears on the final "Boy!"—comes out of the trance during the accusation.

Only the conspirators shout "kill him!"

Cries and confusion amongst the crowd.

Aufidius keeps his foot on the body even after he gets down.

"My rage is gone"—momentary crack; "Assist"—quieter.

The show was ten minutes quicker this afternoon.

EIGHTH PREVIEW (back aisle seat)

The first citizen cut the illustrative gestures on "head . . . eye . . . heart . . . arm."

Coriolanus lost "who's like to rise"—does not use his sword to chase the rabble, but wields his scroll of commission.

Domestic scene played more down centre.

Lighting accidentally went out on Titus Lartius while Coriolanus was in the scaffold.

Aufidius this time kicked sand at Coriolanus in the lead up to the single combat.

Aufidius did not move out of the way quickly enough and was disarmed too soon.

As during the matinée, Coriolanus dropped his bloody kerchief on "my memory is tired."

Volumnia's letter sequence really took off tonight.

"more cause to be proud" directed squarely at the tribunes, as is "every gash was an enemy's grave"—on the first Sicinius pulls a crooked face at Brutus.

As always Virgilia is the only one silent on "Welcome to Rome."

Put back "Oh" after "Look, sir, your mother"—laugh—also reintroduce the business of taking and kissing Volumnia's hands.

Sicinius paces up and down during Brutus's speech on what they should do.

Some laughs now on the preparation for the senate scene—works much better.

"I cannot/Put on the gown"—Coriolanus gestures with his head to the gown held by Brutus to explicate to the audience what Brutus is tendering with outstretched arms.

Soliloquy in the voices scene was more heated.

One voice missing in the final brace.

The first citizen remains in the scaffolding throughout the scene again—no early exit.

The riot scene is still muddy.

No taking of Volumnia's hand until "Let go" in the first persuasion scene.

"You?" after "I talk of that, that know it"—long pause as Coriolanus makes the transition from complete contempt to anger rather than playing anger as a single line—return to laughter and applause at Sicinius.

Drop to silent hatred on "I banish you."

Sicinius tosses a handful of glitter at the people's triumph.

INTERVAL

After the interval quite a few people leave their seats in the main part of the auditorium to exchange them for seats in the stands.

Seem to have cut "I have deserv'd no better entertainment/In being Coriolanus" because McKellen consistently forgets the line.

The Roman citizens' costumes are darker in the second half.

More humour in the guards' treatment of Menenius.

As this afternoon, McKellen is not relying so much on vocal technique— his speeches are really thought and felt.

The whole show is smoother, flowing and under control after the disaster of Friday night.

Before he puts his son on his shoulders, Coriolanus kisses him on the cheek.

"I'll frame convenient peace"—delivered downstage centre, then walk up for the second request.

Tears more subtle and felt—not forced.

"temple built you" and "confederate arms"—emotionally quiet, without the sense of his earlier controlled show.

"O slave!"—violence of exertion almost too much for him—forces himself to calm down and make his apology to the senators.

"Cut me to pieces"—active assertion made in great pain.

"My rage is gone"—emotional again—subdued ending.

11/12/84

11:30–1:00

General Notes

1.1: The weapons must be more prominent when they are pulled out in the first scene.
The atmosphere is neither frightening nor threatening enough.

The way the play is now Coriolanus has a better relationship with Cominius than with Menenius—need to work on the father/son relationship.

1.6: Rehearse the fanfares to make them more integrated and spontaneous, less rehearsed.

1.8: "Officious, and not valiant"—not directed at the point of the soldiers' exit but delivered downstage as Aufidius picks up his shield and sword—must be quicker.

1.9: There is too much light on the Roman soldiers during Coriolanus's moment with the sling.
"The blood upon your visage dries"—work on the exit.

Work especially on part 2 to extract every bit of drama from a section which is not as action-packed.

The matinée on December 8 was clear, light and shorter—recapture that performance.

The Olivier and the play both require a lightness and easiness of delivery, but this must be energized—need a relaxed energy but naturalism loses it.

2.1: The ladies and Menenius were top hole Saturday night.
There should be a continual breaking down of the formality during the triumph.
Good set-up for the hearty laugh on "crabtrees."
On "All tongues speak of him" cut the "flamens" passage—too bad as it now becomes a somewhat sexist speech, as only women are held up to ridicule.
Red banners changed—now three in front, three behind.
Want the triumph to be "supremely vulgar."

1.4: More movement toward militaristic frenzy and pleasure in the battle— it is 'too public school hearty at the moment.'
Need to consider what Shakespeare is saying about what kind of fighting men they are and what kind of war they are fighting—need to push for the same critical reception it would have had among the audience indigenous to its time, therefore do not fight it but use it.
The battle itself hits the right level—the problem is keeping it there afterwards.

2.2: Swapping the cloaks with Menenius should be a private moment.
Further loosing of Cominius's eulogy—"waxed like a sea" needs more sense of mystery—deliver in a hushed tone—sense of flux.

2.3: The voices scene is working well—the first brace must be very happy—"it's a nice day, if he asks for our voice we must grant it"—the second citizen must make the qualification clear.
Better tension and simple energy, but audibility is difficult for the public behind—it is alright to assume that the citizens want to hear what the tribunes are saying, but not that they *do*.

3.1: Coriolanus moves round Sicinius on "peremptory 'shall.'" The tribunes must portray more that they want him to behave the way he is.
The audience knows that they don't really want to stop him, but rather to wind him up and make him hotter and hotter and hotter, and are simply delighted.
There can be no pause between "traitor" and "and shall answer" or Coriolanus would come in and cut him off.
The crowd must dramatize more what the drawing of the sword does to each element of society represented on stage. All movement must stop with the drawing of the sword, so that the focus remains on that central action—it is still messy—unclear focus.

"This man has marr'd his fortune"—Menenius does not yet realize that the senate's sympathies have altered.

Problem with the audience on stage at this point—express their uneasiness at being threatened at swordpoint through nervous laughter, and this dispels the dramatic tension.

"to his utmost peril"—the tribunes come downstage—good.

3.2: Good tone—now one has the sense that there is a lifetime of arguing behind this climactic disagreement.

Focus problem—"I will not do't"—the reaction of the senators on stage takes focus away from the last part of the speech which is the most important—must therefore internalize their reactions.

"all the trades in Rome"—the tone is corrosive and mocking—don't need the illustrative gesture, as it is over the top.

The final "Mildly!" must come as an explosion.

3.3: The tribunes on "In this point charge him home" have already decided on a course of action and are in a state of nervous excitement because they do not know which way the trial will go.

High adrenalin to make the scene as hot as it must be.

'The people, however it falls, must follow us'—*not* 'we've got him—all that's left is the sentence.'

They assume a lawyer's technique to seem tolerant.

It is not the tribunes who wreck the situation, it is Menenius with his patriotic speech about Coriolanus's wounds.

4.1: "I'll do well yet"—the sense has been lost—used to be dangerous and determined.

4.4: Make part 2 more active.

Elegiac feel after the event in the speech outside Antium.

Coriolanus is the dragon searching for his fen—he has not slept for a long time.

Too resigned—he should be ready, and ready to do something extraordinary.

5.3: Fine tuning the scene—sit in a tight circle and play to each other as quickly and as clearly as possible.

5.6: The gunfire sounds weedy—Peter must have the rifle, Des and Guy pistols.

2:00–5:30

1.4: Need more mystery as Coriolanus disappears into the smoke, and a sense of finality as the gates crash shut.

"To th'pot"—add sound effects leading up to Titus Lartius's entrance—then silence when he goes into his eulogy.

The doors now open to reveal Coriolanus driving back two Volscian opponents—he then turns to beckon his troops, the banner in one hand, his sword in the other.

Coriolanus has his back to the audience during the short battle, then turns front for "Oh, 'tis Martius!"—gives the reason for their initial lack of recognition.

Speed up the fliers on "All the contagion of the south."

1.5: Two looters exit right immediately after the banner is thrown, the third dodges left then returns, grabs the standard and runs off right waving it delightedly.

1.9: Make the warriors more into a Roman Third Reich—barbaric spitting out of "Martius"—need less *Henry V* and more Nazism.

This moment in the spotlight is Coriolanus's last happy moment in the play, and it is even now not unmixed as he has not killed Aufidius—afterwards everything is discontent.

The British way of playing this moment would be with a bit of a self-deprecating smile, but this scene is Germanic—need an absolute affirmation of physical prowess.

They are painting a glorious painting of what Coriolanus despises—delight in the very thing which is the last thing that Coriolanus wants.

The soldiers' congratulations of Coriolanus are too matey—need to be more military—not extended shaking of the hand but a brief touch and a nod of the head—get more of a fascist feeling out of it.

One soldier stands on the step behind Coriolanus while the rest salute him, not with their swords but their fists, as the first leads the cry of "Martius."

The tone then changes as Coriolanus tries to bring it back down to earth on "I have not wash'd my nose that bled."

Swords raised as high as possible on the naming.

The raising is formal and contained within the music.

When at ease the shield is up and the other arm placed behind the back—strong stance.

"So, to our tent"—now directed to everyone and not just Coriolanus, as a means of partially clearing the stage—the musicians leave at this point, leaving a single trumpeter to close the scene.

Other soldiers take up their place near the wings, so that the exit may be executed quicker.

Cominius and Titus Lartius must both close in on Coriolanus at his sole request, to give him a sense of both physical and psychological claustrophobia, prompting the forgetting of his poor host's name.

12/12/84

10:30–1:30: Word Run for Cuts

2:30–5:30

1.1: Weapons made more dangerous—no longer long sticks and clubs but cleavers, meat axes and machetes.
Final blocking of the first scene with the citizens taking care to maintain balance in filling the stage.
Menenius puts his cloak on the ground on the first citizen's line rather than during his own speech—the first citizen is intrigued by what he is doing and he holds the focus of the plebeians.
"Follow Cominius"—gesture by Coriolanus for Titus Lartius to go first, but Lartius declines—"Right worthy your priority"—Coriolanus puts his hands on his shoulders in a gesture of thanks, then Lartius moves to follow him out before the exit is interrupted by Coriolanus threatening the citizens.
Constant repetition of "Martius" in close proximity—a feed for the tribunes to be bloody sick of his name, then it is never heard again until the end of the play.

2.2: More tension needs to emerge from the senate meeting where almost everything on the agenda goes wrong—when Cominius was consul there was never any of this bother. Fatal mixture—the first day of the tribunes' power coincides with the very day that Coriolanus is up for consul.
Individual focus must be very strong.
The senators try to rush things through as a squabble could arise at any point due to the inflammability of Coriolanus's temper.
Menenius is very laid back—Mr. Fix-it—everyone else thinks "Oh, my God."
The senate is now divided and do not enter together—entrance from the left and right wings, leaving Cominius, Coriolanus and Menenius to come through the central doors.
The first back-straightening point is the fracas with the tribunes.
"Leave nothing out for length" is said for the tribunes' benefit—all protocol is clear and aboveboard, as they are unfamiliar with the mode of proceeding—it is their first day in the senate as newcomers.
Change back to the original entrance of all from the central doors.
Formalize the entrance to make the juxtaposition of tension greater.
The senators sit down and start the scene immediately, as in the Volscian senate.
Strong reaction to the tribunes' exchange with Menenius, but they must include concern at what the reaction in Coriolanus will be, as all of Rome knows that he hates their guts.

The senate is surprised by Sicinius's little prepared speech as a nuisance of an interruption—they are not meant to speak, nor indeed is Coriolanus—breach of expectation. Sicinius is much more daring, Brutus more protective.

"He doth appear"—after a moment's doubt as to whether or not he is indeed still on the premises—cut.

13/12/84

12:00–1:00

4.5: Aufidius stands down right for the revelation of the stranger's identity, then holds out his sword in threat—Coriolanus approaches to the point where it is at his throat.

Confrontation—tension.
Strong reactions between the two.
Provocation—Coriolanus dares Aufidius throughout the scene, insulting him.

How much does Aufidius know?
He does not know that the aristocracy has turned against Coriolanus, even if he is aware that the rabble has.
Most importantly, he does not know that Coriolanus himself has turned against Rome—the surprise should elicit a strong reaction.
McKellen pointed out that Aufidius is very capable of taking out his pistol and shooting Coriolanus on the spot—hence he must arrest him with his speech—urgency in having to convey the message.

Intention of effect.
Achievement of effect.

Deliberate playing with Aufidius as in the speech before the duel.
"I know thee not! Thy name?"—half pause between—the two should be looking at one another eyeball to eyeball. Actors released by playing into each other's eyes.
Coriolanus should assume that he will be recognized, and therefore should not turn away but face Aufidius—McKellen said that when sitting on the steps waiting for the lights to go down, two people were talking about his one man Shakespeare show and did not recognize him, therefore he *is* well disguised.
Coriolanus's speech becomes more resonant when he can see what Aufidius is about at the moment that he is looking at him.
Verse structure ll. 54–55—on the first question about his name, observe the verse structure even if it is written in prose—there is a definite rhythm to it through the alliteration.

Coriolanus goads Aufidius to the point of resolution.

The relationship between the movement of the actor on stage and the text emerged as Aufidius moved round Coriolanus on "clip," then expressed uneasiness because it did not come out of the text.

"what's thy name?"—the figure standing before him is obviously not a tramp but an interesting figure.

Tremendous pressure prompts the "Jupiter" image.

Aufidius takes all the emotion out of "O Martius, Martius" and delivers the line flatly until the point of "all-noble Martius"—he is just saying 'I believe you,' then the emotion and the togetherness arise out of that.

Until that point the audience don't know whether Aufidius is going to believe him—throughout Coriolanus's speech there is always the possibility of a Trojan horse outside, then afterwards the question becomes 'How am I going to tell him?'

Back away for tension on the embrace speech.

Coriolanus's subtext is 'Oh, let it work,' then 'Oh, we're great friends' on the embrace speech.

Overformalization of the scene before the emotions are fully worked out becomes a trap.

Coriolanus goes to Aufidius on "Let me twine," so that he is the one who first extends his arms—long cuddle—then it is Aufidius who pulls away to give the rest of his speech. Really a moment of great friendliness and passion—much more energy now.

2:00–5:30

3.3: Gap in the lighting design—it does not sufficiently isolate the prosecutors and defenders to guide audience focus.

Visually the strongest representation of the scene is to put Coriolanus amidst the people in the middle of the circle, with the prosecution and defence in the stands above—something not yet explored.

"Draw near, ye people" becomes the justification for the trial scenario, but an awful gap ensues as Coriolanus rocks between behaving properly and breaking out in anger—it is not transmitting properly.

The senate should be up right and the tribunes up left, with the aediles on either side of Coriolanus in the centre. The problem hitherto lay in the duplication of staging for other (i.e. the voices) scenes, but this is sufficiently different.

All enter through the main gates, Coriolanus centre rather than stage right—"Th'honour'd gods" is delivered up centre.

Decision to move Coriolanus up right for the first "hear me speak."

Menenius now stands on a lower level than the rest of the senate.

4.4: Need to find the moment where Coriolanus becomes aware of the citizen's approach.

The citizen enters right, then keeps to the path along the upper perimeter.

Coriolanus approaches to meet the Volscian citizen left of the doors.
Turn again to point out the specific house.

The citizen stops only when Coriolanus makes him stop, then is already exiting on "Farewell" so Coriolanus can move immediately into "O world, thy slippery turns."

Change the lighting again as the soliloquy is now delivered left rather than right of the doors.

Now the citizen remains standing after "Thank you, sir," as though waiting for another question—Coriolanus paces, then turns to dismiss him with "Farewell," ending up in the original lighting position right of the doors.

'If friends can turn into enemies, then fellest foes can become good friends'—suddenly the whole speech clicks with the finding of this fundamental conclusion.

3.3: Fine tuning the mechanics of the scene.

On Coriolanus's entrance the tribunes split—perhaps with some sense of being overheard—they have no idea how long the gates have been open.

The crowd must come down and circle the stage, so that the citizens stand with their backs to the main audience.

Every time Coriolanus opens his mouth the senate must be on tenterhooks, then express relief on "I am content."

This is the fulcrum of the play in tragic terms—if Menenius had not been fool enough through his generous heart to put his foot in his mouth, Coriolanus might have been able to contain himself.

Instead he breaks into a raging fury again: 'I don't want the trial,—just the sentence. Don't make speeches—just pronounce it.'

After "Let them pronounce the steep Tarpeian death," refocus as Coriolanus descends and stands confronting the tribunes—stands at their feet demanding sentence.

The people's "It shall be so" is a confirmation, as they draw in—Cominius then rushes to intercede.

"It shall be so"—both confirmation and an echo of the tribunes' instructions.

Edit Coriolanus's ironic laughter, as McKellen is uncomfortable with it. His silence can be played as an active acceptance of the sentence, whereas Cominius jumps in to stop the pronouncement, as once he is sentenced he is sentenced and nothing further can be done.

In the next run Coriolanus is led by the aediles to the centre of the circle on "Draw near."

The senate is stationed above right, the tribunes above left, and the people draw into a tight circle.

"a grain a day"—Coriolanus picks up a grain of sand.

Cominius runs down on "Let me speak" and crosses left to the tribunes, addressing the people.

Coriolanus comes down centre for the banishment speech, then circles among the people and exits.

The senate waits for the cheer before they exit, as they have left the stage too early until now.

Coriolanus is given no lines during this sequence—he is listening to the people expressing their minds about him. The people close in to see his reaction.

"It shall be so" is not the cry of a lynch mob, but the affirmation of a verdict—delivered with clenched fists upraised.

Menenius's lines will have more impact if delivered from above right— by turning his head Coriolanus can talk directly to him about the tribunes.

3.1: "This man has marr'd his fortune"—'I think he's blown it, and we all do'—Menenius must register this switch in the senate.

"Proceed by process"—must be said *absolutely* to Sicinius.

On the 'gangrened limb' speech Menenius is not fighting enough—he must be responding to a direct threat of murder.

Menenius moves during Brutus's speech, but no one else stirs until "Spread further."

On "Pursue him to his house," Menenius must be in a position upstage to intercept them—needs a physical response from everyone.

No false exit, however, as they await him to lead them off. Slight pause between "Noble tribunes" and "It is the humane way" to give Sicinius and Brutus a chance to regroup and take a short walk downstage as they discuss their strategy.

4.5: The presentation of the throat and the embrace are still performed standing.

The tension is good with the step back after "O Martius, Martius."

Aufidius crosses to Coriolanus's right on "Jupiter."

The embrace is more passionate but less sexual.

The walk round Coriolanus changes the dynamic nicely.

Aufidius must say "Martius" coldly or he lets the audience know too early what is in his heart.

Give more space on the walk round to let the embrace work more intensely.

Aufidius looks at Coriolanus's body with the space between them to let the "scarr'd the moon with splinters" image work—then a long, strong robust hug before "Here I clip." Aufidius expresses his emotion through the use of intense epithets and the obsessive repetition of Coriolanus's name. When Aufidius enters he should not come so far into the circle, as it dispels the tension—better if he remains on the perimeter (this also makes the walk round bigger).

More geniality in the initial questioning—more appropriate to the lord of the house in control of the situation.

With the revelation of his name Coriolanus drops his disguise and turns round fully to face Aufidius.

Coriolanus plays more with Aufidius in the variety of his tone.

After the step back Coriolanus keeps his arm extended, so that his hand still rests on Aufidius's shoulder, keeping contact—the embrace is active on his part as well.

Aufidius must register a facial response when the unknown stranger calls him by his first name "Tullus."

The general flow of events makes much more sense with the dynamic of the writing.

The meeting of the two is the central event of the play.

The lines about contending and contesting are effective when uttered during the embrace—suits the action to the word, as now they contend as hotly for love as ever they did for hate.

Aufidius stands far back to gaze on "but that *I see thee here*"—intense joy.

Once the embrace is over the two do not touch again until the final handshake.

Question as to whether or not Aufidius should carry a sword and dagger—no dagger as they are for conspirators, swords are carried by the leaders.

14/12/84

2:15–5:30

2.3: The third citizen is the voice of moderation—"We have power in ourselves to do it, but it is a power that we have no power to do"—enjoy the second part of the paradox. Juxtaposition with the first citizen who wants to preserve the serious tone of the conversation.

"You have stood your limitation"—'You have won,' then pause before the line about the tribunes.

"Lay/A fault on us" delivered as the citizens begin to go off—this is the pivotal point where the tribunes begin to get restless and there should be movement on the stage.

The first citizen is jumping the gun if he states a decision rather than a possibility on "He's not confirm'd" or the scene will end too early—growing tension with "I'll have five hundred voices of that sound."

Groups gather round the speakers in their excitement.

Big delivery on 'Say what you want, blame us.'

The interest of the scene lies in watching the tribunes spark off each other—move into a gear of excitement, as they try to make the citizens understand.

"He's not confirm'd"—this is news to the tribunes as well, which they catch hold of and run with.

The people actually do blame Sicinius and Brutus in Act 4, but the accusation is aimed at the tribunes themselves rather than at Coriolanus.

4.6: The alliance of Coriolanus and Aufidius is like the joining of the Pentagon and the Kremlin.
Change the line "yet it was against our will" to "yet it was his death we wished for" to make the ambiguous meaning clear for a modern audience and to keep the tone more serious—yet now the line doesn't scan.

2.3: "*Lay*/A fault on us"—"Lay" comes at the end of the line as a blinding idea.
"Repair to th'Capitol"—handshake with the third citizen.
All say in unison "We will so" before the solo line "Repent in their election."
The scene gains energy when all catch fire off each other.

3.3: Sense of Coriolanus really being surrounded by the common cry in this new staging.
The tribunes no longer split on Coriolanus's entrance—both move left.
Coriolanus is more subdued and less ironic on his entrance.
He moves directly to the centre of the stage to address the tribunes.
On "Draw near, ye people" the tribunes are already positioned above.
The citizens are now on the edge of the perimeter to preserve the dynamic of moving in for enclosure as the scene develops.
"Well, say"—the people sit as the court assembles.
"Mark you this" and "To th'rock"—need a judicial air for the sentencing—he is no longer to be tried by process, as he has just condemned himself.
The people have been schooled by the aediles to follow the tribunes, as they do not know which way the trial will go.
One man is so enraged that he jumps the gun and calls for the death penalty, and the tribunes are forced to calm him as it is not yet decided.
Only the first citizen points to the rock, while the rest raise their hands as though voting.
On Sicinius's line "Deserves th'extremest death" the citizens raise their hands in favour, but are held back by Brutus, and the sentencing continues to be legalistic.
The sentence comes finally on "banish him our city"—hit the words as a completely new thought.
The first "It shall be so" is said with gravity rather than hostility—cued by Sicinius—spoken gravely as the decision is made and assimilated, then grows in intensity—pronunciation crisp.
The only emotional line is "Let him away!"
Cominius's interjection is an outrage to the people's court—Sicinius blows up at him, and several citizens rise.
The first two "It shall be so"s are spoken individually from either side of

the court, though all vote silently—then comes the emotional outburst and the final choric repetition.

The citizens sit cross-legged with their feet in the sand, bum on the wood.

"Well, say" is the citizens' cue to sit.

On the final five "It shall be so"s the mob goes crazy—try to get the audience to join in—with justifiable rage, and the formality breaks down completely with Cominius's outburst.

The aediles move in to control the mob.

This scene depicts the attempt of a man to run a people's court and of the people to have such a court—any interruption can only enflame them.

Their cry at the banishment is more an expression of subdued relief than loud joy.

Staccato delivery of "It *shall* be so" for main impact and emphasis.

4.1: Timing the exits to clarify focus.

"smile" is the cue for the young nobility to exit.

Menenius's line "Come, let's not weep" is delivered directly to Volumnia as a final agreement with Coriolanus not to cry but *smile*.

The rest of the speech is then directed to Coriolanus.

1.9: The cries of "Martius, Martius, Martius" must be made to sound less like a rehearsed music cue—more like an acclamation.

The lead soldier speaks the first and third lines, while the second and fourth are repeated as a unison response.

The cue to lower the swords now comes on "blush or no."

2.1: The aedile enters on "and their blaze."

"You are sent for to the Capitol. 'Tis thought/That Martius shall be consul"—no pause—delivered with one breath as the label of the scene. The pause makes more sense before "I have seen."

Excitement in the report—don't miss the greatest public event that's ever happened—akin to a coronation.

Irony in the messenger bubbling over with excitement to tell the tale, as though it is something that the tribunes want to hear.

There is no reason yet for any but the tribunes to be concerned, as Coriolanus is still riding high on the crest of his victory—adds richness to the scene.

NINTH PREVIEW (production seat)

The citizens enter already carrying the proper weapons and are not triggered by the unloading of the bag—the lights gradually dim well into the speeches.

There are more posters on the set and they are now colour-tinted.

Bigger vocal reaction from the citizens on "The Volsces are in arms."

Distraction as two people sat on the lowest tier of the stands—as though part of the Volscian senate!

Domestic scene much better (especially Virgilia)—first big laugh from the audience on "One on's father's moods."

Titus Lartius now delivers his "carbuncle entire" eulogy holding his sword upraised toward the gate, with his back to the audience, instead of down right holding out his arms—on the next line he sheathes his sword instead of leaning on it—much better, less melodramatic.

Despite the reblocking of the fight, revert to the second version of Coriolanus's appearance through the gate, as the new staging is not sufficiently rehearsed.

Personal cut on the farewell to Titus Lartius.

Cut the lap around the stage on the embrace with Cominius.

Much less blood on Coriolanus's body.

Standard bounced on "Make you a sword of me."

Fight moves refined to get rid of awkward moves.

Raising of swords still messy on the bestowal of the agnomen, and the cries of "Martius" need more conviction.

"Oh no, no, no" from Virgilia in response to "He was wont to come home wounded" is less weepy and expresses more relief—good!

The scene with the Roman ladies really taking off—laughter.

On "You are three/That Rome should dote on" they stand side by side but do not link arms.

Sicinius is slow and lacks energy, but Brutus is on top of things.

Change of stool in the senate scene—no longer an ottoman but a purple seat with wooden legs and red tassels.

Laughs again on the preparation to the senate scene—good.

Coriolanus is more respectful to the senate in vocal tone—as the doors shut on his exit we catch a glimpse of him kicking the wall.

Cominius searches more for his words in the beginning—more emotionally felt than definite in tone—more awe on "dying cries" and loses the arm gesture.

Coriolanus's embrace with Cominius on his reentrance is no longer over the top.

More life in the voices scene with the reworking.

Cues are taken up faster and the scene turn-overs are overlapping now.

No long pauses with the first brace—cues are taken up.

With the second brace edit the confusion on the fast delivery.

Coriolanus still kneels on "Indeed I would be consul"—still seems inappropriate.

More joy on "You have stood your limitation"—good.

Big wiggle on the change of gowns provoked giggles from the audience.

Big fuck up with lines as one citizen was not on stage and others were forced to jump in to fill the gap in lines—energy lagged due to the shock— then, unheard of, Titus Lartius lost his line, and Coriolanus dried three times, yet covered.

Riot scene still muddy—the cry of "Sicinius" came in too late.

Coriolanus is more purposeful in the drawing of his sword—freeze by everyone on stage, then all recoil before he chases them offstage.

The citizens depict a more wholehearted searching of the stage for the traitor at the end of 3.1.

During the first persuasion scene one of the young nobles was missing.

Menenius did not enter on cue, so his lines were begun offstage to cover up.

Laughs throughout the persuasion scene.

The people did not respond physically on "The fires i'th'lowest hell fold in the people."

The new staging of the trial scene will work, but is still crude.

Too slow and lacking in energy on "It shall be so"—forgot to raise hands on "death."

The child citizen is no longer present on stage during the banishment scene.

Sicinius grabs the railing on Coriolanus's exit, as though physically collapsing now that the fight is over.

Again one of the young nobles is missing from the farewell scene.

Virgilia attempts to follow her husband all the way up the stairs, but is intercepted and accompanied back down by Menenius.

Virgilia is much improved in her other scenes, but is still over the top in 4.1—she seems completely lost with the role here.

INTERVAL

Aufidius enters wearing a sword rather than carrying a cup of wine.

Coriolanus is really playing with Aufidius tonight, and once unmasked he assumes an aggressive pose.

Aufidius stands with his hand to the sword and only removes it after the step back—moment of tense ambiguity.

The encounter and embrace is passionate and very physical.

Much laughter at the tribunes' gloating.

Child citizen cut from this scene as well.

Only the outer stands are now brought down for the cluster sequence in 4.6 and the persuasion of Menenius to intercede with Coriolanus in 5.1.

Cominius is more emotional in his description of his spurning and finally gives the appropriate gesture on "Thus, with his speechless hand."

Coriolanus is no longer wearing gloves in his scene with Menenius and so draws the letter from his pocket.

Trouble getting the child on his shoulders.

"He turns away"—Coriolanus took a longer walk and so had to double back to get into place for the prostration passage.

Virgilia drops to her knees with the child on "I'll not to Rome."

For the first time Volumnia is genuinely very moving during the persuasion scene.

Sicinius enters drinking but edits the fainting business.

Aufidius and the first conspirator extend their handshake throughout the "Most noble sir" speech.

On "Boy!" there are more tears at the physical agony of the heart attack, and the lines are delivered with somewhat slurred speech as one of the symptoms.

Aufidius did not leave one foot on the body tonight.

"My rage is gone" delivered coldly again tonight, and it does not work—titters from the audience.

Aufidius delivers his orders in a contemplative vein—"Assist" spoken quietly—on "Though in this city" he is almost in tears.

The music is so piercing in intensity before the gates close that it hurts the ears—wonderful.

15/12/84

2:00–5:15

General Notes

1.2: "The gods assist you"—quieter in tone.
   "And keep your honours safe"—pitch it up.

Though the play is nine minutes shorter than Saturday night, it still needs two more minutes off.

Pauses and self-analysis don't work in this theatre—beats must be full of action.

There is only one pause in this play—the moment in which Coriolanus holds his mother by the hand, silent, and even that will not work if they just stand there—and that's why he grabs her hand.

There are still hundreds of pauses in the show—they must be cut.

The coarse acting is disappearing as the show is being taken away from the director, and the actors are living it and being it—relaxation.

Don't strain and don't push—just relax and be it—needs lightness of playing.

The show is now near to what the director dreamed it could be in this theatre at this time and with these actors.

Be proud—the show needs arrogance and a 'fuck you' quality.

Everyone has a wonderful desire to spread the action, but it needs to be shorter and shorter.

It needs to grow and live and get juicier and even more emotional.

The second half is now full of drama and tension and surprise—better than ever before.

1.1: Rehearse the sound cue for "The other side o'th'city is risen" and the entrance of the best elders.

2.1: The gold flecks for the triumph are cut.

1.9: The shields should be either over the heart at attention or in use—it looks terrible with the arm dropped.
Cut the hankie given to Coriolanus to wipe away the blood.

1.6: The holding aloft of Coriolanus must be more mystical and holy.

1.10: "Wash my fierce hand in's heart"—last night's animalism was beautiful.

2.1: Sicinius's "you are known well enough too" needs to be more of a challenge.

2.2: The tribunes at first must be more polite, so that their politeness sparks Menenius's impoliteness—Brutus's second speech then has more kick, as it is Menenius who has begun the confrontation—boardroom behaviour.

3.2: Volumnia's "Do your will" should be spoken directly *to* Coriolanus before she turns to exit, and not while she is walking away (as last night). McKellen and Worth improvise doing the "harlot's spirit" speech on the mirror side of the stage.
"I prithee now, sweet son"—Volumnia really gets him with "sweet son"—'what you called me when I was four.'

4.5: Need an earlier entrance on "Wine, wine, wine."
The Antium scene is smashing, but needs now to lose the pauses which were initially included as a guide to finding your way during rehearsals.
"Or lose mine arm for't"—hyperbole—the most a soldier can do is lose his fighting arm.
Painful pleasure in the use of sexual images—too neurotic last night.

4.6: Sicinius must lose the jogging—that is the kind of eclecticism which this production never indulges in (like motorbikes and copies of the *Times*)—the audience will not be listening, as they are laughing *at* the production.
Need a false exit on "Go see this rumourer whipp'd"—they do not know what to do, then on confirmation of the news they try to go on their way when they are interrupted by further news.
The rewrite has helped the first citizen enormously.

2.3: Like last night Coriolanus should keep the business of dropping the hat on top of the gown of humility when exchanging them for the consul's robes.

4.7: "Rights by rights *falter,* strengths by strengths do *fail*"—hit the active, concrete verb which has been lost until now.

5.1: "You know the very road into his kindness"—cue for Menenius to begin his walk up the stairs, so that he delivers his last speech on the move.

5.3: "Pass, pass" must come from opposite sides of the theatre, so that it sounds as though the guards are calling to one another.
Aufidius must at first stand closer to the centre than to the right, as he becomes too mixed up with the ladies on their entrance.

1.4: Rehearse the fight revealing Coriolanus behind the Volscian gates, so that the third version may be performed tonight.

1.6: Clean up "Make you a sword of me."

1.9: Clean up the entrance of Coriolanus with his arm in the sling, so that the eye is directed to him first and Cominius second.

2.1: Further banners are added now that the gold glitter has been cut.
A pair of red banners fall on either side of the nuntio on "Know, Rome."
Also add two banners near the wings.
Time the flag waving with the trumpets—wave the flags with a big motion so that it really comes over the heads of the audience.

2.3: At the end of the voices scene the circle must keep on tightening as the tension grows.

3.1: Coriolanus uses the space better when he positions himself in the stands right leaning against the wall of the gates, picking out from above who is addressed with each line.

3.3: On "Draw near, ye people" the outer stands are brought down, but the inner ones remain standing by their seats.
The whole cast now sits in the circle to make it fuller, and the spacing is regularized.
The votes come regularly until all are in on the final "It shall be so"—all register a right hand vote to avoid muddiness.
Leave a beat between Sicinius's line and the first "It shall be so."

5.3: "I'll work/Myself a former fortune"—it is not necessary for Aufidius to come so far downstage, as the grouping of Coriolanus's family has now moved upstage—Aufidius begins speaking on the walk down.
The ladies begin their exit on "Come, enter with us," as they do not know that Coriolanus is going to stop again.

4.6: On the entrance of the clusters, only the outer stands are to be brought down—they are to be led back to their seats on the citizen's last line.

5.6: Add the waving of banners and flags on Coriolanus's arrival in Antium.
Whistling, applauding, kissing, hugging, screaming, loud cheers—Coriolanus is now a popular hero ('like David Bowie').
Carry gold glitter in their pockets to throw over him as confetti.
After the assassination one citizen rushes to prevent defilement of the body, but is prevented by two Volscian soldiers.

5.3: "Pass, pass"—the line is said by the guards who have exited to the top of the theatre and no longer into the left and right wings—the shouts stop after Coriolanus's two steps.

OPENING NIGHT (K1)

The fight was worse than it has ever been—Coriolanus was disarmed on the first move again, as a result of having too much blood on his hand—never recovered—moves tentative and some wrong.

Despite the rehearsal, the blocking for "harlot's spirit" remains the same as before.

Tonight the third version of Coriolanus's appearance through the Volscian gates was played.

The banishment scene works much better with the people's court staging.

Virgilia was much better in 4.2, as she did not chew the sand and writhe on the floor but sat on her knees and rocked silently and rhythmically.

During the persuasion Volumnia spit after "a Volscian to his mother"—effective—but otherwise tonight she was too much in love with the sound of her own voice—the scene was more moving last night, as she was more genuinely emotional.

Coriolanus was back to a subtler version of the eagle image during the assassination scene, but the crying on "Boy" still does not work for me.

Aside from the fight going so poorly, the first night adrenalin was flowing, and it was one of the best performances to date—certainly in terms of the second half.

The action seemed to move quickly even though it lost the tempo of last night and was back to its usual length.

Titus Lartius now gives a much more Germanic interpretation of the "carbuncle entire" speech, and it works much better—a carbuncle is a crude stone—if Shakespeare had wanted a melodramatic eulogy he would have used softer sounding words—needs a more stiff-upper-lip delivery—it makes sense to deliver the lines toward the door through which Coriolanus has disappeared rather than out downstage.

17/12/84

SECOND PRESS NIGHT (s.m. box)

Half an hour late in starting due to the switch from the *Mariner* matinée—needed to change the set and refocus the lights.

The show has now found its natural rhythm and is flowing smoothly, but lacks the energy of Saturday night.

The third version of Coriolanus's appearance through the Volscian gates is very impressive.

"Make you a sword of me"—almost orgasmic.

Coriolanus's hands were clear of blood during the fight—ends at the forearm—nevertheless he was disarmed again midway through the first sequence but was up quicker, as there was no need to run for the sword—generally vital and well acted.

During the fight the soldiers ran in too early—Aufidius had been disarmed of his sword but not of his shield.

The lead soldier no longer raises his arm to cue the cheers of "Martius" but uses both hands to raise and lower the bloody helmet rhythmically with the music.

Almost lost the line "dieted/In praises sauc'd with lies."

Menenius lost his lines and repeated "Is he not wounded? He was wont to come home wounded."

Coriolanus kisses his mother's hands on "Nay, my good soldier, up" and rises only as Volumnia names him.

Nice moment as he enfolds his wife within his gown on the kiss.

As on opening night, the speech to the second brace was more distinctly pronounced, so that the audience can follow it even if the citizens cannot—still spoken quickly.

More of a conscious decision for Sicinius on "Noble Menenius,/Be you then as the people's officer."

On "harlot's spirit" Coriolanus mimics Volumnia's gesture—a gross exaggeration of her move on "perform a part."

"Do your will" spoken on her way out after she looks directly into her son's eyes and deliberately turns away.

"Let him away"—no longer as an emotional outburst, but calmly putting up the hand to vote—also performed this way opening night—emotional only on the final five "It shall be so"s.

Coriolanus leaves Virgilia at her usual place on the stairs—she no longer follows him right up to meet Menenius.

INTERVAL

"Not of a woman's tenderness to be"—really felt for the first time.

After grabbing Volumnia's hand Coriolanus went right into his speech—no pause.

Bigger reaction during the assassination scene to being called "Martius."

"Cut me to pieces"—less collapse and bigger on the eagle image.

Really sobbing on "Boy!" so that "The man is noble" becomes ironic.

"mourn you for him" delivered directly to Aufidius, and not a general statement to the Volscian citizenry.

Aufidius reacts more emotionally tonight—must fight to regain control, and it is a few seconds before he can issue his commands for the burial of the body.

13/2/85

CORIOLANUS WORKSHOP: OLIVIER THEATRE

With Alan Cohen, Greg Hicks, Jim Hayes, Nigel Le Vaillant.

Set: Roman/Greek amphitheatre to give the atmosphere of political debate and hard politics.
Pertinent to British society today because of the issues raised.
Creating the feel of the U.N. or House of Commons with the speaker having people on all sides in this hotbed of political debate.
Promenade seats used as acting areas.
No furniture and scenes played overlapping for quick progression.
Only two blackouts—one at the interval, one at the end—to hold the audience's concentration and gain momentum—concentration problem due to the influence of other media.

Costumes: Largely modern for accessibility.
Timeless—the issues raised are universal in the sense of time, therefore instead of all modern or all Roman dress we see more of the fundamental truth relating to here and now. It is more important to concentrate on the language and to make it visually relate to the audience to which it is played.
It is also more equivalent to the original Elizabethan setting, therefore the set is in fact not radical but basic—same with the costumes—the Elizabethans would have used whatever cross-section of costumes they had in stock—no unity in time or place, though largely modern dress.

Language: Difficult language and dense imagery.
Six weeks rehearsal of the play without cuts to make sure that every

image and line was understandable and therefore able to be communicated.

Clarify obscure references and images.

After the end of those six weeks and after running the play, the director decided which passages would probably not be understandable to someone with no knowledge of the text. Thus the psychologically and politically complex play was pruned—finally cut what it was impossible to make understandable verbally and visually.

Trial audiences invited to certain rehearsals—not only to practice crowd control but also to gauge what they did not understand.

Sample cut in 2.1: tribunes' reaction to Coriolanus's popularity in the market square—"All tongues speak of him . . ."—"Seld-shown flamens" image cut—a gesture to illustrate the line is worse theatrically than a cut.

Promenade Seats: Did not want crowd actors, but felt that certain scenes would be enhanced by occurring within the context of a crowd.

Unfortunately can lead to a diffusion of tension if audience reacts self-consciously on stage.

Character: "He who cannot live in society is either a god or a beast."

Coriolanus is not an embodiment of the fascist principle, but of an absolute singular principle—brilliant in own context, but disastrous when forced to function within the context of society.

CHANGE IN STAGING

Before a line-run on February 21 it was announced that the audience participation would be cut for all but three of the present scenes—it has been kept for the opening, the trial and assassination, but cut for the voices, triumph etc.—seeing the show the following day (22/2/85) it was evident that this reworking is a major improvement, as it rids the stage of the distracting self-conscious reactions where crowd involvement is unnecessary.

Appendix A: Textual Cuts

1.1.18–20:   "the leanness that afflicts us . . . their abundance."
1.1.41–45:   "You must in no way . . . to tire in repetition."
1.1.58–60:   "They say poor suitors . . . strong arms too."
1.1.68–73:   "whose course will on . . . must help."
1.1.109–13:   "it tauntingly replied . . . such as you."
1.1.136–39:   "And through the cranks . . . Whereby they live."
1.1.158–59:   "Thou rascal . . . some vantage."
1.1.173–78:   "Your virtue is . . . increase his evil."
1.1.192–95:   "side factions . . . Below their cobbled shoes."
1.1.210–11:   "To break the heart . . . look pale,"
1.1.269–275:   "Besides, if things go well . . . In aught he merit not."
1.3.84–86:   "Come . . . pricking it for pity."
1.4.26–27:   "They do disdain us . . . Come on, my fellows:"
1.4.36–38:   "Pluto and hell! . . . agued fear!"
1.4.41–45:   "If you'll stand fast . . . Not for the fliers."
1.5.5–7:   "Cushions, leaden spoons . . . with those that wore them,"
1.5.13:   "with those that have the spirit,"
1.5.23–24:   "Thy friend no less . . . highest."
1.6.38–39:   "Even like a fawning greyhound . . . To let him slip at will."
1.6.60–62:   "And that you not delay . . . this very hour."
1.6.65–67:   "Take your choice . . . That most are willing."
1.6.78–85:   "None of you . . . Which men are best inclin'd."
1.9.16–19:   "induc'd . . . Hath overta'en mine act."
1.9.21–25:   " 'Twere a concealment . . . Would seem but modest."
1.9.28–31:   "I have some wounds upon me . . . tent themselves with death."
1.9.34–36:   "to be ta'en forth . . . Your only choice."
1.9.44–46:   "When steel grows . . . An ovator for th'wars!"
1.9.53–54:   "More cruel . . . By your patience,"
1.9.59–61:   "in token of the which . . . With all his trim belonging;"
1.9.69–71:   "I mean to stride your steed . . . my power."
1.9.74–76:   "send us to Rome . . . their own good and ours."
2.1.6–11:   "Pray you . . . like a lamb."
2.1.29–31:   "Give your dispositions the reins . . . in being so."
2.1.35–36:   "or else your actions would grow wondrous single:"
2.1.56–58:   "I can say . . . the major part of your syllables."

338

2.1.61–65:	"If you see this . . . known well enough too?"
2.1.69–72:	"you wear out . . . second day of audience."
2.1.79:	"You are a pair of strange ones."
2.1.83–84:	"Our very priests . . . such ridiculous subjects as you are."
2.1.86–88:	"and your beards . . . an ass's pack-saddle."
2.1.113–17:	"It gives me an estate . . . horse-drench."
2.1.129–31:	"and he had stayed . . . that's in them."
2.1.193–96:	"Ere in our own house . . . change of honours."
2.1.211–13:	"Seld-shown flamens . . . win a vulgar station."
2.1.222–24:	"He cannot temp'rately . . . there's comfort."
2.1.227–29:	"which . . . he is proud to do't."
2.2.8–11:	"and there be many . . . upon no better a ground."
2.2.14–18:	"and out of his noble carelessness . . . neither good nor harm;"
2.2.21–23:	"Now to seem . . . flatter them for their love."
2.2.25–28:	"and his ascent . . . their estimation and report;"
2.2.32–34:	"To report otherwise . . . from every ear that heard it."
2.2.124–29:	"Our spoils he kick'd at . . . to end it."
2.3.29–34:	"but if it were at liberty . . . to get thee a wife."
2.3.59–60:	"like the virtues . . . lose by 'em."
2.3.213–15:	"make them of no more voice . . . kept to do so."
2.3.220–24:	"but your loves . . . he bears you."
2.3.236–43:	"from whence came . . . his great ancestor."
3.1.39–40:	"Suffer't . . . Nor ever will be rul'd."
3.1.55–56:	"Or never be so noble . . . for tribune."
3.1.71–79:	"the honour'd number . . . The very way to catch them."
3.1.93–94:	"being but . . . noise o'th'monster's,"
3.1.113–14:	"as 'twas us'd / Sometime in Greece—"
3.1.124–29:	"Being i'th'war . . . so frank donation."
3.1.141–43:	"This double worship . . . without all reason:"
3.1.156–60:	"Your dishonour . . . th'ill which doth control't."
3.1.164–65:	"On whom depending . . . To th'greater bench."
3.1.246–48:	"Whose rage doth rend . . . us'd to bear."
3.2.10–13:	"to show bare heads . . . peace or war."
3.2.15–16:	"Rather say I play / The man I am."
3.2.45–51:	"Tush, tush! . . . in like request?"
3.2.62–64:	"I would dissemble . . . in honour."
3.2.68–69:	"and safeguard / Of what that want might ruin."
3.3.32–33:	"Ay, as an hostler . . . by th'volume."
3.3.54–57:	"Do not take . . . Rather than envy you."
3.3.97–99:	"and that . . . doth distribute it—"
3.3.114–16:	"My dear wife's estimate . . . Speak what?"
3.3.129–31:	"which finds not . . . Still your own foes—"
4.1.3–9:	"You were us'd . . . A noble cunning."

4.1.23–27:	"My sometime general . . . laugh at 'em."
4.1.43–47:	"which doth ever cool . . . yet unbruis'd:"
4.3:	Entire
4.5.10–11:	"I have deserv'd no better entertainment / In being Coriolanus."
4.5.45–49:	"Then thou dwell'st . . . meddle with thy mistress."
4.5.72–74:	"a good memory . . . should'st bear me."
4.5.149–241:	"Here's a strange alteration! . . . In, in, in, in!"
4.6.68–69:	"as spacious as between / The young'st and oldest thing."
4.6.104–7:	"and who resists . . . find something in him."
4.6.115–19:	"And therein. . . . You have crafted fair!"
4.6.135–37:	"As many coxcombs . . . for your voices."
5.1.53–56:	"but when we have stuff'd . . . our priest-like fasts."
5.2.16–22:	"haply amplified . . . stamp'd the leasing."
5.2.28–32:	"Prithee, fellow. . . . Therefore go back."
5.2.46–49:	"No, you are deceived, . . . reprieve and pardon."
5.2.62–66:	"Guess but by my entertainment . . . to come upon thee."
5.2.83–85:	"That we have been familiar . . . note how much."
5.2.99:	"What cause do you think I have to swound?"
5.3.7–8:	"no, not with such friends / That thought them sure of you."
5.3.12–17:	"for whose old love . . . I have yielded to."
5.3.203–5:	"and you shall bear . . . will have counterseal'd."
5.4.17–21:	"The tartness of his face . . . his hum is a battery."
5.4.48–49:	"Ne'er through an arch . . . through th'gates."
5.4.56–58:	"You have pray'd well . . . given a doit."
5.6.22–32:	"who being so heighten'd . . . joint-servant with me,"
5.6.50–54:	"Your native town . . . at your vantage,"
5.6.57–59:	"When he lies along . . . with his body."
5.6.74–79:	"You are to know . . . The charges of the action."

Appendix B: Textual Emendations

1.1.125:	"you'st hear" to "you'll hear."
1.2.27:	"Corioles" to "Corioli."
1.3.98:	"Corioles" to "Corioli."
1.6.10:	"Corioles" to "Corioli."
1.6.37:	"Corioles" to "Corioli."
1.6.75 (stage direction):	*"They all shout and wave their swords."* to a choric cry of "Martius, Martius, Martius!"
1.6.76:	*"All.* O me alone! Make you a sword of me!" now ascribed to Coriolanus.
1.8.8:	"Corioles" to "Corioli."
1.9.62:	"Corioles" to "Corioli."
1.9.74:	"Corioles" to "Corioli."
1.9.80:	"Corioles" to "Corioli."

2.1.23: "*Both.*   Why, how are we censured?" to
"*Sicinius.*   Why?
Brutus.   How are we censured?"

2.1.26: "*Both.*   Well, well, sir, well." to
"*Sicinius.*   Well.
Brutus.   Well, sir.
Sicinius.   Well."

2.1.92:	"God-den" to "Good e'en."
2.1.162:	"Corioles" to "Corioli."
2.1.177:	"Corioles" to "Corioli."
2.2.102:	"Corioles" to "Corioli."
2.2.114:	"Corioles" to "Corioli."

2.3.163: "*All.*   No, no; no man saw 'em." to
"*Second Cit.*   No.
All.   No.
Third Cit.   No man saw 'em."

2.3.252–53: "*All.*   We will so: almost all
Repent in their election." to
"*All.*   We will so.
Third Cit.   Almost all
Repent in their election."

3.1.98:	"lenity" to "leniency."

3.1.184–86: "*All Pleb.* Tribunes! Patricians! Citizens! What ho!
Sicinius! Brutus! Coriolanus! Citizens!
Peace, peace, peace! Stay! Hold! Peace!" to

"*Men.*   Tribunes!
Women.   Patricians!
Senators.   Citizens!
All.   What ho!
1st Aedile. Sicinius!
2nd Aedile.   Brutus!
Brutus.   Coriolanus!
Senators.   Citizens!
All.   Peace, peace, peace!
Citizen.   Stay! Hold!
All.   Peace!"

3.1.197–98:   "*All Pleb.*   True,
The people are the city." to
"*All Pleb.*   True.
Woman.   The people are the city."

3.1.258 (stage direction): "*A noise within.*" to the citizens entering with cries of "Traitor!"

3.2.92:   "*Vol.*   Here is Cominius." now ascribed to Menenius.

3.3.41:   "*Both Trib.*   Well, say. Peace ho!" to
"*Sicinius.*   Well, say.
Brutus.   Peace ho!"

3.3.106–7:   "*All Pleb.*   It shall be so, it shall be so! Let him away!
He's banish'd, and it shall be so!" to
"*First Cit.*   It shall be so!
Second Cit.   It shall be so!
Third Cit.   Let him away!
All Pleb.   He's banish'd, and it shall be so!"

3.3.119:   "It shall be so!" repeated not twice but five times.

4.2.26–27:   "*Vol.* He'd make an end of thy posterity," now ascribed to Virgilia. "Bastards and all." still Volumnia.

4.6.19 (stage direction): "*Enter three or four Citizens.*" to "*Enter a Couple, with Infant.*"

4.6.20:   "*All.* The gods preserve you both!" now ascribed to the male citizen.

4.6.20:   "Good den" to "Good e'en."

4.6.21:   "Good den" to "Good e'en."

4.6.25:   "*All.*   Now the gods keep you!" ascribed to the male citizen.

4.6.121:   "*Both Trib.*   Say not we brought it." now ascribed to Sicinius.

4.6.146:   "yet it was against our will" to "yet it was his death we wished for."

4.6.144–46:   "That we did, we did for the best . . . it was his death we wished for." now ascribed to the Fourth rather than the Third Citizen.

4.6.154–55:   "*First Cit.* The gods be good to us! Come, masters, let's home." now ascribed to the Fourth Citizen.

5.3.19 (stage direction): "*(Shout within.)*" to

> "*First Guard.* Pass.
> *Second Guard.* Pass."

5.6.12–15: "Most noble sir . . . your great danger." now ascribed to the First rather than the Second Conspirator.

5.6.41–44: "So he did, my lord . . . no less spoil than glory—" now ascribed to the Second rather than the First Conspirator.

5.6.90: "Corioles" to "Corioli."

5.6.115: "Corioles" to "Corioli."

Notes

Chapter 1. Rehearsals and Production Work

1. William Shakespeare, *King Richard III* (London and New York: Methuen and Co., 1981), 3.5.1–4.

2. The only character to rival Richard for self-dramatization and sheer theatrical panache is the "serpent of old Nile," Cleopatra, though she is the subject of a divided heroic focus in Shakespeare's later tragedy, *Antony and Cleopatra*.

3. *King Richard III*, 3.5.5–11.

4. See the rehearsal diary for 3/11/84.

5. Hall compares this technique with that employed by the film editor directing the audience's focus (Diary, 3/11/84).

6. Hamlet's advice to the players, *Hamlet*, 3.2.19–20.

7. William Shakespeare, *The Tragedy of Coriolanus* (London and New York: Methuen and Co., 1976), 1.1. 9–10. Hereafter references to *Coriolanus* will appear in the text.

8. See the rehearsal diary for 6/12/84.

9. Trial audiences were also invited to certain rehearsals, both to practice the crowd control and to gauge which sections of the play were not being transmitted effectively.

10. In fairness to the actors involved, it should be noted that this scene received little attention in rehearsal; the director tended to focus on the principal players, often at the expense of such small cameo performances.

11. A complete list of textual cuts in the National Theatre's production of *Coriolanus* may be found in Appendix A.

12. A complete list of textual emendations may be found in Appendix B.

13. That this departure from the original is recognizably un-Shakespearean is attested to by the critic Benedict Nightingale's scathing comments in his review of *Coriolanus* for *The New Statesman;* but one hearing was sufficient to send someone with a knowledge of Shakespeare's stagecraft back to verify the line with the original text. Nevertheless, his concern at this "piece of well-meant vandalism" is an overreaction to an otherwise textually faithful production, and fails even to attempt to consider the motives underlying the change.

14. See the rehearsal diary for 14/11/84.

15. See the rehearsal diary for 3/12/84.

16. In addition to the easy accessibility for entrances and exits afforded by the bare amphitheatrical staging, quick progression of scene changes was further facilitated by the cutting of what little furniture was used at the beginning of the rehearsal process. (This includes Volumnia's day-bed and the cart used by the looters to transport their spoils from Corioli.) The lighting design also contributes to the show's momentum; only two blackouts interrupt the action, one at the interval, the other at the end of the production, so that the audience's concentration is held throughout the two movements of the play.

17. This space-age quality to the military uniforms was especially evident in the earliest version of the costumes, which included octagonal metallic plates attached to the loose-fitting stylized jackets. The subsequent simplification, however, rendered them more attractive and more consistent with the Spartan bareness of the set.

18. See the rehearsal diary for 13/2/85.

19. The decision to costume several of the citizens in middle class attire was made to preserve a sense of visual continuity with the stage audience, which is called to enact the crowd at several points during the play.

20. McKellen's inspired adoption of the white overcoat then prompted the actor portraying his nemesis, Tullus Aufidius, to search the costume department for the black leather overcoat which he wears in the production. This addition to his uniform helps visually to define his character and further intensify the parallels with Coriolanus as his counterpart in Rome.

21. In opposition to this general response of self-conscious embarrassment, several individuals regularly become so engrossed in the action that they perform with an exaggerated theatricality that is amusingly over the top. Such "loonies," as they are technically termed, have been known to join the 'real' actors in the self-appointed task of crowd control, to aid the tribunes to "dismiss the people," even to attempt to physically attack Coriolanus on his way to accept the consulship. Perhaps the temptation to audition for the National Theatre during their brief moments on stage proves too much for these poor souls; in any case, their eccentric behaviour proves a serious, because overly amusing, distraction.

22. I do not mean to criticize excessively the behavior of the stage audience; it is natural that people with no acting training, whose sole experience of the theater has hitherto been in the capacity of passive observer, react tentatively in this unfamiliar and quite daunting situation. Even so, their spontaneous reactions can provide an invaluable contribution to the production when carefully controlled by the actors.

Chapter 2. Act 1

1. Coriolanus's power and dominance over the people is immediately transmitted to the audience by his strong entrance from the top of the stands, right. His isolation within Roman society is also integral to this image of the single man positioned above, with the citizens physically and metaphorically beneath him.

2. See the rehearsal diary for 13/11/84.

3. This gesture not only highlights the reference to "this painting/Wherein you see me smear'd" (1.6.68–69), but also facilitates Coriolanus's upcoming costume change, as he is already half stripped when he leaves the stage.

4. For a full account of the blocking of the fight sequence, see the rehearsal diary for 13/11/84.

5. The difficulty of acting on such a surface was experienced by all members of the company. Their attitude was best summed up by James Hayes at a lecture given on the production: "If Shakespeare had meant us to act on sand he would have set *Coriolanus* on a beach."

6. This entrance solves the problem of masking which was encountered during rehearsals. If Coriolanus enters holding the banner on the diagonal in his right (i.e., downstage) hand, he is obscured by the movement of the flag. To further clarify the story of the fight, it was also necessary to find specific moments for

passing the banners, choosing ground, and drawing the swords. (See the diary entry for 13/11/84.)

7. The actual performance of the fight is extremely complex and physically draining; it was several weeks into performance before McKellen and Hicks were able to "act" the battle in addition to executing its moves for accuracy. During previews, their tentative performance made the blocking seem more stylized than realistic, and on several occasions, as I have already mentioned, an excess of blood dripping down Coriolanus's arms allowed the sword to slip from his hands in the early moments of the fight. The slight error can result in the actors' finding themselves in the wrong position to begin the next sequence, and the consequences are often dangerous. (See the diary entry for the third preview, 4/11/84).

8. See the rehearsal diary for 11/12/84.

9. During rehearsals, Greg Hicks (the actor portraying Tullus Aufidius) added the gesture of indicating his bleeding wounds at this point in the lines, thus implying that the attendance he will receive at the cypress grove is medical. This interpretation is sometimes (although not with regularity) explored in performance.

Chapter 3. Act 2

1. Shakespeare's use of fast-paced cues and repeated phrases to build momentum is again evident in the family's enthusiastic agreement to Valeria's observation "In troth, there's wondrous things spoke of him" (2.1.136):

> *Men.* Wondrous! Ay, I warrant you, and not without/his true purchasing.
> *Vir.* The gods grant them true.
> *Vol.* True? pow, waw!
> *Men.* True? I'll be sworn they are true. (2.1.137–41)

Hall insisted that each repetition of the word "true" must be hit by the actors to set up the pay-off on Volumnia's dismissive "pow, waw," if the line is not to fall flat. The necessity of performing this passage in its entirety was attested to in rehearsal, when Menenius's initial reference to "his true purchasing" (2.1.138) was temporarily cut before being restored for the first preview.

2. See the rehearsal diary for 8/11/84.

3. Coriolanus's attempt to undercut the formality of the occasion is, however, sufficient to return the scene to its original prose form.

4. During rehearsals and early previews Coriolanus removed the oaken garland on "Pray now, no more" (2.1.168) and presented it to his mother when kneeling at her feet; Volumnia then recrowned him with the laurels as she pronounced his name—an ironically appropriate gesture, as it is she who has been the inspiration for his military success. This piece of stage business was cut, however, from the final version of the scene.

5. See the rehearsal diary for 8/11/84.

6. This decision to play up Coriolanus's self-control before the senate led to the cutting of a piece of stage business developed in rehearsal; he originally kicked over the ceremonial stool before exiting at 2.2.77, yet it was felt that such a gesture would prove excessively anarchical too early in the play, and therefore detract from the ultimate shock value of Coriolanus drawing his sword against the people in 3.1.

7. During Cominius's speech the lights gradually dim to give an added sense of mystery and awe to the chronicle, then come up again for Coriolanus's entrance.

8. On "for I cannot/Put on the gown, stand naked, and entreat them/For my wounds' sake to give their suffrage" (2.2.136–38), Coriolanus gestures with his head to the gown held by Brutus, thus indicating to the audience what the tribune is tendering with outstretched arms.

9. See the rehearsal diary for 30/10/84.

10. Texture is added to the crowd's response to the upcoming election by having the "great toe's" loyal followers leave in disgust at the general gullibility of the people a few seconds before their mass exit.

11. In rehearsal and early previews, McKellen added the gesture of kissing the women's hands as he addressed them, and kneeling in supplication on "Indeed I would be consul" (2.3.130). Although it is conceivable that Coriolanus could so far humble himself as to speak in a mild accent and even shake their hands, I find it difficult to believe that he could thus embrace their 'stinking breath,' or indeed that he could bend his knee to any man, let alone a plebeian. Certain it is that he later turns away in disgust at Volumnia's suggestion that he stand stretching his bonnet in his hand, "Thy knee bussing the stones" (3.2.75). This piece of stage business was, however, thankfully cut during performance.

12. This sense of discovery diminishes the focus on Coriolanus and transforms the scene into an exploration of the people discovering that they have a voice.

Chapter 4. Act 3

1. The tribunes had exited through the audience at the end of 2.3 and so are already in position to run down the central aisle.

2. For the purposes of this play there is but one consul, and not a triumvirate.

3. On "O good but most unwise patricians: why,/You grave but reckless senators" (3.1.90–91) Coriolanus addresses the senate in a tone of disappointed disbelief rather than violent anger. The latter emerges whenever he makes reference to the corn or the rabble.

4. See the rehearsal diary for 31/10/84.

5. McKellen's business of pointing to the senators, tribunes and audience during these speeches serves to clarify who is referred to by the complex series of pronouns.

6. See the rehearsal diary for 31/10/84.

7. Hall pointed out in rehearsal that Menenius must wait to deliver the line until after the mass entrance of the citizens, so that this key notion of the play may not be thrown away.

8. This moment of dangerous violence is echoed on a comic level in Coriolanus's pummelling of the servingmen in 4.5.

9. Birtwistle also directed the vocal delivery of the cries of "Martius, Martius, Martius!" (1.6.75 and 1.9.40), and the round of "It shall be so"s in the trial scene (3.3.106).

10. The "canned" riot which was originally played over the speakers during the citizens' reentrance was exchanged during previews for live cries of "Traitor, traitor!"

11. The tribunes originally split on Coriolanus's entrance, as though uncertain how much of their dialogue has been overheard, but this blocking was felt to undermine the strength of their authority in the scene and so was cut.

12. In previews, this ironic tone was so predominant as to provoke laughter from the audience when Coriolanus mockingly shook his head on "And not our streets with war" (3.3.37). This delivery was, however, judged to be too provocative and was therefore subdued during performance.

13. See the rehearsal diary for 1/11/84.

Chapter 5. Act 4

1. During the first preview this entrance was not made soon enough, causing confusion among members of the audience who were already preparing to leave their seats for the interval.

2. During previews, McKellen experimented with giving his former fist salute at this point, but cut the gesture before the show entered performance.

3. In rehearsal, Coriolanus gave an elaborate nod to each character on the stage as he bid them "smile," yet this was simplified to the exchange with Volumnia and Virgilia, as it slowed the momentum of the exit.

4. The danger of the tribunes' repeated false exits appearing comic to the audience was minimized by changing their original direction from down centre to down left.

5. The Arden edition of *Coriolanus* reports a controversy over the speaker of "You shall stay too" (4.2.15); Hall has chosen to ascribe the line to Virgilia rather than Volumnia.

6. Thus the final emblem of part 1 shows an old man and woman standing in the center of the stage, with a keening girl at their feet in the sand; the moment contains all the stark and devastating power of an image from Greek tragedy.

7. This version replaced the earlier blocking which had Coriolanus enter down the central aisle of the auditorium as the lights dimmed to a solo spot on the stage.

8. See the rehearsal diary for 5/11/84.

9. The business of Coriolanus's attack on the servingmen was cut at one point during rehearsals, but was later restored to ensure continuity with subsequent dialogue about the beating, and to preserve the one moment of comic relief in an otherwise uniformly serious work.

The original staging of the sequence had the third servant personated as Cotus, entering from the right vomitory, and carrying a basket of wine. He turned to see the stranger only when he heard the chink of Coriolanus grabbing one of the bottles from his sedentary position in the center of the sand. This was simplified to maintain the quick pace of the interchange.

10. In rehearsal Aufidius carried a cup of wine, suggesting that he had just been summoned from his place at the feast, but it was decided that the sword intensified the sense of danger which Coriolanus must face in thus approaching the enemy leader.

11. The scene was originally blocked with a woman and child picnicking along the upper left hand corner of the sand, but this was cut before the show entered performance.

12. The stage audience in the outer stands was originally invited to descend and join the ranks of the citizens during this sequence, but the blocking was simplified during the run.

13. See page 27.

Chapter 6. Act 5

1. This is another sequence which was originally blocked with the stage audience descending from the outer stands to swell the crowd, but their participation was cut during performance.

2. See the rehearsal diary for 6/12/84.

3. The large document which Coriolanus originally passed to Menenius was reduced to a small, folded paper to indicate the personal, rather than political, nature of its contents.

4. The original sound cue was replaced with live cries of "Pass, pass" for the first preview.

5. Coriolanus crosses left on "He turns away" (5.3.168) in a silent denial of Volumnia's appeal, prompting her to return to the women as she makes her final plea.

6. The supplication sequence was altered late in rehearsals so that the ladies remained on their knees; yet Hall felt that the complete prostration created a more powerful and evocative stage image, and so restored the original blocking.

7. On opening night, Worth punctuated her attack by spitting to the sand on "This fellow had a Volscian to his mother" (5.3.178).

8. This silence comes as an active, rather than a passive moment. Hall maintained throughout rehearsals that pauses do not work in the Olivier theatre, and so Coriolanus's taking of his mother's hand is performed while she is walking away from him.

9. On this occasion, Coriolanus also gave the fist salute as he passed through the main gates, but the gesture was never repeated after this performance.

10. Hall pointed out that the prose of this passage includes an enormous amount of alliteration, which must be observed by the actor without being over stressed.

11. Hall stressed the irony of this imagistic inversion of Alexander as he sits in state to destroy the civilization which created him, thereby not realizing his full Alexandrian potential by fighting *for* Rome.

12. Sicinius drops to his knees as though in an attitude of prayer on "The gods be good unto us" (5.4.31).

13. Sicinius originally fainted at this point, and was carried to the left side of the stage by the aedile as he made room for the carpet, but this business was cut during previews to preserve the serious tone of the scene.

14. The live cries which originally greeted the procession were cut before the first preview, on the grounds that they proved an intrusive piece of naturalism in an otherwise ritualized triumph. Such cheers are saved for the popular welcome which Coriolanus receives on his entry into Corioli.

15. It is because of the scansion of this last line that Hall chose to regularize the pronunciation of the protagonist's name as "Cor-eye-olanus." Yet a case may be made for a short "i" sound, for the name is here uttered by Martius's inveterate enemy; it could be argued that Aufidius gives it an ironic twist as he taunts the Roman with his former attacks against the Volscian state.

16. Coriolanus at first attempted to fully disrobe himself to make his final attack wearing the gladiatorial loincloth of 1.8, but there proved insufficient time to complete the change. He now simply tears off his jacket to reveal the battle wounds which scar his chest and throat.

McKellen also experimented with creating a physical emblem of the "eagle in a dovecote" image by rhythmically raising and lowering his arms while delivering the vaunt, but cut the gesture during previews.

17. The idea of using pneumatic blow-guns to transfer the blood was also discarded as impractical, because of the distance from which the shots are fired.

18. Aufidius experimented with the gesture of extending his arm in an echo of Martius's fist salute, but cut the business before the show entered previews.

19. Hall decided to have Aufidius stand with both feet, rather than just one foot, on Coriolanus's body, despite the problem of maintaining balance, in order to intensify the horror of its effect. Although the Elizabethans would have recoiled from a subtler form of desecration, he felt that the image required added enormity for a modern audience dulled to violent atrocities by their extensive media coverage.

Chapter 7. Ian McKellen on *Coriolanus*

1. At a lecture given at the "Coriolanus Weekend," a series of seminars held by the theater for the general public on 15 May 1985, McKellen elaborated on his technique of approaching a role. He begins with a series of images which prove to him that his character could exist in the modern world: Macbeth is a man who experiences a great moment of illumination in the face of political exposure, like Nixon or Kennedy; while *Richard II* is a play about the deposition of a man who thought he was god—like the Dalai Lama, Hollywood film stars, or Elvis Presley, who was called "the King" and died in misery with his spirit broken. There were a sufficient number of right-wing dictators to provide parallels with Coriolanus, but McKellen chose instead to look for a man with frailties. He finally hit on John MacEnroe, the ultimate athlete who can do anything, but clearly has problems: he needs to perform in public and to win prizes, but despises his public and that part of himself which needs it. One can call him "boy" and "brat," but he is a giant as well; but, McKellen hastened to add, this does not necessarily mean "we are doing a production where Coriolanus and Aufidius play a game of tennis!"

McKellen added that he also found a personal parallel in the role as he himself enjoys the attention of playing in public, but knows people's praise to be no guarantee of success. Only within the self can one find a sense of one's own worth. Thus he picked up on the acting metaphor which runs through the heart of the play, and made it a crucial element of his performance.

2. At the "Coriolanus Weekend," McKellen elaborated on this concept of "playing jazz" with a scene, saying that it constitutes playing the same basic tune, but experimenting with different rhythms.

3. At the "Coriolanus Weekend," McKellen dwelt in greater detail on the problems of performing with actors who have different levels of experience in performing classical drama. He told his audience that Hall's work with the Royal Shakespeare Company had been based on three year contracts, with a company that had a lively understanding of the way in which Shakespeare wrote his words. The actors were invited to understand blank verse to be the most elastic, freest, quickest way of making a point or an argument. Writing in verse is not something beautiful and poetic, but a series of instructions as to how to think, feel and say the words.

With *Coriolanus*, Hall was coming back a generation later, with actors who had no experience with his technique of directing Shakespeare; much time was consequently spent on a quick course in how to speak verse. Although lively and good in its way, it was not helpful for McKellen or Worth, who had long been masters of this style of verse-speaking, and felt held back by the director's worry about the rest of the company.

4. During his lecture, McKellen described the temporal setting for Guthrie's production, which was placed during the transition between the eighteenth and nineteenth centuries, an era with a clear social hierarchy, in which dress was the key to a character's identity.

Chapter 8. Greg Hicks on *Coriolanus*

1. Throughout the rehearsal period Greg Hicks had been an outspoken advocate for the removal of the stage audience.

2. Tim Hick replaced Nigel le Vaillant as the Volscian lieutenant when the latter took over the role of the first citizen in June 1985.

Chapter 9. The Athens Remounting

1. The construction of this single set of doors from blond wood necessitated the cutting of a piece of business in the opening riot sequence, the spray-painting of rebel slogans across Rome gates, as there was no longer a point at which they were out of the audience's field of vision to be retouched.

2. If the plebeian sequences took off, so too was the persuasion scene at its most effective: the pause before Coriolanus grasps his mother's hand was held longer than ever before, yet completely filled the space, and never did Rome gates slam to with more crashing finality than when the funeral party carried the body of Coriolanus through their portals for the last time.

Chapter 10. Conclusion

1. *King Richard III*, 3.7. 95–98.
2. *Hamlet*, 1.3.78.
3. *Macbeth*, 1.5.67–68.
4. Peter Brook, *The Empty Space* (Harmondsworth: Penguin Books Ltd., 1980), 98.